D0468686

PRAISE FO
REVOLUTION AT SEA SAGA

"Nelson's seagoing experience is evident in his clear, convincing description. . . . The characters are strong and realistic, the plot and action believable and brisk . . . a fine adventure series."

—*Publishers Weekly*

"Set sail with Jim Nelson into a world where he will lead you with the same command presence that he led his shipmates as Third Officer aboard the very real twentieth-century sail training ship H.M.S. *Rose*. Plant your feet firmly on Nelson's decks and you will smile as Patrick O'Brian has at Jim Nelson's grace, wit, and humor."

—Captain Richard Bailey, Sail Training Ship H.M.S. *Rose*

"A lively and highly readable account. Exploring the lives of seamen, merchant captains, and Royal naval officers, *By Force of Arms* offers a realistic and minutely detailed account of shipboard life during the period."

—John G. Kolp, assistant professor, Department of History, U.S. Naval Academy

"*The Maddest Idea* is sprightly in style and accurate in historical sweep and detail. Nelson has no apologies to make by sailing in company with [C.S.] Forester and Patrick O'Brian."

—William David Barry, *Portland Press Herald* (ME)

Also by James L. Nelson

By Force of Arms
The Maddest Idea
The Continental Risque

Published by POCKET BOOKS

For orders other than by individual consumers, Pocket Books grants a discount on the purchase of **10 or more** copies of single titles for special markets or premium use. For further details, please write to the Vice President of Special Markets, Pocket Books, 1230 Avenue of the Americas, 9th Floor, New York, NY 10020-1586.

For information on how individual consumers can place orders, please write to Mail Order Department, Simon & Schuster Inc., 100 Front Street, Riverside, NJ 08075.

THE CONTINENTAL RISQUE

REVOLUTION AT SEA SAGA

BOOK THREE

JAMES L. NELSON

POCKET BOOKS
New York London Toronto Sydney Tokyo Singapore

The sale of this book without its cover is unauthorized. If you purchased this book without a cover, you should be aware that it was reported to the publisher as "unsold and destroyed." Neither the author nor the publisher has received payment for the sale of this "stripped book."

This book is a work of fiction. Names, characters, places and incidents are products of the author's imagination or are used fictitiously. Any resemblance to actual events or locales or persons living or dead is entirely coincidental.

An *Original* Publication of POCKET BOOKS

POCKET BOOKS, a division of Simon & Schuster Inc.
1230 Avenue of the Americas, New York, NY 10020

Copyright © 1998 by James L. Nelson

All rights reserved, including the right to reproduce this book or portions thereof in any form whatsoever. For information address Pocket Books, 1230 Avenue of the Americas, New York, NY 10020

ISBN: 0-671-01381-5

First Pocket Books trade paperback printing August 1998

10 9 8 7 6 5 4 3

POCKET and colophon are registered trademarks of Simon & Schuster Inc.

Cover design by Matt Galemmo
Cover art by Dennis Lyall

Maps by Christopher L. Brest/Folio Graphics Co. Inc.

Printed in the U.S.A.

To Nat Sobel, without whom I would still be a poor, dumb sailor, rather than the poor, dumb, published sailor that I am today

And to Lisa

For the Encouragement of the Men employed in this service I am ordered to inform you that the Congress have resolved that the Masters, Officers and Seamen shall be entitled to one half of the value of the prizes by them taken, the wages they receive from the Colony notwithstanding.

The ships and vessels of War are to be on the Continental risque & pay . . .

—John Hancock
October 5, 1775

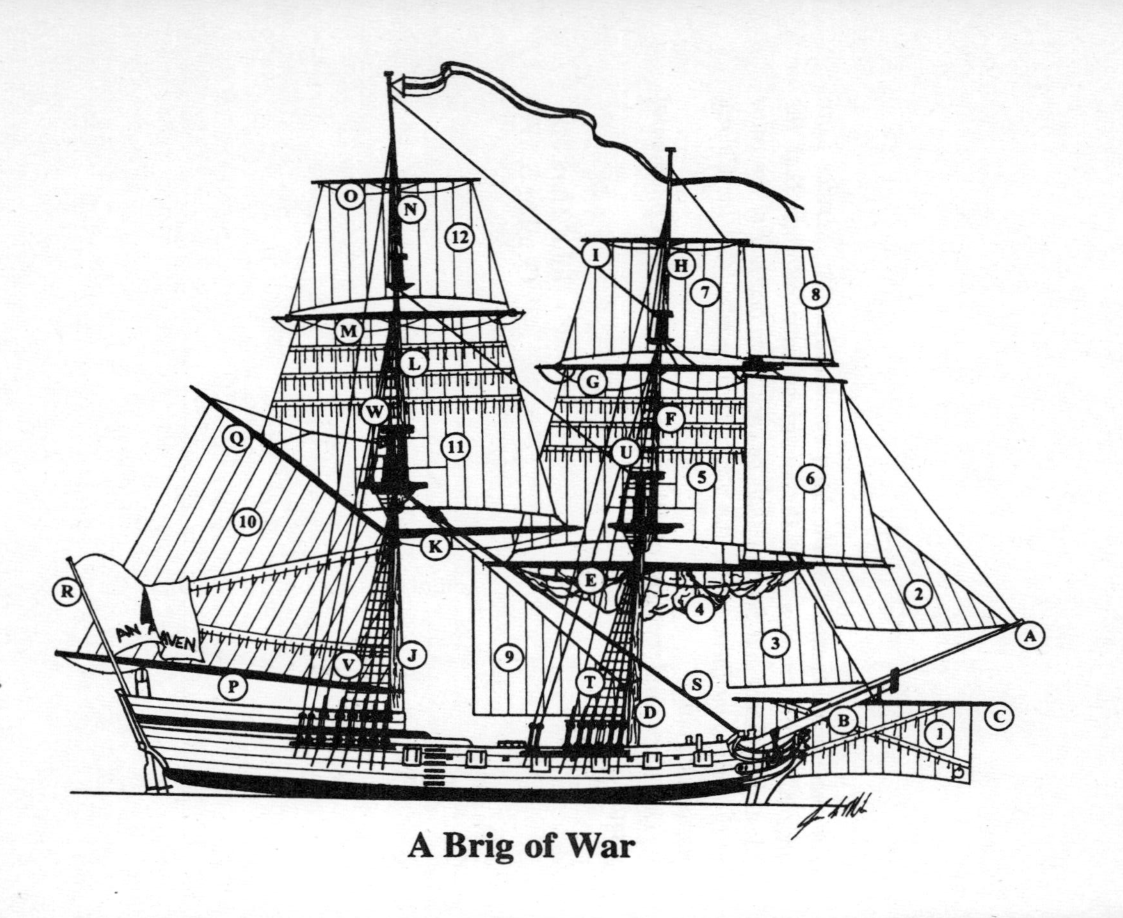

A Brig of War

Sails

1. Spritsail
2. Jib
3. Fore Topmast Staysail
4. Foresail (clewed up)
5. Fore Topsail
6. Fore Topmast Studdingsail (removable)
7. Fore Topgallant Sail
8. Fore Topgallant Studdingsail (removable)
9. Main Staysail
10. Mainsail
11. Main Topsail
12. Main Topgallant Sail

Spars and Rigging

A. Jibboom
B. Bowsprit
C. Spritsail Yard
D. Foremast
E. Foreyard
F. Fore Topmast
G. Fore Topsail Yard
H. Fore Topgallant Mast
I. Fore Topgallant Yard
J. Mainmast
K. Mainyard
L. Main Topmast
M. Main Topsail Yard
N. Main Topgallant Mast
O. Main Topgallant Yard
P. Boom
Q. Gaff
R. Ensign Staff (removable)
S. Mainstay
T. Fore Shrouds and Ratlines
U. Fore Topmast Shrouds and Ratlines
V. Main Shrouds and Ratlines
W. Main Topmast Shrouds and Ratlines

*For other terminology and usage see Glossary at the end of the book

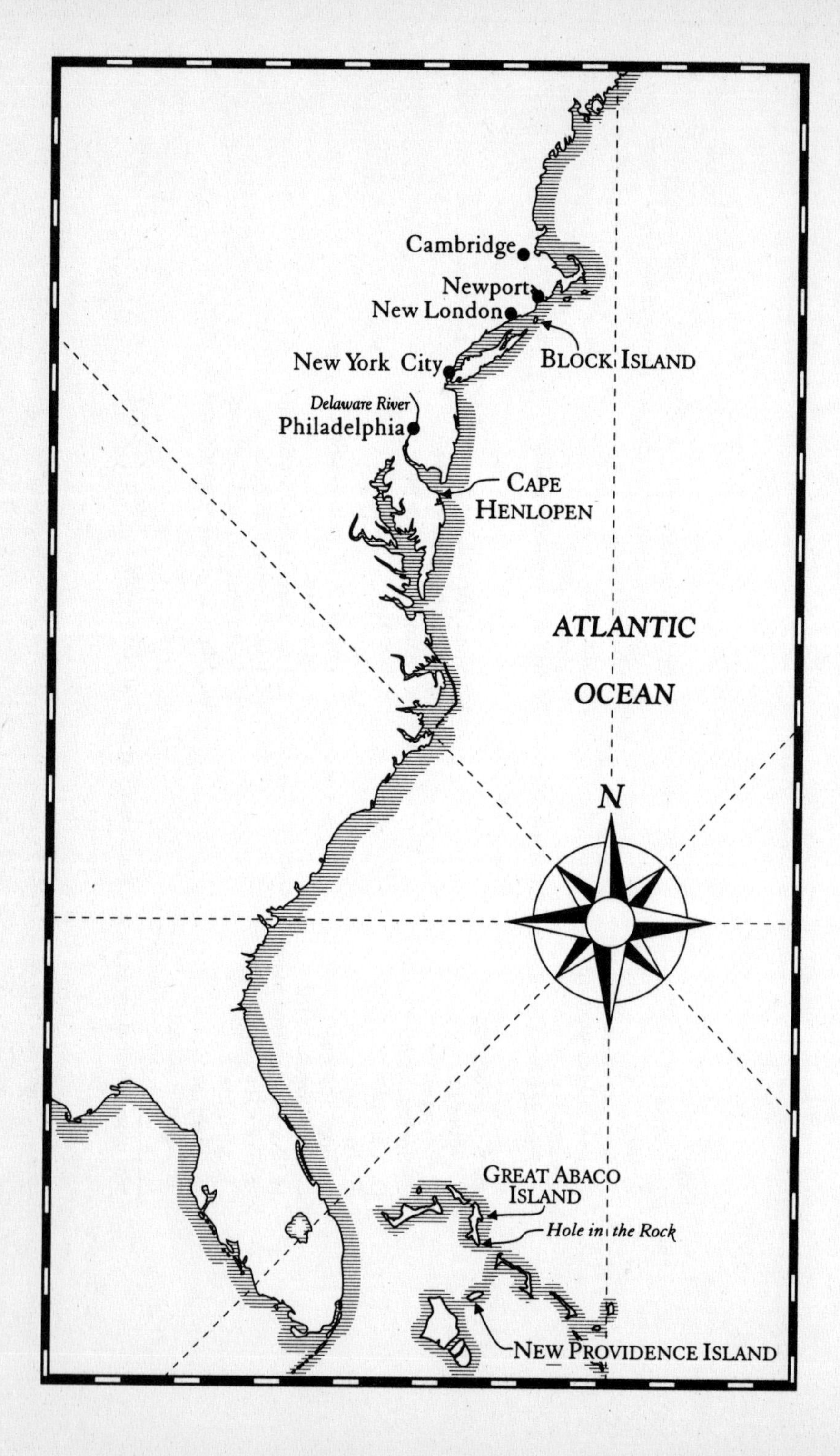
Cambridge
Newport
New London
Block Island
New York City
Delaware River
Philadelphia
Cape Henlopen
Atlantic Ocean
N
Great Abaco Island
Hole in the Rock
New Providence Island

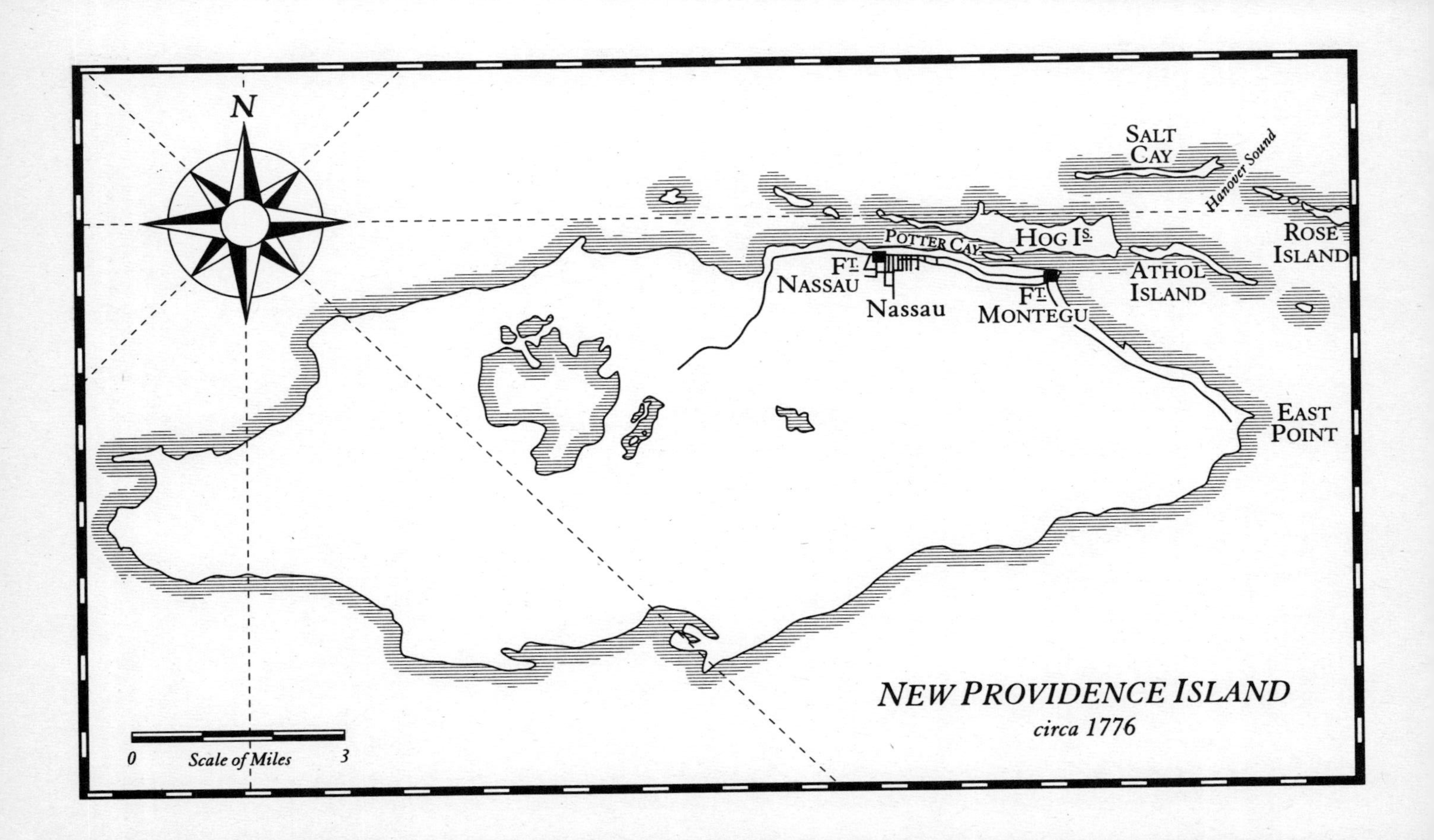
N
Salt Cay
Hanover Sound
Rose Island
Potter Cay
Hog Is.
Ft. Nassau
Nassau
Ft. Montegu
Athol Island
East Point
New Providence Island
circa 1776
0
Scale of Miles
3

PROLOGUE

Second Continental Congress

AT LEAST THERE ARE NO FLIES, HE THOUGHT, BUT THE PRICE YOU PAID for that one minor luxury was the cold, the damnable cold. Stephen Hopkins, delegate from Rhode Island to the Second Continental Congress, pulled his coat tighter against his chest and folded his arms. It was October 5, 1775, and Philadelphia was already cold and wet, a prelude to the coming winter. At sixty-eight years old Hopkins was not as tolerant of such weather as he had once been.

He glanced around the big room in the Philadelphia State House. The delegates from the various colonies were filtering in for the morning's session, though many still remained out of doors, conducting in huddled meetings the real business of Congress. The walls and high ceiling of the room were painted a brilliant white, mitigating the gloom to some degree. The round tables scattered around the floor were covered with rich green cloth, so many little islands, each with a silver inkstand in the middle and a sprout of white quills sticking out at odd angles.

The president's desk sat on a raised stage at the front of the room, flanked on the left and the right by identical fireplaces. Hopkins considered telling the boy to stoke up the fires a bit. He was on the verge of voicing that demand when he heard the familiar clop clop clop of John Adams's walking stick, like someone tapping rapidly on the floor with a small hammer. The Massachusetts delegate moved with his usual frenetic pace across the hall and into the meeting room.

"Well, damn the fire," Hopkins muttered to himself, and then to Samuel Ward, his fellow Rhode Island delegate, he added, "Here's Adams. I'll warrant things will warm up directly."

"Hopkins, there you are," said Adams from across the room, working his way through the tables to the Rhode Island delegation. "I looked for you at your rooms but you had left already."

"I'm willing to rise very early to avoid seeing you first thing in the morning, John," said Hopkins.

"Indeed. Well, you can avoid me no longer. Have you seen the letters from Barry?"

"I have." The letters in question, not yet officially read before Congress, had been carried from England by Capt. John Barry. They reported the sailing of two brigs, unarmed and unescorted, carrying great quantities of military stores and bound away for Quebec.

"I think it likely that we'll see some action now, in the naval line," Hopkins said. "Those members who do not have enough imagination to see the need for a navy in the abstract should at least be able to see the benefit of arming a few ships to capture those brigs."

He ran his eyes over the room. It was now all but full, the many delegates congregating in the hallway having taken their seats, and John Hancock, president of the Congress, was making his usual flamboyant entrance. "Once we turn this corner, we pave the way for the creation of a navy. If you will allow me to thus mix my metaphors."

"In point of fact I agree with you, Hopkins, your literary style notwithstanding," Adams said.

In the front of the room President Hancock brought his gavel down on the desk and called for order, but Adams continued, "I've arranged for Lee to move for a committee of three to draft a proposal to fit out some armed vessels. Once that is passed, I'll require you to nominate myself, Deane, and Langdon for that committee."

"And you reckon you can draft such a proposal?"

"We have already. We need only for the Congress to ask for it."

Hancock once again pounded the desk with his gavel. "I trust you gentlemen will not be too disappointed if we give over our discussion of trade for the moment. We have recently received several letters from England, brought to us by Capt. John Barry, containing information upon which we should consider action. Mr. Thompson, if you would?" Hancock nodded to the secretary.

"Sir," Thompson read out loud, "It has come to my attention, through sundry sources, that there has sailed from this place on the eleventh of August two north country built brigs of no force, last loaded with six thousand stand of arms and a large quantity of powder and other stores for Quebec without a convoy . . ."

Hopkins watched the various expressions across the room as the implication of the letter became clear. He could see on some faces disgust; John Dickinson of Pennsylvania for one, while beside Dickinson, Benjamin Franklin sat expressionless, not even appearing to listen.

I wonder what old Franklin is thinking, Hopkins thought. No doubt he'll favor going after these brigs, thinks we've been too cautious as it is.

Hopkins's eyes moved toward Connecticut's table. Silas Deane sat quite erect, listening intently, like a dog waiting for his master to say "Fetch." New Hampshire, New York, New Jersey, North Carolina, South Carolina, all of the delegates listened closely as it dawned on each of them that they would once again have to make a decision the implications of which were far greater than the immediate effects.

Then finally Thompson came to the end of the letter. At Virginia's table Richard Henry Lee fidgeted and drummed his fingers on the table, anxious to make his motion before any other could be made, as Hancock went through the formalities of having the letter entered into the record.

"Mr. President!" Lee leapt to his feet and called out even before Hancock was quite done speaking. "Mr. President, I move that a committee of three be appointed to prepare a plan for intercepting these two vessels bound for Canada and that said committee proceed on this business immediately."

"So moved," said Hancock. "Does anyone—"

"I second the motion," said Christopher Gadsden of South Carolina.

John Adams leaned over, close to Hopkins. "Now we shall see some lively discussion, I'll warrant."

The first to offer that lively discussion was Edward Rutledge of South Carolina. He rose from his seat beside Gadsden, casting an ugly scowl at his fellow delegate as he did, and addressed Hancock.

"Mr. President," he began, glancing around the room with shifting eyes in his peculiar and annoying manner, "not all of us from the Southern colonies, nay, very few of us indeed, share Mr. Gadsden's enthusiasm for a naval force. A challenge to Great Britain of the high seas, the unprovoked capture of her merchant vessels, would be no less than a declaration of war, a declaration of our desire for independency—"

"If the gentleman would care to put that in the form of a motion, sir," Adams called across the room, "I should gladly second it."

Rutledge stood silent, nodding his head and shrugging his shoulders until the laughter and pounding subsided, then began again. "Sir, I submit that it is the most wild, visionary, mad project that has ever been attempted. We cannot hope to take on the might of the British navy, and such an attempt would bring ruin down on our heads, would destroy any hopes that we might have for reconciliation. It is like an infant taking a mad bull by the horns.

"What is more profound and remote," Rutledge continued,

"such a plan would ruin the character and corrupt the morals of our seamen. It would make them selfish, piratical, mercenary, and bent wholly upon plunder."

"One thing's for certain," Hopkins said to Adams, "Rutledge doesn't know much about the morals of our seamen if he thinks sending them after these brigs will corrupt them any more than they are now."

At last Rutledge finished, and John Adams took the floor. "Mr. President," he began, his voice soft, calm, and reasonable as he began, and building in intensity as he spoke. "As a considerable part of my time, in the course of my profession, I have spent upon the seacoasts of Massachusetts, I have conversed much with the gentlemen who conduct our cod and whale fisheries, as well as the other navigation of the country. I have heard much of the activity, enterprise, patience, perseverance, and daring intrepidity of our seamen. As a result of this personal knowledge I have formed a confident opinion that if they were once let loose upon the ocean, they would contribute greatly to the relief of our wants as well as to the distress of the enemy."

And so it went on through the morning and into the afternoon. Outside the rain let up and a watery sunlight made its way through the tall windows as inside the State House the issue of sending armed vessels after the unarmed ordnance brigs and the greater, the much greater, implications of such action were made to run the gauntlet of debate.

At last the motion of forming a committee was put to a vote, and the motion was passed. Like an actor taking his cue Hopkins moved that the committee consist of Mr. John Adams, Mr. Silas Dean of Connecticut, and Mr. John Langdon of New Hampshire, and that motion too was passed by the same vote as the first. The newly created committee took their leave of the Congress. In an hour they were back.

"Mr. Adams, has your committee prepared a plan regarding the ordnance brigs?" Hancock asked.

"We have, Mr. President, and by your leave I shall read it."

"Pray, Mr. Adams, proceed."

"Resolved, that a letter be sent by express to General Washington, to inform him that Congress having received certain intelligence of the sailing of two north country brigs . . ." Adams read the report, the words couched in his lawyerly language. Hopkins was once again surprised at how such wording could render even the most dramatic documents dull and nearly intolerable to the ear.

". . . he apply to the council of Massachusetts Bay for the two armed vessels in their service, and dispatch the same, with a sufficient number of people, stores, etc., particularly a number of oars, in order, if possible, to intercept said brigs and their cargo, and secure the same for the use of the continent; also, any other transports laden with ammunition, clothing, or other stores—"

"Hold a moment, sir!" John Dickinson was on his feet. Adams stopped and peered with ill-disguised irritation over the top of the paper at the delegate from Pennsylvania. "What is this business about 'any other transports'? The plan was to call for the intercepting of two brigs, two specific brigs. It was not a general invitation to piracy."

"Well, Good Lord, man," Adams replied, "should our vessels ignore any ship just because it is not one of these brigs? Should they let pass a wealth of materials that will strengthen our enemy simply because they are carried on ships that we were not aware of?"

"You go too far, sir, too far by half."

"Point of order, Mr. President," Hopkins called out. "Is this the time for debate?"

"It is not. Mr. Dickinson, please be seated. Mr. Adams, pray continue. We shall have debate after the motion is read."

Adams continued. He read on through instructions for securing the prizes in the most convenient places for the purpose above mentioned, for requesting the governors of Rhode Island and Connecticut to provide the general with ships, for the vessels of war to be on the continental risk and pay.

It was half past eight when the issue came to a vote. One by one the colonies were called, and on the big board that recorded their votes the markers were slid to yea or nay. It seemed to Hopkins that for all the shouting the debate had swayed few opinions. The colonies voted just as they had for the original motion to form a committee.

But that was enough for passage.

"Virginia," the secretary called out.

"Virginia," said Lee in his smooth, confident, aristocratic tone, "says yea."

Hopkins caught Adams's eye and the two men smiled and nodded. Hopkins knew full well what Adams was thinking; it was the same thing that he himself was thinking. They did not yet have a navy, per se, but they had the next best thing. The United Colonies were, as a nation, sending armed vessels out to hunt for British ships. They were taking the war to sea.

CHAPTER 1

The Sound

CAPT. ISAAC BIDDLECOMB TURNED AND STARED OVER THE TAFFRAIL of the *Charlemagne,* brig-of-war. Four miles astern and dead in line with their wake was a British frigate, a powerful enemy in all-out pursuit. Again.

The only odd thing about being thus pursued was how familiar it felt, as if being chased by the Royal Navy were a daily routine. To be sure, they had been chased so often in the past year that Biddlecomb had reason to feel that way. And while the familiarity failed to eliminate his fear, it did much to mitigate it.

They were being overtaken, of that there was no doubt. But in their favor, they were halfway down Long Island Sound, heading for Hell Gate and the East River and the many islands and inlets around New York, with no more than four hours of sunlight left. And that, he felt, with a confidence born of experience, made their escape a near certainty.

He considered the sensation brewing in his gut, the vague terror that was as familiar as the sight of the frigate astern. He was reminded of the time, fifteen years earlier, when as an ordinary seaman he had discovered that laying out on a yard to reef sail in a howling storm was no longer a new and terrifying experience. It had become, rather, an old, familiar terrifying experience.

And so it was here, in late October of 1775, after nearly a year of fighting in a conflict that was not quite a war, for an end on which few agreed, Isaac Biddlecomb found himself once more in the all too familiar position of being chased by a frigate of the Royal Navy.

He had, in the past year, been chased by the frigate *Rose* all over Narragansett Bay. He had been chased by the *Cerberus* through the Caribbean and through these northern waters after leading a mutiny aboard the brig *Icarus*, a vessel of the Royal Navy aboard which he had been impressed. He had been chased by the frigate *Glasgow* in Bermuda, in his ill-fated attempt to liberate British gunpowder from that island, and chased by the two-decker *Somerset* clear across Boston Harbor to the American lines.

So Biddlecomb was not overly surprised when, that morning, with the *Charlemagne* just south of Block Island, the lookout aloft reported the sails of what might well be a man-of-war hull down on the eastern horizon.

And when the strange ship hauled her wind and set studdingsails aloft and alow in what was without question pursuit, Biddlecomb had ordered the brig's canvas stretched, had turned her bow northwest to pass Montauk Point and run into Long Island Sound, and had settled into the monotony of eluding a stern chase. He was tired of being chased and wondered if his grudgingly chosen career as a naval officer would ever entail attacking, as opposed to running away.

"I must say, Captain, your calm demeanor does much to bolster the confidence of your passengers," a feminine voice broke the quiet on the quarterdeck. Biddlecomb pulled his gaze from the frigate's sails and looked over at the leeward side where Virginia Stanton leaned against the rail.

She was dressed in a hooded caraco jacket over a silk dress that flared out at the waist and draped down off of the wire hoops of her false hips. Her hands were thrust into either end of a fur muff to defend against the cold winter air. From beneath her hood and cotton mobcap her brown hair tumbled down around her ruddy face, her girlish smattering of freckles, her playful smile. Biddlecomb could see the toes of her old and well-worn riding boots peeking out under the long skirts. Despite himself and his assumed air of detachment, he smiled as well.

"I am pleased that I can be of some comfort to you, Miss Stanton," Biddlecomb said, smiling broader still at their sham of formality. He wanted to rush across the deck and grab her in his arms and kiss her, a long, lingering kiss, and would have done so had they been alone. "With any luck at all we'll shake them off through Hell Gate or around Long Island," he said instead.

"Hell Gate, is it?" said William Stanton, Virginia's father, who stood beside her at the leeward rail. Stanton squinted at the hilly shoreline of Connecticut, ten miles north of them, then at Long Island, ten miles south. The *Charlemagne* was running nearly dead downwind in a fifteen-knot breeze, running west southwest through Long Island Sound toward the point where that bay narrowed into the East River, with its cluster of islands and the wild dogleg turn through Hell Gate.

"Tide's on the ebb now," Stanton observed. "Water'll be running like a son of a bitch through Hell Gate by the time we get there."

It was an observation by an experienced mariner, and Biddlecomb could hear no implied criticism in Stanton's tone. Stanton, he knew, understood the situation perfectly.

There was every chance that the frigate would not dare follow them through the treacherous passage. Big ships rarely went through that way; indeed, it was rare for any ship, big or small, to risk itself among the rocks, islands, and back eddies of that twisted passage, particularly at the height of the ebb when the water crashed through the Gate like a flash flood.

And even if the frigate did dare to follow them, and assuming they both made it, on the other side were any number of rivers and bays around New York in which they could hide or at least keep ahead of their enemy until nightfall. Once it was dark, the *Charlemagne* could disappear. Virginia's confidence was not misplaced, or so Biddlecomb assured himself, and her obvious admiration of his boldness bolstered in turn his own confidence.

"Did I ever tell you, Isaac, of the time I took the old *Providence* through Hell Gate, back in the winter of '64 . . . or '65, one of those?" Stanton asked.

"No, sir, I don't believe you did," Biddlecomb lied, running his eyes over the *Charlemagne*'s rig and her waist as Stanton launched into the story, as well-worn as Virginia's boots. From long experience Biddlecomb nodded and smiled at the appropriate spots, but his thoughts were on the condition of the vessel under his command. To any observer a mile or so away, or to anyone unfamiliar with the way of ships, she was a lovely sight, well proportioned, her sails set and drawing, her rig taut and blacked down.

But a closer look would reveal the crazing in that facade. Her mainmast was fished five feet above the deck; stout lengths of timber were lashed around the circumference of the mast to take the strain where the actual wood had been nearly shot through. The red paint on the inboard side of the bulwarks and the linseed oil on the outboard side were variegated shades of dark and light where sections of the brig's side had been knocked flat and then repaired and freshly finished. The main topgallant sail and the fore topsail were brand-new and stood out from their worn and much patched brethren aloft. The *Charlemagne* was a tired vessel.

Over a month before she had fought a running battle with the two-decker *Somerset,* racing across Boston Harbor, and was nearly beaten to death before Biddlecomb ran her aground at the feet of the American army encamped in the hills surrounding the city and laying siege to the ministerial army there. Along with the *Charlemagne,* Biddlecomb had brought in a prize, the *Mayor of Plymouth,* loaded to the deckhead with gunpowder, that precious compound of which the American forces were in desperate need.

The praise, bordering on adoration, that had followed that feat had been overwhelming. For the next month, after working the battered *Charlemagne* up the Charles River to Cambridge, Biddlecomb had seen to the *Charlemagne*'s repairs during the day and allowed himself to be toasted in all circles by night. In a year of novel situations he found himself in the most novel, and most pleasant, of all. He was a hero.

They did the best that they could, setting the *Charlemagne* to rights, but Cambridge was not a maritime center and the facilities for repairing a vessel were less than adequate. So rather than hope for a new mainmast they split their damaged spars into long fishes and bound them with rope to the mast and patched their sails in those instances where there was material enough left to patch.

And in those cases where the canvas could not be patched, or the lines long spliced or the spars fished, they tried their best to wrest stores from the few chandlers in the area, but acquiring new supplies, it turned out, was even more difficult then repairing old.

The General Court of Massachusetts had passed an act to issue letters of marque to ship owners with a thought to go privateering, and these private men-of-war were gobbling up stores at a prodigious rate. So confident were the privateersmen in the profitability of their ventures, and so eager were they to get to sea, that they were quite willing to give the chandlers three times the asking price for needed materials, a largess that the beleaguered Continental Army could never hope to match. And so the poor *Charlemagne*, commissioned by General Washington, whose authority over naval matters was at best questionable, had to settle for the scraps left by the privateers.

He had written to William Stanton in Bristol, informing him of his whereabouts and the events that had led him there. He had written to Virginia as well, and if he had not, at the last instant, been able to pour out his affections with as much abandon as he had intended, he nonetheless made it clear that he was not writing with any sense of mere platonic affection.

A dozen times at least he had informed Ezra Rumstick, his longtime friend and the *Charlemagne*'s first lieutenant, that he would be leaving for Bristol forthwith. And every time something—an unplanned meeting with General Washington, crucial negotiations with a chandler, some aspect of the *Charlemagne*'s repair that required his attention—had come up and stopped him. So he planned and waited and fretted about Virginia's feelings for him.

Midway through their third week in Cambridge, Biddlecomb resigned himself to the idea that he would not be going to Bristol anytime soon, and that there would be no new mainmast. The next morning he began fishing the old.

He was supervising the job personally, and by midafternoon it was all but done. " 'Vast heaving!" he called out to the men on the capstan. The line running from the mainmast to the capstan was hauled nearly to the breaking point. He put his hands on it and tried to flex it back and forth, but it was unyielding. Along its length drops of tar were oozing from the strands.

"That's well," Biddlecomb said. He glanced over at the wooden wharf to which the *Charlemagne* was tied. William Stanton was standing there, and beside him Virginia, familiar faces from another place. He stared for a minute, confused, trying to place those faces with this location. Then Stanton leapt onto the gangplank and ran aboard, arms outstretched, and embraced him, unaware of or unconcerned about the tar with which he was liberally splattered.

Biddlecomb squeezed the old man in turn and looked over Stanton's shoulder at Virginia, still standing on the dock. She smiled, her wide smile, in parts amused and mocking and affectionate, and gave him a tiny wave.

He was about to call out to her, his mouth was open, when Stanton released him, grabbed him by the shoulder and half spun him around, shouting, "Rumstick!" as the hulking first officer stepped up, grinning, hand outstretched. There followed half an hour of introductions, congratulations, and technical discussions, during which Virginia stood off to the side, smiling to mask her boredom, and Biddlecomb was able to get no more than a "Good to see you so fit, Captain Biddlecomb" from her by way of conversation.

At last Biddlecomb was able to pull Stanton from the boisterous camaraderie and invite him and his daughter below. "There was some fine Madeira, wonderful stuff, in the great cabin of the *Mayor of Plymouth* that I reckoned to be fair spoils of war," he said. "Won't you join me in a glass? Virginia?"

"Delighted! Lead on, sir," Stanton said, and the three of them, Stanton, Virginia, and Biddlecomb, made their way down the narrow after companionway. They crossed the gunroom and stepped into Biddlecomb's quarters, which carried the traditional, if perhaps, for that cramped space, pretentious title of "great cabin."

"Oh, damn me," Stanton said. "I've a message for Rumstick. Please excuse me for a minute." And with that he was out the door.

And they were alone. "Well, Virginia," Biddlecomb began. His eyes were fixed on her face. Her smile was fading, not gone, but changed into something else: a frustrated desire, perhaps, to say something, a desire for him to say something. He stopped and looked at that smile, but he could think of nothing to say.

And then the desire rushed over him, an aching need, a physical thing, and before he even knew that he was going to speak, he said, "I love you, Virginia."

"I love you too," Virginia said, and suddenly he was across the cabin and wrapping his arms around her small frame and she was wrapping her arms around his shoulders and they were kissing, long and desperate. He could feel the curve of her waist even through the riding cloak and the silk dress and bodice and shift, could feel her breasts pressed against his chest.

He wanted to hold her completely, to feel every part of her pressed against every part of him. He wanted to say so much to her, he wanted to laugh with joy, but he did not. He could not stop kissing her, he could not stop the venting of years of suppressed passion.

From somewhere beyond the cabin he heard the scuttle door open and heard boots on the ladder, but he could not pull away from her. He heard boots coming across the gunroom, and at last he stepped back, his hands still on her waist, seeing nothing but her eyes. Then he dropped his hands to his side and turned just as Stanton stepped back into the great cabin.

"You know, Isaac, about those wedges under the woolding there on your fish . . . ," Stanton began, and his eyes moved between Biddlecomb and his daughter, then back to Biddlecomb. The old man could be obtuse at times, but he was not so obtuse that he could not see what was happening there. The great cabin was silent, and Biddlecomb could hear Rumstick topside calling orders to the men on the capstan.

"Yes, sir, the wedges?" Biddlecomb asked at length, and with obvious relief Stanton leapt into the subject of repairing damaged spars.

"In any event," Stanton said, after giving his advice on fishing spars, "I received a letter from Hopkins . . . you know Stephen Hopkins? Of the Providence Hopkinses? Delegate, former governor?"

"I know of him," Biddlecomb said. Indeed it would be hard to live in Rhode Island and Providence Plantations and not know of Stephen Hopkins.

"Well, Stephen wrote and asked if I'd like to serve his committee, assistant secretary of the Naval Committee, or some such nonsense."

"Naval Committee? What does the Naval Committee do? I wasn't aware that there was even a navy."

"It just happened, officially," Stanton said. "They just authorized the purchase of a few ships and formed this committee. So now there is a navy of sorts, a bunch of merchantmen they're beefing up and turning into men-of-war."

Stanton's tone left little doubt as to his position regarding that plan. "Nonsense, of course, as you well know. If you want a man-of-war, you have to build a man-of-war, like *Charlemagne* here. No merchant brig could have lived through the pounding she's taken. But I reckon there's neither time nor money to build new—"

"So Hopkins asked you . . . ?" Biddlecomb cut Stanton off. If he was allowed to get full under way with this line of thought, Biddlecomb knew from long use, there would be no stopping him.

"Yes. He said they need people working for them that know ships, understand what's required. I reckon my involvement in the Rhode Island navy gave him the idea I know something of naval affairs."

"You know as much as anyone in the Colonies, I should think."

"Well, I was honored, to say the least, and I accepted right off. I had to take Rogers, of course, I'd be lost without him, and I couldn't leave Virginia alone, so we're moving the whole household to Philadelphia."

Biddlecomb glanced at Virginia. She was excited about the trip, he could tell as much, excited to live in the biggest city in the Colonies.

"It was my thinking, you know," Stanton continued, "that you and *Charlemagne* would be best off going to Philadelphia. That's where it's happening, in the naval line."

"You see a place for *Charlemagne* in this navy they're forming?"

"I do. I reckoned when *Charlemagne* was ready, why, we'd all take passage to Philadelphia. Kill two birds, you know. I'd a mind . . . I mean I had thought that, if it is agreeable to you, perhaps *Charlemagne* might just be leased to the Naval Committee. You're to retain command, of course."

Biddlecomb smiled and nodded his head. Stanton was being

as political as he could; despite the familial aspects of their relationship, Stanton was in fact the outright owner of the *Charlemagne* and could do whatsoever he pleased with her.

"A fine plan. I would be honored, of course, to serve as an officer in the navy of the United Colonies, and frankly I'll be quite pleased to see a real navy come together, converted merchantmen or not."

It was another week before they were blessed with the right conditions for slipping past the blockading squadron: quarter moon with a promise of morning fog, light airs from the northwest, and an ebb tide just past midnight. A pilot was summoned, a man whose local knowledge encompassed every shoal, rock and shifting bank of sand, and in the darkness the *Charlemagne*'s dock lines were singled up and topsails loosened off.

"Mr. Rumstick," Biddlecomb called forward. He spoke in a loud whisper; there were enough people in Cambridge of dubious loyalty, and enough time for such people to get word to the Royal Navy, that he did not care to advertise their departure. He was about to follow the hail with orders to set the fore topsail when a coach and four came rumbling and creaking down the quay. The driver reined the horses to a noisy stop as the door was flung open.

"Ahoy, there! Ahoy, is this the *Charlemagne?*" a voice called from the dark interior of the carriage. Biddlecomb wondered if there was anyone in Cambridge who was not startled awake by the noise.

"Yes," he called back hesitantly.

"Are you getting under way?" the man in the carriage demanded next.

It was irritating in the extreme that any degree of secrecy was now lost, and Biddlecomb was not about to begin shouting out his intentions like a town crier. "Look, here—" he began, then the man in the carriage cut him off.

"Of course you're getting under way, singled up and topsails loosened off, I must be quite blind." The stranger stepped out of the carriage struggling with a large bag which he carried over to the *Charlemagne*. The driver of the coach snapped his whip and the vehicle rumbled off into the dark. The stranger dropped his bag on the quay and glared at the sailors staring back at him.

"You there, take this on board," he snapped in a tone that demanded obedience, and much to Biddlecomb's further annoyance a sailor leapt ashore and snatched up the man's bag and carried it on board, as behind him the bag's owner clambered over the bulwark.

Biddlecomb turned to William Stanton, who was standing on the starboard side of the quarterdeck, hoping that he might have some explanation. "I think that may be . . . ," Stanton began, but before he finished the stranger was up the quarterdeck ladder and making his way aft. He was not a tall man, and the lines of his conservative black coat showed him to be plump. His long hair—he wore no wig—was tied back in a queue, and a civilian-style cocked hat was on his head.

"Are you Biddlecomb?" he asked.

"Captain Biddlecomb. And as such I will not—"

"Yes, I am fully aware of who you are. Good show with the powder, by the way. I'm John Adams, and I'm sure there's no need to explain who I am. I shall be taking passage to Philadelphia with you. And I will say simply that the British would willingly lose half their navy to capture me, so please do not take any unnecessary risks. You there"—he pointed with his walking stick to Midshipman Weatherspoon—"take my bag and show me to my cabin." With that he turned and went forward, then disappeared down the scuttle.

"Oh, yes, Isaac," Stanton said, "I'm afraid there was one other arrangement that I failed to mention."

And now, four days later, Biddlecomb stood on the quarterdeck watching either shore of Long Island Sound slip past and enjoyed the relative calm of being chased by a frigate.

From the moment the *Charlemagne* had successfully slipped

out of Boston Harbor, passing at least one British man-of-war so close that they could hear the ship's bell ringing out in the fog, he had endured Adams's presence in the gunroom and his loitering about on the windward side of the quarterdeck, quite contrary to maritime etiquette. He had endured Adams's suggestions and his criticisms and his condemnation of all but a handful of his fellow congressmen.

Fifty yards off the larboard beam a seal rolled its sleek body out of the water. "Oh, Virginia, look at this," Biddlecomb said as the door to the after scuttle burst open and with it came Adams's grating voice, and Biddlecomb knew that his moment of peace was at an end.

"Honest to God, Rumstone," Adams was saying to the first lieutenant, Ezra Rumstick, who was, as he had at every opportunity, tagging behind Adams like a big dog, "if we keep referring to ourselves as 'United Colonies,' we shall never rid ourselves of the notion that we *are* but colonies and not free and independent states, as we should be. It's bad enough that I can't get those blockheads in Congress to refer to us as the United States, I should hope that at least men such as yourself, one of the Sons of Liberty, hotheads though they are, could be depended upon to say 'United States.' "

"Yes, of course, sir," Rumstick said, "and truly I am accustomed to saying 'United States.' I don't know . . ."

Adams moved with his usual brisk pace up the quarterdeck ladder and aft to where the captain stood. "Captain Biddlecomb," he began. Biddlecomb looked over Adams's shoulder to Rumstick and reminded his first officer, through a narrowing of his eyes and a tilt of the head, that it was his, Rumstick's, duty to keep passengers from harassing the captain on his private side of the quarterdeck. Rumstick, by way of answer, merely rolled his eyes and shrugged.

Biddlecomb was in fact shocked to see the degree of sycophancy displayed by Rumstick, an attitude that was most unlike anything he had seen from his friend before. Rumstick stood six foot two and was close to three hundred pounds, the most powerful man that Biddlecomb had ever known. Like any professional seaman Rumstick accepted the ship's hierarchy without question, but beyond that he had never been known to behave so like a serf in the presence of his lord and master, radical revolutionary that he was. When Biddlecomb mentioned it that morning in the privacy of the great cabin, Rumstick had said simply, "But, Isaac, that's John Adams," as if that were all the explanation required.

"Captain Biddlecomb," Adams said again, "I trust you have made some provision to elude that frigate?"

Biddlecomb looked Adams in the eye for long seconds before replying, "I have, sir."

"Isaac, you may recall, has a long history of getting out of such situations," Stanton said, crossing over to the weather side. "I should think that this situation is a trifle compared to what he just did in Boston."

"Yes, and bravo I say, but it is this frigate, not the one in Boston, that concerns me." Adams's voice conveyed not the least bit of fear; he seemed to view the frigate now chasing them as the same type of minor irritant that plagued every aspect of his life.

"I'm not certain they'll care to follow us through Hell Gate," Biddlecomb said, "but even if they do, I should think we'll be able to keep away from them until nightfall. In any event it would take a bit of extremely bad luck for them to run us down now."

He said the words with little enthusiasm; indeed, he was hardly thinking as he spoke. The chief of his attention was drawn down into the waist, just forward of the break of the quarterdeck, where the carpenter was sounding the well, gauging the depth of water in the *Charlemagne*'s bilge with the iron sounding rod. Biddlecomb was not at all comforted by the carpenter's expression.

It had occurred to Biddlecomb five minutes before that the motion of the *Charlemagne* was somewhat sluggish underfoot, but he had noticed that sensation at other times when the wind was so far aft of the beam and so he dismissed it.

The men had been working the pumps an hour per watch; a lot of pumping, but not an excessive amount for a vessel that had seen such hard use without heaving down. Still, the water that had just flowed from the pumps was clear and clean: not water that had long been in the bilge but water fresh from the sea.

The carpenter pulled the sounding rod out of the well. His expression was, if anything, more distressed than before. He handed the rod to his mate and disappeared below.

"Hancock!" Adams was saying, quite loud, apparently in response to some comment of Rumstick's. "Oh, Hancock's fine as a delegate, but, by God, did you know that the man wanted to be commander in chief of the army, in Washington's stead? Can you think of it? I mean, Washington's no Alexander himself, but Hancock?"

"Isaac, is there something wrong?" Stanton asked in a low voice, glancing over the taffrail at the frigate, now three and a half miles astern. Biddlecomb's quarterdeck face, his expression of unflappable calm that he had developed through long practice, failed to conceal from Stanton his churning stomach and his sense of pending disaster.

"I should think we'll hear from the carpenter directly," Biddlecomb said, "and then I'll be able to answer that."

Less than a minute later the carpenter burst out of the after scuttle like a startled pheasant and fairly ran up the quarterdeck ladder and aft. He stopped in front of Biddlecomb, saluted, and without waiting for acknowledgment said as calmly as his heaving for breath would allow, "We sprung a plank, sir, right up by the bow, and damn me to hell if we aren't taking on water like a son of a whore."

Biddlecomb nodded his head. It was what he had suspected, and it was, by any definition, a bit of extremely bad luck.

CHAPTER 2

Hell Gate

"OH, THIS IS MARVELOUS, CAPTAIN," SAID ADAMS. "TELL ME, WHICH are we to do first, drown or be captured?"

"I'm not certain, Mr. Adams," Biddlecomb said, considering the options available, two of which Adams had just mentioned, "but when I find out, I'll be certain to let you know. Now . . ." He turned to the carpenter.

"Clearly we must jettison the guns," Adams said. "We shall start that immediately. Rumstone—"

"Mr. Adams," Biddlecomb said calmly in a tone that did not admit to questioning, "if you presume to give another order aboard my vessel, I shall have you restrained below."

"Well, for God's sakes, man!" Adams searched the other faces of the quarterdeck for support and, seeing none, stamped off to the leeward side and leaned against the bulwark, arms folded across his chest.

"Mr. 'Rumstone'," Biddlecomb said, "please roust out the watch below and set hands to the pumps," and then, turning to the carpenter, continued, "Tell me about the leak."

"It's the hood-end, right up against the stem, sir, starboard side, about three foot below the waterline, and it's coming in like a son of a whore. Don't know if the plank's sprung or rotten clean away or what."

"Too big a hole to drive a plug in?"

"Lord, bless you, sir, yes. Too big even for a piece of beef."

"Very well. Please see to the pumps. Take whatever hands you need to keep them going. Mr. Sprout!" Biddlecomb called out to the *Charlemagne*'s bosun. Sprout hurried aft with the odd rolling stride he used whenever he was in a hurry, the result of a large body and squat legs. "Mr. Sprout, we're taking on water, right up against the stem on the starboard side. We'll have to fother a sail over it, just a spare staysail or whatever you have, we've no time for fancier."

"Aye, sir," Sprout said, saluting and hurrying forward.

"Mr. Rumstick." This was the order he least wished to give, but he had no choice. He had to relieve the pressure of the water on the bow. He was tempted to look over his shoulder at the frigate following astern, but he fought it down. "Mr. Rumstick, we'll have the studdingsails in, then clew up everything save the topsails."

"Aye, sir," Rumstick said, then turning forward bellowed, "Hands aloft to take in studdingsails!"

Every man aboard, Biddlecomb was certain, was aware of their situation, there being no more efficient system on earth for disseminating information than shipboard rumor. Those men not racing aloft in obediance to Rumstick's orders were peering over the side and aft, gauging how long it would be before the frigate caught up with them. Ten minutes ago the estimate would have been four hours at least. Now, with the sails coming in as fast as they could be fisted, it would take less than half that time.

At the larboard rail Stanton was explaining to Adams, "He has no choice but take in sail. The faster we go the more the water comes in through the bow and the more likely it is that we sink."

That was exactly right. Biddlecomb looked at the shoreline to the north and south of their position. The closest land was ten miles off. If he crowded on sail, he could probably run the *Charlemagne* aground before the frigate came up with them. But if he crowded on sail, then the chances were better than even that they would sink before reaching land, and if he headed for shore under topsails alone, then the frigate would catch them before they were halfway there. His only option was to keep running directly away from their pursuit. But that in itself would not save them, it would only mean freedom for an additional hour or so.

"I have no doubt," Virginia was saying, "that the captain has some scheme to keep us from capture."

The captain in question stared at the frigate astern, pretending not to listen to the conversation on the leeward side, and wondered if Virginia really believed that. He couldn't imagine that she did. She was an insightful woman, startlingly so at times, and he doubted that she could believe with certainty something of which he himself was entirely unsure. His hand moved to the hilt of his sword, the beautiful sword that he had liberated from its last owner, a lieutenant in the British navy, and grasped the handle as if it were a talisman.

"Understand," Adams said to the Stantons, "that I am not without some knowledge of maritime affairs. I have spent a considerable part of my time, in the course of my profession, upon the seacoasts of Massachusetts. I have conversed much with the gentlemen who conduct our fisheries, as well as the other navigation of the country . . ."

As Adams continued to explain his intimacy with shipping, Biddlecomb stared absently aloft. Men in each top were folding the studdingsails that had been pulled in, and men on the topgallant yards and the foreyard were stowing sail.

A month before, this evolution would have been done twice as quickly. But a month before, the *Charlemagne* carried a much different crew, both in terms of numbers and experience. Naval stores were not the only things that were going first to the privateers. With the promise of easier discipline, shorter enlistments, and vastly greater profits, all of the best seamen in the Colonies were opting for the private men-of-war.

Biddlecomb had a few holdouts; his officers and petty officers had stayed with him, as had a core of men: Woodberry,

Ferguson, and a few others who had been with him since his days as a merchant captain. But many of the Charlemagnes had melted away and, he imagined, were even now seeking out rich prizes aboard the fast, heavily manned privateers.

More than twenty minutes later Sprout announced the sail properly fothered over the hole, and in that twenty minutes the frigate had gone from being a distant concern to being a genuine and growing menace. She was, by Biddlecomb's estimate, now two miles astern and visibly closing the gap.

"I imagine that patch won't hold if we set studdingsails," Biddlecomb said to Sprout, who was now aft on the quarterdeck. "But we must set plain sail at the very least, or we might as well let her sink."

"I wouldn't place a wager on the patch holding even with just plain sail set, sir," Sprout said. "There wasn't the time for me to do it the way I'd have liked—"

"I understand, Mr. Sprout," Biddlecomb said, then called out for topgallants and foresail to be set once again. It was a game of chance, one that they had to play. The increased pressure brought on the patch by their increased speed could tear the fothered sail clean away. But if they did not sail faster, then they would be overtaken. As it was, their chances of staying ahead of the frigate until nightfall did not look promising. Not promising at all.

"Mr. Rumstick, we'll clear for action, if you please," Biddlecomb said, and one shouted order brought men swarming over the deck, casting off the great guns, laying out rammers and swabs and tubs of smoldering match.

The *Charlemagne*'s gunner was new to his post. Biddlecomb had innocently introduced the former gunner, William Jaeger, a veteran artillery officer of the Prussian army, to an old acquaintance of his, Henry Knox, a bookseller from Boston. It turned out that Knox was now an artillery officer himself. The two became fast friends and Biddlecomb at last had no choice but to dismiss Jaeger from service aboard the *Charlemagne* in order that he might join Knox's unit. But Jaeger had taught the Charlemagnes well, and they were fast and efficient in preparing the brig for battle.

Midshipman Weatherspoon dashed up from below. At fifteen years old he was already a veteran of a number of desperate fights aboard the *Charlemagne*. He took his place on the quarterdeck, relieved, no doubt, to be free of the navigational trigonometry that so baffled him, but which on most days Biddlecomb insisted he study.

"Isaac, is there anything I can do?" Stanton asked quietly, stepping over to the weather side.

"Yes, in fact, if you would take the conn, that will relieve me of one thing, at least." Stanton had sailed these waters many times—more times, in fact, than Biddlecomb—and he would be more than capable of seeing to the *Charlemagne*'s navigation.

"Gladly," Stanton said, stepping over to the helmsmen.

"Mr. Stanton has the conn," Biddlecomb said to the helmsmen.

"Captain?" Stanton said, his voice now loud enough to be heard around the deck. Never had Biddlecomb's mentor, the man for whom he had worked for fifteen years, from cabin boy to master, addressed him as "captain," and he was a bit taken aback.

"Yes . . . Mr. Stanton?" he said, adjusting with some difficulty to their changing roles.

"What course?"

"Keep her headed for Hell Gate," Biddlecomb said as if he had a plan and that were a part of it. He turned and looked over the waist. The ship was cleared for action, the men at their posts, and Rumstick was heading aft to report the time that it had taken. Once again they would settle down and wait, though now any sense of monotony was quite gone.

Two hours later, two hours of watching the frigate draw inexorably nearer, Biddlecomb realized that she was the HMS *Glasgow*, freshly repaired after the damage that he himself had inflicted on her two months before. She was a mile and a half astern, no more than that, her buff bowsprit and oiled jibboom thrusting high above the water, all sail set to studdingsails and royals, the churning foam under her bow boiling halfway up the cutwater.

He recalled the last time they had been in this position, the *Glasgow* racing to catch the *Charlemagne*. At that time her jibboom was gone and her bowsprit jury-rigged and her fore topgallant gear torn away. There had been no fear of capture then. But this time his was the crippled vessel. He wondered if Capt. William Maltby was still in command. If he was, then Biddlecomb could expect no mercy from that quarter.

He realized that he was gripping hard on the quarterdeck rail. Fear, physical fear, and panic at the hopelessness of their situation were seeping in around the edges of his thoughts. He remembered the parties in Cambridge given in his honor, the secret delight he took in his role of hero. A flush of embarrassment swept over him. Some hero, some pathetic pretender of a hero.

But he was not beaten yet, he would not be controlled by his fear. Nor was he ready to hand the *Charlemagne* over after all they had been through. While there was still sea room, there was still a chance.

He could make out the little town of New Rochelle just beyond the starboard bow, where Long Island Sound began to constrict into the East River, with its islands and spits of land reaching out into the water. The tide was on the ebb, sweeping them and the *Glasgow* downriver. Another few miles and they would have no choice but to race through Hell Gate and into New York Harbor; they would not be able to turn and sail back against the tide.

Biddlecomb tried to picture it in his mind: the *Charlemagne* working through the wild turn at Hell Gate, past Hallet's Point, then between Frying Pan and Hog's Back, the *Glasgow* just astern by then, if not alongside. They would be safe in that narrow water, but once they shot out the other side, once in New York Harbor, they were lost. The *Glasgow* would be on them.

Suddenly Biddlecomb felt his grip on the rail ease, felt the twist in his stomach and the tingling on the soles of his feet that heralded the first awakening of an idea. He looked astern at the frigate. The timing on this would have to be perfect.

"Mr. Rumstick, Mr. Sprout, lay aft please," he called out, and the odd sound of his own voice made him realize how silent the ship had been for the past twenty minutes. But now a buzz ran through the men as the first officer and the bosun made their way aft. Biddlecomb saw some grin, and some of the older hands whispering to those new to the *Charlemagne*. They knew by now, as well as he did, the signs of a plan springing to life.

The confidence that they had in him was, by his own estimate, completely out of proportion with reality, but it was clear that his merely conferring with his officers gave the men faith. He felt as if there was a veil between the quarterdeck and the waist, a thin gauze, and if those men forward had the insight to pull the veil back, they would realize that there was nothing was there.

"Mr. Sprout, what is the state of the sheet anchor?" he asked.

"It's secured for sea, sir, but the cable's bent and it would take just a few minutes to let her go." Sprout gave the answer that Biddlecomb had expected.

"Very good. We'll make ready to let it go, but I don't want them"—Biddlecomb indicated with a nod of his head the frigate that was now a mere mile astern—"to see what we're about. So, Mr. Rumstick, I'll thank you to brace up a bit sharper on the port tack. The clew of the foresail should hide the activity on the channel."

Rumstick looked over his head at the sails, then turned his face into the wind, and Biddlecomb could see the look of disapproval forming. "Yes," he said before Rumstick could object, "I know the sails will set like washing hung out to dry, but we'll just have to endure it for the time being." Beside hiding the men on the channel, the poor set of the sails would allow the *Glasgow* to catch up a bit; she was overhauling them quickly, but not quite quickly enough for the plan that was coming together.

"Sharper port tack, aye, sir," Rumstick said, good subordinate that he was, and hurried forward, Sprout at his heels.

The sails did indeed look like laundry on a line, and the *Charlemagne*'s speed fell off noticeably, but that was fine with Biddlecomb. The frigate had closed a great deal of distance; with her towering rig and her longer waterline and the *Charlemagne*'s inability to carry anything beyond plain sail, Biddlecomb guessed that the *Glasgow* was going half again as fast as the brig. But they were just passing Prospect Point, racing down toward Throg's Neck and the East River, and she was still three-quarters of a mile astern; too far away for Biddlecomb's purposes.

The after-scuttle door flew open with a crash and John Adams emerged on deck, a pistol in each hand, a pouch over his shoulder. Biddlecomb had not even noticed that he was gone. He stepped up to the quarterdeck and handed one of the weapons to Virginia. She took the pistol with the ease of familiarity and held it sideways as she drew back the cock and pulled the trigger, nodding with approval at the resulting spark.

"Vir—Miss Stanton, I must insist that you go below," Biddlecomb said with the tone in which he couched all of his commands. "I think the hold would be best, for the present."

Virginia smiled at the suggestion, as if she found it genuinely amusing, but before she could speak, Adams spoke for her.

"Really, Biddlecomb, I've been talking with the girl at some length now about firearms, and I'm convinced that she has a great deal of expertise. As it seems clear we are to get into some type of fight, I should think you would want every able shot on deck."

"Well, certainly, but . . . she's . . ."

"A woman, yes, I've observed as much, but if she can shoot straight, we shouldn't hold sex against her."

Virginia was smiling broader now, and Biddlecomb knew that his red face was as much a source of her amusement as anything, and he knew that that in turn was making him blush harder still.

"Very well, you may remain on deck for the present," he said, then called for Rumstick to lay aft before anything more on the subject could be said.

"Mr. Rumstick, I've a mind to slow us down a bit, let them close up on us. Get some hands out on the bowsprit and lash up the fore staysail as some kind of sea anchor, then lower it away on its halyard. The foresail should hide you from view."

"Aye, sir," Rumstick said, and once again hurried forward, calling out the names of half a dozen of the more experienced hands to come with him.

Not ten minutes later the fore staysail was under the bow and adding its considerable drag to the barnacles and kelp that were already slowing the brig. Biddlecomb turned to the frigate, sweeping the deck with his telescope. The spritsail, braced square, hid his view of the figurehead and the foredeck, and only glimpses of the raised quarterdeck were visible around the fore- and mainsails. He could see clusters of blue coats, the officers relegated to the leeward side. There seemed to be no excitement, no running about, no fingers pointing. That at least gave him hope that his intentions had not been divined.

"You know, Biddlecomb," John Adams said from a foot away, his voice, loud as ever, making Isaac jump, "this is marvelous, marvelous. Makes a man feel alive!"

Biddlecomb took the telescope from his eye and looked down into the shorter man's face. Adams was smiling, grinning really, a broad and genuine grin of pure exhilaration. "I can quite see why you become so fond of this."

"To say I'm fond of it, Mr. Adams, may be going it a bit high. I suppose if I had some kind of a priori assurance of escape, this part would be more enjoyable, but as it stands, I really can't say that I'm having fun. Still, I'll admit I do like the telling of the story after the outcome has been determined in my favor."

"Quite right, Biddlecomb. Bravo. But I tell you, man, you sit in that fly-infested State House and listen to those chuckle-heads drone on and on about reconciliation and Petitions to the King and the invulnerability of the damned British Navy and you'll realize just how edifying your part of this thing is. You're doing something here, taking real action. Well, in this instance you're running away, but you understand my drift. You can take the initiative, do something. God but I wish I could command Congress the way you can your ship."

"I see your point, though I would venture to say that anything, even something as thrilling as being chased in a sinking ship by a greatly superior force, becomes a bit of a bore with repetition."

"I should imagine. Now, what's our plan?"

Biddlecomb was about to assure Adams that he, Adams, would learn of the plan the moment that the British did, when he was interrupted by the *Glasgow*'s bow chaser. The report of the gun was loud, the frigate now less than a half a mile astern, and as if to serve as a further warning the echo of the gun came again and again from the close by shore.

But there was no damage to the *Charlemagne*, and Biddlecomb doubted that the frigate's bow chasers would even bear on them. The gun was primarily to unnerve the Americans, and judging from the uneasy glances aft and the heads craning over the bulwark and looking astern it was having just that effect. Adams, however, grinned harder and fingered the butt of the pistol he had thrust in his waistband. Like aqua vitae to a midwife, Biddlecomb thought.

"Miss Stanton, I think it time you went below," he called out.

"I'll go below directly, Captain," said Virginia, heading forward toward the break of the quarterdeck.

They rounded Throg's Neck and turned more westerly, and Biddlecomb ordered the yards braced around. They were into the East River now, encompassed by the colony of New York. He could see the water piling up around the rocks that thrust out of the water near the shore, could see flotsam carried swiftly in the fast-moving stream.

Stanton stood just to weather of the helmsmen, hands clasped behind his back, his feet apart, the white hair under his cocked hat whipping around in the following wind. He wore a stoic, disinterested expression, but Biddlecomb was not fooled. The old man was enjoying himself and found this every bit as exhilarating as Adams. More perhaps, for Stanton had spent his youth and early manhood at sea. His had been the life of a sailor and an adventurer, not the life of a city attorney.

Only in his later years had he been forced to give that up to tend to a merchant fleet grown too large to manage from shipboard and to raise his daughter ashore (as a girl she had accompanied him to sea many times) after her mother's death. Biddlecomb tried to imagine how Stanton would feel about his protégé kissing his daughter.

Isaac glanced over at the space of deck where Virginia had been standing and was surprised to find her standing there still. "Miss Stanton, I thought you were going below."

"I am, just this minute, Captain."

"Well, please do so," he said with more irritation in his voice than had been there a moment before.

"Captain," William Stanton said in a low voice, and Biddlecomb stepped over to him. "Might I suggest that you let at least two hundred feet of cable go before you make it off? With the bow weak as it is, snubbing it up short might tear it clean out, but with enough scope the weight of the rope will take up the shock immeasurably."

"Quite right, William," Biddlecomb said, smiling despite himself. Stanton had figured out what he was about to do.

The *Glasgow* fired again, the sound louder, much louder now. She had closed to less than a quarter of a mile and was drawing perceptibly nearer every moment. Past the bow Biddlecomb could see the north and south shores of Hell Gate,

Montresor and Buchannan's Islands and Hallet's Point, two miles away. The *Charlemagne* was going too slow; at that rate they would be under the *Glasgow*'s broadside before they even made it to the Gate, and that would be an end to things.

"Mr. Rumstick, send someone to cut that fore staysail away. Just cut it!" Biddlecomb waited, ten seconds, twenty seconds, and then the *Charlemagne* lurched forward as the sea anchor was cut free. She felt lighter underfoot and he could sense, without measuring it against the shore, that they were moving faster.

He stepped aft to the taffrail and peered down into their wake, afraid that the sail would hang up in the rudder and continue to slow them down. But the gray bundle of canvas emerged from beneath the counter, undulating and sinking in the river. By the time the *Glasgow* passed over it, it would be embedded in the muck.

He looked up at the *Glasgow*, towering over them. Less than three hundred yards astern. Along her yellow sides he could see the gunports raised, the great guns run out. He had hoped they would not do that, not yet. He had hoped to avoid her broadside. But now that would be impossible.

The land to the north and south was passing swiftly, more swiftly than was warranted by the mere fifteen knots of wind that was blowing over their transom. The current was carrying the *Charlemagne*, sweeping her down to Hell Gate, and sweeping the frigate along with her.

"Make your head right for Hallet's Point," Biddlecomb called forward to William Stanton.

"Right for Hallet's Point, aye," Stanton replied, then turning to the helmsmen called, "Port your helm a bit . . . good, steady as she goes."

Virginia was standing by the lee rail ramming a wad down the barrel of her pistol. "Miss Stanton, damn it, down below with you, please."

"Aye, aye, Captain," Virginia said with a smile, and a playful tone that made Biddlecomb even more angry.

"Hands to braces!" he called forward, turning to matters of more immediate concern.

The *Glasgow* was coming up, coming much faster than he had realized, and he wondered if he had hung on to the sea-anchor a bit too long. If he had, there was nothing for it now. The frigate's bow chaser roared out again, but Biddlecomb knew from hard experience that the closer the frigate came, the less likely it was that her bow chasers would bear, aimed, as they were, at an angle away from the frigate's centerline.

The *Charlemagne* flew past the gaping entrance of Flushing Bay to the south, past the Two Brothers to the north. Buchanan's Island was broad on the starboard bow, on the larboard was the wooded area known as the Pinfolds, and beyond the bowsprit, less than half a mile away, was the entrance to Hell Gate. From where he stood it did not even look like a channel, appearing more like a narrow inlet, but that was only because the far end of the passage was hidden by the dogleg. It was time to issue orders.

Biddlecomb stepped up to the break of the quarterdeck. "Listen up, you men!" he shouted, and all heads turned aft. "Sail trimmers, stand by sheets and halyards. On my order I want you to let 'em fly, just cast them off, you hear? Gun crews man the starboard battery, get ready to fire on my command. Mr. Sprout, please lay aft. Carry on."

A buzz of speculation ran fore and aft, but the men moved to their stations and Biddlecomb was satisfied that they understood and would carry out their duties. With a quick word to the bosun he explained what he wanted and sent him forward to attend to it. Biddlecomb then stepped over and said, "I'll take the conn now, William." He could not help smiling, a smile that was equal parts conspiratorial and filial.

"Aye," Stanton said, smiling as well, then in a loud voice announced, "Captain has the conn!"

"Now . . . Virginia, will you get the hell below?" Biddlecomb shouted, noticing that she had moved to the break of the quarterdeck and stopped. "William, will you see her below?"

"Aye," Stanton said with a look of resignation on his face, "I'll try."

Biddlecomb stood by the helmsmen, feet at shoulder width, hands clasped behind his back, and watched the mouth of the Harlem River opening up to starboard and the entrance to Hell Gate gaping before them. Even from there he could see the confused, swirling chop of that treacherous spot of water near the tip of Hallet's Point know as the Pott.

He looked aft. The *Glasgow* was no more than one hundred yards astern, charging down like an enraged bull, overwhelming, great guns thrust from her side. Maltby, if it was Maltby still in command, intended no doubt to hang on the *Charlemagne*'s heels through Hell Gate and then beat them to flotsam in the wider part of the East River beyond, destroy them under the eyes of the citizens of New York. And that was fine; he could intend whatever he pleased.

Biddlecomb swiveled around. The shoreline was close by, to north and south, and under his keel all of the water of Long Island Sound was funneling through the narrow hose of the East River and screaming into the nozzle of Hell Gate. This was the moment.

"Helm hard a-port! Put your helm hard a-port!" he shouted at the helmsmen, though they were less than five feet away. The two men at the tiller could not have been more surprised by the command, but they were experienced seamen, and though their eyes went wide, they pushed the long tiller over.

The *Charlemagne* heeled hard as she slewed around, turning broadside to the wind, broadside to the frigate tearing down on them. "Sail trimmers, let fly! Let it all go! Larboard battery, fire as you bear!"

Overhead, topgallants and topsails came flogging down, the perfect symmetry and power of the sails collapsing in a loud, banging confusion. The *Charlemagne* continued to turn, and now the frigate was right on their beam, fifty yards away. The American brig swung up into the wind until her bow was facing the bow of the oncoming frigate.

"Midships!" Biddlecomb shouted, and the helmsmen pulled the tiller in and the *Charlemagne* came to stop, her bowsprit pointing upriver, the *Glasgow*'s jibboom just overlapping her own as the frigate passed down their side. "Mr. Sprout, let go!" Biddlecomb shouted and the bosun let fly the ring stopper and the anchor plunged into the East River. The heavy cable paid out through the hawse pipe as the brig gathered sternway.

The forwardmost gun on the larboard side banged out as the *Glasgow* hurtled down on them, passing less than twenty yards away on their larboard side. The calm of the frigate's quarterdeck was gone; now men, officers and seamen, were rushing around in pandemonium. The captain alone seemed undisturbed, standing by the starboard rail of the quarterdeck, a covey of midshipmen off to one side. He did not look like Maltby, but a man taller and thinner.

The *Charlemagne* fired, again and again down the line, and the gun crews flung themselves to reloading, hoping to get off a second shot in the few seconds that the two ships would be broadside to broadside.

And then the *Glasgow* fired, one gun after another as she passed the now anchored *Charlemagne,* the whistling, screeching shot from her long nine-pounders tearing up the shrouds and ripping chunks from the masts and bulwarks. They were firing chain shot, chain over round shot, and it was ripping standing and running rigging alike. At least one of the Charlemagnes lay dead, his blood pooling on the deck. But the brig's anchor was holding fast, and the current had the frigate and was sweeping her past, sweeping her into Hell Gate, and they could do nothing to stop it.

Gun for gun the *Charlemagne* and the *Glasgow* pounded away at each other as the British man-of-war flew past. Biddlecomb could see chunks of wood flying through the smoke, and he knew that the Charlemagnes were having some effect. But it was the current that would save them, if they were to be saved. He could see a gang of men on the frigate's bow struggling with the best bower, and he smiled to himself. It was too late. They would not get that anchor down in time to stop themselves.

He heard a pistol shot close by, then another and another. William Stanton and Virginia and John Adams were at the quarterdeck rail, searching out targets through the smoke. An officer hung dead in the *Glasgow*'s shrouds, his arm and leg tangled in the ratlines. "Virginia, goddamn it, get below!" Biddlecomb screamed, wondering if Virginia had killed the man. Her face was as expressionless as her father's as she spit a ball down the barrel, cocked the lock, searched out a target, aimed, and fired again. Only Adams still wore his idiotic grin.

"Virginia, son of a—" Biddlecomb shouted, but she was ignoring him and he did not have time to dedicate to this problem.

And then the *Glasgow* was past, her quarter galley sweeping by at Biddlecomb's eye level, swinging away from him. She was turning, coming up into the wind, her captain trying to check her forward motion before she was pulled into the grip of Hell Gate. Biddlecomb could not believe his luck, or the poor judgment of the *Glasgow*'s captain. It was the most foolish thing that he could do.

The *Glasgow* heeled hard over, turning up into the wind, just as the *Charlemagne* had. She was careening sideways into the narrow part of the river, her sails coming full aback, studdingsails collapsing and flogging in a tangled and unholy mess. The frigate swept sideways into Hell Gate with greater and greater force as the current and the backed sails increased her sternway. She was completely beyond human control, completely at the mercy of wind and tide.

Thirty seconds later she went aground on Hallet's Point. She stopped, not the sudden, jarring stop of a ship hitting a rock, but a more gentle cessation of movement as she sank, rudder first, in the mud. The tall rig shuddered and swayed as the frigate came to rest, pinned against the bank by the tons of water that flooded through the Gate. It would likely be days before she would float again.

The *Charlemagne* was quiet, unnaturally quiet, though Biddlecomb realized that a part of that at least was the result of the broadsides impairing his hearing.

And then the entire brig exploded in cheers. Men leapt up and down and waved their hats over their heads and clapped each other on the back. Biddlecomb felt strong arms around him, Stanton pounding his shoulders, Adams clasping his hand and shaking it.

"Marvelous, Biddlecomb, marvelous! Bravo, I say!" Adams was saying, and to Biddlecomb's dulled hearing his voice seemed a normal volume. "Now I should think we can get a landing party together and attack the frigate over land, maybe one thrust by land, do you see, and one from a boat. Shall we tell off the men? I'll be happy to take command of the shore party."

"A fine idea, Mr. Adams," Biddlecomb said, "but in the interest of republicanism I think we shall go to Philadelphia first, and there you can take up your plan with the full committee." And before Adams could reply, he called for hands away aloft to set the sails to rights, and for Mr. Sprout to rig the capstan.

CHAPTER 3

The Naval Committee

STEPHEN HOPKINS MADE HIS WAY TOWARD THE PHILADELPHIA waterfront, leaning into the bitter autumn wind, assaulted by the leaves and the sand that swirled around the sidewalk bordering Chestnut Street. Windows set into the tall blocks of homes that lined the street cast their light on the walkway, revealing the patchwork of bricks amid the shadows.

The wind seemed to grow more tenacious with each block, coming off the river and tumbling down the street. Hopkins kept one gloved hand on the top of his wide-brimmed, black hat to prevent it from lifting off and flying away. The other he kept thrust deep into the pocket of his coat. It was November 5, and though it was not yet seven o'clock in the evening, the city was as dark as it would be at midnight.

He paused at a corner of Third and waited while a coach and four rattled past, a beautiful vehicle with two servants dressed in superb livery on the back and a driver hunched forward over the reins. It rolled past and the sound of the iron wheels was soon lost in the wind and Hopkins continued down toward the waterfront. He could smell it now: brine and fish and tar carried on the cold air. He turned on Water Street, that familiar corner, and paused for a moment, staring at the tavern across the street.

Through the small, distorted panes of glass he could see a

crowd of men in the room downstairs, many of whom he recognized by now, though he did not associate with them. They were ship's captains and small-time merchants and shop owners who came to the tavern nightly to drink their rum and beer and forget the troubles that went with being ship's captains and small-time merchants. Like them, Hopkins came nightly to the tavern, but for reasons quite different.

His eyes moved up to the second floor, to the single window that looked out over Commerce Street. The window was open to defend against an overly zealous fireplace and the clay pipes on which even now the six men inside would be pulling away. Hopkins could hear a voice, John Adams's voice, over the muted din coming from the tavern downstairs.

Hopkins could not make out what the Boston lawyer was saying, he could only catch the odd word, but that was all that he needed to hear to know what Adams was talking about. He heard the words "Hell Gate" and the expression "—so I made it clear to—" and the rest was carried away by a gust of wind. Hopkins smiled to himself. He was happy to arrive late and miss hearing once again of Adams's adventures aboard the *Charlemagne* and how he, Adams, had been instrumental in their escape.

Hopkins continued to stare at the window, indulging himself in his private thoughts. For the past week, since its creation on the thirtieth of October, the Naval Committee had met there and plotted how they would, over all objections, create a navy for the United Colonies.

They were intelligent men, and dedicated: John Adams, Silas Deane, and John Langdon, the original committee of three who had drafted the plan to intercept the ordnance brigs. Christopher Gadsden of South Carolina, who many years before had served as an officer in the British navy and who was dedicated to the idea of sea power. Richard Henry Lee of Virginia, who always joined with the New Englanders in calling for the most radical action, and Joseph Hewes of North Carolina, who had broken with the Society of Friends, to which he and his family belonged, rather than endorse their denunciation of Congress.

The committee meetings had so far proven to be exciting and stimulating, the most enjoyable duty Hopkins had performed since coming to Philadelphia.

Dramatic things were happening concerning American naval power. A Committee to Headquarters, consisting of Benjamin Franklin, Benjamin Harrison, and Thomas Lynch had returned from a meeting with General Washington filled with enthusiasm for what the general was doing regarding the organization of the fleet.

A less charitable man than Hopkins might have said that the committee was unduly influenced by Washington's naming three of his ships the *Franklin,* the *Harrison,* and the *Lynch,* but still their enthusiasm for men-of-war infected the Congress as a whole. On the fifth of October it had taken Herculean effort to convince Congress just to arm two ships to go after the north country brigs. By the thirtieth of October they had happily authorized one hundred thousand dollars to form a fleet and had created the Naval Committee.

We few, Hopkins thought, we happy few, we band of brothers. He did not feel like a brother to those men. He was more than twenty years older than the next oldest man on the committee. He felt more like a father. He glanced down the dark street, then stepped over a dubious puddle at the curb and made for the tavern's front door.

He walked up the steep stairway toward the second floor. He could see the light seeping out from under the door, could hear Adams's voice quite clearly now. The attorney had just fired his first pistol shot into the frigate, to some great effect, he believed, and was quickly reloading when Hopkins opened the door.

"Ah, Hopkins, you're here!" Adams said. "And just in time. I was just relating to these gentlemen . . ."

Hopkins shut him up with a wave of his hand. "I've heard

it before, John," he said, struggling out of his heavy wool coat. "At my age I have heard it all before."

He tossed his coat over a chair and looked around the room. They were all there, all of the other members of the Naval Committee, all seated in their familiar seats, relaxing, smoking, and drinking in their familiar postures.

The room itself was just another second floor of another tavern, like a thousand that Hopkins had seen in his life. The ceiling was supported at regular intervals by heavy wooden beams, two feet apart and perhaps five and a half feet from the floor. One wall was taken up with a big brick fireplace that sucked as much warmth out of the room as it gave off, but which was, given the confines of the room, enough to make it almost unbearably hot. Most of the space was taken up by a big oak table, brought there on Hopkins's request, and around which the Naval Committee sat, the smoke from their pipes forming a gray cloud, like low-hanging fog, in the upper two feet of the room.

Hopkins glanced over toward the sideboard on the wall opposite the fireplace. There were bottles of beer, wine, and a bottle of Jamaican rum, especially for him. He wished very much to have a drink, but he pushed the temptation aside. He would have a drink later, probably quite a few, as he did most nights, but he would not start until their business was done. That was a resolve that he had not broken yet.

"Gentlemen, let us plunge in here, headfirst," Hopkins said, and the various conversations stopped as the Naval Committee listened respectfully to their patriarch. "Stanton has draw up the list of ships and officers we've appointed, so let me read this out. Not all of these men are confirmed, but I reckon they'll accept. Seems everyone's ready to be an officer. I just hope there's as many want to be foremast jacks."

He pulled a sheaf of paper out of his waistcoat where he had tucked it away from the wind. "So. The ship *Black Prince,* renamed *Alfred,* flagship, of twenty-two guns, Dudley Saltonstall flag captain, John Paul Jones, senior lieutenant. The ship

Sally, renamed *Columbus,* of twenty guns, Abraham Whipple commanding. The brig . . . the brig *Sally.* I guess it's another *Sally.* Well, half the damn ships in these colonies are called *Sally* or *Nancy.* The brig *Sally,* renamed *Cabot,* of fourteen guns, John Burroughs Hopkins commanding . . ."

Hopkins read through the list, which was approved for presentation to the Congress as a whole, and the discussion moved on to the organization of the Marine Corps, which the committee had just created five days before. The talk went well into the evening as the committee worked through the structure, the number of officers, the number of troops, the duties, and the pay of the nascent corps.

It was well past eleven o'clock when Hopkins, glancing at the bottle of Jamaican rum sitting patiently on the sideboard, called for an adjournment.

"First there's one other matter I would like to discuss," said Adams, "as we're on the subject of ships and officers. You have heard, no doubt, of some of the events that took place on my passage to Philadelphia?"

As it happened they had and did not wish to hear more, so Adams continued, "The *Charlemagne* is not a converted merchantman, she was built to be a man-of-war, and she is being offered by William Stanton, her owner and secretary to this committee, for employment in the navy."

"Another ship in the navy?" asked Lee. "Does Mr. Hopkins have yet another unemployed relative? His brother is the commodore, his nephew has command of the *Cabot.* Whipple is . . . Gadsden, what relation is Captain Whipple to Mr. Hopkins?"

"Married to his niece, if I am not mistaken."

"Whipple is married to his niece. Pray, sir, who in your family is there left to employ?"

Hopkins smiled despite himself. After forty years in the rugged world of Rhode Island politics, he was most adept at finding positions for his kith and kin. It was like having a fondness for drink, it was difficult to stop.

"The *Charlemagne,* as it happens, comes complete with her

own captain," Adams interrupted. "A most capable man, and if you do not believe me, I shall relate the story again."

"And," Joseph Hewes said, "a Rhode Islander, I believe?"

"Yes, but he's no relation to Hopkins," Adams said. "Is he, Hopkins?"

"None that I'm aware of."

"The thing of it is," Adams continued, "that while his commission is dated back to August, giving him quite a bit of seniority, that commission was issued by Washington, and I suppose technically it's not valid. So I think it would be proper if we were to issue him a commission now, a naval commission."

"If we were to commission him now," Silas Deane said, "he should be junior to all of the officers already commissioned. I don't see how we could give him command of a vessel."

"Oh, Good Lord, Deane, the man brought his own boat!" Adams said. Deane had already arranged for his brother-in-law, Dudley Saltonstall, to take command of the flagship, *Alfred,* and Adams suspected that more Deanes were seeking employment. "Should we perhaps make a rule that if you bring your own vessel, you get to be captain? No, gentlemen, in all fairness I say we postdate his commission to the date that Washington issued it."

"But that would make him the most senior captain in the service," Gadsden pointed out.

"Very well, then, we'll postdate his commission to be the same date as the others we issued, so he'll be on an equal footing with the others. I mean, really, gentleman, Biddlecomb's one of the only people who has actually done something. The powder he brought in changed everything in Boston. And you should have seen him in the East River. Face like a marble statue, never flinched as that frigate was coming right up our backside. Spun her around and dropped the anchor like it was a yachting holiday, made an absolute fool out of that frigate captain. As you know, I've been around shipping all my life, done hundreds of admiralty law cases, and I've never heard of the like. Fantastic!"

"I have no doubt that he is a fine captain," Hewes began, searching for the political turn of phrase, "but there does seem to be a preponderance of captains from New England, and Rhode Island in particular. I know"—he held up his hand to stop Adams before the lawyer's protest began—"I know that yours are more seafaring colonies than ours, and it's no surprise the captains should come from there. And I know that the commander in chief is a Southern man. But as you gentlemen may recall, we issued a commission to a Mr. Roger Tottenhill from North Carolina, an able mariner, has been going to sea since his youth. He was not available when we were manning the four ships we have now, but he's just applied to me for some employment in the navy. Perhaps we could see him posted as first officer aboard the *Charlemagne?*"

"And this Tottenhill is what relationship to you, sir?" asked John Langdon, a partially suppressed smile on his face.

"Well, Mr. Langdon," said Hewes, smiling as well, "it happens that he is married to my cousin, but that has had no influence on my suggesting him for the post aboard the *Charlemagne*. Just as Mr. Hopkins and Mr. Deane were in no way influenced by their own relationships to the commissioned officers now serving in our naval force."

"The *Charlemagne* has a first officer, a man named Rumstone, and he's—"

"And his commission," Hewes interrupted, "it was also issued by Washington?"

"Well," Adams said, "in fact Washington gave Biddlecomb a blank commission, let him fill the thing in, but nonetheless—"

"John," Hopkins interrupted, "perhaps we should consider Mr. Hewes suggestion." It was clear that this Rumstone's claim to a commission was of dubious legality, but there was a greater issue to consider. Though the Southern colonies were almost equally represented on the Naval Committee—there were three Southerners and four from New England—they were greatly underrepresented in naval officers. Experience and nepotism had leaned the committee heavily toward the northeast, and there were rumblings in Congress that this was not an American navy at all, but a New England navy. If they were to get the cooperation of the entire Congress, then the entire Congress had to feel they had a stake in these affairs. John Adams, Hopkins knew, understood this.

"If this committee needs further convincing," Hewes added, "let me mention that Tottenhill has put recruiters to work at his own expense. He expects to have thirty or so seamen coming shortly from North Carolina who can be used to fill out the *Charlemagne*'s crew."

This news sent a murmur through the committee. The delegates were well aware of how the privateers were already depleting the Colonies' supply of able seamen.

Hopkins spoke, making a decision for the committee. "We can issue Rumstone a commission tonight. He'll be junior to everyone, but at least he'll be properly commissioned, and he can continue on as second officer aboard *Charlemagne*. We'll appoint Tottenhill as first, and we'll write out a commission for the *Charlemagne* to take her into the navy. We'll have to put a contingent of marines on board, fifteen or twenty, I should think, and some sort of marine lieutenant."

He paused as he considered the amount of work that still needed to be done, thanks to John Adams's poorly timed suggestion. His eyes flickered over at the sideboard and the bottle of Jamaican rum. "To hell with it, we'll do it in the morning, get William Stanton to bear a hand with some of this."

He stepped over to the sideboard and pulled the cork from the bottle, splashing the pungent rum into a cup. "Rum with you gentlemen?" he asked. "Mr. Lee, will you have a glass with me? Of course. Mr. Adams, some wine with you?"

He could feel the men in the room relax, like releasing a breath after holding it. He had that effect on these men, could alter their moods at his will. He knew it and it amused him. "Now, gentlemen," he said, distributing glasses of liquor to the Naval Committee, "we were discussing Hesiod's *Works and Days* at close of business last night, if I am not very much mistaken, and how Hesiod's vision of the perfect society was one in which no man would ever have to go to sea."

It was nearly midnight before the jovial and fairly intoxicated Naval Committee left off their discussion of classical Greek literature and adjourned for the night. Joseph Hewes was the last to leave, bidding his fellows good-night and hesitating on the sidewalk outside the tavern as he watched them disappear down the black street. Then he turned and stepped inside again, not to the upstairs room but to the tavern on the street level, where he knew Roger Tottenhill would be waiting.

The lieutenant, the newly appointed lieutenant, was indeed waiting, sitting at a table in the far corner, a mug clutched in both hands, deep in an animated and one-sided conversation with a bored-looking man sitting beside him. Hewes had feared that the meeting would go on as long as it had, leaving Tottenhill to wait for hours, drinking all the while. Hewes was afraid that he was already quite in his cups.

He stood by the door for a moment, unseen, considering the young man in the expensive blue coat and silk breeches and stockings. Tottenhill was twenty-nine years old, handsome in a fine-boned way, with dark brown hair tied back in a queue. He came from a good family, a wealthy family, and had the concomitant breeding and manners. Hewes's cousin, of course, would not have been allowed to marry anyone less.

The man at Tottenhill's table nodded his head at some point that Tottenhill had made, then glanced away, clearly not listening. That, unfortunately, was the other side of Tottenhill's character.

He was an extraordinary bore.

To be sure, that was a minor flaw compared to, say, cowardice or dishonesty or infidelity, but still Tottenhill had raised this annoying trait to something like an art. It was most difficult to be around the man for long, and that was why he was rarely asked to ship out a second time on a vessel aboard which he had served. Hewes had neglected to mention that to the committee as a whole.

The congressman made his way across the still-crowded tavern to his cousin's husband's table.

"Roger, I apologize for the delay," he said, shaking his head at the publican's inquiring glance.

"Joseph, not at all, not at all!" Tottenhill smiled his broad, genuine smile. "Please, be seated. I know how these politicians can go on." Tottenhill stood and pulled the chair out for Hewes, waving to the publican for two fresh drinks. "Joseph, this is—"

"Thomas Page," said the bored man at the table, who looked entirely relieved to have the flow of Tottenhill's conversation interrupted.

"I was just telling Thomas here about the privateering in the last war. I recall once in France . . . no, wait . . . was it Spain? In any event . . ."

At that the grateful Thomas Page stood. "Forgive me, sir, but the hour is late and I must be off. Good evening."

"Good evening. A pleasure," Tottenhill said, but Page was already halfway to the door.

"Things went very well, you'll be pleased to hear," Hewes began, not allowing Tottenhill to start up again. The publican set the unwanted drink on the table in front of him. "Better than I had hoped. As it happens, Adams just this evening brought us the news that another vessel is available for the service, the brig *Charlemagne*. You're to be posted as first officer. Her captain and crew are Yankees, but there's little you can do to avoid that, they're all Yankees.

"The best thing is that the *Charlemagne* is man-of-war built, she's not a converted merchantman, and that gives her the chance to be the best ship in this fledgling navy. She's a good vessel for you to serve aboard."

"Excellent. This is marvelous, as much as I dared hope for. First officer! In fact, it puts me in mind—"

"It's the least you deserve, I should think," Hewes cut him

off again. "In all fairness you've sailed as first mate for three years now, and if this war had not come about, you'd be a ship's master soon. Not to mention the fact that you've recruited a good number of seamen, which the *Charlemagne* desperately needs."

"They're good men, good Southern boys, and they're ready to fight. Perhaps you know my agent, Jedadiah Huck?"

"I do not."

"Jedadiah Huck of the Wilmington Hucks? He's a good man, fanatical about the cause for independency. He's recruiting the best seamen he can find. The last of them should be here by next week, latest. You know, in my experience the southern man always makes the best sailor because—"

"There's talk of expanding the navy. We spent most of tonight discussing a plan to build a fleet of frigates. They'll be fine ships, fast and powerful, and command will go to those who distinguish themselves. I hope that such an opportunity will present itself to you."

"As do I, Joseph. But in my experience one can make luck, if you see what I mean. I don't intend to sit on my haunches and hope that such opportunity will come my way."

"As well you should not. Good. I'm pleased with your attitude. But . . . there's one other thing . . ."

"Yes?"

Hewes paused, staring down at the filthy tabletop, searching, as was his habit, for the right words. "There is some concern," he began in a hesitating voice, "some concern among the Southern colonies that this navy is increasingly becoming a New England navy. I thought at first there was a note of excessive suspicion in that, but now I'm not so certain. The only captain not from New England is Nicholas Biddle, and he's from Pennsylvania, which is hardly the South. There are no Southerners . . ."

"If there is something I can do . . . ," Tottenhill began, his voice sounding unsure.

"I don't know. The best that you can do is serve with distinction, then we'll get you a command. But . . . keep your eyes open, you understand? I should like to know what's really going on. We need a representative from the South to break this New England cabal. Do you understand me?" Hewes knew he was not expressing himself well.

"Oh, I certainly do, Joseph, I certainly do." Tottenhill smiled and took a long pull of his drink. The light from the lantern mounted on the wall danced across the wet sheen on his eyes as he looked off into the clouds of smoke that gathered around the low ceiling beams.

Hewes cleared his throat and stared into his mug. Tottenhill was an eager young man, always agreeable, which made Hewes uneasy. He hoped that the lieutenant understood, truly understood, what he had been trying to say.

CHAPTER 4

The Sea Lawyer

THE SMALL MERCHANTMAN, AROUND TWO HUNDRED TONS BURTHEN, worked her way past Cape Fear and into the Cape Fear River, homeward bound for Wilmington in the Colony of North Carolina. The wind was over her quarter and the tide was with her; the first bit of luck, her master mused, since they had pulled their anchor from that very river two months before.

Under topsails, jib, and fore topmast staysail, she worked her way past the marshy fields covered with brown winter grass to larboard and starboard. She was not handled well—those few of the crew who were not sick or injured were sullen and uncooperative, going about their duties grudgingly, not acknowledging orders, not acknowledging their shipmates. The master drummed his fingers on the quarterdeck rail. He was desperately anxious to be home.

At last the final, gentle bend in the river straightened out into the long stretch of water that led like a road to the docks and anchorages of Wilmington, that lovely town.

Ten minutes later the ship rounded up and the anchor plunged into the river. The vessel eased back into the current until her hawser was taut. Her topsails hung in great disorderly folds of canvas, her hatches needed breaking open, there was the customs inspector to meet, a thousand details to attend to. But the master had one concern that took precedence over all of that.

"Mr. Luther," he called to the first mate, "pray get the boat over the side and fetch the sheriff out here, as quick as you can."

Amos Hackett lay in the dark hold of the merchantman, his hands and feet bound in iron shackles made fast to chains that were in turn fastened to the deck with big iron staples. He felt the rage come over him, possess him, blind him, a more profound blindness than even the blackness of the hold.

The rage did not make him want to lash out, did not make him want to strike anything, the way stupider men did when thus overcome. He rarely felt the urge to hit someone. His was a more subtle violence, and he was proud of that. Chaos, anarchy, was his balm, manipulation was his release. Nothing made him feel as genuinely calm as watching men around him fall apart, victims of his guile.

It had been good for a while, on that voyage. He had really stirred things up. But it had not lasted, and the old man had shown a surprising degree of determination in locking him down. And so for the past five days he had been shut up alone, with only his thoughts. Amos Hackett now knew what his own private hell would be.

He felt the ship heel to starboard and knew they were rounding up into the wind. He was enough of a seaman to understand the nuanced motion of a ship. His career had begun twenty-five years ago, at the age of nine, when his father, a common laborer and a violent drunk, sent him to sea as an apprentice, after receiving, Hackett was certain, some payment for him. Even an idiot would learn something of ships in that time, and Hackett was no idiot.

Suddenly the hold, which had been silent save for the slap of water on the hull, was filled with the rumble and shudder of the hawse paying out from the cable tier and running out of the hawsehole one deck above. They were anchoring. Now there would be the devil to pay and no pitch hot. Hackett felt the rage overwhelming him again and he cursed softly and violently, spewing out a string of obscenities that grew increasingly filthy and vituperative. It made him feel better, but only a little. He needed a drink. He needed to see someone hurt.

He heard the ship's boat lowered away, and sometime later—he had no notion of how long—he heard it bump against the side of the ship, returning from the town. A minute later came the sound of shoes on the ladders, voices, and the dim, swaying light of a lantern coming closer as some party made its way down to the hold.

"Amos Hackett, hello again." Hackett glanced sideways up at the group of men standing over him. The chains did not allow him anything more than a kneeling position, and that further inflamed him. The light, dim as it was, hurt his eyes.

"Sheriff, is that you? God damn me, but I'm glad to see you. Tell them to get these chains off me. It ain't legal."

The sheriff was smiling. "But of course, Amos. You there"—he turned to two armed seamen and the ship's carpenter standing behind him—"pray let Mr. Hackett, Esquire, out of them chains."

The group stood silent as the chains were removed from Hackett's raw wrists. "You can't get up to the gallows if you're chained up down here, now can you?" was all the sheriff said before leading the small band back to the deck. Hackett was manacled and flanked by the two armed seamen, who took every opportunity that presented itself to shove him along and curse him for stumbling.

They stepped through the after scuttle and into the bright autumn afternoon. The sunlight brought tears to Hackett's eyes, and he felt them well up and roll down his cheeks. His clothes were torn and filthy, and in the fresh air on deck he was aware of how badly he stank. He felt his rage come to a boil again. He had to let it out. He had to talk.

"Sheriff, Captain Barry here chained me up, chained me like a dog for no reason. It ain't legal and I want him arrested. I'm going to bring charges against him." This was a lame attempt; no thought had gone into it. He was just talking, but it made him feel better, as if he had some control. "I suggest you get these irons off my wrists."

"Ain't legal, you say?" the sheriff asked. "Well, now, Captain Barry, who, I should point out, is a gentleman and a citizen of long standing in this town, not the son of a drunken cur, says you was undermining his authority and leading a mutiny. And this ain't the first time we've heard the like about you. Now, who do you reckon I should believe?"

"Mutiny? It's mutiny, is it? A man can't have a genuine grievance without being arrested for mutiny, and the cook laying out food what ain't fit for a dog? And the men asking me would I please go to the captain and beg him do something to make our lot better, and me going, humble as you please—"

"That's quite enough, Hackett. Captain Barry . . ." The sheriff held up his hand to restrain the master, who was making a move as if to strike Hackett. Hackett was in turn cowering as if his life was being threatened.

"There, Sheriff, you see now how it is!" Hackett yelled, pointing with cuffed hands an accusatory finger at the master.

"Shut your gob, Hackett," the sheriff said and then to the armed seamen added, "Get him in the boat."

Hackett slumped in the stern sheets of the boat as they drew nearer the town of Wilmington and its all too familiar jail. He had not intended to lead a mutiny, that was the thing of it. He had just been amusing himself, just letting the rage pay out.

It was the first time he had sailed with Barry. Indeed, it was the first time with most masters with whom he sailed, as it was rare that any captain would ship him twice. Had Barry not been desperate for able-bodied men, the stock of seamen being much depleted by the privateers, Hackett doubted that he would have found that berth. His reputation was spreading. He should really have left Wilmington as he had planned. But he had not.

He had been aboard Barry's ship only two days when he

first saw the rift. The cook was an old-timer, adept at wielding the kind of authority that cooks can have, if they play the game well, and that one did. Half of the crew liked the man, or at least pretended to. The other half did not, but they kept that opinion enough to themselves that it caused no real friction. Until Hackett came aboard.

The first move had been the most enjoyable, and surprisingly effective. He had caught a rat, deep in the hold, and with his sheath knife had deprived the animal of its tail and four feet. It had been amusing enough to watch the filthy thing squirming around in the light of the lantern, trying to flee on bloody stumps. But that was nothing compared to the reaction of the men—none of them friends of the cook—who found the rat's body parts in their food.

That alone had started a near riot. First accusations, then plates, then fists, had flown around the forecastle. Blood might have been shed if Hackett had not stepped in as peacemaker, pleading with both sides to be reasonable.

The captain had thanked him for that, the stupid bastard. They were only three days out at that point. It had promised to be one of the most enjoyable voyages yet.

The boat thumped against the wooden dock and Hackett was lifted, none too gently, from the stern sheets while the sheriff, preserving as much dignity as he could, clambered out after him. "Come on, then, Hackett, off to the jail. You know the way, been going there since you were weaned. Recall how you used to visit your father, even before the first time you was thrown in there?"

They started up the narrow street, sloping uphill away from the river. The sheriff would not let up. "Most decent families, you know, Hackett, have their own pew in church. Yours got its own cell in the prison. Hey? Your own cell in the prison? The Hackett cell?"

People were stopping to watch the procession go by. Hackett could see the heads shaking, the children's eyes averted by their parents. The better sort. He loathed them. All his life they had looked at him like that, shaking their heads. He envisioned doing to their children what he had done to that rat.

After the initial riot things had gone well. In his role of peacemaker and new man in the forecastle, he had no former loyalties, and thus the ears of both factions, which made it that much easier to stoke everyone's suspicions and anger. He had never seen a crew so divided, so angry and unhappy. Oh, it was great fun, for a time.

They came at last to the jail. "In you go, Hackett. Into the Hackett cell." The sheriff found this concept thoroughly amusing and would not stop. Hackett remained silent, staring at the stone floor. Raising any objection would only make the idiot sheriff go on at greater length. He knew the sheriff. They had known each other for many years now.

What was so utterly maddening to Hackett was that the whole thing, the whole wonderful frolic, had fallen apart through his own stupidity. He was not content to just enjoy what he had wrought. He never was, and he was ashamed of that weakness. In such instances he felt the need to share his triumph, to gloat, to explain to those more stupid than he, and that was pretty much everyone, just how clever he had been.

Always, on any crew, some sycophant was ready to lap up his words, and on this voyage Tom Elphinstone was that man. He followed Hackett around, agreed with everything he said, waited for more. On a night watch, 3 A.M., Hackett found himself alone with Elphinstone on the quarterdeck, taking their trick at the helm, the mate having gone forward to stop a fight from breaking out. It was a rare thing on shipboard, to find yourself alone. Hackett could hold it in no longer.

"I done this, you know."

"What?" asked Elphinstone.

"This whole thing, about the cook? I started the whole damned thing. I brought the crew down, tore the ship apart, because I wanted to. And I could do it because I'm smarter than any of these sons of bitches, including you."

Stupid, stupid! High aloft in the rigging was the only safe place on shipboard to tell a secret. He knew it and he ignored it. But who would have thought that the captain would have been awake at that hour? Of course it was his own fault that Barry could not sleep. But who would have thought? The old man's skylight was open, the skylight just behind and below where they stood, and it communicated from the quarterdeck right into the great cabin. Barry heard every word.

But Hackett didn't realize his mistake for some time. Barry was smarter than he had thought, the whore's son. Barry brought Elphinstone into the cabin the next day, along with both mates, and made him talk. And when they had forced from him everything he knew, they extracted from him, on pain of great punishment, a promise to report to them anything more that Hackett said.

And Hackett said a great deal. He found in Elphinstone an eager follower, one who devoured his tales. It made him wild now to think of how he had regaled Elphinstone with stories of his clever manipulations. He had even confessed to things he had not done! And all of it going straight aft to the great cabin.

Three days after his confession on the quarterdeck Hackett was in chains.

"Reckon you'll get your trial next week," the sheriff said as he prepared to shut the heavy iron door of the cell. "Mutiny, it'll be."

"Mutiny, that's a lie. You gonna arrest Captain Barry for chaining me up like a dog?"

"No, Hackett, of course I'm not, you stupid whore's son. That ain't even worthy of you." The sheriff seemed about to leave, then paused. "Barry says he has a witness, fellow that'll tell everything you done." He was being particularly talkative. Hackett wondered if he was lonely. He hoped so.

"He got someone willing to lie about what I said. I didn't do nothing. It'll be that bastard's word against mine."

At this the sheriff burst into laughter, and Hackett felt the rare urge to physically, personally, beat someone.

"Oh, well, you'll hang for certain, if that's the case!" the sheriff said. He stepped out of the cell and closed the door and three minutes later Hackett could still hear him laughing at the far end of the hall.

Nothing was more horrible to Amos Hackett than to be left alone with his thoughts. He was terrified of death, in fact, because he had some vague notion that death would be like his time in the merchantman's hold: aware, thinking, feeling his rage increase, yet unable to talk to anyone, unable to release it.

The prison cell was little better. He could move, at least, and he could see. He had the sheriff or guard to speak with three times a day when his meals came. But each day that passed brought him closer to a hopeless trial and then the gallows and then the black nothingness of the hold.

He heard keys jangling in the door. He looked up quickly. Breakfast was not an hour past, there was no call for his door to be open. He felt a sudden dread, like a cold draft. Whatever this was, he had no doubt it was bad.

"Hackett, this gentleman here is Jedadiah Huck. He wants to have a word with you," the sheriff said. Behind him was a middle-aged man, pudgy, red-faced, in some sort of uniform. On his head was a wig that might have been better discarded some years before.

"Amos Hackett?"

Hackett glared at him for a long moment before saying, "I reckon you know who I am."

"I understand that you're an able-bodied seaman? Can hand, reef, and steer?"

"Aye."

"Well, Hackett, pray allow me to explain the situation to you. You are to be brought up on some quite serious charges, I'm told. Hang you, I've no doubt. However, there might be a way to spare your life."

After another long silence, Hackett said, "Go on."

"These colonies are on the verge of a great struggle with England over certain rights. The Continental Congress is putting together a navy of the United Colonies. They need able-bodied men such as yourself to join them. If you are willing to volunteer for the navy, we could see that you are pardoned of your crimes."

Silence again, and this time it lasted for some while. This could not be right. It was far too good to be true. Let him go simply for volunteering for some navy? Did this Jedadiah Huck know what crime he was accused of? No captain would want him on board a ship if he knew. But the offer had been made.

"That's it? Join this navy and I'm pardoned?"

"If you are indeed an able-bodied seaman, yes. That's it."

This navy might possibly be a right hell. He had heard stories of the British navy: floggings, hangings, lousy food. This Continental navy could be worse.

But still it would not be worse than the darkness. As long as he was alive, there was hope, and as long as he was on shipboard, among a ship's crew, there was a chance for even better.

"Very well, then. I'll join."

"I figured you might, Hackett," said the sheriff. "I'll miss seeing you hang, but at least we're free of you. But if you come back, I promise we'll hang you when you do."

"Hold a moment," Hackett said. The suspicion was back again. "Tell me again why you want me?"

Huck cleared his throat. "Our colonies are locked in a battle for our freedom. We need every man we can get to defend our God-given liberties."

"Oh, my arse," said Hackett. "Give it straight."

The pudgy man shrugged, deciding, apparently, that the truth would do no harm at that juncture. "Some gentleman . . . Lt. Roger Tottenhill . . . gives me a dollar a head for each able-bodied man I recruit. I don't give one damn what you done, as long as I get my head money. Once you report on board the ship, you're his problem."

CHAPTER 5

Philadelphia

SOMEONE WAS GIVING ORDERS CONCERNING THE REPAIRS ON THE *Charlemagne*'s bow, someone that Biddlecomb did not recognize. He, this stranger, was standing by the cutwater and waving his arms, apparently pointing out to the shipwrights how far back to strip the planking, and Biddlecomb was not pleased.

The *Charlemagne* did not, at that moment, look like the third most powerful vessel in the navy of the United Colonies, though such she was. Rather she looked like a forlorn wreck, rolled over on her larboard side twenty yards from where he and Virginia stood.

Three days before, they had pulled up to the yard of Wharton and Humphreys on a thankfully slack tide, standing on and off under topsails while another brig—Biddlecomb later learned it was the merchant brig *Sally* undergoing conversion into the United Colonies brig-of-war *Cabot*—was warped quickly out of the way.

With her pumps working nonstop to keep up with the flow of water coming in around the fothered sail, an army of sailors and dockworkers had stripped the *Charlemagne* of guns, stores, and top-hamper. That done, she had been hove down, rolled over on her larboard side, bringing the leaking starboard bow out of the water.

The *Charlemagne* seemed to breathe a great sigh of relief, pleased to be free of the damaged top-hamper, grateful to be pulled from the water, like a man stripping off coat and shirt on an unbearably hot day. It made Biddlecomb happy to see his beloved brig in the graving dock, finally getting the proper attention.

And now some interloper was giving instructions concerning the work on her bow, saying to the lead shipwright, "No, you cannot simply put a dutchman in there, you must rip the planking back to the first cant frame, and three strakes above that and below to see there's no more rot. You don't know what's going on under there, the whole damned bow could fall clean off." Standing in a half circle around him and peering down from the hull above were the gang of shipwrights who had been working on the brig.

It did not matter to Biddlecomb that the man was right, or that ten minutes later he would have issued the same instructions himself, the fact remained that someone he did not know was giving orders concerning his ship.

"Could that be Mr. Wharton?" Virginia asked, tightening her grip on his arm.

It was part of their routine now to stroll over to the shipyard after breakfasting with William Stanton in the Stone House, where they had their lodging. The mornings were lovely, brittle and cold, but even abominable weather could not have quashed the general excitement with which Philadelphia was infused in those latter days of 1775.

"No, I met Wharton yesterday, that's not him. Here's Mr. Humphreys now." Biddlecomb nodded toward the young man walking in their direction, clad in Quaker black, a bundle of draughts held awkwardly under his arm. "Mr. Humphreys, sir, a word, if you please! Who, pray, is that gentleman giving directions to your lead shipwright? The one there pointing toward the cutwater, in the blue coat. Is he one of your people?"

Humphreys squinted though spotted glasses toward the

Charlemagne and shook his head. "No . . . good morning to you, Miss Stanton . . . that's Mr. Tottenhill, your first officer. Came by this morning, first thing. I'm surprised you didn't recognize him."

"Indeed," said Biddlecomb, quite taken aback by this information, and, after bidding Humphreys good day, added, "This is passing strange." Tottenhill was now poking at the exposed frames with a long scrap of wood. "Let's see what's acting here."

Biddlecomb and Virginia stepped over the frozen mud of the shipyard, making their way to the *Charlemagne* around piles of snow-covered timber. The big men-of-war, big at least by the standards of the Colonial Navy, were tied to the dock, receiving the last of their new top-hamper. Biddlecomb had known the flagship, *Alfred,* in her earlier life as the merchantman *Black Prince*. The second ship, which, like the *Andrew Doria,* had formerly been named *Sally,* was reborn as the *Columbus* and was commanded, to Biddlecomb's delight, by his former superior officer in the Rhode Island navy, Capt. Abraham Whipple. Both ships mounted twenty-four nine-pounder guns, the biggest men-of-war the colonies could assemble.

"You, sir," Biddlecomb called out as he approached Tottenhill. "Who are you? What are you about?"

Tottenhill turned and regarded his captain with a face full of annoyance. "I'm Lt. Roger Tottenhill, sir, first officer of the brig-of-war *Charlemagne,* if it is any business of yours."

"I should say it's some business of mine. I'm Isaac Biddlecomb, Capt. Isaac Biddlecomb, commander of this brig that you fancy yourself to be first officer of."

Tottenhill's face changed as if a cloud had been whisked away from the sun. He smiled broadly. "God, I beg your pardon, sir! We've not met, I thought you were one of these infernal rascals from the dockyard, set on doing as little work as they can." The lieutenant extended his hand. "Lt. Roger Tottenhill, sir, from the proud colony of North Carolina, at your service."

Biddlecomb shook the proffered hand and remained silent as Tottenhill introduced himself to Virginia, bowing and, much to Isaac's annoyance, kissing her hand. When at last the scraping was done, Biddlecomb said, "I am still confused by this first-officer business. I have a first officer, Ezra Rumstick, who has been with me this past year. Who told you that you were to be first officer?"

"It's politics, sir, and I apologize. I know Mr. Rumstick by reputation, and I'm not all that pleased to try and fill his shoes, but the Naval Committee decided that his commission, issued by Washington, do you see, who didn't really have the authority, ain't valid. They reissued him a commission, but that makes him junior to me. They were going to post me aboard as second lieutenant, but I'm afraid the new commission made Rumstick the most junior officer in the service, so they had to make me first." As he spoke, the lieutenant rummaged around in his blue coat, finally pulling from an inner pocket a packet of papers, which he handed over.

Biddlecomb took the papers without a word and unfolded them. "There is quite a bit of politics, I fear, in the Congress, and . . ." The lieutenant continued to speak though Biddlecomb, looking through the papers, did not continue to listen. There was a lieutenant's commission, months old, and instructions to assume the position of first lieutenant aboard the *Charlemagne,* signed in Stephen Hopkins's scratchy hand. "Hmm," Isaac said, refolding the papers and handing them back to Tottenhill. "Does Rumstick know of this?"

"I don't know, sir. Sir, if you please, I'm sorry about this, really, and about how I greeted you. I don't want us to get off on the wrong foot here. I know you and Mr. Rumstick have been close, but it's not like he's left on the beach, he's to be second officer. And I'm an experienced officer, sir. I've been an officer in the merchant service for five years now. And in the last war I sailed aboard a privateer. I was just a boy, of course, an apprentice seaman, but I saw a scrape or two."

"Well . . . ," Biddlecomb said, mustering his composure after the shock of having a new officer thrust upon him. This navy thing, he reminded himself, was not all fancy balls and sycophancy. It involved, among other things, considerably less autonomy than he was accustomed to as a merchant captain. But this was too much.

"I suppose those are as good credentials as we're likely to find. Better than my own were a year ago. I'm sorry as well, sir, for doubting you. The organization of the navy has been so . . . informal up until now, I'm not accustomed to superior officers and Naval Committees and such. Yes, very well . . ." Isaac did not want to start an argument, nor did he wish to offend Tottenhill, so he did not voice his thoughts, which were that Tottenhill would not remain in his post for long. Rumstick was Biddlecomb's first lieutenant. There would be no other.

He smiled at Virginia, then looked Tottenhill in the eye. "I—"

"Sir, if I may be so bold, shall I tell you about the cant frames here?"

"Yes, certainly." There was no harm in indulging Tottenhill. He would, after all, most likely remain aboard the *Charlemagne* in some capacity. Second lieutenant, perhaps. It was important to establish some rapport with him.

And besides, Tottenhill had already launched into his explanation. "I reckon they're sound enough. You know, I've seen vessels going down the ways with cant frames rotten. We had a merchantman built in a local yard. It was in '65. Or was it '66? Yes, '66. No . . . yes, '66. In any event, the shipwright had taken frames out of a wreck, do you see—"

"Mr. Tottenhill, pray, I'm in a bit of a hurry," Biddlecomb lied, "so perhaps we can confine ourselves to the *Charlemagne?*"

"Oh, yes, of course. In any event, I was looking at the rabbet, there, and thinking perhaps it could be cut an inch or so deeper, give a better fit to those hood ends. Half this planking at least will need replaced, but . . ."

For the next forty-five minutes, until Virginia's eyes were glazed over with a boredom that was beyond what Biddlecomb considered acceptable for someone in his company, he allowed Mr. Tottenhill to drone on about the repairs to the bow. Issac found himself constantly nudging the lieutenant back onto the subject, like conning a ship through conflicting currents that were trying to throw it off course. At the end of the first twenty minutes he found himself fidgeting and interjecting such things as "Yes, yes, of course" and "To be sure, right," signs that he too was becoming intolerably bored. Though Tottenhill appeared to possess a decent knowledge of the subject, for the first time in his life Biddlecomb had found a discussion of naval architecture something less than fascinating.

"And, sir, I'd just like to say as well what an honor it is to sail with you. I've heard a great deal, of course, about the *Icarus* and the powder to Boston. And just lately they're talking about—"

"Yes, well, thank you, Mr. Tottenhill. Ah, I look forward to working with you, and, well, welcome aboard, I suppose. Now, I'll let you carry on. Miss Stanton and I really have to shove off." Isaac shook the first lieutenant's hand, took Virginia again by the arm, and tromped off across the shipyard, past their own frozen footprints.

"Am I mistaken," Virginia asked, "or is he a bit long-winded?"

"You are not mistaken, dear." The man was beyond long-winded. Biddlecomb was certain that he had never in his life endured such a breathless monologue, and he included in that assessment several talks with lawyers and politicians. And now, through some official machinations to which he was not even privy, he would be stuck with the man, forced to live with him and his monotonous chatter on a small ship at sea for the Lord knew how long.

He had learned long ago how awful it could be to have even one annoying person aboard a ship. An irritating sailor was bad enough, but Tottenhill would be, if not first then most likely second officer. As captain, Biddlecomb would not be able to avoid him. If this had been the merchant service, then he would have left Tottenhill on the beach. But this was the navy, and it was, apparently, not his decision to make.

"Needless to say I intend to protest to the Naval Committee. Nothing against Tottenhill, but this is intolerable, after all that Rumstick's done," Isaac said as he and Virginia made their way back down Water Street.

"I wonder how Ezra will take this," Virginia said.

"I don't know. Not well, I'll wager."

Rumstick did not take it well, not well at all, but it was to his credit that no one, save for Biddlecomb, realized as much. "We have a bit of a problem, Ezra," Isaac said over dinner in the warm, homey front room of the Stone House. "The Naval Committee's saddled us with a new officer for *Charlemagne*. Fellow named Roger Tottenhill. North Carolinian. Talks a lot, but he seems to know what's what, far as ships are concerned."

"New officer, huh?" said Rumstick after swallowing a bite of mutton and pudding. "What do you mean? Third lieutenant? Officer of marines?"

"Ah, well, that's the problem. As it happens, the committee it seems appointed him first lieutenant. They apparently decided he was senior to you, since you were just officially commissioned the other day. Needless to say I was not aware of any of this, and just after dinner I intend to straighten it out. I'll go see Adams, he's on the Naval Committee, and he's gotten quite a bit of wear out of our little adventure at Hell Gate. Owes us, I reckon. I'll get him to put things to rights. But, ah, for the moment, that's how it lies."

Rumstick sat in silence, an uncomfortable silence that seemed to last an exceptionally long time. "Of course, I can well see how that happened," he said at last. "Washington never had the authority to appoint naval officers, nor should he have. You recall, Isaac, that was just some fill-in-the-blank affair, that commission. But that's good, now I'm official. Junior-most in the service, mind, though I've done more fighting than any other five put together, been a prisoner twice, but now I'm official. What do you make of this Tottenhill? Good officer?"

"Fine, he's fine. But he's not the *Charlemagne*'s first officer. You are."

"Please, Isaac, I beg you, don't go and make a big issue out of this. Just leave it be. It ain't always for us to know why them politicians do what they do."

Biddlecomb, however, did make an issue out of it, or tried to at least, despite Rumstick's halfhearted protest. With dinner done he trudged through the snow and frigid wind west down Chestnut Street to the State House, where, behind shut doors, the Continental Congress wrestled with questions of war and reconciliation. The clerk who guarded the door left it in no doubt that Biddlecomb would not be admitted, regardless of how large a ship he commanded, so he took a seat in a high-backed chair in the lobby outside and waited.

For the next hour and a half he waited, while, from within the chamber, he could hear muffled shouts and the occasional pounding of walking sticks on the floor, like the far-off tramping of an army. Then suddenly, and quite unexpectedly, the doors flew open and the delegates issued forth, some walking quickly, some strolling in clumps, but nearly all still talking, still arguing, still cajoling.

"Mr. Adams! Mr. Adams!" Biddlecomb called, pushing his way through the crowd to the short lawyer. Adams broke off his discussion with a man that Biddlecomb believed to be the famed Dr. Franklin. "A word, sir, if I may?"

"Yes, of course," Adams said. "Franklin, this is Captain Biddlecomb, of whom I have spoken. Biddlecomb, Dr. Franklin, of whom you and everyone on God's earth has heard. Franklin, the captain seems to be showing me an unusual degree of respect this afternoon, which must mean he has some great favor to ask, so I will bid you good day for now. Come, Biddlecomb, let's go above stairs and I'll hear you out. On my quarterdeck, eh?" With that the delegate from Massachusetts led the way up the wide stairs to the balcony that overlooked the lobby in which the delegates were clustered.

"Now, sir, what might I do for you?"

"Well," Biddlecomb began, cursing himself for a fool for having sat in the lobby for an hour and a half letting his lurid imagination run to thoughts of Virginia rather than thinking of what he would say to Adams. "It seems that the Naval Committee has elected to appoint a first officer to the *Charlemagne*. A Roger Tottenhill. Now, I have no doubt that Tottenhill is a fine man—"

"Yes, yes, Tottenhill. Hewes's man. Decided that the other night."

"Sir, no man has done more for this cause than Ezra Rumstick, the man who has been first officer up until now. He deserves to continue in that office."

"Oh, I have no doubt of that. I was most impressed with his actions during the Battle of Hell Gate. I'm sorry he must be demoted."

"Why must he be? Just change the damn . . . the orders."

"Tottenhill is sponsored by Joseph Hewes, who is also a member of the Naval Committee. This was done at his request."

"And it is my request, the request of the captain of the *Charlemagne*, that it be undone."

"The request of the great naval hero, eh?" Adams smiled not unkindly. "I'm sorry, Biddlecomb, really. There is so much more going on here than you could even imagine. Why do you think I was so envious of the way you ran your ship, giving out orders and having to placate no one, not even me? See here: Hewes is from North Carolina. Without the Southern colonies . . . states . . . we can't hope to win this war or even get an agreement on independence. We must be united.

"But as it stands, the navy is largely a New England affair and that makes men like Hewes suspicious. The fact is that it is far more important to me to keep Hewes happy than it is to keep you happy, and I mean that as no offense to you. As powerful as I might be in this Congress, I still must play these games, and I'm afraid Rumstick must accept his lot. Besides, did Tottenhill not bring thirty sailors with him? You were a bit shorthanded, as I recall."

"Yes, he mentioned something about more hands being on their way, along with mentioning every other damned thing in creation. But see here. Tottenhill . . ."

What was he going to say? Tottenhill talked too much? It sounded ridiculous, and only someone who had spent a lifetime at sea, who understood the workings of a floating society, could appreciate how intolerable and detrimental it was to have an officer as incompatible as Tottenhill. Adams would point out that Biddlecomb had met Tottenhill but once, and he would be right, and the argument that once was enough to see how intolerable Tottenhill could be would sound equally ridiculous.

He could threaten to resign, have a tantrum like a petulant child, but that would resolve nothing. Biddlecomb had the unhappy and humiliating realization that he was not nearly as important in the great cause as he had believed himself to be. He had no leverage here.

"I'm sorry, Biddlecomb, truly I am. I think highly of your man Rumstick, I do. But the minute you set foot ashore, you lost that autonomy that you so enjoy at sea. I for one found it much easier to face a broadside than to watch over my shoulder for the figurative knife in the back. My advice is to go back to sea and stay there, avoid Naval Committees as best you can, and if you're lucky, this Tottenhill will get killed or get a command of his own."

The atmosphere in the city was charged, crackling with the energy generated by preparations for war and the national and international implications of the fight that was increasingly regarded as inevitable.

Fort Ticonderoga was taken, and Washington, for all his difficulties, still held the British under siege in Boston. There were rumors that Benedict Arnold was about to take Quebec.

The British, for their part, had done little to assuage the Colonies' fear and anger, laying Falmouth to waste, shelling that city from the harbor and destroying a generous share of homes just as the weather was turning cold. A decade and more of simmering tensions were coming to a boil, bubbling and spilling over.

And on through December the fleet gathered in the Delaware River as one after another of the merchantmen were beefed up, pierced for gunports, armed, and pronounced men-of-war.

Biddlecomb gritted his teeth and endured Tottenhill's incessant chatter during those times when he was not able to avoid the lieutenant. He found the sensation of listening to his first officer not unlike that of hearing the high-pitched squeal of a rusty carriage brake, the kind of sound that makes one clench one's fists and grimace until it is gone.

Every night he resolved to be more tolerant of the man, and every day he found it increasingly impossible.

Two days after Christmas the *Charlemagne* was eased back into the water, her round bottom pushing aside the heavy pieces of ice that floated like wreckage up and down the river. Her bow was rebuilt, her masts and rigging new and freshly set up, her paintwork repainted to mask any sign of the recent repairs. She was like a man waking up refreshed from a long, deep sleep.

The New Year came, the year 1776, and among the many causes for excitement and expectation was the small fleet of warships, the *Alfred* and *Columbus,* the brigs *Cabot* and *Andrew Doria* and *Charlemagne,* warped from their moorings to the docks that jutted out into the Delaware River.

In their tavern room the Naval Committee drafted their orders for Commodore Hopkins, and in the great cabin of the *Alfred,* Hopkins drafted his signals for the fleet. Over the sides and down the gaping hatches of the ships flowed barrels of food and water and gunpowder, sailcloth and round shot, paint, tar, brick dust and sand, as well as a stream of men, all in preparation for getting under way.

This was not a mere resistance of British authority. It was not a defensive action brought on by British aggression. This was American aggression, a first strike, an act of war. The Navy of the United States of America was ready to fight.

CHAPTER 6

The Continental Fleet

BIDDLECOMB STARED OUT THE SMALL WINDOW IN THE *CHARLEMAGNE*'S quarter gallery and watched the ice in the Delaware River undeniably breaking up.

There was a thin swath of open, running water down the middle of the river, which was close to a mile wide at that point, and then the ice took up again, a flat, white expanse that melded with the colony of New Jersey on the far side. But cold as it was, it was warmer than it had been the past few days, and the stretch of open water was noticeably wider.

Once the ice was gone, the fleet would sail. Biddlecomb was not all that anxious to leave Philadelphia and the wonderful fun that he was having there. He was not anxious to leave Virginia. He was not anxious to be trapped aboard the *Charlemagne* with Lt. Roger Tottenhill.

As if prompted by his captain's thoughts, Tottenhill knocked on the cabin door.

"Come."

The first officer opened the door and stepped into the cabin, ducking under the deck beams.

"Ah, Mr. Tottenhill, is it dinnertime already?" Biddlecomb asked, glancing down at the papers strewn across the surface that was both desk and dining table in that confined space.

Protocol had forced him, at last, to invite Tottenhill to dine with him.

"It lacks one bell to dinner, sir, but I thought perhaps this might be a good time for me to report on our readiness."

"Yes, quite right, of course. Please, be seated. A glass of wine with you? I still have two bottles of a tolerable Madeira."

"Thank you, sir, I should be delighted." Tottenhill eased himself into the chair that Biddlecomb was more accustomed to seeing Rumstick occupy. He filled two glasses, handed one to Tottenhill, and sat again behind his desk.

"I had hoped to have the powder stowed down before dinner, but I'm afraid we shall not," Tottenhill began. "I was not at all pleased with the way Mr. Rumstick was placing it, too far from the magazine by half. I was forced to roust it out and have it restowed properly. I find in these smaller vessels that the dead rise—"

"I see," Biddlecomb interrupted, nodding his head. "This surprises me, I must say. Mr. Rumstick is a very experienced seaman. I don't know as I've ever seen him make a mistake in that line."

"Well, sir, I don't know as you could even call it a mistake, it was more that there was a better way to do things. When I was aboard the privateer, we were very much navy fashion, and I learned a great deal about such things. I credit Mr. Rumstick's mistake to ignorance, no more."

"Indeed," said Biddlecomb, pressing his lips tightly together. "Well, very good then. How are we in the article of water?"

Their discussion of the *Charlemagne*'s readiness continued for twenty minutes, until the ringing of eight bells on the deck above. Biddlecomb found little to complain about in Tottenhill's report; the brig was all but ready for sea, and the first officer was aware of every article on board, quantity, quality, and location, as well as the exact number of strakes down the ship was loaded by the head and by the stern. The *Charlemagne*'s captain loved the subject dearly, which made it all the more incredible to him that Tottenhill could render it so dull.

"If we get any more shot aboard, let's stow it down in the after locker," Biddlecomb said. "She likes it best another strake down astern, but I reckon she's just about right now." A knocking at the door interrupted the thought, and rather than making his next point about the bread room, Biddlecomb called out, "Come!"

Rumstick stepped in, bending far lower than the others had to to avoid striking the deck beams, and behind him Mr. Midshipman Weatherspoon, who stood straight upright, his hatless head just a quarter inch below the overhead.

"Gentlemen, come, sit," Biddlecomb said, gesturing around the desk, which, during his conversation with the new first officer, he had managed to clear of papers.

"Thank you, sir," said Rumstick, taking his seat. He nodded to Tottenhill. "Mr. Mate," he muttered.

"Please, Rumstick, 'lieutenant,' not 'mate.' This is a navy vessel," Tottenhill said with a smile, and looking at Biddlecomb, said, "We'll break him of his merchantman's habits yet, eh, captain?"

"Let's bear in mind, Mr. Tottenhill, that Mr. Rumstick was fighting this war long before any of us knew there was a war." Biddlecomb smiled at Rumstick, and Rumstick gave him a quarter smile in return. Rumstick had not used the title "mate" out of ignorance, he had intended for it to be insulting. The incident concerning the powder clearly had not been as amicably reconciled as Tottenhill had suggested.

"Mr. Weatherspoon," the captain continued before Tottenhill could speak again, "this here is your purview." He handed Weatherspoon several sheets of paper, the first of which was headed "Signals for the American Fleet." "Commodore Hopkins has come up with a fairly catholic collection of signals there. I'll thank you to see that we have all of the necessary ensigns aboard."

"Yes, sir," said Weatherspoon, looking over the signals. " 'Catholic,' sir, like papist?"

" 'Catholic' like all-encompassing. You'll find, Mr. Rumstick, that there are signals for fog, something we could have used on our last voyage, as you'll recall."

"That's certain," Rumstick said. "I seem to remember you were making some grand fun of Captain Whipple for his set of signals, and when it come time—"

"I recall," Tottenhill interrupted, "in '62, aboard the *Falcon,* we had occasion to devise a set of signals. It was a singular incident, quite a funny story, really."

For five minutes, until their dinner arrived (an excellent fricassee of winter hare with potatoes and a plum duff pudding, courtesy of the carpenter's wife, who was now acting as cook for the gun room and great cabin, yet another pleasure they would lose when they put to sea), Tottenhill regaled them, bored them, in fact, with the tale of the *Falcon*'s exploits. "I was fourth lieutenant then, we called our officers lieutenants, not mates, Mr. Rumstick, man-of-war fashion, when all of this took place. It was—"

"If you'll excuse me, Lieutenant," Biddlecomb interrupted, it being his duty, as he saw it, to save his guests from further tales that Mr. Tottenhill might relate, "I should like to inform the company of what I know concerning our future."

That, more than anything, was bound to command attention. The cabin fell silent and the three men leaned forward expectantly, so expectantly in fact that Biddlecomb was forced to laugh. "Forgive me, gentlemen, but you look so like children in a confectioner's I couldn't help myself. And I'm afraid that I'll disappoint you. I can tell you we sail on the tide tomorrow afternoon, and that we are rendezvousing at Cape Henlopen, but beyond that I know nothing."

In a moment of silence they digested this news. "No idea where we're bound, or what we're to act?" Rumstick asked.

"None, I'm afraid. But it looks to me as if this ice is breaking up, and we only need three or four days at the very most to fetch Cape Henlopen, and I should think then we'll find out what our mission is to be."

"The Chesapeake, I should guess," said Tottenhill, speaking with the smugness of one who has privileged information. He kept his eyes on his plate, cutting a generous bite as he continued. "Lord Dunmore, the former royal governor of Virginia, is ravaging the countryside with his improvised fleet. I believe we are to teach him a lesson." With that Tottenhill put his fork in his mouth and glanced around the table for reactions.

"Well, ain't that something," said Rumstick. "I'd have thought we was bound for Narragansett Bay, clear those rascals out of there. That's where the fleet is most needed, not in your Southern colonies."

Tottenhill swallowed quickly. "You see, sir, there is your problem, your damned regionalism. This is not, sir, a New England navy, it is a navy of the United Colonies, and I will thank you to remember that."

Tottenhill was angry, genuinely angry, and Biddlecomb found the outburst more surprising than anything else. He could see Rumstick flaring, see that the second officer was prepared to give it back with interest to the first. "Gentlemen, I have no doubt that the Naval Committee . . . ," Biddlecomb began with some weak platitude, the best he could concoct in the instant that he had to prevent a confrontation, then was happily interrupted by voices outside the great cabin door.

"Yes, right here, good man," someone was saying, a voice that Biddlecomb did not recognize. "No, you needn't stand like you've a ramrod up your backside, you'll be here for a while. . . . Yes, good. Carry on."

In the great cabin the four men listened intently to this odd exchange, and Biddlecomb was on the verge of standing up to investigate when there came a knocking on the door.

"Come," he said. The door opened and a uniformed officer stepped in, though both the uniform and the officer were unknown to Biddlecomb and, judging from the others' expressions, to anyone in the cabin.

He was in his late thirties apparently, with wisps of gray sneaking in among his light brown, unpowdered hair, his head unencumbered with a wig. He wore on his upper lip a thick mustache in a style rarely seen in the Colonies, but in his case it seemed to go with his generally amiable expression. His eyes, as he looked around the cabin, had a pleased and vaguely amused look, which reminded Biddlecomb of Virginia Stanton. He wore white breeches and a white waistcoat and over that a striking green coat with white facings.

"Ah, gentlemen, you are at dinner," he said. "I apologize for this interruption," then as if as an afterthought, he snapped to attention and swept his hat off in a salute, saying, "Elisha Faircloth . . . beg pardon, Lt. Elisha Faircloth, Second Battalion, Fourth Company of American Marines, sir!" He gave a quick bow and smiled, as if expecting applause for his performance. "I took the liberty of posting a sentry outside your cabin door, Captain, navy-fashion and all."

"Indeed." Biddlecomb could think of nothing else to say. He stood and extended his hand. "Capt. Isaac Biddlecomb, your servant."

"An honor," said Faircloth, shaking the captain's hand, "but of course you need no introduction; not many in this town that don't know Captain Biddlecomb."

"Indeed," Isaac said again, this time embarrassed. "Allow me to present my first officer, Lt. Roger Tottenhill, and my second, Lt. Ezra Rumstick. And this is Mr. Midshipman Weatherspoon."

Hands were shaken all around, and after a chair had been found for Faircloth and the last of the fricassee passed his way, he said, "Fourth Company's been assigned to the *Charlemagne*, something of a last-minute thing, I'm afraid. Don't believe they knew you were coming. Only twenty men, good lads all. 'Lads,' I say; half of them are old enough to be, well, my older brother, in any event." He glanced around the table with his half-amused expression, the flesh around his glinting eyes crinkling as he smiled. His gaze settled on the Madeira. "Ah, I am mad for Madeira. Might I?"

"Of course, of course, how rude of me," said Biddlecomb, pouring a glass.

"Your coat, Lieutenant, is it a marine officer's uniform?" Tottenhill asked.

"No, not an official one. There are no official uniforms as of yet, I don't believe, but some of us have taken to wearing these coats, hope to convince the Congress to make them official, what? Dashing color, ain't it?"

"I believe it was a requirement of Congress," Rumstick spoke for the first time since Faircloth's appearance, "that the men enlisted in the marines was to be able seamen. Is that the case, do you know, Lieutenant?"

"Able seamen, well . . . I'll be honest, there was quite a rush to sign up for the battalions, those drums and all, recruiters marching through the streets, quite stirring to those of adventurous spirit. I think it may be that they were none too discriminating in signing men up."

"And you, sir?" Biddlecomb asked, looking up at Faircloth from his plum duff. "Might I enquire as to your background? Were you employed at something before accepting your commission?"

"Employed? Oh, Lord, no. I'm a gentleman, sir. My father wanted me to join the Philadelphia Light Horse. Can't bloody stand horses, miserable animals, much prefer a rational ship under my foot to some insane animal under my arse."

"We are of one mind in that, sir," Biddlecomb said. "Do I take it then that you are not a seaman?"

"Well, as it happens, my uncle has a yacht, so I am not without some knowledge of the sea. And I have been studying, oh, yes. Mountaine's excellent *The Seaman's Vade Mecum.*"

Glances were exchanged around the table, and at last Biddlecomb said, "Well, Lieutenant, I suggest you get as much studying in as ever you may in the next twenty-four hours, for after that, your training, I assure you, shall begin in earnest."

"This yacht, sir, it was quite a large one," Faircloth added quickly. "Perhaps I did not represent myself well."

Further inquires into Faircloth's maritime abilities were interrupted by a rather loud discussion beyond the door.

"I got a message for the captain," came a voice, loud and irritable. It was Ferguson.

"All right, then, I'll announce you. What's your name?" the marine sentry replied.

"Ferguson."

The sentry knocked on the door and opened it, just a crack. "Ferguson for the captain," he called.

"Very well," Biddlecomb called, and then to the officers seated at the table said, "This is rather silly, don't you think?"

Before any could voice an opinion, Ferguson stepped into the cabin and saluted. "Beg your pardon, sir, and sorry for all the noise. I guess we're doing things different now, being in the navy and all. Bloody marine—"

"What is it, Ferguson?" Biddlecomb asked.

"Beg pardon, sir. The recruits from North Carolina is here, and a mangy lot they is, sir."

Mangy they were, but that did not stop Tottenhill from giving Ferguson a thorough dressing down for saying so. The captain and officers left their dinner to go topside and greet the new men, who had arrived just in time. There were twenty-six in all, making up about a third of the *Charlemagne*'s company. They were dressed in rags for the most part, unwashed and with hair and beards long and unkempt, giving Biddlecomb the suspicion that most of them had been recruited from prison.

That worrisome fact aside, Biddlecomb could tell in one glance that they were seamen. Seaman had a quality that no landsman could imitate. They had a way of looking about the ship, assessing it rather than staring in wonder, a way of standing, a certain angle at which they wore their hats, that indicated better than any credentials to which they laid claim that these men were at home on shipboard. Of that at least he was thankful.

"Welcome aboard the *Charlemagne*. I am Captain Biddlecomb, this is First Lieutenant Tottenhill, Second Lieutenant Rumstick, Lieutenant of Marines Faircloth, and Midshipman Weatherspoon and Mr. Sprout, the bosun. The rest of the ship's company you'll meet in time. Get your dunnage and Mr. Sprout will show you where you mess and swing your hammocks."

Mr. Sprout led them below. They seemed to have precious little dunnage, as far as Biddlecomb could see.

"They seem a bit ragged, but I have no doubt they'll do fine," Biddlecomb said as the last of them disappeared below. "I am grateful to you, Mr. Tottenhill, for bringing these men."

"It was no great trouble, sir. The people of North Carolina are most disposed to protecting our liberties, you see. We've always been an independent people. In the last war—"

"Sir? Captain Biddlecomb? Beg pardon?" a voice from the quarterdeck steps interrupted Tottenhill's speech. It was one of the North Carolina men. "Sir, I wanted to thank you, on behalf of the men, for giving us this chance to serve."

Biddlecomb considered the man addressing him. He was of average height, tending toward being overweight, with long brown hair bound in a queue, the way men wore it who had been long at sea. His expression revealed nothing, he might have been asleep for all one could see in his face, but his narrow, darting eyes seemed far more disingenuous than his tone of voice, and it put Biddlecomb immediately on his guard.

"You're welcome . . ."

"Hackett. Hackett, sir, pleased to make your acquaintance. And, if I may be so bold, sir, the men have come a long way, and we're none of us too well off. I . . . well . . . I was elected by the North Carolina men to speak for them, sir, and ask, could we get some issues of slops, sir? Clothes, and a bit of tobacco, if we could? And we figured the men aboard has had their tot today, and of course we haven't . . ."

"Elected?" Faircloth said to Biddlecomb. "Quite a republican notion, I should say."

"Indeed. However, there is no room for republican notions aboard this ship, Lt. Faircloth," Biddlecomb replied. "We are a perfect tyranny here, and I the tyrant. Listen here, Hackett," he said in a louder tone, addressing the sailor before him. "You men shall be issued proper clothes before we sail, have no doubt. But understand this: I do not much care for elections and spokesmen and discussions of shipboard operations, is that clear? Do not ever let me hear of you voting for this and that. This is no democracy. You follow orders on this ship and that is final."

"But, sir, I only—"

"Hackett, for your own sake I suggest you shut your gob and go forward. Understood?"

"Aye, sir." Hackett's expression revealed nothing: no anger, no humiliation. With no more than a flash of his eyes, he was gone, forward and below.

"Really, sir, perhaps you were a bit harsh with him," Tottenhill began. "My men have come a long way to volunteer, and they deserve some consideration."

"Lieutenant, that man is a sea lawyer, through and through," Biddlecomb replied. "I can spot the breed a mile distant. He wasn't asking out of concern for his fellows, he was poking around the quarterdeck, looking for the soft spots, and he didn't waste much time, did he? With that type you cannot give them an inch, I assure you. No one knows better than me what damage a few well-placed words can do."

" 'I have great comfort from this fellow,' " Faircloth said, nodding toward the hatch down which Hackett had disappeared. " 'Methinks he hath no drowning mark upon him; his complexion is perfect gallows.' "

"*The Tempest.* Well said, Mr. Faircloth," said Biddlecomb, genuinely pleased to discover someone aboard with whom he shared an interest. "Gentlemen, shall we go below again? I believe there is still a bottle of Madeira that has yet to suffer shipwreck."

They sat down at the table again, taking their former seats, but it was different now. Rumstick was sullen and angry, as he had been before, but now Tottenhill was as well. Biddlecomb filled glasses all around, exchanging pleasantries with Faircloth, talk of theaters and books, while Weatherspoon looked on, oblivious, and the two lieutenants sulked. Apparently Tottenhill was not happy with Biddlecomb's treatment of Hackett. Apparently he took it as a personal affront. And that was too damned bad.

He had better get over that, Biddlecomb thought, or he'll see what trouble really looks like.

CHAPTER 7

Government House

JOHN BROWN, PRESIDENT OF HIS MAJESTY'S COUNCIL, BAHAMAS, SAT on the wide second-story veranda of Government House, sipping a rum punch and waiting for the house's occupant to say something. Anything. This silence was a great irritant to him, as if the governor were so occupied with weighty matters that he could not, for the moment, speak. Brown knew for a fact that the most pressing matter on the governor's mind was the digestion of his breakfast in preparation for dinner.

The royal governor of the Bahamas, Montfort Browne (the similarity of their surnames was yet another source of irritation, and quite often confusion), was bent at the waist, as best he could, peering through a brilliantly polished brass telescope mounted on the equally brilliant legs of a tripod.

Spread out below the two men was the town of Nassau, cut into squares by the cobblestone streets, which were covered with a fine layer of dust. Each square was cluttered with pretty houses built of gray bricks cut from coral and accented with brilliantly painted wood shutters.

Government House, situated as it was on Mount Fitzwilliam, gave them a commanding view of the town and Hog Island beyond, separated from the island of New Providence by a strip of water that constituted the harbor at Nassau. To the west, beyond the far tip of Hog Island, the Atlantic Ocean stretched away, the light aqua-green color of the shallow water melding into the deep blue of the open sea.

"This fellow who is here to see me, who is he, again?" Governor Browne asked, never taking his eye from the telescope's eyepiece.

Brown sighed with exasperation, but quietly, so as not to be heard, and said, "He is Capt. Andrew Law, an army officer, though I do not know of what regiment."

"Well, Babbidge," the Governor said to his secretary, the half-pay lieutenant James Babbidge, who sat a respectful distance away, "you're the army fellow here. What regiment is he with?"

"It would appear, Your Honor"—Babbidge always called the governor "Your Honor" in the company of others—"he is of a light company, the King's Own Regiment of Foot, the Fourth, I do believe."

"King's Own, eh? Another one of Gage's men?"

"Howe, sir," Babbidge corrected the governor, no doubt aware that Brown would not do so again. "General Howe is in command in North America now."

"Howe, right. Six of one . . ." Governor Browne lapsed back into silence, shifting the telescope to the east. In the harbor directly in front of Government House, swinging from a mooring, was His Majesty's schooner *St. John*, the island's only representative of the Royal Navy. Even without a telescope Brown could see that she looked tired, her rigging slack, her paint dull and rubbed off in spots, her spars possessed of a generally sagging quality. She gave the impression that she was ready at any moment to roll over and take a nap, and she did not inspire the confidence and awe that so often accompanied the ships of the greatest navy on earth.

Brown pulled his eyes from the harbor and looked instead at the governor, a boundless source of amusement to him. From the side the governor's midriff was shaped exactly like a half of an egg, and Brown marveled that his breeches, now stretched to the utmost of the fabric's limits, did not carry away entirely.

But the governor did not have the flabby, lethargic quality of a fat man; Brown often wished the governor were more lethargic by half. He was over six feet in height and carried his weight well, and the extra five stone did not seem to slow him in the least.

The governor straightened and reached out a hand for his coat, which Babbidge obediently handed him, shaking it to smooth out nonexistent wrinkles. The governor struggled into the garment and adjusted the stiff wig on his head, all the time looking down at Fort Nassau, the odd-shaped, many-sided, sprawling fortification that sat perched on the shore, four hundred yards away.

"Damned stupid place for a fort," he said. "Damned stupid. Anyone who captured Government House could make the place untenable. A couple of big guns up here and you could enfilade the place. Enfilade it." Governor Browne had reached this fairly obvious conclusion the week before and had not yet tired of mentioning it. "Well, show the captain in, Babbidge."

Babbidge disappeared through the open door and reappeared a moment later, stepping to one side and saying, "Capt. Andrew Law," and then, "Captain Law, the Royal Governor Montfort Browne, and Mr. John Brown, President of His Majesty's Council."

After handshakes and how-do-you-dos were exchanged all around, and Babbidge was dispatched for a cup of rum punch for the captain, the three men sat and the governor said, "What can we do for you, Captain? We've no troops here, you know, the Fourteenth Regiment of Foot was withdrawn last fall, packed off to Boston."

"Yes, sir, I am aware of that." Law was what one might call swarthy: dark hair and eyes, skin either naturally dark or much weathered, it was difficult to tell, and his tone and features revealed nothing of the man. He seemed to Brown to be much practiced in making himself an enigma, and the president of

His Majesty's Council guessed that the governor would find him a bit disconcerting.

"I have come to make you aware of certain intelligence concerning the rebellious element in North America," Law continued. "There is a fleet fitted out and attempting to get to sea, in fact they may already be out, and it is believed, on good authority, that their destination is New Providence. As you say, the Fourteenth Foot was removed, and it is no secret that there are no regular troops on the island, just as it is no secret that there is a great quantity of military stores here, ripe for the taking."

Law took the cup of rum punch from Babbidge, who had returned to the veranda, and sipped it while the others absorbed this information. At last the governor spoke.

"Bah! We've heard this before, rebels coming to attack. When was it, Brown, last June? When that infamous Linzie showed up here with his transports, ready to take all our powder and shot on Gage's orders, leave us defenseless as babes. We sent him packing, sir, depend on it. So why should we believe you?"

"Well, Governor," Law continued patiently, "we know that the rebels have had designs on this island for some time. In November of last year the Secret Committee of their Congress resolved to attempt something." Law held up his hand to ward off the governor's protest. "Don't ask me how I know this. In any event, they have not had the means to attempt anything. Until now."

The veranda was silent as the government men absorbed this intelligence. "What are you suggesting, sir?" Governor Browne asked at last.

"Nothing, Governor. I am suggesting nothing." Law stood up and walked to the edge of the veranda and leaned on it, letting his eyes rove over the enviable view. "Allow me, however, to mention some options. If you have faith in your militia, then you might consider resisting an attack. If not, you might hide your supplies in the interior of the island or charter one of those ships out there to take your military stores to some place safe. To Governor Toyn at St. Augustine's, perhaps. These, as I see it, are your options."

Governor Browne drew himself up to full height and looked at the assembled men. "We must evacuate the forts, send the stores to St. Augustine. We shall round up all the militia, and whatever free Negroes we can find. We must act at once."

Governor Browne was a man of great decisiveness, making up his mind and then changing it with staggering rapidity.

President of His Majesty's Council Brown, however, was more thoughtful, and he considered this decision, wondering whether or not he should change Browne's mind for him. If the supplies were gone, then New Providence would be defenseless in the face of the rebels. But worse, much worse, he, President Brown, would be without any leverage, without any cards to play. That was why he had not allowed Linzie to take the supplies before. It had been his decision, the governor having been gone from the island when the captain arrived.

"Indeed we must, Governor, but I beg you consider the other options the captain has suggested."

"Such as? Move the stores to the interior? Let some infernal tool of the rebels betray their whereabouts?"

"No, that's too much of a risk, I'll warrant. Though it occurs to me that if the rebels come here and we are without guns and powder, then we must necessarily surrender without a fight. And if the rebels find we have frustrated their designs, then they could take their revenge on the town, and us with no way to defend ourselves. But of course you are in command of the militia, and therefore in the best position to know if they will follow your orders."

"That is a fact, I am in command of the militia." The governor paused and looked down at Fort Nassau. "The fort's in abominable condition, the damned parapet might come crashing down if we fire more than one gun at a time. Montegu's in good shape, however, but it's damned small."

The governor frowned and stared down at Fort Nassau.

Brown could almost hear the debate in the governor's head. He was considering, no doubt, how it might look to the home government if he gave up the town without the slightest vestige of a defense.

"Damn it all, we will not just roll over and give up this island to a bunch of damned rebels. I can just imagine what they'd say back home if we did that," the governor exploded. "We'll keep our arms, sir, and if they come, we shall stand and fight!"

"Very good, Governor," Captain Law said, his voice betraying no opinion of the governor's decision. Brown studied Law's face; nothing was given away, but Law had not missed a bit of what had transpired. Not that it mattered. The military supplies would remain on the island, and if the rebels came, then there would still be some options available, beyond immediate surrender.

Brown felt the warm trade wind blow across the veranda, making the napkins flutter, then settle again. The same trade wind that would carry the Yankees south. And for President of His Majesty's Council John Brown, it would carry more than just rebel ships, oh, yes. It would carry opportunity as well.

CHAPTER 8

Downriver

"GENTLEMEN," STANTON SAID, RAISING HIS GLASS AND PREPARING to give the same toast he had given three times already, phrased differently, to be certain, but substantially the same. The others at the table, Virginia, Rogers, Rumstick, and Biddlecomb, all raised their glasses high.

"I give you the First American Fleet! Ten long years of blood and toil have been leading up to this moment, the moment when the United Colonies of America would put to sea their own mighty armada!"

Biddlecomb raised his glass, clicking it against the others, toasting the five vessels tied up to Willing and Morris' Wharf: two ships and three brigs, converted merchantmen all, save for the *Charlemagne,* and she much battered, which had now become a mighty armada.

He caught Virginia's eye and smiled broader still, and she smiled as well and winked. For a decade Virginia had been the only woman in Stanton House, and her father had long since given up any attempt to corral her into playing the lady; now she had her dessert and brandy with the men, and if she had lit up a pipe, Biddlecomb would have been only mildly surprised.

The conversation flowed like the Delaware River, which was now all but free of ice, drifting to subjects other than the American Navy and the upcoming fleet action. That was very much to Biddlecomb's liking; he was tired of the subject and loath to exchange this lovely city and fine company for the freezing terror of the Atlantic Ocean in the height of winter.

It was nearly midnight when the party, the farewell party, came to a close. Stanton and Rumstick and Rogers, arms linked, staggered out of the sitting room, their usual bonhomie much augmented by wine and port. They stood in the foyer, exchanging loud good-nights and congratulations.

"Captain Biddlecomb?" Virginia said softly, her teasing smile playing across her lips. She stepped close to him, her long, delicate fingers smoothing the ruffle on his shirt. "I would not think it amiss if you were to come by my room, say at two bells in the middle watch, as you sailors put it. So I can say farewell." Her seductive tone could not hide the note of timidity in her voice. Then she turned and walked, fairly glided, out of the room.

For the next hour Biddlecomb, in stocking feet, paced back and forth across the floor of his room. There was much for him to think about. In the morning he would be getting under way in command of a man-of-war in the first fleet of the American Navy, with an unknown first officer and a crew half-comprised of new recruits and jailbirds, bound away for the wintry Atlantic.

But of course he was thinking of none of that, and even when he attempted to distract himself by forcing those other considerations to the forefront of his mind, they did not stay there for long. Rather, his mind was standing fast in Virginia's bedroom, in Virginia's bed, where, he hoped, he himself would soon follow.

Through the window, which he had cracked open, it suddenly feeling very warm to him, Biddlecomb heard the sound of two bells ringing out from the men-of-war tied to the dock three blocks away. He stiffened and felt his stomach knot up, felt the telltale tingling on the bottom of his feet, the harbinger of some pending action.

He looked at himself in the mirror, adjusted his ruffled shirt, smoothed his breeches, and shook his head in disgust at this nervous and agitated state. It was not as if this would be his first time, far from it. He had been a sailor for years, and as such had experienced all of those things for which sailors were famous, including those shore-side pursuits. But that memory did nothing, absolutely nothing, to assuage his anxiety.

He walked slowly down the hall, grimacing at every squeak of the floorboards. He moved past Stanton's door, and Rumstick's, behind which he heard the loud and familiar snoring. His footsteps would never be heard over that din.

He came at last to Virginia's door, breathed deep and knocked twice, the lightest of raps. He waited, thinking that she had perhaps fallen asleep or changed her mind. He considered knocking again, or skulking back to his room, then he heard the latch lift and the door swung open.

Virginia looked out through the partially open door, looked into his eyes and smiled. She was dressed in her nightgown, a loose-fitting silk affair, low-cut in the front and clinging to her here and there, giving a suggestion of the slim body beneath. Her head was uncovered and her long brown hair hung down her back and forward over her shoulders.

Behind her the single candle standing in a tin sconce shaped like a fleur-de-lis on the wall cast a warm circle of light, giving the gauzy fabric that draped down around the big four-poster bed an ethereal quality while the rest of the room was lost in shadow.

Virginia opened the door wider and stepped aside and Biddlecomb stepped in. "Captain Biddlecomb," Virginia said with a hint of her teasing voice, then shut the door. "Isaac," she said, this time with an odd note of vulnerability as they stood looking at each other.

"You look wonderful," Biddlecomb said, and inside he grimaced and cursed himself for being such a stupid, awkward calf. Such an idiotic thing to say! But Virginia smiled, a shy, girlish smile, not at all what he was used to, and she looked at his face and then down at the floor.

The light from the candle lit the one side of her face and played off the shimmering surface of her nightgown. Biddlecomb was overcome with desire, a hunger that would be sated before all else. He reached out and put his hands on her little waist, and she looked up and threw her arms around his neck and they kissed, pressing hard against each other. He ran his hands over the smooth silk, feeling her body under the cloth, ran his hands over her back and shoulders and she pulled him toward her, kissing him with a reckless need.

He reached his arm down and scooped her up, their lips never coming apart, and carried her over to the bed, her weight far less than he would have imagined. He pushed the curtains aside and laid her down and laid down with her.

"Isaac," Virginia breathed the word. His lips ran over her face and her eyelids and her neck, he kissed the beautiful, smooth expanse of skin above her breasts. He felt his desire increasing, ready to break over him like a squall.

His hand ran down the length of her body, over her hips and her waist and her hard stomach. He felt her hands running through his hair, her breath coming faster, and he moved his hand up along her side and cupped her breast, warm and firm. She let out a little moan and moved under him, and he felt her hand on his, pressing his hand harder against her breast. He ran his lips over her face, and then she pulled his hand away, saying, "Isaac, no. I'm sorry. I'm sorry."

Biddlecomb rolled back, propping himself up on his elbow, stroking her face with his hand. She looked like a trapped bird, confused and afraid. "I . . . I am sorry, Isaac, I love you so much." It was not the Virginia Stanton he knew, not the unflappable Virginia Stanton. Now she was vulnerable and frightened, for the first time in his memory, and despite the frustration, the inordinate frustration that he felt, he loved her far more then than he ever had before.

"I'm sorry," she said again. "It's not you, it's me." Biddlecomb wrapped his arms around her and pulled her close to him, and she pressed her face against his chest, her hands clasped across her chest. He could feel her tears on his skin.

"It's all right, it's all right," he said. "I love you so very much." They lay like that for a long time. Biddlecomb ran his fingers through her thick hair. "Fair's fair," he whispered at length. "I did write you a note once, alluding to our upcoming marriage."

Virginia pulled away from him and looked up at his face. Her eyes were rimmed with red, but she was smiling. "You did too. And will you keep your word? Will you marry me?"

"Of course I will, of course I will." What in the hell was he saying? Had he at last agreed to something to which his courage would not admit?

An hour later Virginia's breathing became rhythmic and pronounced as she fell asleep in his arms, and Biddlecomb knew that if he did not leave then, then he might fall asleep as well, and morning would find them in that compromised position. He rolled her gently on her back, and wisps of her hair fell across her face and her silk nightgown pulled taut, revealing the sensual curves of her body. He felt the desire flare up again, like a fire one had thought extinguished, and he fought down the urge to run his hand over her.

"Are you going?" she asked in a sleepy voice, and her eyes slowly opened.

"Yes, my love." He leaned over and kissed her, and she kissed him back.

"Are you angry with me?"

"No," he said, not knowing if it was the truth. Yes, it was the truth. He loved her, he was not angry with her.

"And you'll marry me?"

"Yes, I'll marry you."

"Should I make you do it tomorrow, before you sail? You might change your mind, given time to think."

"Well, I suppose . . . ," he said, equivocating, trying to guess if she was joking, if he was ready to keep his promise immediately. The thought, in truth, was far more intimidating than the thought of taking his battered brig into the North Atlantic.

"I'm joking," Virginia said, closing her eyes and rolling half over, throwing her arm over his legs. "You can wait 'till you return. I don't want you to rush headlong into anything." The old Virginia was waking up.

"I'll marry you when the fleet returns. Now you go to sleep, and I'll see you in the morning. I have to go back to the ship quite early. But you will come see me off, won't you?"

"Of course, my love, my sweet Isaac." She kissed him again.

Biddlecomb did not wait until the morning to return to the *Charlemagne*. No sooner had he made his way back to his room than he realized that sleep was no longer a possibility, plagued as he was by his frustrated desires and his apprehension for the future, his unwillingness to leave Virginia and Philadelphia, his concern over his promise of marriage, and his anxiety over the myriad things that plagued commanders of ships the world over.

He pulled his blue coat on, and his heavy wool coat over that, pushed his cocked hat down on his head, and made his way down the cold and silent streets to his ship, his beloved *Charlemagne,* tied to the wharf.

He crunched through the snow, inches deep, and struggled to the foot of the brow, walking carefully over the icy surface. He stepped gingerly onto the wooden plank; in the dark it was hard to tell wood from ice, and he was halfway up when a voice from the deck called, "Halt! Who goes there?"

Biddlecomb stopped and looked up, unsure if he should laugh at the histrionic challenge. He did not recognize the man at the gangway, one of Faircloth's marines, only about half of whom he had met.

"Who goes there?" the marine asked again.

"*Charlemagne,*" Biddlecomb replied, the standard means of indicating the captain of a vessel.

"Yes, this is the *Charlemagne,* and who are you?"

Biddlecomb might have laughed if he had not been in so

foul a mood, and he might have given the man a dressing-down, but the marine was only following orders, and doing so conscientiously, and a captain could not lambast a man for that. He even managed, ten minutes later, to give the marine a "Well done," after he had been held at bayonet point on the brow while Lieutenant Faircloth was summoned.

"God, I am sorry for this, sir," said Faircloth, dressed in his bottle-green coat, boots, and wool undergarments. He thrashed his arms across his chest as he followed Biddlecomb across the deck.

"No need to apologize, Lieutenant." Biddlecomb stepped below with Faircloth hurrying beside him to usher him past the other marine posted at the great cabin door. "We shall all have ample time to get to know one another, and to pick up the finer points, such as who is the captain of the vessel. Good night, sir." No sooner had he shut the great cabin door than he regretted taking his irritation out on Faircloth, but it was too late to rectify that.

Thunderheads of excitement about the sailing of the fleet had been building over Philadelphia, and the next morning they broke. With the first clear light at dawn one could see that the ice was thinner than it had been in weeks, with large pieces breaking away from the solid sheets along the banks and swirling away downstream. By the afternoon watch the river would be clear enough for the fleet to sail, and sail they would.

The crowds began to gather along the quay just as the last of the supplies were struck down and hatches battened securely for sea. Commodore. Esek Hopkins, younger brother of Congressman Stephen Hopkins, his face creased by a lifetime at sea and looking every one of his fifty-seven years, paraded the wharf, a lieutenant and three midshipmen trailing behind like bridesmaids.

"Hopkins is on a rhumb line for our brow, Captain," Rumstick mentioned, nodding to the entourage just stepping off the *Cabot*. "Reckon he'll expect a side party and all."

"I reckon you're right. Do we . . . ah . . . do we have a side party? Has that detail been told off?"

Rumstick smiled. "I got it well in hand, Captain."

And, as usual, he did. The ship's boys turned out with white gloves, and Faircloth's marines, dressed in identical bottle-green uniforms, much to Biddlecomb's surprise, stood ready to present arms. Their drills were ragged, but not overly so, considering that the very Marine Corps itself was not above two months old.

As Biddlecomb stood at the end of the line of marines, he was not surprised to see Tottenhill slide up next to him, a look of grave injustice on his face. "Sir, Mr. Rumstick has set this whole thing up without consulting me. The side party is my responsibility, not his, and I resent the intrusion."

"Mr. Tottenhill, did you think to organize a side party at all?" Biddlecomb was becoming tired of this. "Did you have the gloves for the sideboys and alert the bosun and his mates and the marines? . . . No, I thought not. Please be so gracious as to thank God, at least, for Rumstick's foresight, if you cannot bring yourself to thank Rumstick himself."

Tottenhill stepped back, his pride wounded deeper still. Biddlecomb knew it and did not want the wound to fester, so he said, "Still, Mr. Tottenhill, I will see that Rumstick clears these things through you in the future." He felt like the headmaster of a boarding school.

"Biddlecomb, Biddlecomb, God damn my soul to hell, right to hell," Commodore Hopkins said, stepping up the brow and shaking Biddlecomb's hand over the noise of the side party. Shoulder-length, salt-and-pepper hair fell out from under his cocked hat and was tied loosely behind, and his craggy and lined face with its protruding hawk nose was softened somewhat by his smile. He ran his eyes over the *Charlemagne*'s rig and along her deck. "Lovely, lovely. Stanton always built the best, none of your false economy you see too much of in America, too much by half. It's good to lay eyes on you again."

Biddlecomb had known Hopkins for ten years at least, just as he had known Whipple, commanding the *Columbus,* and Hopkins's son, John Hopkins, commanding *Cabot,* and, for that matter, Dudley Saltonstall, flag captain aboard the *Alfred.* New England ship captains all, and all, save for Saltonstall, from Rhode Island. "It's good to see you as well, sir, and joy on your promotion."

"Joy, my arse, we'll see how much joy I get out of it. You ready for sea?"

"Ready in all respects, sir."

"Good, good. *Alfred*'s still got a few hands ashore, run or just waking up in some whorehouse. *Cabot*'s waiting on a midshipman and four marines, and *Columbus* is short a few as well, I believe. We'll wait until eight bells in the forenoon watch and not a minute more, then we go. I'll fire a gun from *Alfred* and we'll all raise our ensigns. I sent an ensign over; does your signal midshipman have it ready to go?"

"I'm certain he does, sir," said Biddlecomb, certain of no such thing, but certain at least that Weatherspoon would be made to find an ensign if he had misplaced the one Hopkins had provided. With a thought toward future subterfuge Biddlecomb had brought aboard the ensigns of a dozen different nations, and he hoped that his own country's flag was among them.

"Good then. Wait for my gun, then raise the ensign, and we'll start to cast off, get under way in grand style. Won't need to warp out, this blessed breeze will lift us right off the dock. *Alfred*'ll go first, then *Columbus,* then *Cabot,* then you and *Andrew Doria,* right up the line."

They waited for the gun, waited through eight bells in the forenoon watch, then one bell in the afternoon watch, then two bells and three bells, with midshipmen from the flagship racing down the quay every twenty minutes or so to explain the latest delay.

Stanton came aboard, and Virginia, to bid their farewell. Biddlecomb pumped Stanton's hand and thanked him for his blessings, and he kissed Virginia on the cheek. Her eyes said more and said it better than any words he had ever spoken to her. He hoped desperately that he was able to convey to her in that all too public farewell all that he wanted to say: his love and his commitment—grown stronger in the light of day, but he could not rid himself of the image of her lying on the big bed, and it distracted him.

At last the Stantons went ashore and joined the crowd lining the quay and Water Street three deep. Ten minutes later the *Alfred*'s gun went off. On the flagship's quarterdeck Isaac could see the first lieutenant, a young Scotsman with red hair whose name he could not recall, hauling away on the flag halyard.

The ensign rose up the staff, a flag of red, white, and blue stripes, the union jack in the canton. The Grand Union Flag. From the ships and the crowd on the shore came a shout like rolling thunder, wave after wave of cheering as the ensigns went up on the other men-of-war.

The cheering did not abate, indeed it grew louder, as *Alfred*'s topsails fell and the yards were hoisted and her inner jib jerked up the fore topmast stay and was set aback. Her bow swung majestically away from the dock, the ship pivoting on the one stern line held fast. Then that too was slipped and the flagship moved out into the river, free of the shore at last, her round bows nudging the heavy chunks of ice aside.

The *Columbus* followed, portly Abraham Whipple standing like a stunted tree on her quarterdeck, his eyes everywhere, seemingly oblivious to the frenzied crowd on the shore. Then came the *Cabot*, momentarily delayed by a gasket left tied on her jib, but that was soon cast off and the brig followed the two larger ships downstream.

Biddlecomb smiled, quite involuntarily. His feet were tingling with excitement. This was what he loved above all else, the moment when the brig became an extension of himself, every action aboard the vessel a reaction to his spoken word.

The sensation was only heightened by the hundreds of people watching and cheering. He was the focal point now of the great military show, and he loved it.

"Get the main topsail on her, and topgallants as well, if you please," Biddlecomb said to Tottenhill, and Tottenhill ran forward to see that done. "Mr. Rumstick, I would like the best bower cockbilled, in case we must drop it quickly. In any event we don't have above two hours of daylight left, and I rather doubt Hopkins will choose to feel his way through this ice in the dark."

Fifteen minutes later the anchor was hanging from the cat-head, and the topgallants, which had just been set, were clewed up and stowed, the extra canvas having made the *Charlemagne* surge ahead and threaten to overtake the slow-moving ships sailing downriver under shortened sail. The lovely city of Philadelphia was off the starboard quarter and disappearing astern, and the crowd that had lined the waterfront was gone.

The fleet pushed through the broken ice, one mile, then two miles downriver. The sun moved quickly toward the western horizon, and the sky, the flawlessly clear winter sky, was orange and red in the west, then white, pale blue, dark blue, and black in a great variegated arc overhead. A low, marshy, frozen island appeared off the starboard bow, an island that Biddlecomb had known for years as Mud Island but which had apparently been caught up in the general sweep of patriotic fervor and renamed Liberty Island.

"Signal from the flag, sir," said Weatherspoon, and then in a less certain tone he added, "I think."

Biddlecomb looked over at the *Alfred* as Weatherspoon rifled through the list of signals for the fleet. The flagship's main topsail was clewing up; an odd thing to do if it was not meant as a signal. The ensign, which was absent from the ensign staff, was hoisted again, tied in a long bundle like a hammock. "Main topsail clewed up, ensign hoisted with a weft," he prompted the midshipman.

"Oh, here it is, sir. 'Fleet to anchor.' But it doesn't look like he's going to anchor, sir."

"No, indeed," said Biddlecomb. The *Alfred* was making for one of the long piers that jutted out from the island, apparently intending to tie up there. It was not clear if it the commodore wished them to do so as well, and he had given the signal closest in meaning, or if he genuinely wished for the fleet to anchor. As Biddlecomb speculated on this point, he saw the *Columbus* heading for the pier as well. "Mr. Tottenhill," he said. "We'll be warping alongside the northern pier, there. Please see things laid along."

Hopkins had no choice, of course. There would be just enough daylight for the ships to safely tie up and not a minute more. And it was just as well. It had been a hectic day, and at least half of the crew, he was certain, were still suffering from the farewell celebrations of the night before, himself and Rumstick included.

From the head of the Delaware Bay one could walk overland to the head of the Chesapeake Bay in an afternoon, but it would take them five days at least to sail out into the Atlantic and beat south against wind and current, if that was indeed where they were bound. Now they could stand down to an anchor watch, and all hands would be well rested for getting under way and reaching blue water tomorrow night. Still, he had envisioned covering more than two miles on the first day of their expedition.

The five vessels heaved themselves against the stout wooden docks to the clacking of five capstans. An hour of hectic activity aboard the *Charlemagne* and then quiet, the pervasive quiet of winter, as the men were stood down to an easy anchor watch and most of them sought shelter below.

Biddlecomb slept well that night, as if he were still ashore, undisturbed by any violent motion of the brig, or any motion at all, and dreamed of the noble expedition to which they would sail on the morning tide. He woke before dawn, dressed and stepped out onto the quarterdeck just as the first hint of gray appeared in the east. And even in that thin light he could see that they would not be sailing on a noble expedition. They would not be sailing at all.

From the western shore of the Delaware River to the eastern, from Pennsylvania to New Jersey, the river was a flat expanse of ice, thick and impregnable, and in it the American fleet was frozen solid.

CHAPTER 9

Icebound

THE GOOD HUMOR FELT BY THE MEN OF THE NAVY AND MARINES OF the United Colonies, which started with the cheering crowd and had stayed with them the two miles they had made downriver, did not abate with the prospect of being indefinitely frozen in ice. The men laughed and shoved each other across the slick decks and flung snowballs at each other, starboard watch against larboard, as they tumbled out at first light.

Biddlecomb, standing on the quarterdeck, was at least happy to see that his own disappointment was not shared by the others.

"I suppose," he said an hour later to the *Charlemagne*'s assembled officers, gathered around the table in the great cabin and hungrily consuming what they imagined would be the last fresh eggs they would see in some time, "that we might as well exercise with the great guns. The men seem to have a tolerable level of seamanship, but I imagine those that just joined us have little experience in gun drills."

"I don't know about seamanship, sir," Tottenhill said. "Most of the hands, and I mean the older hands as well as the new men, seem far too slack. That isn't a problem with my North Carolina boys, but some of the others . . . this ain't a merchantman, we can't have merchantman ways."

"Many of these men have been with me for a long time,

some back to my time as a merchantman," Biddlecomb said. "Pray don't let their outward appearance fool you; it amuses them to make a show of being chuckleheads, but when it counts, they are the men I would rely on most."

"I understand, sir, and no doubt you're right, but, with all due respect, this is an actual navy now, not a collection of privateers, doing what they will."

"I'll take your words under consideration, sir, if you will remember that there are no 'North Carolina boys.' These men are Charlemagnes first and Americans second. Another cup of coffee with you?" Biddlecomb said with more irritation in his voice than he had intended to reveal. It apparently did not occur to Tottenhill, and Biddlecomb was amazed to realize as much, that every time he criticized the manner in which the *Charlemagne* was run, he was criticizing her captain.

"With your permission, sir, I shall drill my marines in the . . . don't tell me, the chief part of the deck there . . ." Faircloth began to touch the parts of his body, starting at his head and moving down, stimulating some aid to memory. "The waist," he said at last. "So bloody confusing. You have the head of a ship, and the waist, but you don't come to the foot until you consider the parts of a sail."

"More confusing still when you consider that the head is where you put your bottom," Rumstick said. "You are well into your *Seaman's Vade Mecum,* I perceive."

"Quite. Fascinating stuff. Did you know that on a topsail or a topgallant you have a clewline, but on a course sail the very same line is called a clew garnet?"

"I believe I've heard that."

"Lieutenant Faircloth, please, drill your marines, with my blessing," said Biddlecomb. "I've meant to ask you about their uniforms and arms. Surely they did not provide those themselves?"

"No, not at all. I'm afraid that for the most part the men who signed up for the marines were not men who could afford such a rig. Except perhaps the officers; you have Mullan there, the proprietor of the Tun Tavern, he was made a captain, and Sam Nicholas, who's in command on this expedition, he was owner of the Conestoga Wagon, that well-loved public house. I reckon most of the officers owned taverns, and most of the privates were their customers."

"So you outfitted your men?" Rumstick asked.

"Well, certainly. I mean, the damned Light Horse of Philadelphia, I went to school with most of those spoiled bastards, you know, prancing around in their finery. I wasn't about to get involved with them, riding those damned horses. They snub their noses at the army, and my seamanship isn't yet quite up to snuff for the navy, so it was the marines. But I couldn't let my lads look like some tag and rag militia."

"Those are nice muskets they have, and uniforms. They couldn't be cheap," Rumstick observed.

"No, they were not. But I hope the Congress makes those green coats official. They look marvelous, I think."

Ten minutes after they had finished their breakfast, and with no warning to anyone save for the officers, Biddlecomb ordered the *Charlemagne* cleared for action. Mr. Sprout, the boatswain, ran from hatch to hatch, blowing his boatswain's call as if he were possessed and pushing the men to their stations, aided in that last effort by the gunner and Mr. Weatherspoon.

The older men, the core of the *Charlemagne*'s crew, who had fought on Narragansett Bay and had sailed with Biddlecomb to Bermuda, instructed the others in the drill, showing them the most efficient ways to prepare the brig for combat. A full fourteen minutes and forty-three seconds later, Rumstick appeared on the quarterdeck and declared the brig cleared for action, but still Biddlecomb was satisfied.

"That's good, for the first go-round," he said. "We must shave five minutes at least from that, but for now that's good. Now let us drill at the great guns. Dumb show only, I fear. The commodore will never let us use even an ounce of this precious gunpowder."

And thus the routine was established, a routine that varied

little, day to day, except when Biddlecomb would call for the brig cleared away at odd hours, day and night, to keep the men from becoming complacent. The time needed to clear for action dropped steadily away until they broke the ten-minute mark, and then the nine.

The men went about their duties cheerfully, quickly, and willingly. The *Charlemagne* was a happy ship, but it was a fragile happiness, Biddlecomb had no delusions about that. Nothing could eat away at a ship's moral more effectively then being stuck—becalmed, windbound or icebound—and he hoped desperately that the ice would disappear faster than the men's good humor.

On the seventh of January the *Katy*, now renamed *Providence* and officially a vessel of the navy of the United Colonies, managed to push its way down from Philadelphia and join the fleet in their frozen world. She rounded up and dropped anchor in the small patch of open water, fifty yards from the *Charlemagne*.

They fired a salute to the flagship, then hoisted a flag of their own, a yellow flag with some device in the center. Biddlecomb put the signal telescope to his eye. It was the rattlesnake he had seen on the marine recruiter's drums, and the motto Don't Tread on Me. He smiled. Don't tread on me, indeed, he thought. With this small but growing fleet the United Colonies could at last deliver a genuine and possibly lethal bite. The motto was altogether more uplifting than Washington's somewhat pathetic An Appeal to Heaven.

At last, on the seventeenth of January, twelve days after the ice had enveloped the American fleet, it broke up again. Biddlecomb could hear it cracking as he made his way through the gunroom and onto the quarterdeck. The air was still cold, but less cold than it had been, and the rising sun was no more than a dull white spot behind a thick cover of clouds, the unfailing harbinger of warmth. Water dripped like rain from the rigging overhead, and the deck was a uniform wetness rather than a variegation of patches of ice and planks.

"It looks like we may be under way today," he said to Tottenhill, who had moved over to the leeward side upon the captain's arrival.

"God, I hope so, sir." Tottenhill stared at the eastern horizon, never meeting Biddlecomb's eyes. He seemed to be increasingly morose, and it concerned Biddlecomb and would have concerned him more if he thought they would be stuck in the ice for very much longer.

He felt a hint of guilt about Tottenhill; he did not invite his first officer to the great cabin as often as a captain might be expected to do. But neither would he allow himself all of the blame. It was hardly his fault that Tottenhill made himself so obnoxious that his captain could not stand his company. He wondered if the first officer was being likewise ignored by his fellows in the gunroom.

Nor, he assured himself, was that entirely the source of Tottenhill's black mood. Biddlecomb had seen this sort of thing before, often enough to know that breaking free of the land and finally having blue water all around would shake Tottenhill from his funk, as Isaac had seen it shake others from theirs. But in the meantime he resolved, again, to be more tolerant of the lieutenant.

It was only nine o'clock in the morning when Biddlecomb's prediction proved accurate. The *Alfred,* after considerable fuss, loosened her fore topsail and sheeted it home, the signal for coming to sail, then worked her way off the pier and began her slow progress downstream.

The other ships of the Continental navy—the *Columbus* with her high, black sides; the *Cabot,* yellow-sided, like the flagship; the *Andrew Doria;* the *Charlemagne,* and now the little *Providence* and the smaller *Fly* schooner, which had come up from the Delaware Bay—followed in her wake. They sailed line ahead, a smaller version of one of the great fleets of the world. For the rest of the morning and into the afternoon the fleet pushed seaward, moving past the frozen fields and the mouths of ice-choked rivers.

By the end of the afternoon watch the Delaware River was

growing wider as it flared out into the Delaware Bay. Biddlecomb had hoped desperately to reach that wide expanse of water before nightfall; there would be little chance of being frozen in there, and with anything like moonlight they would be able to continue on after nightfall, continue their progress toward the sea.

But he could see now that that would never happen. Reedy Island was four miles ahead, the Bay ten miles beyond that, and the sun, what sun there was, was already dipping rapidly toward the horizon. What was worse, the river, wide as it was, was choked with floating ice, and it was starting to impede their progress.

With great reluctance, he ordered the *Charlemagne*'s best bower cockbilled and then her warps laid along as he saw the *Alfred* making ready to anchor off Reedy Island. An hour later the fleet was riding at their hooks. Biddlecomb stamped his foot in frustration. He wished the commodore had taken the risk, had pushed on through the dark and the ice, imprudent as that choice might be.

It was black night, and the cold settled in on them like the hand of death. And the next morning they were once again frozen solid in a perfect field of ice.

The good humor that had marked the first episode of their being icebound was entirely gone now, like a joke carried too far. There was no laughing, no snowball fights or roughhousing among the men. They just stamped up on the deck and glared out at the ice and muttered profanities to themselves, and that was the full extent of conversation to be heard on board.

And so began again the routine that had been so firmly established at Liberty Island, forty miles upstream. The ships were cleared for action, the guns run in and out, but now it was done grudgingly, sullenly, and the time it took to clear away grew longer with each day. Tempers flared, harsh words flew across the deck when words were spoken at all.

"We'll stand down to an anchor watch, rotate your men

through the week," Biddlecomb said to his officers, Rumstick and Tottenhill, Faircloth and Weatherspoon. They were all assembled on the quarterdeck, bundled in coats and scarves and greatcoats, their heads and ears bound in cloth under their cocked hats to keep out the numbing, pervasive cold.

"You know the routine, you've been doing it for a goddamned month now." He spat those words out. He was sick of trying to bolster morale. A captain needed some morale himself before he could bolster others, and his was entirely exhausted. He could well imagine how the foremast jacks felt.

Seven bells rang out, eleven-thirty at night, and he was still wide-awake, weighted down by three blankets and still miserably cold. He had been thinking about mutiny and what it took to spark that in a ship's crew: boredom, misery, internecine fighting among the officers.

He reckoned that all of those elements were there aboard the *Charlemagne*. There was boredom aplenty, and the cold brought all the misery one could ask for. There was palpable tension among the officers, at least between Tottenhill and Rumstick. He did not know how Faircloth felt; the man was hard to read.

But despite all of that, he was not worried, at least not about a mutiny. For one thing, even if the crew did successfully mutiny and take the *Charlemagne,* they would still be stuck in the ice. The marines from the other ships could stroll over and shoot them at their leisure. What was more, it was too damned cold to mutiny.

These thoughts were in his head as he drifted off, and they added to his confusion when he jerked awake some hours later, woken by the sound of a shout topside. What was that? he wondered, sitting up, staring into the absolute blackness of the caboose. Had he dreamt it, an extension of the morbid thoughts he had been entertaining before he fell asleep?

And then there was another shout and a clang of steel on steel. Biddlecomb flung the covers aside and his feet hit the cold deck just as a pistol went off. His hand reached out and wrapped around the brass-bound grip of his sword, sliding it out of the scabbard as he flung the door to the caboose open.

He was thinking back to his earlier conclusions as he raced through the great cabin to the gunroom, running for the weather deck, thinking, "They will not mutiny, they will not mutiny, this cannot be a mutiny."

CHAPTER 10

French Leave

IT WAS NOT A MUTINY.

Biddlecomb burst out of the scuttle onto the weather deck, his sword in a defensive position, ready for whatever might come. But nothing did. It was quiet, and as far as he could tell, no one was on deck.

He felt the numbing pain of the ice on the deck through his stocking feet. He looked forward, peering into the shadows, suddenly afraid that he was losing his mind, then Rumstick and Tottenhill and Faircloth, each in various states of dress, came tumbling out on deck.

"Sir, what's acting?" Rumstick shouted, looking around as Biddlecomb had done.

"I . . . ," Biddlecomb began, then they heard it—a low moaning coming from the shadows around the booms amidships. The four men approached cautiously. One of the foredeck men was lying there, clutching his head.

"Goddin, what happened? Were you shot?" Biddlecomb asked, crouching down beside the man.

"Oh, no, sir," Goddin said, as much of a moan as anything. "They hit me with a belayin' pin. Took French leave."

"Took French leave?" Biddlecomb asked. *French leave* was forecastle vernacular for deserting. "Who?"

"Dunno, sir. About twenty of 'em I reckon. Went over the side."

"How . . . who's watch is this?" Biddlecomb demanded of the assembled officers.

"Mr. Weatherspoon's, sir," Tottenhill supplied.

"And where in hell is he?"

"Went after 'em, sir," Goddin said. "Lit right after 'em, over the ice. It weren't his fault, sir, they just all come up at once. Only me and three others on deck, and the others went with 'em. Mr. Weatherspoon tried to stop 'em, came at 'em with his hanger, but they took a shot at him and was gone."

Biddlecomb stood and stared out over the ice. Weatherspoon had chased twenty deserters, men who had already shot at him, out into the frozen night. The boy was brave, if not as thoughtful as he might be, and Biddlecomb was suddenly very afraid for his safety, a paternalistic fear that surprised him.

"Mr. Tottenhill, get all hands on deck. Mr. Rumstick, tell off ten of our men, some of the old hands, and issue muskets and cutlasses. Mr. Faircloth, I want your marines turned out and ready to march in five . . . three minutes. I'm going to go below and dress, and when I come back, I want my party assembled and ready to go and get those sons of whores back."

Biddlecomb dressed quickly; breeches, sea boots, sword, coat, cross belt onto which he clipped his brace of pistols. He threw his heavy boat cloak over his shoulders, wrapped his head in a wool scarf, and jammed his cocked hat down over that. By the time he returned to the weather deck, all of the Charlemagnes were turned out.

Faircloth's marines were dressing ranks, and because of the speed with which Faircloth had driven them to turn out, it seemed as if the ranks were the only things that were properly dressed. But it did not matter. Muskets and cartridges were all that Biddlecomb required of them.

"Mr. Tottenhill, form the men up by divisions."

With a few shouted orders the men that were left fell in by their divisions, and Biddlecomb, standing on the ladder to the quarterdeck, ran his eyes over them. Most of the deserters, he saw, had been from the North Carolina contingent, which surprised him not in the least. There were only a few of the North Carolinians still aboard, including Hackett, who stood in a back row, glancing around and apparently trying not to laugh.

That at least was a surprise. The very moment that Biddlecomb had heard the sound of the pistol shot, he had thought of Hackett. But Hackett was still on board.

There was no time to ponder that situation. "Mr. Rumstick, tell off your men and come with me. Mr. Faircloth as well. Mr. Tottenhill, you will remain here, in command."

"Sir," said Tottenhill, "as first officer I think it is my place to go—"

"Mr. Tottenhill, enough. Every one of these damned deserters is one of your North Carolina villains."

"Sir, I must . . . how can you insinuate that? North Carolina is—"

"Look, Tottenhill, every one of those useless bastards was recruited from prison, even I can see that. Hell, I'd let 'em go if it wasn't for the example that would set."

Biddlecomb stepped down from the ladder and over to the gangway as Tottenhill stammered something about his agent, Jedadiah Huck. "Come on," Biddlecomb said to the armed men in general.

"Sir," Tottenhill said, tagging behind him, "shall I send word to the flagship? The commodore will no doubt wish to know about this."

"Good God, no, Mr. Tottenhill. Not a word." The last thing Biddlecomb needed was for Hopkins to hear how a third of his crew had deserted. He climbed down to the ice and turned his back on the *Charlemagne,* marching carefully over the slick surface to the dark shape of Reedy Island in the distance. Behind him he heard the clamber of thirty armed men following his lead.

It was a wickedly cold night, and the wind howling through

the fleet's frozen rigging sounded like lost souls on Judgment Day. And Judgment Day it shall be, Biddlecomb thought, if those sons of bitches are stupid enough to stop long enough for me to catch them.

It was not hard to follow the deserters' trail. The frozen river was covered with a thin layer of snow, which the fugitive band had beaten into a visible path, heading straight for the island. Biddlecomb quickened his pace, and behind him he heard the others, whose steps had fallen into a steady rhythmic march, do the same. Rumstick came huffing up to walk on his left side and Faircloth on his right. Both men had sense enough not to speak.

At last they came to the edge of the island, where the white frozen water melded with the shore, gently sloping up from the flat sheet of ice that was the Delaware River. Biddlecomb stopped and heard Sergeant Dawes give a grunt of an order, and the men stopped as well.

"Rumstick, what is that, do you suppose?" Biddlecomb pointed to a dark shape looming up from the white snow. It was some distance away, but in the dark it was hard to tell how far.

"I think that's an old barn or some such. I've seen it from the ship. Some old building."

"Right." Biddlecomb remembered now. He too had seen it often enough. A barn or some sort of long-abandoned structure. He knew that if the deserters had even a little sense, they would not have stopped for a minute, but as he did not credit them with any sense at all, he was hopeful that they might have sought shelter there.

"Come on," he said, and led his troops up the low-sloped shore, slipping on patches of ice concealed beneath the snow.

The barn was looming in front of them, twenty feet away. Biddlecomb could see a light of some kind burning inside. Was it possible the deserters had been so stupid as to stop?

"Hold up!" a voice called from the black monolith in their

path. It was a familiar voice. Israel Bennett. Waister. A recruit from North Carolina. An idiot. "Who's that?"

"You know full well who it is, Bennett. That is you, is it not? This is Captain Biddlecomb. Now come out of there this instant."

"Not likely. We've got Mr. Weatherspoon here, Captain, and I swear to God we'll blow his head off if you try and stop us!"

"Oh, damn it all to hell," Biddlecomb muttered. "Now they have a hostage. Mr. Faircloth, surround the building with your men. Make sure none of these bastards are lurking in back there. Mr. Rumstick, keep your men here with me."

"Here!" Bennett called. "What're you about? I told you I'll do for the midshipman if you try to stop us!"

"Yes, and I shall grieve for his death, Bennett, and then there will be nothing to stop me and my men from killing every one of you sons of bitches, so for the moment let me suggest that Mr. Weatherspoon is worth much more to you alive." Biddlecomb could feel his fury building. Of all the stupid situations to find himself in, standing in the bitter wind, arguing, threatening his own men just to get them to return to duty.

He waited for Bennett to say something. It was no surprise that Bennett was taking the lead, he was the brightest of the lot who had deserted, though that was not saying much, not much at all. At the moment he seemed to be wrestling with the conundrum that Biddlecomb had presented.

"I said leave us be," Bennett shouted at last.

Biddlecomb clamped his mouth shut until the desire to make a scathing reply passed, then shouted, "Listen to me, all of you, there's nowhere you can escape to. If you kill Weatherspoon, I'll have the marines shoot you where you stand. But if you give up and come back to the ship, then I shall be willing to let this go with a minor punishment. No tot for a week. That's a small price to pay for a hanging offense."

It was quiet again, and over the sound of the wind he could hear muffled talk from within. The tones were urgent; sharp words spoken softly, disagreement. He felt the wind creeping in under his boat cloak and began to shiver.

This impasse could go on all night, and then the sun would rise and Hopkins and all of the other captains would see him here, like a fool, trying to urge a third of his men to come back to his ship. Those stupid bastards. He would happily let them all go if that did not leave him seriously undermanned with no hope of finding replacements. And he would look like an incompetent fool in the eyes of his brother captains.

"You and your bloody marines move back to the edge of the ice," Bennett called out, "and we'll all talk about it."

Something about his voice was not quite right, some chink in the armor of his determination. Biddlecomb imagined that not all of the deserters were so bold in the face of thirty muskets. He could picture the uncertainty, the disagreement. It was time to make a move, a bold move, and he was angry enough, fed up enough, that he was willing to do anything, radical as it might be.

He pulled the pistols from his shoulder belt, one in each hand. "I'm coming in, Bennett. I want to talk to you, face-to-face."

"Keep back, Captain, or by God I'll shoot Weatherspoon!" Bennett's voice was higher pitched, his words coming out faster than before. He was frightened, but he was smart enough to know that shooting Weatherspoon meant certain death for himself. At least Biddlecomb hoped he was smart enough to know that.

He marched up to the door and pushed it open with his foot. A lantern was sitting on the frozen dirt floor, partially shaded, and standing in a semicircle around the lantern were the deserters, twenty or so uncertain-looking men. Biddlecomb saw the odd belaying pin and even a pistol or two clutched in nervous fingers. These desperate fugitives looked to him more like children caught in some poorly conceived illicit activity.

Except for Bennett. He stood in the center of the ring, and in front of him was David Weatherspoon. Bennett's left hand was holding tight to the midshipman's arm, and his right held a pistol behind the young man's ear. "Drop them pistols, Captain."

"Are you all right, Mr. Weatherspoon?"

"Yes, sir. Don't let these bastards go to save me, Captain." In the light of the lantern Weatherspoon's skin looked pale and his eyes were wide, but his mouth was set and Biddlecomb could tell that his teeth were clenched to keep his fear at bay.

Biddlecomb knew of few people, himself included, who had as much physical courage as the midshipman. If only he had the wits to match. But he was still young, and there was always the hope that maturity would help, though as it stood, old age did not seem as likely for Weatherspoon as it had even an hour before.

"That's enough!" Bennett roared. He was angry and frightened and frustrated, all at once. The others shifted nervously, looking from Bennett to Biddlecomb and back again. "I said drop them guns or by God I'll blow this little bastard's head off!"

And that, for Biddlecomb, was the end. He felt his anger overcoming his senses, overcoming his reason, moving him to action as if it had charge of his body, which indeed it did. In two steps he was across the floor, his left arm outstretched, the pistol in his hand pressed against Bennett's head. "You drop *your* pistol, you mutinous, black-balling son of a whore! Drop it now or I'll blow *your* head off!"

"I mean it, Captain," Bennett said, his voice softer this time, speaking with an audible quaver. "I mean it—"

He was cut short by the sound of Biddlecomb cocking his pistol, the satisfying metallic click of the lock snapping in place filling the barn, the loudest and most authoritative of sounds.

And then there was silence again. They all stood there, absolutely still, Bennett's gun to Weatherspoon's head, Biddlecomb's gun to Bennett's head, and the rest watching on, waiting for someone, something, to break the deadlock.

A movement to Biddlecomb's right. He caught just a glimpse of it on the edge of his vision and one of the deserters screamed, "You Yankee son of a bitch!" and flung himself across the hard-packed floor.

Biddlecomb half-turned, his right arm coming up, the thumb of his right hand drawing back the lock as the man was on him. He saw his pistol press against the assailant's shoulder as the man reached out at him, reaching for his hand, reaching for his neck.

He pulled the trigger just as he felt the man's hand on the gun at Bennett's head. The recoil jolted his arm back and spun the assailant around, tripping him, tossing him to the hard floor. Biddlecomb turned back to bring the gun to Bennett's head again, but now Bennett and Weatherspoon were struggling for the pistol, pointed at the ceiling, all four of their hands locked on the weapon.

Then suddenly Weatherspoon released his hold on the gun, and Bennett, with nothing pulling against him, reeled back and Weatherspoon drove his fist into the man's face. Bennett fired in surprise, the flash illuminating the far corners of the building, and then the deserters flung themselves at Biddlecomb and Weatherspoon, belaying pins raised like clubs.

The big door to the barn burst open and Rumstick and his sailors came charging in, the marines right on their heels.

"Stop it! Hold up! Shoot the next bastard that moves! Shoot anyone that hits the captain!" Biddlecomb heard Rumstick's voice roar out, heard a pistol shot that once again lit up the barn with its flash. They all froze, the deserters and Biddlecomb and Weatherspoon, as the armed men spread out across the floor.

"Take care to fire by rank!" Faircloth shouted, and with amazing precision, for they had learned their drill well, the marines fell into two ranks, one kneeling, one standing, all twenty muskets pointed at the deserters, who were now backing away.

"Front rank, make ready!" Ten locks clicked into the firing position.

Biddlecomb saw one of the deserters, then another, raise their pistols at the marines, ready to give off the one last defiant shot. They would kill perhaps three of the shore party before they were gunned down like driven and fenced-in deer. If one of them fired, it would mean suicide for all of the North Carolinians.

"Hold up! Hold up!" Biddlecomb shouted, stepping in front of the line of marines with their perfect muskets in perfect rows and the sailors with their sea-service weapons pointed haphazardly. "Listen here, you men, I made an offer outside and I shall honor it, if I can trust you to honor your word. No tot for a week for any of you, and no court-martial, if you return to your duty and do not try anything like this again. That is more than generous. What say you?"

He stood running his eyes over the men as they wrestled with their decision. What there was to consider Biddlecomb could not imagine; they had little choice in the light of the muskets pointing at them.

God, how he hated to coddle those whore's gits! But he needed them if he hoped to sail and fight the *Charlemagne*. He could not let them desert if he hoped to keep his dignity intact, his reputation among the other captains. If he wished to remain Captain Biddlecomb, *the* Captain Biddlecomb.

And needing them did not mean just having them aboard. He needed them to be part of the crew: active, willing, not sullen and grudging. They would not be active and willing if he had them flogged, and certainly not if he had them hung. He had stood up to them, had shot one of their own. Now was the time for mercy.

One of the men looked over at Bennett, then at the others, and then tossed his pistol aside. "I reckon that's fair, Captain. I accept." That raised a great murmur from the men, a nodding of heads as one by one they tossed aside their weapons and looked sheepishly at the floor.

"You stupid bastards!" Bennett shouted. "You think he's telling the truth? You think—"

"Bennett!" Biddlecomb shouted, and the force of his voice was enough to shut the man up. Bennett would have to be flogged if he came back. Flogged or hung. There was no choice. Not after putting a gun to Weatherspoon's head. But after his flogging he would be back among the men, sullen, angry, spreading his poison. That would never do. And hanging him meant a court-martial, and admitting to the other captains that his ship's company was falling apart and he was not able to stop it.

"Bennett, get out of here," Biddlecomb said.

"What?"

"Get out of here. Go."

"Where?"

"I don't know. Wherever it was you intended to go when you ran. Just get out of here and never let me see you around the fleet again or I will personally run you up on a halter."

Bennett looked around, thoroughly confused. "No," he said at last. "No, I ain't going to leave."

"By God, you are one stupid idiot," Biddlecomb said, stepping over to him and once more pressing the pistol to his head. "Either you leave or I kill you here." He wanted to kill him for his sheer irrational stupidity alone.

Then, as if to emphasize the likelihood of Biddlecomb's pulling the trigger, the man whom Biddlecomb had shot let out a groan, a deep, guttural, agonizing sound. That was enough for Bennett. He jerked his head away from Biddlecomb's gun and ran for the barn door, pushing it open without breaking stride and disappearing into the dark. For half a minute they could hear his footsteps crunching in the snow, and then he was gone.

Biddlecomb turned to the deserters, who had now rejoined the company of the *Charlemagne*. "Very well, you. Get back to the ship. A couple of you, help that one." He gestured toward the figure who was now thrashing around on the floor. Two men lifted the wounded sailor up and along with the others shuffled out of the barn in a ragged line, flanked on either side by the marines and followed by Rumstick's sailors.

Pray God this is an end to it, he thought.

At least they did not mutiny.

CHAPTER 11

Capital Offense

"THAT SON OF A WHORE, THAT BLOODY SON OF A WHORE," AMOS Hackett snarled under his breath as he glanced aft at his captain, the Yankee Biddlecomb. He hated Biddlecomb even more now than he did after Biddlecomb had dressed him down over the slops back in Philadelphia.

He hated him because of the deserters. Because he had handled the deserters to perfection.

He ran his eyes over number five gun, on which he worked the rammer and sponge when at quarters. It was the fifth week of their being frozen in the ice, and they were once again going through the absurd dumb show of clearing for action. The men were moving slowly, their morale as low as Hackett had ever seen. It was fertile soil for mischief.

His tools, the rammer and sponge, were in their proper place, as was the priming wire, the tub of slow match, and the bucket of water.

The only instrument missing, for which the rest of the gun crew was busily searching, was the linstock. Hackett did not join in the search. To his certain knowledge the linstock for number five gun was being used by the men of number three gun, while the one previously belonging to number three gun was lost in a dark corner of the bilge. He knew that because he had hidden it there himself.

The deserters. Hackett had started the idea of a mass desertion, murmuring low suggestions to his messmates, and had found in Bennett an eager audience. "You best believe if there's any danger, them Yankees will send us North Carolina boys in first," Hackett had muttered. "We're just here to stop bullets for them."

"You're right, Amos, God damn my soul you are right," Bennett had said. And then it started, the whispering, the planning, the threats to any who might tell tales. They had all assumed that Hackett would come with them. Indeed, he had all but said he would. The stupid bastards, as if he would do something that foolish! As if they could ever have gotten away, even if they had not been so stupid as to stop at that barn.

There had been some harsh words when the others saw that Hackett was not running with them, but in the end there had been no time to argue about it, and Hackett had promised to hold up the search as much as he could.

And he did just as he promised. Of course he held up the search not one second, but that was as much as he could do.

"Here, Captain," Hackett said to the captain of his gun, "them sodomites have our linstock, I recognize it." He pointed with his chin in the direction of number three gun.

"You got our linstock there?" the captain asked, his voice thick with accusation.

"Sod off," the captain of number three gun replied.

A week before, Hackett had begun to perceive some animosity between the old crew members at number five gun and number three, and he was curious to see if he could make that flare up.

The ship's company was falling apart around him; he had only to find the fissure, the thin crack between factions, and stick his knife blade in. Then the fun would begin.

As he had done with the deserters. It had been a fine thing. Hackett never thought that they would get away, but he figured that their attempt, and the subsequent punishments, would really set the crew against the officers, to his greater amusement.

But the bastard Biddlecomb had played it just right: stormed in on them, shot one of them in the shoulder to show he wouldn't be taken advantage of, scared them all half to death, and then let them off easy. Hackett found himself growing angry again, thinking about it. They came back aboard more in awe of Biddlecomb than anything. Well, he was not done with that Yankee son of a bitch, not near done.

He turned to the captain of number three gun, desperate to vent his anger.

"Give me that, you son of a whore!" He yanked the linstock from the gun captain's hand. "There, look at this. Got the number five carved in it. You recall I carved that there just the other day, in case these bastards done something like this."

The men of number five gun took a step toward number three, and the men of number three took a step toward number five.

"Well, this here's about what I'd reckon from a bastard like you," the captain of number five growled.

"Give me that, you great horse's arse!" The captain of number three lunged at the linstock, but Hackett swept it out of the way and shoved the gun captain back, hard.

"Leave off, you thieving bastard. I'll go to the captain with this," Hackett said. He could feel the rage building.

"You're the thief, fucking buggering bastard. Give that here!" The captain lunged again. Hackett dropped the linstock and caught the man up by the collar with one hand and with the other delivered two quick blows to the side of his head. It felt good, in that instance, with all the hatred toward Biddlecomb building up. If he could not start a riot, at least he could vent his anger by pounding someone. He struck the man again. He felt his control slipping.

And then Tottenhill was there, that stupid, miserable jellyfish Tottenhill, grabbing both of them and pulling them apart, shouting, "Stop this, this instant! I order you to stop!" Hackett punched the gun captain again, was hit himself in the jaw.

"Stop this!" Tottenhill shouted again.

Hackett loathed that idiot first lieutenant, had wanted to do for him for a while. Don't, don't, he warned himself, but he was beyond control. He half-turned, grabbed Tottenhill by the collar, and pushed, sending him sprawling to the deck.

That was a grave mistake. Hackett knew it the instant that his fist had wrapped around the first officer's collar, but by then it was too late. "God help me, I'm sorry, I'm sorry," Hackett pleaded, letting go of the gun captain and kneeling beside Tottenhill. "Forgive me, sir, it was an accident," he whined.

Tottenhill pushed the supplicant aside and leapt to his feet, clutching the elbow on which he had fallen and grimacing in pain. "Master-at-arms! Master-at-arms! Put that man in irons, now! Lock him below!" Tottenhill shouted, and the master-at-arms, aided by the gunner and Mr. Sprout, grabbed the surprised Hackett and restrained him.

"No, sir, please, no! It was an accident!" Not the chains, not the black hold, not the solitude, Hackett thought.

"Lock him below!" Tottenhill said again, and Sprout and the master-at-arms dragged Hackett away.

"Damn it. Damn it all to hell," Biddlecomb said softly. He did not want to make a great issue out of this; that would not help the fragile mood of the crew. If Rumstick had been there first, he would simply have knocked Hackett flat and kicked him around and that would have been an end to it. But now he had no choice but to support the first officer.

"What did you have in mind, Mr. Tottenhill?" Biddlecomb asked as Tottenhill stepped back onto the quarterdeck. The captain spoke softly; this was not a conversation he wished to be overheard. "We could stop his tot, put a wooden collar on him, some 'shameful badge of distinction' as the navy rules put it."

Tottenhill looked surprised, shocked even, at the suggestion. "He struck me, Captain."

"I can order no more punishment than a dozen lashes. Anything more requires that we convene a court-martial."

"Then convene a court-martial, sir." The first officer spoke in a loud whisper. "He struck a superior officer. He might have broke my arm. I want him tried, sir, and I want him hung."

And despite the godlike powers he possessed aboard his vessel, Biddlecomb had no choice but to accommodate his officer's desires. If the first lieutenant wanted a court-martial, then a court-martial he must have. Biddlecomb thought of Adams's quite unrealistic vision of a ship captain's autonomy. This was the price Biddlecomb paid for the cheering crowds and the thrill and pride of commanding a ship in the Continental navy.

Tottenhill joined him for dinner that afternoon. Biddlecomb had extended the invitation the day before, before Tottenhill had forced him into this disciplinary corner, before the first officer had further soured his already sour mood. Isaac had hoped the dinner would improve their strained relationship, which was growing more strained by the day.

It was not a success.

CHAPTER 12

Court-Martial

THE *RULES FOR THE REGULATION OF THE NAVY OF THE UNITED Colonies* laid out that a court-martial should consist of three captains and three first lieutenants, and if available, three captains and three lieutenants of marines. Since, as it happened, every captain and lieutenant of both the navy and the marines for all of the United Colonies was frozen in within one hundred yards of each other, that otherwise tall requirement was easily met, and the result was a crowded great cabin aboard the flagship *Alfred*.

Biddlecomb sat on the starboard side, right against the ceiling, not a member of the court-martial but a grudging witness. His head was inches below a rather stiff portrait of the commodore's wife, Mrs. Desire Hopkins, painted, he mused silently, some years after that appellation was quite applicable.

Second Lieutenant Ezra Rumstick, who sat beside him, was also a witness, though even more grudgingly so than his captain. He sat in the *Alfred*'s great cabin with arms folded, looking around.

"What is the name of the flagship's first lieutenant?" Biddlecomb asked, as much to try to engage Rumstick in conversation as to assuage his frustration at forgetting. "The Scotsman with the red hair?"

Rumstick leaned forward and glanced at the man in question,

who was carrying on an animated conversation with Captain Saltonstall. "He's one of these fellows with three surnames. John Jones Paul, or Paul Jones, I think. Paul John Jones? One of those. I forget."

Across the cabin, and as physically far away from his fellow officers of the *Charlemagne* as he could get in that space, sat Tottenhill, arms and legs crossed, foot wagging nervously up and down, as he glared impatiently around the room.

Two tables had been pushed together to make one long enough to seat the twelve-man court, and it ran from one side of the cabin to the other with barely enough room to squeeze in on either side. This despite the fact that, by Biddlecomb's estimate, one could have placed two and a half great cabins from the *Charlemagne* in the *Alfred*'s.

It had already been a long morning, but the officers called to sit were still milling about. They had begun to assemble at nine o'clock, walking across the ice and waiting their turn to go up the flagship's side. At last all were aboard and below in the great cabin and served coffee and soft tack and butter and jam. It was a break in the dreary, icebound routine, a pleasant social occasion, and all seemed to share in the amiable atmosphere, save for Biddlecomb and Rumstick, the miserable Tottenhill, and the vastly more miserable Hackett, who spent the morning in chains and under guard on the *Alfred*'s gundeck.

"Well, call me a son of a whore," Commodore Hopkins said. He was seated in the middle of the table, the only one yet seated, and reading over the *Rules for the Regulation.*

"Who here knew we was supposed to do a damned divine service twice a day? Whipple, did you know that? Captain Saltonstall? Has anyone done that? What a blackballing waste of time. I thought I read these sodomizing things. Damned lawyers' clerks and parsons. Listen to this: 'If any shall be heard to swear, curse, or blaspheme the name of God, the commander is strictly enjoined to punish them for every offense by causing them to wear a wooden collar,' et cetera, et cetera. 'If he be a commissioned officer, he shall forfeit one shilling for each offense, and a warrant or inferior officer, sixpence,' " he read, and then without a hint of irony added, "Well, I'll be God damned."

"Sir?" Tottenhill interjected, the higher than normal pitch in his voice sabotaging his attempt to sound like a man in control.

"Yes, of course, Tottenhill," said Hopkins. "I guess we had best get on with this thing." The commodore stood up and called the room to attention, announcing that the court-martial was about to commence. "Let's see here, Whipple, you slide in there, then Saltonstall, and you marines, Captain Nicholas, there, come in on this side, amidships. Good, and you lieutenants outboard."

Whipple with some difficulty squeezed his big frame around the end of the table, followed by Dudley Saltonstall and the others, shuffling sideways to their places until at last all were seated and ready.

After the morning's festivities the court-martial itself was something of a let-down. Tottenhill stood and in an unemotional, mechanical way described the events of the previous morning, then Biddlecomb stood and confirmed what Tottenhill had said. Mr. Rumstick was called and related much the same story, though with a painfully obvious attempt to soften up the event. But at last, and under direct questioning, he was made to admit that Tottenhill's presentation of the facts was in no way inaccurate.

Finally Hackett was called, and in a stammering voice, shaking, Biddlecomb guessed, as much from stage fright as from fear of capital punishment, he related the events. His story did not differ in any material way from that of the officers, save for his claim that he didn't push Tottenhill but rather fell into him, accidently knocking him to the deck, and that when he pushed him, he forgot that the man was an officer. Other than the fact that the one statement seemed to contradict the other, he was fairly convincing.

Forty-five minutes after testimony began it was over. Hackett was removed from the great cabin and the *Charlemagne*'s officers sat facing the twelve-man court.

"Well, I reckon he's guilty as charged," Commodore Hopkins

said. "But let's have a vote on it. All who say he's guilty say 'aye.' "

Twelve "Aye's" were muttered along the table.

"Well, that's that. I guess now we figure a punishment."

"Sir." Tottenhill stood and addressed the court. "The *Rules for the Regulation* says striking an officer is punishable by death or any such punishment as a court-martial shall inflict."

"Does it?" Hopkins asked. "Jones, hand me that. Death, that's going it a bit high." Hopkins flipped through the pages of the *Rules for the Regulation.* "Here it is. . . . No, you're mistaken, sir, the death thing is for mutiny. Striking an officer is just 'on pain of such punishment as a court-martial shall order to be inflicted.' "

"But, sir, he struck a superior officer, and, damn it, sir, I cannot speak to the other ships, but things are too lax, too lax by half, on the *Charlemagne.*" Tottenhill's voice grew louder, his face more animated as he spoke. "We need discipline, we need an example set. Where I am from, we do not countenance such things. We do not let our discipline slip. We take our military regulations seriously, sir." Tottenhill was practically yelling by the time he finished, and when he stopped, the great cabin was silent.

The tirade, unexpected as it was, left the court stunned and not a little embarrassed. Tottenhill remained standing, standing at attention. Biddlecomb caught Rumstick's eye, and Rumstick raised an inquisitive eyebrow at the condemnation of Biddlecomb's command.

"Yes, well, thank you," Hopkins said at last, breaking the embarrassed silence. "Biddlecomb, what say you?"

"Well, sir, I'll admit that morale has not been high, not since we were frozen in this second time. I doubt it's been high on any ship here, what with the cold and the smallpox. But I don't see a hanging doing much to improve it."

"Neither do I," said Hopkins with finality. "But we need to order something, he is guilty. Let's say two dozen with the cat? Gentlemen, two dozen at first light tomorrow?" Heads nodded along the length of the table. "Good, two dozen it is."

"Sir—" Tottenhill began, but Hopkins stood and thankfully cut him off.

"Two dozen is the decision of this court, and it is fair and final. And, sir, we are all under a great strain here, pray do not be so quick to call for a court-martial in the future. It is not for all the vessels in this fleet to solve your own problems. The court is adjourned." And then turning to Abraham Whipple, Hopkins added, "Hey, Whipple, that was done pretty smart for our first court-martial, what say you?"

I have made a mistake, a foolish mistake, Tottenhill thought as he and Biddlecomb and Rumstick stood together on the *Alfred*'s quarterdeck, waiting their turn to run the gauntlet of ceremony and descend to the ice.

The beginnings of that realization had nagged at him all night, and the court-martial had cemented it. He had sat there like an idiot, like a pariah, while the Yankee officers had chatted and laughed in their familiar way, unwilling to embrace him as a fellow officer, making an outcast of him. Just like Biddlecomb, who only grudgingly invited him to dinner, and that rarely, and never tried to engage him in conversation. It was clear now that one could not be a fellow officer without being a fellow Yankee.

He should never have lost his temper with Hackett. He could see the truth in what Hackett was saying; it had been an accident, he had not intended to strike a superior officer. After all, Hackett was one of his people, a Southerner, a North Carolinian.

If he was under an undue stress, it was only to be expected. Hackett no doubt felt as ostracized in that Yankee ship as he himself did. It was little wonder that the North Carolinians tried to desert, with the way they were treated, officers and men alike. It was time, Tottenhill realized, to start thinking about who his friends were.

"Lieutenant." Biddlecomb turned to Tottenhill, a tone of conciliation in his voice. "I think the court's decision was fair. Two dozen is a severe enough punishment under the circumstances.

Any more or less would be injurious to discipline. As to your comments concerning discipline aboard—"

"Sir," Tottenhill cut him off, "I understand what happened today, do not doubt it. I understand very well." He was tired of Biddlecomb's attempts at placating him. He would have no more of it.

"Lieutenant, this is a difficult time for all of us. I expect you to stand with the other officers and help to maintain discipline."

"And I would like to think that other officers would stand by me, sir, though that might be more than could be hoped for."

Biddlecomb stared into Tottenhill's eyes for a long moment, then turned away.

There, that's shut him up, Tottenhill thought, with a glow of triumph.

CHAPTER 13

"On Pain of Such Punishment . . ."

"WHAT DO YOU THINK TOTTENHILL MEANT BY THAT?" BIDDLECOMB asked Rumstick. They were standing together on the *Charlemagne*'s quarterdeck, an hour after leaving the *Alfred*'s great cabin. Biddlecomb was still angry over the first officer's remarks.

"No, don't bother to answer," he added as Rumstick made to speak. "I know what he meant. Son of a bitch!" In his younger days Isaac had been better at hiding his impatience. But as he grew older, and since he had made captain, he felt that ability slipping away. He wished that he could fool Tottenhill into thinking that they were friends. He did genuinely respect the man's seamanship. He just couldn't stand his company.

Tottenhill spoke little that day, and the next morning when Biddlecomb ordered Mr. Weatherspoon to graciously offer to stand the lieutenant's watch so that Tottenhill might join the captain, Rumstick, and Faircloth for breakfast, the midshipman returned with a polite declination.

As a result Biddlecomb felt obligated to invite the midshipman to breakfast instead, and Weatherspoon happily accepted, chatting amiably for the better part of an hour, unaware that his captain was silent and unresponsive, pushing his fried pork around his plate with his knife. Rumstick, whose appetite was undiminished, nodded once in a while, but was, for the most part, equally silent, leaving Faircloth to maintain the conversation with the midshipman.

"Ezra" —Biddlecomb looked up, cutting Weatherspoon off in midsentence—"we do have a cat-o'-nine-tails for this morning, do we not?"

"I don't know. I figured the bosun would come up with something," said Rumstick, surprised by the question. "Weatherspoon, hop up top and see if the bosun has a cat-o'-nine-tails prepared."

Two minutes later Weatherspoon was back, Mr. Sprout in tow, and Biddlecomb, who was at that moment again resolving to be more patient with the first officer, was reminded of the bloody spectacle that was about to take place aboard his brig, thanks to Mr. Tottenhill.

"God, I'm sorry, sir, but I didn't make a cat," the bosun said. "Don't really know how. I had figured that Mr. Rumstick, having been in a British brig-of-war and all . . ." His voice trailed off in embarrassment.

"That's understandable, Mr. Sprout. We should have discussed this. On the *Icarus*, Rumstick and I had plenty of chance to see how a cat is used but not how one is made. Pray go forward and see if there are any aboard that know how to make a cat and set them to it."

An hour later Mr. Sprout returned to the great cabin. "We got a cat-o'-nine-tails all lashed up, Captain," he said. "Old fo'c'sle man, Neeley, done it. Good hand with the fancy stuff." He paused, and an uncomfortable silence filled the cabin. "Anyway, sir, we got a cat now."

"Well"—Biddlecomb met Rumstick's eye—"I guess there's nothing now stopping us from . . . carrying out punishment. Mr. Rumstick, please see the men assembled to witness this."

Rumstick and Sprout disappeared forward, and less than a minute later the brig was filled with the sounds of bosun's calls and shouted orders and stamping feet. Biddlecomb silently strapped on his sword and pulled on his cloak. He picked up his copy of the *Rules for the Regulation of the Navy of the United Colonies* and stepped from the cabin.

The rising sun revealed an overcast and mournful day: a thick, gray-mottled cloud cover and a wind that stung like driving rain, whistling out of the southeast. The men stood at a semblance of attention, shuffling around and blowing on their hands for warmth. Only Faircloth and his marines, drawn up along the break of the quarterdeck, remained stationary, nearly identical in their beautiful green uniforms and small cocked hats.

There was a uniformity now among the men as well. Most of them had come aboard with only the poor clothes on their back, but now, on Biddlecomb's insistence, they were dressed in trousers, shirts, and blue jackets from the slop chest.

He wished that their spirits were as uniform as their clothes. The protective wall formed by the marines made him think, and it was not a comfortable thought, of the Praetorian Guard. Was it absolutely necessary that he be so protected from his own men?

"Mr. Tottenhill, Mr. Rumstick," he called his officers over to him. "Let's get this over with quickly. Get Hackett up here. I'll touch on the germane rules and then we'll carry out the punishment."

Hackett was brought up from below, his hands and feet in shackles, and he and his shipmates stood impassively, save for their fending off the cold, as Biddlecomb skimmed through the *Rules for the Regulation*. "Amos Hackett, you stand convicted by a court-martial of the crime of striking a superior officer and are sentenced to two dozen lashes upon the bare back. Mr. Sprout, secure the prisoner."

The armorer knocked the shackles away, and Sprout instructed Hackett to remove his shirt. When he did, the prisoner's wrists were bound to a grating leaned against the starboard bulwark. Sprout pulled the cat-o'-nine-tails from its red baize bag—Biddlecomb was surprised to see that Neeley had had the time to craft that as well—and ran the nettles through his fingers.

"Do your duty, Mr. Sprout," Biddlecomb said, and the cat came down on Hackett's back, and the first blood of the voyage was spilled.

Biddlecomb glanced up at the men assembled and watching the flogging and did not like what he saw. In his brief time aboard the British brig-of-war *Icarus* he had learned a great deal about floggings. Among other things he knew that a ship's company would accept the punishment if, in the opinion of the lower deck, it was warranted. But Biddlecomb recognized the grimaces, the set faces he was seeing now, and he knew that the men were not at all pleased with what was happening.

He heard Sprout say, "Twelve," and looked down at the grating. Hackett was hanging limp, and only his sharp intake of breath with each stroke told Biddlecomb that he was still conscious. His back was a series of red ribbons, and the blood was seeping into his trousers and pooling on the deck. With each stroke of the cat he jerked under the impact. This despite the fact that Sprout was clearly going easy on him, letting the wicked tips of the nettles strike the grating and not his bare skin.

Biddlecomb ground his teeth together hard and twisted his hands behind his back. He had known this moment would come and had dreaded it, dreaded it more than combat. He recalled those many times, standing on the *Icarus*'s deck, witnessing a flogging, hating the man who had ordered it. Were his own men having those same thoughts now? Biddlecomb could here a murmur rising from the watching crowd.

And finally Sprout said, "Twenty-four," and the horror was over. Hackett was cut down, supported by two of his messmates, and carried below to be attended by the *Alfred*'s surgeon, who had come aboard for that purpose.

Lieutenant Faircloth, that generally cheerful officer, stepped up onto the quarterdeck, looking more morose than Biddlecomb had ever seen him. The captain turned to his other officers. No look of satisfaction was on Tottenhill's face, no expression of any kind. That was fortunate for him, for Biddlecomb was ready to dress him down mercilessly if he had looked even a little smug.

"All right," Biddlecomb said. "We'll drill with the great guns until dinner, then issue canvas for make and mend and stand down to an anchor watch for the rest of the day. Mr. Faircloth, I don't know what your intentions are, but perhaps it would be best to keep your marines under arms for a while. Drill them or something so they don't actually appear to be on an alert."

"Aye, sir." Faircloth nodded. Biddlecomb was not certain why he had ordered that, did not know what it was that he feared, but somehow it seemed a good idea to have the marines and their weapons at the ready. He looked out at the white ice stretching away to the far shore and cursed it, cursed it out loud, unconcerned with who might hear or what they might think.

Fifteen hours later, Amos Hackett lay facedown on a bunk swung from the beams at the forward end of the berthing deck. His little area was screened off from the rest of the deck by a canvas screen hung from the overhead, giving the convalescing man some small degree of privacy.

Hackett was rated as a fore topman, able-bodied, but he was able-bodied no longer, and the mere act of breathing caused him pain enough to make him gasp. From the other side of the screen he could hear the cacophony of snoring from his sleeping mates, but he was awake, his back and his mind on fire.

He cursed the navy and the ship and the officers. And mostly Biddlecomb, who could have prevented this flogging, who had let that idiot Bennett go and had quashed the insurrection that he had so carefully begun. He fantasized about his revenge. It would be his, and it would not be too hard to come by. Not with the way the men were feeling now.

He heard footsteps on the deck overhead, the middle anchor watch prowling around, making certain that the brig was safe and that no more of her company managed to escape their frozen hell by slipping over the side and running across the ice to shore.

There was a small hatch just above him, and a ladder that descended almost to the head of his bunk, the forwardmost scuttle to the berthing deck. Those men who had come to see him had come and gone through that hatch. Now he heard the familiar groan of the grating being lifted, surprising at that time of night. He twisted as best he could to see who was coming, but the effort caused him renewed agony and he gave it up.

He heard steps on the ladder, and the grating easing back in place, and he waited in the dark to see who was there. Some member of the watch coming to see if he needed anything, coming to listen to his sorrows. A figure, a shade in the dark, appeared at his side, standing motionless, looking at him.

"How are you, Hackett?" the visitor asked in a whisper. Hackett lay still, peering into the shadows. He could make out the person's outline, could see the suggestion of a white waistcoat under a darker coat, white breeches.

"Poorly," Hackett said, and then, "Who is that? Lieutenant Tottenhill?"

"Aye."

Hackett was silent for a moment, wavering between anger and confusion, and then anger won the day. "I got nothing to say to you, hear? What do you want?"

"I was hoping to have a word with you."

"I got nothing to say to you. You was the one had me flogged, wasn't you? And just because you slipped on the deck?"

"Yes, and I was wrong. I have come to offer you this, by way of apology."

Tottenhill's shape had become more defined as Hackett stared into the dark, and now he saw the lieutenant's arm reaching out toward him. He reached out as well, and his hand touched the cold glass of a bottle, and at the same time he whiffed the familiar, comforting smell of rum.

There was no man on earth he would less wish to drink with than Tottenhill, but here was an officer offering him rum. Such opportunities did not come along often. He took the bottle and took a long swallow of the liquor, feeling it warm, not burn, as it went down. He had never tasted rum this good. He took another drink.

"I am dreadfully, dreadfully sorry about what has happened to you," Tottenhill continued as the fore topman drank. "I can see now it was an accident, tempers flaring because of this ice and all. I never . . . well, I don't know what it was I wanted. I lost my head a bit too, I suppose. Had the master-at-arms lock you down. I just wish to say that I am sorry."

This was all very surprising to Hackett, and difficult to understand, and the rum, which he was drinking steadily, was not helping. "Why in hell would you want to apologize to the likes of me? You, a gentleman and an officer, and me just some poor rat in the forecastle?"

"Here's the thing of it, Hackett. This is a Yankee navy, if you haven't noticed; Yankee captains and Yankee officers. Now, I may be an officer and you may be a foremast jack, but we are both sons of the South, if you follow. They've got no use for Southerners like you and me. Don't think I get treated with any respect. You better reckon on more floggings, for you and anyone who isn't from New England. You should know that Biddlecomb is convinced that the desertion the other night was all the fault of the Southerners. He's mad, and we are all of us Southerners in for a bad time, unless we look out for each other."

Hackett took anther pull from the rum. "I understand, sir."

And he did understand, understood far more than Tottenhill might have guessed. Here was a rift in the crew far worse than he had imagined: Southerners versus Yankees. The best part of it was that the rift apparently existed among the officers as well. In the dark, and despite the pain, Hackett smiled. "You're right, sir. I can see that now. It all makes sense, when you lay it out for me like that."

"Good, good. Listen, I have to go now. I just wanted to make sure you were all right, as all right as you can be, anyway, after being so ill-used. Let me take that bottle; if Biddlecomb catches you with that, he'll flog you again, on top of the stripes you've already got. You get some sleep now."

Hackett saw Tottenhill move, like a shadow in the dark, and felt him pull the bottle from his fingers.

"Sir," Hackett said as contrite as he could, "bless you, sir, for . . . for coming to me like this."

"Think nothing of it. We fellows from North Carolina must hang together, you know, look out for each other. Get some rest now." Silently Tottenhill went up the ladder and was gone.

Hackett lay still for a long while, thinking over the strange meeting he had just had. Tottenhill was reaching out to him, actually reaching out to him even after he, Hackett, had quite purposely taken the opportunity of the fight to lay him out flat on the deck. And still Tottenhill was coming to him with a genuine offer of friendship, and showing him the perfect way to get the entire crew worked into a frenzy of self-destruction.

"Stupid bastard," he said out loud.

CHAPTER 14

Blue Water

THEY WERE FREE OF THE LAND, FREE OF THE LAND AT LAST, AND Biddlecomb's heart swooped with the long blue rollers, soared with relief and optimism. They had left Cape Henlopen in their wake two days before and had seen nothing but blue water in that time. It was like the final fulfillment of a dream long held, and he had not felt this uplifted since Virginia had invited him to her room that night over a month before. He loved every minute of it, and even the big storm building on the northeastern horizon could not diminish that fact.

The crew, however, did not seem to share his joy. He had to admit that, at least to himself. Isaac Biddlecomb's jubilant mood and former predictions notwithstanding, their southerly progress and liberation from the accursed ice seemed to have had little if any effect on the dark and brooding attitude of the men.

He stood at the weather rail of the quarterdeck, one hand on the main topgallant backstay, and squinted aloft. They were carrying full topsails and foresail, pressing their luck in the mounting wind. He looked out to weather. The gray sky, threatening at sunrise, looked positively ominous now.

Between the *Charlemagne* and the horizon to windward was the *Andrew Doria,* the first reef tucked in her topsails, and a mile ahead of her the lumbering *Columbus,* already making heavy weather of it, though worse was yet to come. The rest of the fleet was visible to leeward, with the flagship almost hull down, leading the way south.

"Mr. Rumstick," Biddlecomb called to the officer of the watch, and Rumstick made his way across the slanting deck. "I reckon we're in for a rough night. Been building all day and it's still building."

"Aye, sir, I reckon so."

"This is hardly the thing to bring good cheer to the men." Biddlecomb could not help but smile.

"No, but it'll take their minds off their woes."

"Well, they seem to have a lot of woes, whatever the hell they might be, so they'll need a lot to keep their minds off it. Let's turn out the watch below. I'll have the second reef in both topsails and strike the topgallant masts and yards to deck."

"Second reef in the topsails and strike the t'gallant gear, aye, sir." The *Charlemagne*'s bow rose on a wave, rearing up like a startled horse. The two men took a firm grip on the rail as the wave passed under the ship. Then the bow dropped, crashing into the sea and sending a great shower of spray aft that soaked them as thoroughly as if a hose had been turned on them.

Rumstick looked up at Biddlecomb and smiled, despite the water streaming off his face and dripping from the end of his nose. "At least we ain't in the ice anymore, sir."

"And I say amen to that, Brother Rumstick."

Six days earlier, on the morning of the eleventh, the eleventh of February, after several days of mounting temperatures, they had woken to find the ice around them reduced to floating pieces. The largest was as big as a ship's boat, but they were sufficiently scattered to allow the American fleet to weigh anchor and make its way downstream.

They ran down the last twenty miles of the Delaware River and into the wide Delaware Bay. It was five weeks since they had left Philadelphia, five weeks frozen in the river, five weeks to travel sixty miles downstream. But it seemed even longer, much longer than that.

It took them thirty-six hours in the light air to run the length of the Bay and come to anchor in the ice-free, glassy water of Holekill Road. They were joined there by the sloop *Hornet* and the schooner *Wasp,* fitted out in Baltimore and just come around to join the fleet.

Biddlecomb stood on the *Charlemagne*'s quarterdeck as the longboat was swayed over the side. A red pennant hung limp from the *Alfred*'s ensign staff, the signal for all captains to come aboard the flagship.

Dinner in the flagship's great cabin was an amiable affair, loud and raucous as a tavern, and as crowded as well, with the commodore, nine captains, Captain Nicholas of the marines, Jones, and the *Alfred*'s surgeon. The Yankee sailors crowding the great cabin, old and young, were not men given to subtlety or much refinement, and that added greatly to the public-house atmosphere, as did the quite extraordinary consumption of wine, slings well to the northward, canhooks, and various other intoxicating concoctions.

At last dinner was done and rum punch served out, and the commodore called the group to order.

"All right, gentlemen, listen here. We get under way tomorrow, so I reckon you should have some tolerable idea of what we're about. This here"—he held up a folded paper—"is the orders from the Naval Committee of Congress, and when I read them to you, you'll see what a bunch of"—and here Hopkins reeled off a string of obscenities, that Biddlecomb, despite having been a sailor for sixteen years, found genuinely shocking—"lawyer's clerks they truly are."

Hopkins held the sheet of paper up to the light coming in from the stern windows and read, " 'To Esek Hopkins, Esquire, Commander-in-Chief of the fleet of the United Colonies, Sir. The United Colonies, directed by principles of just and necessary preservation against the oppressive and cruel system of the British Administration whose violent . . .' They always write this kind of horse shit. Who do they think they're talking to? Preaching to the goddamned choir. If we didn't already know this crap, we'd be out making our fortunes on some privateer, eh, Whipple, like the last war, instead of sitting on our arses here.

"Anyway, let's see . . . 'and hostile proceedings by sea and land' et cetera, et cetera . . . 'Continental Congress have judged it necessary to fit out several armed vessels . . . you are instructed with the utmost diligence to proceed with the said fleet to sea and if winds and weather will possibly admit of it to proceed directly for Chesapeake Bay in Virginia . . . you are immediately to enter the said Bay, search out and attack, take or destroy, all the naval force of our enemies that you may find there,' blah blah blah.

" '. . . should be so fortunate as to execute this business successfully in Virginia you are then to proceed immediately to the Southward and make yourself master of such forces as the enemy may have both in North and South Carolina . . .' "

Now brows were furrowing around the table, and several captains were exchanging glances. "That's getting to be something of a tall order, ain't it, Commodore?" asked Hoysteed Hacker of the *Fly*.

"Oh, it gets better, sir, depend upon it," Hopkins said, and turned again to the orders. " 'Having completed your business in the Carolinas you are without delay to proceed Northward directly to Rhode Island, and attack, take and destroy all the enemies' naval force that you may find there.' "

A howl went up from the captains as a dozen different points were offered up in loud and louder voices. "Rhode Island?" said Nicholas Biddle, fairly shouting to be heard over the rest. "After we get the tar beat out of us down South? That ain't some cobbled-together bunch of merchantmen, there, that's an honest-to-God British squadron. What have they got there, two frigates?" The last he directed at Captain Whipple.

"Two frigates and then some," Whipple said. "The *Rose* and the *Glasgow*, and the frigate *Cerberus* is always poking around.

You can ask Captain Biddlecomb here about them." He gave Biddlecomb a conspiratorial wink. "They got the *Nautilus* too, and the brig *Bolton,* and the Dear knows what else. That's quite an assignment we've got there."

"And our men sick already, before we've even got to sea," added John Hopkins of the *Cabot*. "I've got twenty down with the smallpox, and my surgeon won't give odds on how many'll live."

"Silence, please, gentlemen." The commodore held up his hand and the great cabin fell silent. "Your objections have been duly noted. Of course only a covey of goddamned, rutting lawyer's clerks would expect us to maintain on a cold coast like this with so many men down sick. In any event, here's the last part I want to read to you.

" 'Notwithstanding these particular orders,' et cetera, et cetera, 'if bad winds or stormy weather, or any other unforeseen accident or disaster disable you so to do, you are then to follow such courses as your best judgment shall suggest to you as most useful to the American cause and to distress the enemy by all means in your power.' "

Hopkins tossed the orders from the Naval Committee on the settee behind him. "All right, listen here. Your orders are simple enough. Just keep company with the flag while we make our way south. Watch for my signals. If you get separated"—Hopkins pulled nine identical sealed envelopes from a haversack on the table—"these here are your orders and the rendezvous. Read 'em whenever you want, I don't go in for that 'open them at this or that goddamned latitude' nonsense. I don't know how you could mend it if you but do what I've just told you." He picked up a bottle of Jamaican rum and said, "Now, on to new business."

By the time Biddlecomb climbed with elaborate care down the *Alfred*'s side and into the waiting boat, he felt decidedly unwell, having been eating and drinking, smoking a pipe, and shouting with his fellow officers without respite for the past five hours.

He boarded the *Charlemagne* on the larboard side to avoid the ceremony that must accompany the captain's official boarding on the starboard. His head was in no condition to endure the shrieking bosun's calls, nor did he feel he could manage another civil word. But four hours later, after a restorative nap, he called to the marine sentry to pass the word for the first and second officers.

Tottenhill and Rumstick arrived at the same moment, as did the cabin steward with a pot of coffee.

"Gentlemen, sit." Biddlecomb indicated the chairs in front of the table. "Coffee? Ezra, I need not ask. Roger? No? Is there anything I can get you? Wine, beer?"

After Tottenhill had declined all offered refreshment, Biddlecomb sat behind the desk and took a long and luxurious sip of coffee. "I've just been to the flag, as you know, and the commodore has informed us of our orders. Or, perhaps I should say he has informed us of the orders the Naval Committee gave. You were right, incidentally, Lieutenant, about the Chesapeake and Lord Dunmore."

At that Tottenhill's otherwise neutral expression took on a hint of his former smugness. "I enjoy the confidence of some well-placed people, sir."

"Indeed. Well, as I said, there might be some difference between what we're ordered to do and what we actually do. The orders the commodore read were a bit . . . ambitious for this little fleet. What's more the commodore's orders give him some discretion to disregard the committee's orders if he must, and he put some particular emphasis on those words.

"In any event, I have here"—he held up the orders given him by Hopkins—"the instructions for the ship should we be parted from the fleet. I'm going to open them, and as the first and second officer I thought it best that you be acquainted with them as well, in case something should happen to me."

Biddlecomb picked up a butter knife and sliced at the seal. The three men sat in silence as Biddlecomb read through the orders, evoking the captain's privilege to be rude if he so chose. He frowned as he read the words and fathomed their intent.

It had occurred to him that Tottenhill might be one of those men who felt as if he were being persecuted, felt as if there were a grand conspiracy against him and his kind. The lieutenant had already made several oblique references to "Yankees." Biddlecomb had seen this sort of thing before, and he recognized the signs. In the forecastle it could be disastrous, and he hated to think what it could mean on the quarterdeck. These orders would not make Tottenhill sleep any easier.

"Well," Biddlecomb said at last, looking up at his officers, "it's all quite straightforward. We are to keep company with the flag, observe signals, the usual. If we are to get separated and cannot find the fleet after four days, then our rendezvous is"—he looked down at the orders again, to make certain of what he had read—"the southern part of Abaco, in the Bahamas. No doubt he has in mind Hole-in-the-Rock. You'll remember that, Ezra."

"Abaco?" Tottenhill said. "What in hell is the commodore about? Why should we rendezvous at Abaco for an attack on the Chesapeake Bay?"

"I can't say with certainty. The commodore did not make his intentions known, but, ah, I think perhaps we are not going to the Chesapeake."

Tottenhill looked at Biddlecomb and then at Rumstick with something accusatory in his glance. Biddlecomb wondered if Tottenhill thought them a part of whatever nefarious plot he was imagining. "The orders were for the Chesapeake," he said.

"Well, for God's sake, Isaac ain't the damned commodore, is he?" Rumstick said in a loud voice. "He don't write the orders for the fleet." The second officer had, up until that point, displayed what was for him a near saintly patience, but Biddlecomb could see it wearing thin.

"I don't suspect that you . . . gentlemen quite appreciate the deprivations that Dunmore is carrying out in the Southern colonies," Tottenhill said, biting off each word.

"Roger, I don't know what the commodore has in mind. But understand, this is a cold coast, and a dangerous one this time of year. The *Charlemagne* alone has eighteen down with the smallpox, and we're doing better than most. I think it reasonable—"

"Did you know about this?" Tottenhill asked suddenly.

"'Did you know about this, *sir?*' " Biddlecomb corrected.

"Well, did you? Sir?"

"Lieutenant, despite my lofty and, as you seem to think, autonomous station, I follow orders, just like you. And I generally don't know what they are beforehand, and I'm generally not asked if they meet my approval."

Tottenhill stood up quickly, nearly knocking his chair over. "Beg your pardon, sir, but I have matters to which I must attend."

Biddlecomb stared into his eyes. "Sit, Lieutenant." When the lieutenant remained standing, he said, "That's an order."

When Tottenhill was once again sitting, Biddlecomb continued, "I have been trying to fathom what you're about, Lieutenant, and I'll own I can't. But you will hear me on this. This is a navy of the United Colonies, and we follow the orders of the man appointed by the Continental Congress to lead this fleet. Or, more to the point, I follow his orders. *You* follow my orders, quickly and unquestioningly. You may depend upon it that whatever I order is for the good of the ship and the country. Depend upon it, but don't question it. Understood?"

Tottenhill glanced at Rumstick and back at Biddlecomb with just a hint of a furtive, trapped-animal look. "Yes, sir," he said in a neutral tone. "May I be dismissed?"

The captain held him in his gaze for a moment before saying, "Yes."

"Whatever you're thinking, Ezra," Biddlecomb said as Tottenhill shut the great cabin door behind him, "pray keep it to yourself."

That was three days ago. Since then the activity had been nonstop, getting the *Charlemagne* ready for sailing offshore.

Biddlecomb had been certain that that work, and the blue water that followed, would take the men's minds off their troubles. But he had been wrong.

He felt the *Charlemagne* twist in the big sea with an odd, corkscrew motion. A burst of water came in through the forwardmost gunport and ran inches deep along the deck.

Well, he thought, if fine weather will not distract them, then what we're in for now surely will.

CHAPTER 15

Hornet *and* Fly

BIDDLECOMB FELT THE *CHARLEMAGNE* HEEL FARTHER OVER, HEARD the note of the wind in the rigging rise in pitch. The shrouds and backstays on the weather side were straight and taut, to leeward they bowed out, the slack running gear twisting and flogging in the wind. He looked up at the six unhappy souls aloft, three on the main topmast crosstrees, three on the fore, struggling to send the light spars down.

Biddlecomb waited for the gust to pass, for the note of the wind to come lower, and for the brig to stand upright again, but it did not. Rather, she heeled over another three degrees, and the whistling wind rose to a shriek. Fore and aft, men stumbled and grabbed on to anything solid or fell on hands and knees to the deck.

He looked aloft once more, willing the men to move faster, to get the uppermost masts and yards down on deck, but he knew that they were doing the best they could. Even on deck it was hard to stand; seventy feet up, they were getting a wild, terrifying ride. To a landsman it would be inconceivable that a man could do anything but hang on to the swaying, bucking mast. But the men aloft were pressing on with their work, preparing to send down to the deck spars weighing hundreds of pounds.

The main topgallant yard was hoisted from a horizontal to

a vertical position. It hung there from the yard rope, the line on which it would be lowered to the deck, and the three men on the crosstree struggled to keep it from swinging out of control, like a giant pendulum. They wrestled it out to the backstay to which they would toggle it and send it down.

Benjamin Woodberry was one of the three, the most able man aboard and a seaman who had been with Biddlecomb since the merchantman days. He stood by the topgallant mast, one arm gently hugging the pole as if it were his child, as if he were four feet off of solid ground.

He handed the man at the backstay a becket and toggle; the short rope was standing out straight in the wind, as was Woodberry's clubbed hair. The man reached for it, and as he did, the *Charlemagne* rolled away to windward and the yard slipped from his grasp.

Biddlecomb tensed up, his hands balled into fists as the spar swung inboard again. "Ahhh!" he said through clenched teeth as he saw the topgallant yard smash into Woodberry's arm, heard the man scream even over the howling wind.

"Mr. Rumstick," he began, intending to have Rumstick send some men aloft to help Woodberry down, but Rumstick himself was already in the main shrouds, going up himself.

It took Rumstick ten minutes to help Woodberry down to the maintop, and Biddlecomb could wait no longer.

"Mr. Tottenhill," he called, and the first officer stepped aft, wrapped in oilskins, moving with confidence on the rolling deck. There was a steadiness about him, a lack of fear or concern in that sea that gave Biddlecomb confidence. Perhaps he was wrong about the man, perhaps his fears, amorphous as they were, were misplaced. If nothing else, Tottenhill was a decent seaman.

"Mr. Tottenhill, we'll tuck deep reefs in the topsails and the foresail, and the second reef in the main!" he screamed. The wind had built to a steady forty knots and was gusting much higher than that, laying the *Charlemagne* hard over until the sea boiled over her leeward rail and ran feet deep along the waterways, crashing against the triple lashed guns like surf against a rocky shore.

"Aye, sir!" Tottenhill shouted back, and staggered forward, rounding up the men, pushing them in various directions as Sprout did the same. Slowly, deliberately, the men clambered up the weather shrouds, pausing and clinging tight as the ship rolled to windward and threatened to chuck them into the sea, then climbing again as the ship rolled away.

Ten of the marines came tromping aft to tend to reefing the mainsail, ostensibly under the command of Lieutenant Faircloth though actually taking directions from Midshipman Weatherspoon.

Faircloth staggered up to Biddlecomb's side and peered aloft. "Striking topgallant gear, sir?"

"Yes. Probably should have done it an hour ago."

"God, what a storm!" Faircloth shouted as the wind made his cloak flog like a slow drumroll. "Are we . . . I mean to say . . . is there any . . . danger?"

"Danger?"

"Well, sir! This storm! Sure you've not seen worse than this?"

Biddlecomb looked at the marine officer, pale, wet, huddled under his coat, and he laughed, a loud, genuine uproarious laugh. "Lieutenant, are you afraid?"

"No, sir, I am not!" Faircloth shouted, and Biddlecomb could see that that was true. *Concerned* might have been a better description. "I was just interested in knowing our situation, sir!"

"Well, Mr. Faircloth, for one thing, you would be right to be afraid, you should be afraid every time you venture out on the big ocean. But that aside, this storm is no more than a trifle. I shouldn't give it a second thought."

"So we are in no danger, sir?"

"Not from the storm. But once the sun goes down, we shall be in mortal danger of running into one of the other ships in the fleet. I hope they have the sense to spread out more than they are doing now."

At last the main topgallant mast was on deck, lashed to the booms, and the vessel properly snugged down for foul weather. It had been a slow process, with nearly a score of men down below in the sick berth with the smallpox, and the ship's company, unused to working together at sea, struggling to coordinate efforts. Woodberry's left hand had been crushed by the runaway yard, and one of the men from North Carolina was knocked insensible by a flailing staysail-sheet block.

The deck was crowded with all able hands, including the cook and the cooper. Fore and aft they were hauling taut and lashing down, rigging up preventers, lifelines, and leeclothes and seeing that the tarpaulins covering the boats were keeping dry the two small pigs and three dozen terrified chickens housed therein.

A semblance of daylight was still left when the brunt of the storm rolled down on them, flashing lightning all around and carrying in its breast a freezing, driving rain. Then with the setting sun even the little visibility that they had enjoyed was gone.

The storm would be bad, Biddlecomb knew, but if the storm had been his only concern, then his mind would have been at ease, for the *Charlemagne* was a solid brig, just out of the yard, and he had weathered storms much worse than this.

But now there was more than just wind and sea with which to contend. He peered anxiously into the dark and strained his ears above the roar of the wind and the groaning of the *Charlemagne*'s rig and timbers to catch some sign of the other ships. He would not have cared to be within half a dozen miles of another ship on that wild night, and he knew that the entire fleet was closer, much closer than that.

Despite the extraordinary circumstances, the ordinary routine of the ship was maintained. The glass was turned by a shivering, wet ship's boy, who then unlashed the bell rope and struck out eight bells, and Tottenhill and his larboard watch relieved Rumstick and his starbowlines.

Had this been a merchantman, with her diminutive crew, Biddlecomb would have had all hands on deck, no doubt through the night. But aboard the *Charlemagne,* brig-of-war, the larboard watch alone was larger than a merchant brig's entire company, and for the time being he was able to stand the watches down.

"We'll maintain this heading as long as the wind remains as it is!" Biddlecomb shouted to Tottenhill, who was standing only a few feet away. "If it builds any more, we'll have to heave to or run with it! Station lookouts on every quarter, keep a bright lookout for the rest of the fleet! That's our greatest concern now!"

"Aye, aye, sir!" Tottenhill shouted, and relayed the instructions to the men on deck.

Biddlecomb looked over his shoulder. Ferguson was at the helm, backed up by another able seaman. That was good; Ferguson had also been with him since the merchantman days, and he was as good a helmsman as Biddlecomb had ever seen.

"Mr. Tottenhill! I'm going below for a moment! You have the deck!" There seemed to be no immediate danger, and Biddlecomb wanted desperately to change his clothing, get some dry stuff on and his oilskins on over that. He had not been below for six hours, standing all that time on the quarterdeck in soaked clothes.

"Aye!" Tottenhill nodded and Biddlecomb fought his way forward, then down below to the great cabin.

He flopped down on the settee aft and peeled the coat off his back. Overhead the skylight was open, just a few inches, and water poured in with each leeward roll of the brig.

He pulled himself to his feet and was reaching up to close it when he heard from the quarterdeck above Tottenhill's voice, high-pitched with excitement, shouting "Fall off! Fall off!" Then Ferguson replied—it sounded like an argument—

but Biddlecomb did not hear the words for he was already through the great cabin door and rushing for the scuttle.

He burst through the scuttle onto the weather deck, into what seemed to be utter bedlam. The thunder rolled overhead, louder than any sound of wind or sea. A bolt of lightning struck the water, and in the light of the long, jagged shaft he saw the schooner *Fly* to windward, not fifty feet away, looming over their starboard side and racing down on them as if she meant to crash into their bow.

Biddlecomb turned and ran up to the quarterdeck. Tottenhill and Ferguson were face-to-face. "Fall off, God damn your eyes! You insolent whore's son!" Tottenhill screamed.

"What the hell is this!" Biddlecomb screamed over the wind. "Ferguson—"

"*Hornet*'s there, sir, right there! I seen her just when Mr. Tottenhill seen the *Fly!*" Ferguson screamed, pointing into the darkness over the leeward side, water streaming down his face and off his beard. "If I falls off, we'll be right aboard her!"

Biddlecomb looked around. He could no longer see *Fly*, but he did not have to. She would slam into them in seconds, and the two ships would hang up, smash themselves to pieces in the steep seas. They had to fall off, as Tottenhill had ordered. But what if Ferguson was right?

"Mr. Tottenhill, back the main topsail! Back it now!" Biddlecomb shouted.

"In this wind? Are you mad? We must fall off!"

"Back it, do it now! The rig will hold! Now go!"

Tottenhill hesitated, just for a pause, then ran forward.

This was a bad situation, and Biddlecomb knew it. He had just countermanded an officer's orders on the word of a foremast jack. A Yankee foremast jack. Nothing could be worse for discipline, and nothing could do more to stoke up Tottenhill's distrust. But Ferguson was a good hand, and they were talking about the life of the ship.

"If you're wrong, Ferguson, I'll make you wish you were a dead man!" Biddlecomb shouted, but the threat was lost even to his own ears as the thunder exploded again, and in the concomitant lightning Biddlecomb saw that Ferguson was not wrong; the *Hornet* was right to larboard, charging down on their larboard bow as *Fly* was converging on their starboard. In that black and wild night the three ships had come together as if the maneuver had been carefully planned. In a second all three would be a tangled and shattered mess.

Another bolt of lightning, and a big sea rolled under them and *Fly* was lifted high so that Biddlecomb had to look up at her, with her low sides and deep-reefed sails. Then *Fly* went down and *Charlemagne* up, and Biddlecomb could see, in another flash of lightning, the panic on the *Fly*'s deck, and on the *Hornet*'s as well.

And then it was black again. Biddlecomb braced himself for the collision. He could hear Ferguson shouting an Our Father while the man beside him, taking an alternative route, cursed like a madman.

Biddlecomb felt the *Charlemagne* jerk under him, felt the motion of the brig change, and he knew that the main topsail was aback. Through the dull roar of the wind he could hear the groaning of the mainstays. The main shrouds and backstays, windward as well as leeward, were slack. They bowed to the wind and flogged with the *Charlemagne*'s roll as the main topsail took the full force of the wind on her forward side.

It was not how the sail was meant to be set, it was not what the rig was designed to endure, and Tottenhill was not wrong to think this a bad idea. Biddlecomb worked his way forward to the break of the quarterdeck and stared overhead. He could just make out the topsail, pressed hard against the mast, the stays and braces quivering with the load. "Hold on, you son of a bitch," Biddlecomb muttered to himself. Tottenhill was in the waist, staring aloft as well, and Rumstick was beside him.

From out in the night, carried on the wind, came the sound of shouting, screaming, and the rending of wood. *Fly* and *Hornet* had struck. With a backed main topsail the *Charlemagne* had effectively stopped short and the two other vessels had run past her and struck each other. A lightning flash, and Biddlecomb was able to see them, lying side to side, grinding together as the seas worked the two vessels against one another. Their rigs were entangled and they were spinning off to leeward, quite out of control.

He twisted his hands together. He could do nothing to help; trying to keep station on them would put them all in greater danger, it would be safer for everyone if he kept his distance. Still, that knowledge did not lessen the anguish of seeing his fellows in such danger. But if he had not done what he did, there would be three vessels in that mess, rather than two.

"Mr. Tottenhill!" he screamed, and the first officer looked over at him. "We'll brace the main topsail around again!" he shouted, gesturing with his hand, and as Tottenhill and Rumstick pushed men into position to carry out that order, Biddlecomb made his way aft. He was bitterly cold; his coat and oilskins were below, and the clothes he was wearing were soaked clean through.

"Here she comes, Ferguson, meet her!" Biddlecomb shouted to the helmsman. Ferguson nodded and followed Biddlecomb's gaze aloft, where the rig slatted and banged. In the frequent flashes of lightning it looked like some great tangle of cordage.

The deep-reefed topsail began to swing around. Biddlecomb could see in the waist an inordinate number of men heaving away on the brace, trying to haul the sail against the wind. The leech of the sail turned into the wind and the sail began to flog, and then it came around fast and filled with a bang, and the *Charlemagne* began to plunge forward again.

Biddlecomb met Tottenhill stepping up to the quarterdeck as he himself was making his way below. "Mr. Tottenhill, I'm stepping below! I'll be back on deck in—"

"Ferguson disobeyed my order!" Tottenhill shouted.

Biddlecomb stared at him for a moment, blinking away the spray and rain that ran in his eyes. He obviously had not heard the lieutenant correctly. "What?" he shouted.

"Ferguson willfully disobeyed my order!"

Biddlecomb shook his head. This was quite beyond comprehension. "Are you mad? We'd have been aboard the *Hornet* if he'd obeyed you!"

"That is beside the point! The men cannot go second-guessing orders! He disobeyed me!"

Biddlecomb stared at Tottenhill and realized, to his amazement, that Tottenhill was right. Strictly speaking, Tottenhill was right. But being right and being smart were not always the same thing.

"Are you going to have him arrested, Captain?" Tottenhill shouted over the wind.

"No, sir. And neither are you. This is just something that happened, you've been going to sea long enough to understand that. It's not your fault, your order was a good one, as far as you knew, but if Ferguson had obeyed it, we'd most likely be dead. Just let it drop, Lieutenant, for the sake of the ship's morale." He turned away from Tottenhill and made his way below, out of the still-building storm.

Some twenty hours after the collision of the *Hornet* and the *Fly,* the wind and seas had settled enough for Amos Hackett to move with some ease around the sick berth. His back burned and tingled from the wounds inflicted by the cat, but in general he was as hale as before his punishment, and only histrionics and a genuine desire to avoid work kept him on the sick and injured list. That and the knowledge that once back on the lower deck, where even the little privacy afforded to the sick was gone, Lieutenant Tottenhill would no longer come to visit him, no longer provide him with rum and the tantalizing stories of treachery among those in command of the brig.

He rolled off his hanging cot and placed his feet on the cold deck planking, swinging with the still considerable roll of the brig. He looked around, getting his bearings, then as the brig rolled to larboard, he stood up and made his way aft. He stopped at the aftermost cot, starboard side, and knelt beside it, rocking back and forth as the cot swung.

"Hey, Billy Allen, you awake?" he whispered.

"Yeah." Allen's face, pale, splotched with the smallpox, was just visible in the shadows of the cot.

"How're you doing, mate?"

"Better, Amos, better. Fever's broke. I think the worst of it's passed."

"That's good news, Billy, good news. And by the way, I was right." He paused, waiting for Allen to ask.

"What was you right about?"

"About that Yankee bastard Biddlecomb and his coddling his damned Yankees, is what. Lieutenant Tottenhill told me. That lubber Ferguson was on the helm, damn near run us aboard the *Hornet* in this storm on account of he wouldn't take orders from Tottenhill. Called him a 'rascal Southerner' and refused to take orders, and Biddlecomb just said, 'Let him be.' And me, I gets my back scratched on account of an accident, and Mr. Tottenhill wanting to let me off and forget it."

"That bastard," Allen echoed.

"Yeah, well, like I said, those of us from North Carolina that was stupid enough to volunteer, like you and me, we don't have a fart's chance in a gale of making it through this cruise. Them Yankees'll do for us—"

"You shut your fucking gob, there, Hackett," came a voice from the larboard side.

Hackett turned and peered into the dark. "Who's that? Woodberry?"

"Never you mind, you blackballing liar. Don't you go spreading lies about Captain Biddlecomb."

"Yeah, Woodberry. Sure, you got no call to complain. You're one of his Rhode Islanders, one of them coddled ones. I reckon you'll go and tell Biddlecomb or that Rumstick what I said, and I'll get flogged again for telling my mates the truth."

"I don't go telling tales, you son of a whore, and you best do the same."

"Is there something you figure you're gonna do to stop me?" Hackett growled.

"I got a broken hand, Hackett, got broke striking the topgallant yard. That's while you was down here pretending you was still hurt. But once I'm on the mend, we'll see about this, you and me."

"Oh, that's fine, just fine. I'm ready whenever you are, you coward." Hackett fell silent and listened to the working of the ship and the groans of the sick men. He was, in fact, terrified of Woodberry. If it came to a fight, Woodberry could tear him apart, even with his hand broken. Hackett had no delusions on that score.

But it would not come to that. Hackett, who reckoned himself a man with vision, could see great things happening on this cruise. He had Tottenhill convinced that he was a solid friend to him. And the foremast jacks, those from his home colony and those from Philadelphia sprung from jail and resentful of any authority, were lapping up his tales as a cat laps milk. He did not imagine that Biddlecomb would be in command of the *Charlemagne* much longer.

CHAPTER 16

Bahamas

PRESIDENT OF HIS MAJESTY'S COUNCIL JOHN BROWN TOOK A SIP OF his now cold tea, placed the Wedgwood cup with its intricate white and blue pattern on the equally intricate saucer, and shifted uncomfortably in his chair.

Seated across from him on the veranda of Government House was Capt. George Dorsett, a merchant captain and frequent guest there. He had arrived fifteen minutes before, clearly agitated and with something of great import to relate. Still, Governor Browne had insisted on leading him out to the veranda, pouring him tea and introducing him to Brown and Babbidge, who already knew him at least as well as the governor did.

Nor was the governor blind to Dorsett's anxiety; Brown was certain that the governor was performing these absurd rituals to demonstrate his own unflappable nature. Brown had found it amusing at first, but now it was starting to annoy.

"And now tell me, my dear Dorsett, what brings you by here in such a rush?" the governor asked at last.

"Well, since you see fit to ask," Dorsett said with irony thickly applied, "I happened to see the rebel fleet, the American rebel fleet, yesterday around noontime."

The governor sat silent with the look of one quite unsure of what to think. Dorsett was going to make him ask for more information, no doubt as punishment for the governor's behavior.

"Where did you see them? What were they about?" the governor asked.

"They were on the southwestern side of Abaco, and I reckoned they were making for Hole-in-the-Rock. I can only imagine that their objective is Nassau."

"Well, I don't know if I agree. I mean, they could be intending anything. What makes you think they had Nassau in mind?"

Brown spoke for the first time since greeting Dorsett. "Well, Governor, I hardly think Hole-in-the-Rock is their objective. There's nothing but coral and lizards in Hole-in-the-Rock. And you'll recall that captain . . . that army captain warned us back in January that they might move on Nassau."

"That's right, Captain Law, that strange fellow, he did say as much. Damn them and their impudence, we shall see about this." Governor Browne stood up abruptly, nearly knocking his chair over as he did. "Captain Dorsett, I wish I could breakfast with you, but I must act on your information at once.

"Babbidge." The governor turned to his assistant, who was seated beside him. "Run down to Fort Nassau and have them fire off three guns to alert the militia. Not the great guns, probably knock down the ramparts if we shot them, just that signal gun by the gate. We'll have the people assemble there, and the free blacks as well, and we'll issue arms.

"Brown"—he turned to the president of the Council—"go round up the Council and have them meet at the fort. Tell them to bring their arms. We'll be ready to give these rebel bastards a proper greeting."

"Certainly, sir," Brown said, slowly getting his feet. "It's just . . . well, it's nothing."

"No, go ahead and say whatever you're thinking, man."

"Well, sir, it has occurred to me that we are a colony as much as America is a colony. Are you quite certain of where the citizens' loyalty lies? And the free blacks? I certainly hope that the people, the people you propose to arm, are more loyal to the King than they are sympathetic with the Americans."

"Hmmm . . ." The governor looked down at the table as he considered this line of reasoning.

Brown, taking a more introspective tack, considered his motivations for doing what he had just done. Was he manipulating the governor, making him change his mind, simply because he could? Simply because it amused him? It would not be the first time he had done so. But this time they were not talking about an allocation of funds or enforcement of some ordinance. The situation unfolding now could genuinely result in the sacking of Nassau.

But of course the sacking of Nassau was only one consideration. Another, more important one was how this could work to the benefit of himself, President of His Majesty's Council Brown. There was no way of knowing how long it would be before the Americans descended on Nassau, and it would be of benefit to no one in the government to have the citizens—especially the free blacks—walking around armed for any length of time. People got ideas when they had guns in their hands. No, he was making the right decision, changing the governor's mind for him.

"That's a good point, Brown, a damn good point." The Governor turned and hurried over to the edge of the veranda, his thin legs bearing his ponderous weight with surprising speed. "Babbidge!" he shouted down to the street below. "Babbidge, come on back here! . . . No, never mind that, just come on back."

The governor walked back to the breakfast table. "We can assemble the militia in ten minutes, have 'em armed and ready to fight. No reason to get them all warmed up now. Captain Dorsett, I must ask you to keep this a secret, this rebel fleet. Tell no one."

Dorsett looked more confused than anything about what had just transpired. "Yes, Governor."

"Very good. Now, Captain, can I interest you in some proper breakfast?"

Hole-in-the-Rock was no more than an indention in the southwest end of Great Abaco Island, but it had the status of a sheltered harbor by virtue of a spit of coral, a cable and a half long, that jutted out from the land and offered some protection to vessels anchored within. Biddlecomb had been to Hole-in-the-Rock on various occasions: wooding and watering or riding out some freak storm that had blown out of the west. There was little other reason to call there.

He stood on the quarterdeck of the flagship *Alfred* and surveyed the American fleet at anchor. He had never seen Hole-in-the-Rock so busy, and it reminded him of Barbados, or Boston in the old days.

A swarm of boats pulled between the shore and the ships at anchor. On the *Columbus* the crew was preparing to set up their lower shrouds for a full due, and on the *Andrew Doria* they were swaying aloft a new main topsail yard to replace the old one, sprung during the storm. The weather was beautiful, a perfect winter day in the Caribbean where it was just a bit too warm to be entirely comfortable in a coat. It was only the ominous absence of the *Fly* and the *Hornet* that cast a pall on the scene.

"Look at those lubbers aboard *Andrew Doria,*" said Lt. Thomas Weaver, second officer aboard *Cabot,* who, for reasons unknown to Biddlecomb, was standing beside him on the flagship's quarterdeck. "They've got the yardarm caught under the mainstay."

Biddlecomb looked back at the *Andrew Doria*. Sure enough, the new spar was hung up on the mainstay, and the crew was running around, pointing and waving their arms. He could not help but smile. Behind his back he could hear Lieutenant Jones supervising, in his thick Scots burr, the preparations of the *Alfred*'s great guns. He sounded quite knowledgeable, though Biddlecomb was fairly certain that Jones had no more experience with naval matters than he himself did.

"Ah, Biddlecomb, sorry to keep you waiting." Commodore Hopkins stepped aft, pushing his shirt into his breeches. "It's that goddamned salt pork. I ain't been off the head beyond fifteen minutes all morning. So you were telling me that *Fly* and *Hornet* hit after you backed your topsail?"

"Aye, sir. We were pretty much stopped and they went past and struck. Their rigs were tangled, but I couldn't see any damage beyond that. Of course I lost sight of them within half a minute."

"Ah, they'll be fine, depend on it. They'll come limping in here in a day or two, if they ain't heading for some whorehouse in Baltimore. Now here's what I really want to talk to you about. In case you haven't guessed it, we ain't going to the Chesapeake. I have it on good authority that there's quite a lot of powder, guns, and shot in Nassau and no regular troops to guard it. Just militia, and we know what they're worth. We're going to cram all the marines in the fleet on board the *Providence* and those two sloops and sail right into Nassau harbor, sweet as you please."

The two sloops to which he alluded were of the Bahamian variety, each about one hundred tons with shallow drafts and wide beams and long booms and gaffs thrust out over their sterns. They had had the bad fortune to be at anchor in Hole-in-the-Rock when the American fleet had sailed in, and Hopkins had immediately dispatched boarding parties to take possession. Now they swung at their anchors with a forlorn look, like prisoners of war held captive in the midst of their enemy's camp.

"We'll keep the fleet below the horizon while the sloops and *Providence* land the marines at the base of the fort and take it, lock, stock, and barrel. Then the whole fleet will sail in and anchor. I don't reckon we'll have much of a fight."

Biddlecomb considered the plan and saw that it was good. The sloops were the most innocuous vessels one could find in these waters. Their sailing into Nassau harbor should raise not the least suspicion. And then another thought occurred to him.

"Sir, what is my role to be in all this?"

"Biddlecomb, I've known you for some years now, and I know more of your reputation. I think this thing's right up your alley. It needs someone who can think on his feet, as it were, bluff his way through if need be. Hate to take you away from your command, but I need you for this.

"I want you to take command of the bigger sloop. Weaver here . . . have you met Weaver? Lt. Thomas Weaver, second on my son's brig, this here's Capt. Isaac Biddlecomb. Biddlecomb, this here's Weaver. Weaver knows these waters inside and out. He'll take the smaller sloop. Hazard has the *Providence*, of course. Captain Nicholas is in command of the marines. You're in charge when you're under way, Nicholas is in charge once you're ashore. Is that agreeable?"

Biddlecomb's mind ran through the plan again, searching for some objection, but he could find none. "Perfectly agreeable, sir."

"All right then, it's all settled. You'll get under way with the sloops just before sunset, and the fleet will follow an hour later. Only fifty miles or so to Nassau, as you know, so you might have to back and fill some to get there just at dawn. In any event, you two have a world to do. I won't keep you here. Report back aboard the flag at, say, beginning of the first dogwatch, and we'll go over this in some more detail."

"Aye, sir," the two officers said together, and then one more thought occurred to Biddlecomb. If he was going to take command of the sloop, then Tottenhill would be in command of the *Charlemagne*. That should not bother him, but it did.

"Sir," he began, stopping Hopkins as the commodore was walking away. "Sir, one more thing. I was wondering . . . uh . . . do you, in your capacity as commodore, hypothetically speaking, have the authority to, say, move a second lieutenant up to first and a first down to second?"

"Oh, for the love of God, Biddlecomb. Look here, the Naval

Committee, in their infinite wisdom, have seen fit to make all the appointments for first and second lieutenants, and I ain't got the authority to change that. So if Tottenhill is giving you some problem, I suggest you deal with it yourself and don't prance around like some schoolgirl asking where babies come from!"

The commodore turned and walked away. Biddlecomb felt his face flush red. He had as much as admitted to his superior that he could not handle his officers, had crawled to Hopkins for help in solving his own shipboard problems. He had opened his mouth without thinking, something that he generally did not do, and he was experiencing the consequences that generally followed those times when he did. He cursed his stupidity under his breath and stomped off toward the gangway and the *Charlemagne*'s gig waiting below.

The *Charlemagne* had the same powderkeg quality that the *Icarus* had had, right before he had led the men in mutiny. Biddlecomb knew that, had known it since the second time they had been frozen in the Delaware River, but stepping back aboard after the flagship's almost jovial atmosphere made his own company's discontent seem that much more acute.

But on board the *Icarus* the cause was so evident: a sadistic bosun and an inexperienced captain too weak to rein the men in, a captain who had completely lost control.

But the cause of the Charlemagnes' grievances he could not guess. Was it so far from the quarterdeck to the lower deck that he could not tell what was thus affecting the men? He had a sudden and terrible fear that to the men on the tween deck the problem was as clear as it had been to him aboard the *Icarus,* but like the captain of the *Icarus* he was blind to it. Biddlecomb's had always been happy ships; he had no experience in dealing with this situation.

A minute after stepping aboard he had his officers assembled on the quarterdeck. "As you may have guessed, we are not going to the Chesapeake," he said. "Rather, we are going to Nassau."

For the next ten minutes Biddlecomb related to the officers what he knew of Hopkins's plan and the part they would each play in it. "Mr. Tottenhill, you will, of course, have command of the *Charlemagne* in my absence. As I think the chief of the work will be aboard the sloop, I would like to take Mr. Rumstick with me, if you have no objection."

"None, sir," said Tottenhill, and from his tone it was clear that he sincerely would not mind having Rumstick gone from the *Charlemagne*.

"Mr. Rumstick, is that all right?"

"Fine, sir," said Rumstick, equally sincere about his willingness to forgo serving under Tottenhill's command.

"Excellent. Then I'll let you go to make your preparations," Biddlecomb said.

The sun was half an hour from setting, a great red ball in the western sky, streaking the low clouds along the horizon with bands of red and orange, when the *Providence* and the two sloops began to win their anchors. Capt. Isaac Biddlecomb stood on the quarterdeck rail, holding on to the aftermost backstay for support and staring out at the *Charlemagne* two cables away. She was a beautiful sight, her lofty spars and oiled sides tinted red by the setting sun. From a distance she appeared to be as serene a vessel as one might find.

"Short peak!" Ezra Rumstick called out from the sloop's bow, and Biddlecomb reminded himself that everyone would be better served if he were concentrating on the vessel he was supposed to be commanding. Particularly as the Bahamian sloop, with its shallow draft, huge gaff-headed mainsail, and diminutive jib, was unlike any vessel he had ever sailed before.

He turned his eyes inboard. The deck was jammed with men, sitting, standing, and milling about. The two hundred and twenty marines in the fleet, reinforced with fifty sailors gleaned from the various ships, were spread among the two sloops and the *Providence*, none of which were of any great size. Looking around the deck, Biddlecomb was reminded of the days on Narragansett Bay when he and Whipple had loaded their vessels with cattle and ferried them away to deprive the *Rose* of fresh meat.

The sloops had the universal quality of working boats, from the thick paint built up on their sides and the sloppy long splices in the running gear to the odd mixture of smells: sweat and fish and fried food and a nameless substance sloshing in the bilge.

As inconvenient as it was to the ship handlers, who had to elbow their way through the crowds of marines to get to halyards and sheets, human decency dictated that Biddlecomb allow the men to remain on deck until the last possible moment. But when they approached Nassau, he would have to order all of the marines down into the low hold, where the smells were considerably worse and would no doubt be augmented by the smells of the marines themselves, made sick by the odor and motion of the vessel.

"There's the signal from the flag, sir," said Ferguson, who was standing below and behind Biddlecomb at the sloop's big tiller. Biddlecomb looked over at the *Alfred*. The ensign was hauled halfway down the staff, fluttering in the light breeze, then hauled up again: the signal for the expeditionary force to get under way.

"Mr. Rumstick, let's get some hands on the halyards," he called out.

"Aye, sir! You marines, bear a hand here. Clap on to that halyard there, this mainsail'll be heavy as a bastard!" Rumstick began to maneuver the marines into position, placing the halyards in their hands. There was an air of excitement aboard the sloop, a lighthearted quality that Biddlecomb had not felt aboard the *Charlemagne* for some time.

This was in part due to the fact that all of the men aboard were New Englanders. Not one of the men shipped in Philadelphia was there, nor any of the North Carolinians. Most of the men who had been with Biddlecomb since his merchant days were there as well. He had left it to Tottenhill to tell off the men who would be a part of the landing party, and the lieutenant had taken the opportunity to rid himself of as many Yankees as he could, and the Yankees seemed quite pleased to be gone.

"Haul away, sir?" Rumstick called aft.

"Yes, Mr. Rumstick, haul away." Biddlecomb pulled himself from his reveries.

Slowly the great mainsail peeled off the boom and spread out as the gaff was hoisted aloft. "Easy there on the peak, you motherless lubbers!" Rumstick shouted. "Keep it parallel with the deck, the poor bastards on the throat are doing all the work!" With that and sundry other curses the sail was hoisted, the halyards sweated taut and belayed.

"Back the jib. We'll break out the anchor now, if you please," Biddlecomb called, and a moment later a voice called out, "Anchor's a-trip!" and the bow of the sloop began to pay off with the nimble vessel free from the ground. "Meet her, steady as she goes, Ferguson," he ordered from his perch on the quarter-deck rail, and Ferguson swung the tiller amidships.

The sloop heeled over and gathered way, close-hauled to weather the spit of land that protected Hole-in-the-Rock from the Atlantic Ocean, slipping past the anchored fleet. From one of the ships a voice called out, "See you in Nassau!" and then another shouted, "Save some rum for us, boys!" and then from every ship the men cheered.

The sun dipped below the horizon, and Biddlecomb's sloop, with the *Providence* and the other sloop in her wake, stood out from Hole-in-the-Rock and met the long, gentle swell of the open sea.

CHAPTER 17

Trojan Horses

JOHN BROWN SLEPT LITTLE THAT NIGHT, DESPITE THE TWO SNIFTERS of brandy and the cool, comforting winter weather.

He was concerned over his decision to change the governor's mind about alerting the militia. He had assumed that the American rebels would be a bit backward in their attack, that they would lie at Hole-in-the-Rock for some time, preparing, voting, forming committees, whatever it was that American rebels did.

But what if they did not? A competent admiral would strike quickly, and Brown had no way of gauging the competence of the American commander, though from the news he had heard, from Concord and Ticonderoga and Bunker Hill, the Americans had been acquitting themselves with some distinction. It was not impossible that the fleet was on its way now, and his, John Brown's, options would be greatly reduced if the island was caught unaware.

He threw off his thick cover and climbed out of bed, fumbling around for his breeches. He dressed quickly in good, plain working clothes, slung his cartridge box and telescope over his shoulder, picked up his musket, and stepped quietly out of his house.

It was an hour before dawn and the streets of Nassau were deserted. The coral-brick houses that lined George Street were dark, their bright-colored shutters, gray looking in the faint light, closed over the windows. Brown took a deep breath. The air carried on it flowers, drying fish, and conch, a hint of the ocean.

He turned and looked south. Mount Fitzwilliam and Government House loomed over him like some ancient monolith. He could see a lantern burning in the kitchen; the house servants would have been awake for an hour already, preparing for the day, but the governor himself would not be awake until two hours after sunrise, if even then.

He walked down steeply sloped George Street, feeling the uneven cobblestones through the soles of his boots, hearing the crunch of the ubiquitous sand. The morning was beautiful, cool and moist and quiet, an atmosphere that did not lend itself to thoughts of imminent attack.

Brown turned left on Bay Street, walking along the waterfront. The smell of brackish water and moldering conch shells was stronger here than it was on the slopes of Mount Fitzwilliam, and the quiet was broken by the creaking of ships against the wooden piers.

Before him stood Fort Nassau, that odd-shaped, crumbling, largely indefensible fortification, framed against the darker sky. A wooden palisade twelve feet high formed the first line of defense against anyone who might bother to attempt a frontal assault. Brown walked along the palisade to the gate, where a bored guard stood half inside his guardhouse. No regular troops were left on the island; the men of the local militia took turns manning the fort, a dozen men at any one time. In the deep shadows Brown could not tell whether the guard was awake.

"Who goes there?"

"John Brown, President of His Majesty's Council."

"Oh, good morning, Mr. Brown." The guard laid his musket aside and lifted the heavy latch from the gate. "A bit early for an inspection. Are you expecting some trouble?" he asked as he swung the gate open. "I heard some rumors about a rebel fleet from America."

"We must be always prepared," said Brown, the most noncommittal statement he could think of. He stepped through the palisade and across the open stretch to the front gate of the fort proper.

The fort itself was a more substantial affair than the palisade. An impressive, castlelike main gate was the only break in the thirty-foot-high stone walls topped with forty-six heavy guns, twelve and eighteen pounders. Over the battlements of the main gate, which rose half again as high as the walls, flew an enormous, if a bit tattered, British flag. On paper the fort was quite formidable.

But in fact, over the past thirty years it had received only the most perfunctory maintenance, and the integrity of those massive walls and the heavy guns was dubious at best. Its poor repair, along with its vulnerable location, made Fort Nassau one of the last places President of His Majesty's Council Brown wished to be if the island were attacked.

The main gate was opened for him by another guard, who had also heard rumors of an American fleet and who received the same noncommittal answer.

Brown paused briefly and in the gray light of false dawn surveyed the inside of Fort Nassau. Around the perimeter of the fort the ground had been built up into wide, flat ramparts twenty feet high, leaving just ten feet of wall visible above them. These ramparts, extending out thirty feet from the walls like an earthen catwalk, had once been hard-packed dirt but now, from long neglect, were covered with a fairly even carpet of grass. On that built-up area the cannons rested, each peeking out of its embrasure, some looking out over the city, some looking out to sea.

The central area of the fort, the parade ground, was a great rectangle twenty feet lower than the rest, at the same level, in fact, as the land outside the fort. This too was covered with grass, and at either end a set of stairs led up to the ramparts. Nothing moved within those walls.

Brown stepped quickly along the western rampart to the crooked corner at the far end of the fort that jutted out over the harbor. A line of black guns, wet with the morning dew, stood staring out over the water. Brown turned and looked toward the east. The gray line on the horizon, the lessening of the blackness, was more pronounced now. In half an hour it would be dawn, and he would know if he had been needlessly worried, or if he had made a terrible mistake.

Biddlecomb felt ready for the dawn and the action that it heralded. The crowd of marines that had packed the wide flush deck of the sloop for the easy sail down from Abaco were now below, poor devils, jammed into the low, stinking hold. If anyone on shore bothered to look, they would see only six men aboard the sloop.

A ship's forecastle tended to contain the most heterogeneous assortment of men one was likely to find, with the possible exception of a prison, and the ships of the American navy were no exception. Biddlecomb had taken advantage of that to glean from the fleet a sufficient number of black sailors to man the sloops, as someone watching from the shore would expect to see aboard Bahamian vessels. They were dressed alike, deck hand and officer, black and white, in loose trousers and shirts, with the one distinction that he and Rumstick wore blue jackets, much battered, and the men did not.

The three vessels—the two sloops and the *Providence*—lay hove to. The wind had built during the night and was now blowing close to twenty knots from the northwest, blowing them into Nassau harbor faster than they cared to be blown.

The rest of the American fleet was somewhere to windward, hopefully ten miles or more to windward. When the sun came up, they would have to be below the horizon, out of sight from Nassau, so as not to create alarm in the city. Hopkins would have to be careful, with the wind blowing as it was, tending to drive his fleet toward the island. Biddlecomb hoped that Hopkins had hove the ships to hours before.

Now the sun was coming up, and the high point on the island that had been just visible at first light resolved itself into Mount Fitzwilliam and Government House, that familiar landmark to vessels approaching from the west. It was time to go in.

Biddlecomb picked up his speaking trumpet and stood on the leeward rail of the quarterdeck. The two other vessels were downwind of him and his voice carried on the breeze as he called, "Mr. Weaver, Mr. Hazard, do you hear?"

"Aye!" he heard Weaver's voice, and then "Aye!" from John Hazard.

"It's time to go in. Keep your marines hidden until we're alongside the dock. Keep astern of me, but don't make it look as if we're in formation. No hailing from this point on! Understood?"

Two more "Aye's" were returned, and the three vessels were put under way once more, turning off the wind, their long booms jutting out over their leeward rails. Biddlecomb leaned against the weather rail, arms folded across his chest, trying to enjoy the peace of the morning.

Rumstick stepped up and leaned against the rail beside Isaac, in the casual manner of the Caribbean merchantmen. It had been just over a year since the two of them had been arrested by the British marines, pulled from Sabine's Tavern in Providence, Rhode Island, and it had been a hell of a year. Biddlecomb could not image this situation, this calm before the fight, standing into danger, without Rumstick there.

Not that Biddlecomb felt particularly calm at that moment; his stomach had taken a round turn and the soles of his feet were tingling like mad. But he knew that if, say, Tottenhill were standing there, and not Rumstick, he would be feeling considerably worse.

When at last the sun peeked over the eastern horizon, New Providence Island was clearly visible off the starboard bow and Hog Island the larboard. The half-mile strip of water that separated the two and that constituted Nassau harbor opened up before them. Biddlecomb swept the shoreline with his telescope, but Fort Nassau was still lost in the deep shadows of the land.

The two other sloops were astern of his, in no particular formation and giving no indication that they were all sailing in company. They were just three little vessels that were waiting for daylight to enter the harbor. He could see the black deckhands moving slowly about, the officers lolling about the quarterdeck in a markedly unmilitary fashion. He could see no reason that anyone onshore would think things were in any way amiss.

He ran his eyes over the western horizon, now just revealing itself. Nothing was to be seen there, thankfully, and he was halfway turned around again when his eye caught something that it had long ago been trained to catch: a distant sail. He stopped and turned back. A ship was there, and behind it he could see another.

"Here we go," Rumstick said. They had passed the westernmost point of Hog Island and were now entering Nassau harbor. Fort Nassau, with its long battlement bristling with big guns, was visible now.

Biddlecomb put his telescope to his eye and trained it on the sails to the westward, growing more visible with each passing minute. He had hoped that he was wrong, but he knew that he was not, and the image in the glass confirmed it. It was the American fleet, hull up. He could see them as clearly as he could see Hog Island. There was no surprise now, and it would not take a great leap of imagination for the people onshore to guess that the three sloops were a part of that fleet.

He heard Rumstick give a short, quick intake of breath, and a second later he said, "That ain't . . . is that . . . ?"

"Oh, son of a bitch!" was all Biddlecomb could think to answer.

* * *

John Brown sat on one of the eighteen-pound guns and stared with his telescope over the battlement to the western approaches to the island. He had felt a moment's anxiety when the dawn had revealed three vessels standing into Nassau harbor; he had thought that they were under attack already. But he saw that they were just Bahamian sloops of the kind that one saw everywhere in the waters around the islands. The mixed crew, black and white, lolled around the deck in a way that no naval officer would tolerate.

"What is it, sir, if I might ask?" asked the militia captain, whose name Brown could not recall, and who upon being made aware of the important visitor had hastily dressed and joined Brown on the rampart. "Is it them rumors of a rebel fleet that concerns you, sir?"

"Well, that does not appear to be a fleet, rebel or otherwise," Brown said, nodding toward the sloops. He hoped that the relief was not evident in his tone. To have Nassau captured without a fight due largely to advice that he had given the governor would be utterly humiliating to him. But apparently he was safe for the moment.

He swept the glass farther west. The distant horizon was just coming visible, and he moved the telescope slowly, taking in each section of ocean as it was revealed. He looked at empty sea, then more empty sea, and then, to his complete surprise, his lens was filled with sails.

He sucked in his breath, and the knot of tension in his shoulder, which had been dissipating over the past five minutes, bound up again and shot sparks of pain up his neck.

It was the rebel fleet; it could be nothing else. There were two ships and three brigs, just as Dorsett had said, and they were standing in to Nassau harbor with all plain sail set. Brown felt a deep and sudden nausea, like the first pangs of mal de mer, that comes with the realization that one has made a dreadful mistake.

But President of His Majesty's Council Brown had not become the man that he was by rolling over at each adversity.

The fleet was an hour away at least, and that was quite enough time to rally the militia and arm the citizens. What was more, those big ships would have to run the hail of iron that they would pour from Fort Nassau.

"Captain, I want the signal gun by the gate fired three times to rally the militia. Send a crier though the streets as well, and I suppose send someone to alert the governor. Get a gun crew up here at once and as many more as you can muster. I believe the rebel fleet is in the offing."

The captain saluted and was gone, and Brown turned and looked seaward again. He wondered if the masters of those little sloops realized how close they had come to being scooped up by the rebels. No doubt they did and were all running for their lives. It was odd to see three together like that, and to see them entering the harbor just at dawn. The fishermen who ran those boats were rarely that active.

"Damn me!" Brown said out loud as he whipped the glass to his eye. Not above eight people were on the deck of each sloop, black men and white and all dressed in rags, like every Bahamian sloop he had ever seen.

But one of them, the far one, was not a Bahamian sloop at all. It was a sloop, to be sure, but the high freeboard and plumb bow bespoke a northern build, and though Brown knew little about ships, something about that one sloop said to him "Yankee."

He heard feet on the soft ground and was suddenly surrounded by the gun crew. He turned to the first man he saw. "Quick, run and tell the captain to leave off firing the signal from the gate. We'll use the guns here to rally the militia. I believe we have an absolute herd of Trojan horses here," Brown continued, waving toward the sloops, "charging into the harbor."

From the blank looks on the men's faces he guessed that the allusion had eluded them all. "Look, I want to fire three of the big guns as a signal, but I want the guns shotted and aimed generally in the direction of those sloops. But not at them, mind you."

If they are the enemy, then we may frighten them away, he thought, and if not, well, no harm done. As long as we don't hit them.

Biddlecomb had his back to the American fleet; he could not stand to watch Hopkins's solid plan crumbling before his eyes. But there was still a chance. The militia in Nassau might not recognize the fleet for what it was, or if they did, they might believe the sloops to be innocent vessels running from the obvious threat. In any event he would press on, despite his feeling decidedly unwell, until it was clear that their plan would no longer work.

"I reckon we'll be alongside in ten minutes," Rumstick said, and Biddlecomb nodded in agreement. Ten more minutes was all they needed, ten minutes of indecision or complacency on the part of the citizens of Nassau, and he would take the island with a minimum of bloodshed or possibly, hopefully, none at all.

He looked at Fort Nassau, low and menacing, directly off the starboard beam. He was about to tell Rumstick of the last time he had been there, back in the smuggling days, when he saw the flash of light, orange and red and yellow, a tongue of fire shooting out from the fort. And simultaneously came the belch of gray smoke, the dull roar of the gun, and a spout of water shot up between his sloop and the *Providence*.

"I don't think we're fooling them any longer," Biddlecomb observed.

Another of the big guns fired, sending up another spray of water, one hundred feet from the first. And then a third gun, and with it a crash and shudder as the deck trembled underfoot and the air was filled with a burst of splinters.

The cannonball had struck the sloop and torn away four feet of the vessel's low bulwark, taking with it all hope of bloodless conquest.

CHAPTER 18

Hanover Sound

BIDDLECOMB STARED IN DISBELIEF, NOT AT THE DAMAGE, WHICH WAS minimal, but at the near miraculous sight of everyone still on his feet. On either side of the yawning hole in the bulwark men stood frozen in surprise and gaped at the splintered wood. The ball—it could not have been smaller than a twelve-pounder—had passed right through a knot of five men and gone on its way, leaving the crew of the sloop unscathed.

"Now that was some lucky," said Rumstick.

"A foot lower and that would have been right in the hold," Biddlecomb said. "I doubt the scantlings on this little thing could stand up to a heavy gun like that." The cloud of gun smoke was lifting off Fort Nassau in a solid blanket and drifting away downwind. "I don't want to think what a twelve-pounder ball would do to those poor bastards down there."

He did not want to think of it, but he did; a twelve-pound ball tearing through the sloop's frail sides, tearing into the mass of close-packed, helpless men. The whole ship would be a slaughterhouse in minutes.

He swept the walls of Fort Nassau with his telescope. He could see no further activity, but that did not mean that it was not happening, that more guns were not being loaded and run out. He would need another ten minutes to lay his sloop alongside and disgorge the marines, and in that time, firing from the stable platform of the fort, the defenders could blow him out of the water.

"Any signal from the flagship, Mr. Rumstick?"

The second officer was silent for a moment as he squinted aft through his telescope. The fleet was not far off, just over half a mile, but it was difficult to see without full daylight. "Hard to say, Captain," he said at length. "Course, the signal to disengage, which is what I reckon I'm looking for, is a white flag at the ensign staff. And since we're looking bow-on, I can't see the ensign staff, which, as you might recall, is on the taffrail. I guess old Hopkins didn't figure on this case."

"You men," Biddlecomb called forward. "Get some lumber and shore up the bulwark there. Nail something over the hole." It would not do to let the men mill about unoccupied, waiting for the next murderous hail of fire.

Lieutenant Faircloth crawled out of the forward hatch and walked aft. He had left his bottle-green jacket below and thrown a filthy blanket over his shoulders to hide his perfectly white shirt from watchers ashore. He stepped aft, glancing curiously at the missing section of bulwark. "Trouble, sir?"

"Possibly. We've not done too well as far as surprises go." Biddlecomb indicated with a jerk of his thumb the American fleet less than a mile astern. He hoped that he did not sound even half as nervous and angry as he was. His shoulders ached with tension as he braced for the fusillade that would murder the poor men below.

"Oh, dear, a bit of miscalculation, what?" Faircloth said. "Are we to proceed with the plan?"

"Until Hopkins signals otherwise. Though I think we can abandon any hope of pulling this off without bloodshed."

"Here, sir," Rumstick said. "They're running something up the jack staff, where we can see it. There's a bright boy . . . white flag, sir. Disengage."

"Thank God, before the butcher starts running up his bill. Forward there," Biddlecomb shouted along the deck, "we're going to bear up. Hands to sheets."

"Shall I signal the others, sir?" Rumstick asked.

"Yes. And damn the idiot flags, just shout to them."

Rumstick put the speaking trumpet to his mouth and shouted, "Stand by to bear up. We are disengaging!" and from the first sloop, and then the second, the response "Aye!" floated across the water.

"Port your helm," Biddlecomb ordered the helmsman, who pushed the tiller to larboard. The sloop swung up into the wind and the sails were drawn in tight as she turned close-hauled to retrace her course out into the Caribbean. Fort Nassau was over the larboard beam now, silent and menacing. In their wake the other two vessels, the *Providence* and the second captured sloop, swung around, and together the three Americans took up their headlong and ignominious flight from Nassau harbor.

"I told you to miss them, you stupid idiot, whoreson bastard!" Brown shouted at the gunner, now standing twenty feet below him on the parade ground.

The first two shots had fallen perfectly between the lead sloop and the second, sending spouts of water high in the air. But the third had scored a direct hit, smashing a huge section in the vessel's bulwark and killing the Lord only knew how many men. If that sloop was some innocent Bahamian trader, perhaps running for the protection of the fort, then Brown would have some tricky explanations ahead of him, and he was not certain that even his quick tongue was up to the task.

"It were an accident, sir," the gunner wailed from below the rampart. "I've never hit nothing before in my life. But look at this gun, sir! What am I to do about this?"

The gun was something of a problem. The recoil had torn the ringbolt, to which the breeching was attached, clean out of the crumbling wall, and both gun and carriage, a total of about thirty-seven hundred pounds, had flown backward off the rampart and plunged twenty feet to the parade ground below.

The other two guns had remained in place, but just barely.

The ringbolts on their breechings, though they had held, had been jerked halfway out of the wall. If fired again, they would inevitably join their comrade, lying on its side on top of the shattered remnants of its carriage. As formidable as the battlements of Fort Nassau appeared, the great guns, it seemed, would be good for no more than one or two shots apiece at most before they hurled themselves off the gun platform. Brown wondered if anyone else—the invading Americans, for instance—knew that.

He turned his attention from the disabled gun—he had no time for that now—and looked out over the stretch of water sandwiched between New Providence and Hog Island. The sloops had not changed course, sailing inbound in a loose formation. "Damn your eyes to hell," Brown muttered another curse at the unfortunate gunner and his lucky shot. Someone was nailing a board over the hole that the gun had blasted in the vessel's bulwark.

And then, suddenly, like a gift from heaven, the three sloops spun on their heels and headed back the way they had come. There was nothing ragged in the movement, it was perfectly coordinated and clearly done on some signal.

Brown wanted to cheer out loud.

Such an evolution could only have come from naval vessels, working in consort. They were Trojan horses after all, and he had not allowed Nassau's wall to be knocked down. Not much separated the hero from the goat, but in this case at least he had come out the former.

As his elation subsided, he became aware of the commotion on the far side of the fort and coming closer. He turned from the joyful sight on the water to see what was going on.

Governor Browne had arrived, and trailing behind him like the tail of a shooting star was the omnipresent Babbidge and a dozen militiamen representing those wealthiest islanders who lived close to Government House.

The governor himself might have made an imposing sight, with his cartridge belt and powder horn around his shoulder and his beautiful musket clenched in his meaty hand. The effect was ruined, however, by the worried expression on his face, bordering on terrified, and the fact that he was still in his nightshirt.

The long white garment hung down to his knees, and the fringe, along with his legs (surprisingly thin for so big a man) and his deerskin moccasins, were covered with mud and dust. His head, generally topped with a wig, was bare, and his short hair stood up straight in all directions, making his scalp look very like a sea urchin.

"Brown, Brown, there you are," the governor said, huffing across the parade ground and clambering up the steps to the rampart. "What the devil is going on? Are we being invaded?" He was breathing fast and his face was far redder than usual.

"There, sir," President of His Majesty's Council Brown pointed grandly at the retreating sloops. "Those three vessels. I suspect their holds were crammed with rebel soldiers. As you can see, I have driven them away."

"Yes, indeed. . . . Why do you think they had soldiers aboard?"

"Because, Governor, yonder is the American fleet."

"Oh, sweet Jesus," the governor said as he followed Brown's pointed finger to the ships, a formidable-looking force, standing into the harbor.

But even as he said the words the Americans began to change course. On some unseen signal the two ships and three brigs swung away from the watching men. They turned north, presenting first their broadsides and then their sterns to Fort Nassau, heading back the way they had come. The three sloops followed a quarter mile astern, sailing line ahead out of Nassau harbor.

"Well, they're not going for good, I can assure you of that," the governor said as new apprehensions replaced the relief he had just experienced. "Look, Chambers is over there with his sloop, what is it? The *Mississippi* . . . what is it?"

"*Mississippi Packet*, sir."

"Right. Let's get the gunpowder aboard her, send it off to Florida, keep it from falling into the hands of the damned rebels. Yes, we'll begin immediately, before they return. Show those damnable rascals." The governor turned to the crowd of militia below on the parade ground, which even since his arrival had increased in size, and began to issue orders.

"Sir," said Brown, stopping him in midsentence. "I beg you, consider this. If you send the sloop out now, in broad daylight, there is a better than even chance the rebels will see it and intercept it. Then we are defenseless, and they will both have the powder and be enraged at our attempt to keep it from them."

"Oh," the governor said, and then turning visibly angry, his heavy face flushing, his jaw working, continued, "See here, Brown, you always have some damned thing to say, don't you? It was your idea to not alert the militia, and we came damn close to having those rebels crawling right up our backsides!"

"My duty, Your Honor, is to advise as best I can. I said simply that we can have the militia turn out in a matter of minutes and"—Brown gestured to the assembled men below—"they did, as you trained them. As to the powder, if you believe Captain Chambers can elude the rebel fleet, the entire rebel fleet, then I certainly support your plan to send the powder off."

"Fine, very well. We'll make a stand, fight these bastards off. Show them back home we can do without their damned army. Protect the island ourselves. Babbidge, pick thirty or so steady men and go reinforce Fort Montegu, in case those rascals are thinking of sneaking in from the east, which I reckon they are. I'll join you as soon as I go make myself a little decent and see that my poor wife and aunt ain't too upset. Brown, you take charge here. Men!" he said in a loud voice, addressing the militia who stood looking up at him.

Brown could see that the governor was working himself up

into a patriotic oratory fervor, and he braced himself for what would follow.

"Now is the time to stand fast in defense of your homes, your wives and daughters," Governor Browne said in his deep, speech-giving voice. "Now is the time that you must fight for your king and stand like the solid walls of Fort Nassau, this mighty fortress, against the treasonous onslaught!"

The militiamen gave the speech a cheer of sorts, and Babbidge began to tell off men to march with him to the eastern end of the island. "Very good, Brown, I'm off," said the governor. He turned to leave, paused, and then turned back again. "What the devil is that cannon doing down there?"

It was a fairly dejected band of American rebels that met in the great cabin of the flagship *Alfred* three hours later. Once the fleet had come about, once they realized that they had been discovered, Hopkins led them to the north and then east, skirting around the far shore of Hog Island and working their way through the tricky reefs.

As Fort Nassau disappeared from sight, Biddlecomb allowed the marines up on deck. They poured out of the hold, sweating, coughing, some looking a most unhealthy color, and for the rest of the trip they milled about the waist, talking loud and impeding the work of the sailors.

Hanover Sound, to which they were bound, was, from the level of the deck, indistinguishable from the open sea. It was only from high aloft, looking down, that one could see that the Sound was in fact a deep indentation in the reef, something like a harbor in a submerged island. In that sheltered area, amid the long, low-lying islands to the northeast of New Providence, the American fleet anchored.

Biddlecomb had just luffed his sloop and was waiting for the first sign of sternway before ordering the man forward to let the anchor go when Rumstick reported, "Signal from the flag."

"I can well imagine," Biddlecomb said, then shouted, "Let go!" to the sailor in the bow.

"All captains to repair on board."

The sloop's boat, which, for lack of space on deck, had been towed astern, was brought around and manned, and Biddlecomb took his place in the stern sheets for the short trip to the flagship.

"Hold a minute, Ferguson," he said to the seaman at the tiller. "Take us by *Charlemagne* first; we'll see how things are going there."

"Aye, sir." Ferguson pushed the tiller over, and a moment later the boat was gliding under the *Charlemagne*'s counter and alongside her starboard quarter.

"Ahoy, *Charlemagne!*" Biddlecomb called out, and Tottenhill's head appeared over the quarterdeck rail, and then, oddly, Hackett's as well.

"No surprise that bastard's made his way aft," Ferguson muttered, and before Biddlecomb could ask him what he meant by that, Tottenhill called out, "Oh, sir!" and then turning forward shouted, "Side party! Smartly now!"

"No, belay that, Mr. Tottenhill," Biddlecomb called. "I'm going aboard the flagship. I just wanted to see that everything was all right."

"Fine, sir. Couldn't be better."

"Have you enough hands?"

"Quite, sir. Plenty."

And hardly a Yankee among them, Biddlecomb thought. Probably the happiest you've been in months, you miserable bastard.

Stop that, he thought, that kind of thinking will not help at all. He ran his eyes over the *Charlemagne*. She looked good, but not excellent.

"Perhaps you could get a boat in the water and square up the yards a bit, Mr. Tottenhill. And I think a fresh pull on the backstays would not be amiss."

"Aye, sir," Tottenhill said, but his tone was different now. He seemed to bristle at the suggestion.

Don't get too used to being in command, Biddlecomb thought. "Very good. Carry on. I don't know when I'll be back aboard."

"Aye, aye, sir."

Biddlecomb glanced around the deck, that part of it that he could see from the boat. "Where's Weatherspoon?"

"Masthead, sir."

"Why?"

"I caught him in the cable tier, sleeping, when he said he was working on his trigonometry."

"I see." Biddlecomb had to smile. As an apprentice he had spent a good deal of time asleep in the cable tier when he was supposed to be at more productive pursuits.

Tottenhill gave a crisp salute, which Biddlecomb returned, and the boat was under way again, pulling forward along the brig's length to duck under her bow.

"Kinda odd, sir, ain't it, Hackett being up on the quarter-deck?" Ferguson said casually, too casually to be genuine.

"What do you mean?"

"I just mean . . . well, nothing. Just, Hackett didn't seem to be doing nothing. No work back there, I mean. I reckon he and Tottenhill are friends from back home."

"I don't know about that," Biddlecomb said, then after a pause added, "Ferguson, what are you trying to say?"

"Nothing, sir."

And that, Biddlecomb was certain, was not true. What was Ferguson implying? That Hackett was exerting some influence on Tottenhill? That was not possible. Even Tottenhill, Biddlecomb had to imagine, could see what a weasel and a sea lawyer Hackett was. He wished that Ferguson would just say what he was thinking.

But he would not. Biddlecomb knew that that cryptic warning was the closest that a sailor like Ferguson would come to informing on a fellow foremast jack, despised though he might be. Without further comment Ferguson pulled the boat alongside the *Alfred*'s boarding steps and Biddlecomb climbed aboard. He was led by a midshipman to the great cabin, which was, once again, filled to capacity with officers of the navy and marine corps.

This gathering, however, had none of the jovial, festive atmosphere of the meeting at Cape Henlopen, or Hackett's court-martial. The American Navy had just failed in it's first ever attempted action, and the faces in the great cabin reflected that.

"Biddlecomb, good, you're here," Hopkins said as Biddlecomb stepped into the great cabin and saluted. "Sorry about that whole thing getting buggered up like that. Damn wind set us further east than we thought, of all the stupid, blackballing mistakes. Sun comes up and we're right on the buggering bar. Take any casualties?"

"No, sir."

"Well, thank God for that, anyway. Steward, a rum punch for Captain Biddlecomb. Step up here, Captain, we're trying to figure out what in hell we'll do now." The other captains, as well as Lieutenant Weaver, late of the second captured sloop, and Lieutenant Jones, who always seemed to make himself present at these occasions, were gathered around the great cabin table, across which was spread a chart of New Providence Island and the surrounding waters.

Biddlecomb took the rum punch, which was the last thing he wanted at ten o'clock in the morning, from the steward and made a halfhearted attempt to push his way to the table. Lieutenant Jones was making an animated point about a landing sight and gesturing to the chart, but Biddlecomb was still thinking about the *Charlemagne*. He felt as if his ship were breaking up under him, and he did not know what to do to prevent it. In any event, it was clearly not helping things, allowing Tottenhill to run amuck. As much as he hated to do it, he would have to send Rumstick back aboard. It was the only way to assure that discipline would be maintained.

"Perhaps Captain Biddlecomb has something to add? Captain Biddlecomb?"

Biddlecomb looked up at Abraham Whipple, who had just spoken his name, the second time in a tone calculated to snap him from his reverie. "Yes, I'm sorry, what?"

"Lieutenant Jones is proposing that he lead a landing party here"—Whipple placed a finger like the trunk of a young sapling on a point on the chart—"just south of Fort Montegu."

"No, that's no good," Biddlecomb said without thinking, distracted as he was with other concerns.

"And why not, sir?" asked Jones, a hint of confrontation in his voice. "The batteries from the ships could keep the fort well occupied until the marines were landed, I've no doubt."

"No, no, it's not a question of the fort. The whole shoreline there is steep-to coral and a lee shore. The boats would be smashed to pieces if they tried to land there, and even if they weren't, the poor bastards would never be able to get ashore." Biddlecomb turned to Lieutenant Weaver, who was maintaining a respectful silence. "Isn't that right, Lieutenant?"

"Yes, quite, sir. There's no landing anywhere along that northeastern shore."

"Well, then, what's your plan, Biddlecomb?" Hopkins asked.

"My plan?" Biddlecomb had simply answered a question, he had no plan. He looked around at the dozen faces looking back at him and decided that he would not admit as much to this crowd.

"I think Lieutenant Jones had the right idea," he began, hoping to assuage the lieutenant, who was clearly upset, "with a landing, but not at that point. Right here at East Point"—he leaned over and put his finger on the chart—"is the place to land the marines. Right around here the shore becomes less steep, and here, while it's still rocky, you do have some shallows of sorts to land men. Would you agree, Weaver?"

"Yes, sir. There's no sand beach at all to speak of around there, but you can definitely get boats ashore just above East Point."

"Well, good, then," Hopkins thankfully interrupted. "We land there, just north of East Point. We've lost our chance at surprise, and we ain't going to get it back, but the marines are already on the sloops. No reason to wait. Biddlecomb, you got the local knowledge, so we'll just keep things the way they are. You're in charge of the landing, Captain Nicholas will lead the attack against Fort Montegu, and we'll see how things go from there. Gentlemen, shall we return to our ships?"

As the meeting broke up, Biddlecomb stared out of the salt-stained windows of the great cabin at the two captured sloops riding easily at their anchors. He was, once more, responsible for landing marines on a hostile coast. He would put them ashore, under enemy fire if the enemy had any sense, and would then participate in the attack on a strongly held and alerted fortification. How in the hell did it happen that he was in charge?

Lt. Roger Tottenhill stood at the leeward rail of the *Charlemagne*'s quarterdeck, the captain's sacred spot, aloof and alone. It felt good to be there. It felt good to be in command, and to be free of Faircloth and his arrogant ways. It felt even better to know that Rumstick was gone as well, and not second-guessing him, telling Biddlecomb lies about his abilities. He was relishing the moment, trying not to think of the future when the Yankee cabal would be back.

"Sir, beg pardon." Hackett appeared once more on the quarterdeck and saluted. "It ain't my place, sir, but I had a thought, and, well . . . please, never mind."

"No, go on, Hackett, what is it?"

"Well, sir, the men have been working awful hard, sir, and they were disappointed something cruel about being turned away from Nassau harbor, on account of them Yankees making such a hash of things, sir."

"Yes, I understand," Tottenhill said. Behind his back he could hear Woodberry shift uncomfortably. The seaman was seated cross-legged on the deck, long-splicing a chafed section of the main topsail outer buntline.

"Disappointed something cruel," Hackett said again.

In fact Tottenhill had been thinking just that thing about the men's hard work and their disappointment, but he was not certain he cared for any of the men's actually saying as much, not even Hackett, his friend and chief advocate on the tween decks. Woodberry made another noise, calculated to get Tottenhill's attention. The lieutenant found that irritating in the extreme.

"So, I was thinking," Hackett continued, "perhaps a splice of the old main brace, sir? It would do a great deal, to lift the men's spirits."

"Splice the main brace, eh?" The suggestion made Tottenhill uncomfortable. Issuing an extra ration of rum, which was what Hackett was suggesting, might well lift the men's spirits, but did they need lifting that much? They might think him weak if he did it.

But again, here he was chaffing under Biddlecomb's lack of consideration, yet ready to deny this little thing to the men. And they had been working awfully hard, as Hackett said. Biddlecomb, inconsiderate whore's son that he was, would never do the men this little favor.

"Sir? Beg pardon, sir." It was Woodberry. Tottenhill knew that the Yankee, Biddlecomb's pet, would not resist giving his entirely unwanted opinion. "Beg pardon, sir?"

"Yes, Woodberry, what is it?"

"Well, sir, I couldn't help but overhear what Hackett here said. Now I like my rum as much as the next man, but I don't know as up-spirits is the best idea now, sir. And the men'll all think Hackett talked you into it, sir."

Tottenhill felt his irritation mount with every word Woodberry said. "You presume to tell me how to run my vessel? Who do you think you are? I shall do what I think right, and if I want your counsel I'll ask for it, and I don't imagine that will happen anytime before the conversion of the Jews."

"Sir, I just meant—"

"Oh, I know what you meant, never doubt it. If you do not want a tot, then you need not have one. In which case I'll thank you to get a broom and see to sweeping out the cable tier."

"But, sir, the buntline—"

"Damn the buntline, get a broom and get below before I stop your tot for good!"

Woodberry took a long second to glare at Hackett, and then at Tottenhill, before mumbling, "Aye. Sir," and shuffling forward.

"Very well, Hackett," Tottenhill said with finality. He knew that after his display with Woodberry he could no longer deny Hackett his request. "The men have earned as much. Fetch the purser and tell him I have decided to issue an extra tot today."

"Thank you, sir," Hackett said, saluting crisply. "The men will be wonderfully grateful." And saying that he hurried off forward.

The distribution of the rum, like anything done by a well-trained and properly motivated crew, was carried out with amazing speed and efficiency. Not above four minutes later, Hackett settled on the heel of the bowsprit, displacing two of his messmates, and took a long pull from his tin cup.

"There. And didn't I tell you I could get that stupid bastard to issue us a tot? That's a shilling apiece, you gentlemen owes me, by my reckoning," Hackett said, barely containing his triumph.

"And we'll pay you once we gets it, mate, and you'll just have to wait till then," said Michael Jenkins, a fellow North Carolinian. "I'd like to see you get away with this with bloody Biddlecomb or Rumstick aboard."

"Sod Biddlecomb and sod Rumstick, them Yankee sons of bitches," Hackett said. "They don't run things here, any more than that dumb arse Tottenhill."

"You're getting a bit full of yourself, ain't you, Captain Hackett?"

" 'Captain Hackett'? I like that, I like that full well. Sets good on me, don't it?" Hackett took another pull of his rum and stared out at the flagship, with all the fleet's boats clustered around it.

It had been a productive twenty-four hours. Sneaking down into the cable tier to steal a nap, he had come across Weatherspoon doing the same thing. He raised a great ruckus, pretending to believe the sleeping midshipman injured or dead. Now Weatherspoon was relegated to the masthead as punishment for taking a caulk. With the other Yankees off the ship Hackett had made great advances in Tottenhill's confidence, and with Tottenhill in command it gave him great freedom to work his will.

He smiled as he thought of how suspicious he had been when first recruited. He had been afraid that the navy would be a floating hell, but in fact it was turning out to be the highlight of his career at sea.

And now was the time to prove once and for all who ruled on the lower deck.

"Look here, you bastards, you owe me a shilling each," he said.

"We ain't got a shilling, dumb arse, like I said," said Jenkins.

"Okay, then. What say you gentlemen help me in a little job and we'll forget all about the shilling."

Hackett looked at the five men sitting around him. His courtiers. His court jesters. They looked suspicious, as well they might.

"What job?"

"It's just a little thing. Got to do it right now, so drink up, boys. But don't you worry, you'll like it as much as I will."

The five tilted the last of their rum into their mouths, then sat silent, waiting for further instructions from Hackett. And Hackett, like a chess master, ran over in his mind his next move, and his move after that and his move after that. There was so much more to do. Oh, my, yes, there was so very much more yet to do.

CHAPTER 19

East Point

THE LIGHT OF THE SINGLE LANTERN ALLOWED WOODBERRY ONLY THE dimmest view of the cable tier, even after his eyes had adjusted to the dark. The cables themselves, great heaps of cordage like monstrous coiled snakes, occupied the majority of the space.

The tier itself was none too big, and moving around in that confined place was awkward. That, coupled with the low overhead, made Woodberry uneasy; he was used to the vast spaces on deck or aloft. Being thus confined induced a slightly panicked feeling.

On the deck under his feet he could feel the dried filth that had been carried aboard with the cables, the muck from the bottoms of rivers and harbors where the *Charlemagne* had anchored. He slashed at it with his broom, feeling the pain from his partially heeled hand shooting up through his arm. It felt good, a perfect complement to his mood.

The dim light prevented him from really seeing what he was doing, but he did not care. It was sweltering in that lowest part of the ship. He felt the sweat drip from his face. His hands were slick on the handle of the broom.

His anger, already great and still building, was not at his being given this miserable job, nor was it at his being denied an extra tot.

He was not even angry at Hackett for playing his little games.

Woodberry had been in enough ships to see Hackett's kind rise and fall. And he knew that generally, eventually, they fell, and when they did, they fell hard, with a healthy push from their shipmates. He was angry because Hackett seemed to be winning his game, tearing the crew apart along sectional lines, North and South. And Tottenhill, his infernal tool, too thick to see it, was helping him along.

He kicked at a rat that he could barely see and swept the dried dirt into a pile. He heard footsteps, bare feet, on the berthing deck overhead. He paused in midsweep and listened. The steps were coming down the ladder, aft.

He stepped out of the circle of light and peered in that direction. Whoever was coming, he doubted that they were his friends. Most of his friends were off with Biddlecomb on the sloop, as he would have been, had it not been for his broken hand.

"Woodberry, how are you doing? Careful you don't miss any dirt, now." Hackett stood in front of two other men, just beyond the edge of the light from the lantern. The two men behind him carried belaying pins, which they were making a halfhearted effort to hide.

"Come to bear a hand, Hackett? Be the first work you've done since you come aboard."

"Aren't you a funny one. No, I come to have a talk with you."

Woodberry remained silent. One of the men at Hackett's back was Gray. The other, deeper in the shadows, appeared to be Allen, but he was not certain. If they wanted to mix it up, he could take the two of them down, belaying pins or not. He did not think Hackett would participate in anything that could get him hurt.

At least he could take them down on deck. The thought of fighting in that narrow space, with the serpentine cables at his back, made the panic rise up again. He could taste it in his throat.

He pressed his lips together. He remembered that his hand was broken as well. If they made him do this, he would make them pay.

"You think you're cock of the tween decks, don't you, Woodberry? Well, I just want you to understand who runs things now."

Woodberry's hand moved automatically for the handle of his sheath knife and rested there. "Captain Biddlecomb runs things on this ship. Not you and not me."

"Ain't that nice, you and your little Biddlecomb."

Woodberry heard more steps behind him, coming from the forward ladder, the soft, barely audible sound of hard, bare feet on planking. He took a step back and looked in the direction of the sound. Jenkins and another man. Four against one on the cable tier was pushing the odds. If he could get up on deck, even the berthing deck, he would be all right. If he could get Ferguson down here, they could do for these sons of whores. But Ferguson was off on the sloop.

"I brought some witness with me, Woodberry, you bastard, so they can hear you say all proper that I'm first man on the tween decks," Hackett said.

"Sod off."

"Sod off, is it?" Hackett took a step closer, as did the other four, moving in on Woodberry, further confining him. The sweat on his forehead felt cold.

"Sod off, is it?" Hackett asked again. "You better say it, if you know what's good for you."

"Even if I said it, it don't make it true," Woodberry said, though he knew that he was wrong about that. If he was forced to admit in front of others, even Hackett's men, that Hackett was first man on the tween decks, then that would virtually guarantee that he was. It was like a gun crew, he thought. If the gun captain gets knocked down, the next man steps in. And on the lower deck he was captain and Hackett was the next man.

"You got something to say, Woodberry, you buggering coward?"

Coward. Woodberry was consumed with fear, a sensation that he was not accustomed to, because of the damned confines of the cable tier. His eyes darted around; he felt his palm slick on the handle of his knife. The fear, the thought of being afraid, made him sick.

"Come on then. Coward," Hackett said. He took another step. He was smiling and Woodberry knew that he could see the fear, and he knew that Hackett would think he was afraid of the threats, not the space, and he could not stand that.

"Son of a whore!" Woodberry roared, and lunged at Hackett, grabbing handfuls of his shirt and jerking him closer and bringing his knee up into Hackett's groin as he did. He could see the pain and fear in Hackett's eyes, smell the panic on his breath in that instant before Gray brought the belaying pin down on the knuckles of his broken hand.

He let go of Hackett's shirt, gasped in pain, and reached with his other hand for his knife. He felt Jenkins's hand on his arm, felt the sheath knife jerked from the sheath the instant before his hand reached it. He heard the sound of the knife hitting the ceiling as Jenkins flung it away.

He wheeled around and with his good hand hit Jenkins full in the face. The pain of the blow seemed to explode in his hand and shot up his arm. He knew he had broken at least one finger. But the effect of Jenkins was much worse than that. He flew back as if struck by round shot, and he and the man behind him, unable to step aside in the narrow space between cables and ceiling, fell into the darkness beyond the lantern's reach.

There was an ache in Woodberry's head and in his shoulders and he realized, dumbly, that he was being struck from behind, oddly ineffectual blows. He turned back and caught Gray's belaying pin in midswing and wrenched it from his hand. Hackett had stumbled away, doubled over against the cables.

Woodberry's terror of the confinement was gone, swept

away by his rage. The tight space was his ally now, preventing his attackers from massing on him. He punched Gray, remembering in the last instant his shattered hand and holding back as his fist made contact. The blow was weak, and it hurt Woodberry much more than it hurt Gray.

"Ahhh, son of a bitch!" Woodberry roared, grabbing his left hand loosely with his right. He felt a blow to his kidneys; Jenkins was up and hitting him from behind. He had half-turned when the man behind Gray, having clambered up on the narrow space on top of the cables, struck him on the side of the head with his belaying pin.

The blow swung him around, facing Jenkins. He had just the briefest glimpse of Jenkins's bloody face before he was struck again. He felt himself going down, and he grabbed ahold of Jenkins with both hands, determined to take the man down with him.

He felt Jenkins's arm around his neck as he pounded the man's stomach with both fists, screaming in pain each time he drove his shattered hands into the man's ribs. He felt Jenkins's grip loosen, felt repeated blows on his head and back.

"Bosun! Bosun's coming!" Woodberry heard someone—it might have been Hackett—whisper. Jenkins released his grip and Woodberry half fell to the deck. He felt feet stepping over him as his assailants fled forward.

"You son of a bitch!" Woodberry grabbed at Gray as he rushed past, but Gray squirmed out of his grip and was gone.

"What in the hell is acting here?" He heard Sprout's voice on the deck above. "Hey, there! What . . ."

Sprout's feet stepped onto the ladder. He was coming down to the cable tier. Sprout knew what was going on, and he would certainly have recognized the sounds of a fight. You didn't spend a lifetime at sea without recognizing those sounds. He would demand an explanation, and Woodberry would have to refuse or make up some obvious lie. The problems of the lower deck stayed on the lower deck. Bringing a problem like this aft would do more damage even than admitting that Hackett was first man of the tween decks.

Woodberry pulled himself to his feet and hurried forward. He made his way awkwardly up the ladder, unable even to touch the rungs with his battered hands, just as Sprout descended into the cable tier.

"Son of a bitch," Biddlecomb muttered to himself as he stared at the *Charlemagne* from the stern sheets of the boat as Ferguson steered for the Bahamian sloop. He did not have time to worry about what was going on there, he had an invasion to lead. He would send Rumstick over, let him worry about it, though that was just as likely to make things worse as better.

The boat pulled up alongside the sloop, and Biddlecomb stepped quickly up the two steps of the pilot ladder hung over the side. "Mr. Rumstick," he called, and the second officer stepped over and saluted.

"Look here, Ezra," he said in a low voice, "I've just been aboard *Charlemagne* and things aren't looking too good there. I don't know what's acting, but the mood is . . . brittle. You know what I mean? Like things are ready to break. Like they were on the *Icarus*, just before . . ."

"The mutiny?"

"Just so." Biddlecomb sighed, stealing himself to say what he had to say. "Ezra, I need you to go back aboard *Charlemagne*. Tell Tottenhill it's my orders. I'd make you acting first officer if I could, but I can't. Still, it'll do the men good just having you there."

"Humph," was all Rumstick said, frowning and looking across the water at the brig. If he was trying to hide his disappointment, he was doing a poor job. Biddlecomb knew full well what he was thinking. Not only did he not want to be stuck on the *Charlemagne,* under Tottenhill's command, he did not want to miss the action that was about to take place, the first offensive move by the American Navy and marine corps.

"He ain't going to want me aboard, Isaac. He'll take it to mean you don't trust him."

"Then that'll be the first damn thing he's got right in a while. Whatever he thinks, I'm still the captain of that bucket, he still does what I order him to do." Biddlecomb turned and followed Rumstick's gaze over toward the brig. "I would be delighted if he would disobey a direct order, then I could rid myself of him, but he's too clever by half for that."

"Why not take him with you aboard the sloop, here, and put me in command of *Charlemagne?*"

"A good try, Lieutenant, but I think not. It's never done, a captain and a first officer out of the ship at a time of action."

"And you don't want to be around the son of a whore any more than I do."

"And as captain that is my prerogative. I'm sorry, Ezra. And pray send Weatherspoon back with the boat. He can serve as my aide."

Then, much to Biddlecomb's relief, Rumstick shook his head and grinned. "Good God, what I do sacrifice for my country. Good luck, sir." He saluted smartly and then hopped down the ladder into the waiting boat.

Ten minutes later the three sloops and the schooner *Wasp* were under way, once again leaving the anchored fleet in their wake. With their shallow draft they eschewed the deep water to the north, moving boldly over the reefs where the larger vessels of the fleet could not follow.

They made their way nearly due south, sailing a beam reach in the warm, ten-knot breeze. They skirted past the eastern end of Athol Island, and there, spread out before them, with East Point straight ahead and the east entrance to the harbor off the starboard beam, was the island of New Providence.

Biddlecomb, standing at the leeward rail, put his telescope to his eye and stared at Fort Montegu three miles away. A plume of smoke was rising from the square, gray fort, but he could see no sign of activity beyond that. Not that it mattered much to him; his vessels would never be within range of the fort, and when it did come time to attack that stronghold, he would gladly abdicate leadership to Captain Nicholas, now aboard the *Providence*.

The deck of the sloop was crowded with marines. There was no need for secrecy now, and with the day growing warmer Biddlecomb did not have the heart to force them below, as inconvenient and irritating as it was to have them lolling about as if it were a county fair. He had at least declared that the after edge of the main hatch was the official start of the quarterdeck, and no one, save officers, came aft of that without his permission, thus keeping a portion of the deck clear for himself.

Lieutenant Faircloth, leaning on the rail next to Biddlecomb, breathed a deep lungful of the Caribbean air. "Marvelous! Absolutely marvelous! Is it always this fine in the Caribbean?"

"Well, it's a good deal hotter in the summer, and the hurricane season can be a bit of a problem, but, yes, in general I'd say it's always pretty nice. Have you never been here?"

"Hardly been out of Philadelphia, save for a little time in London and New York. I think this adventuring life suits me well."

Biddlecomb could not help but smile. "Pray, wait till we've had some real adventure before you decide how much you like it."

They continued south, through the translucent, light blue water, a color that could hardly be believed, past the dark patches where kelp covered reefs rose up to just below the surface. Biddlecomb guessed, from the reaction of the marines who lined the rails, peering and pointing down into the water and out at the lush island, that Faircloth was not the only man aboard who had seen little in his life beyond Philadelphia.

"And two and a half, and two and a half," the leadsman chanted. Two and a half fathoms; plenty of water still for the sloops. East Point was straight ahead, and half a mile off. They stood on for another five minutes, and then Biddlecomb hailed Weaver and Capt. John Hazard of the *Providence* and Hallock of the *Wasp,* ordering them to anchor in his lee. Together the four vessels rounded up and dropped their anchors and their sails together and came to rest on the placid water.

"The die is cast," Biddlecomb said to Faircloth.

"Right, well, let's get across this damned Rubicon and get on with it." The marine lieutenant was smiling, very much enjoying himself. "Sergeant Dawes, let's get these men formed up and ready to get in the boats!"

The two boats being towing astern were hauled alongside, and awkwardly the heavy-laden marines clambered over the bulwark and took their places on the thwarts. The same scene was repeated on each of the other three vessels, and soon eight boats full of sailors and marines were pulling for the rocky beach just north of East Point.

Biddlecomb sat in the stern sheets of the first boat, his knees forced up close to his body by the crowding, and scanned the shoreline through his telescope.

He had always thought it a lovely island, but the happy feeling that had attended past landfalls here had deserted him now. This time he was not just going ashore, he was leading an invasion.

The *Providence*'s boat reached the shore first. The crew tossed oars and the forefoot made a horrible crunching sound as it ran up on the rocky shallows that constituted the beach. The men at the bow jumped out, the water coming up to their knees, and hauled the boat farther ashore. Captain Nicholas stood and pushed his way through the marines and hopped down into six inches of ocean.

Biddlecomb's boat was next. "Toss oars," Ferguson called, and the two banks of oars went up and their boat hit the shore, making a sound at least as bad as that of the first boat. The sailors tumbled out, followed by the marines and then Weatherspoon and then the captain.

He adjusted his sword until it hung at the proper angle, then marched farther up the beach. All of the boats were ashore now, eight in all, and the ninety or so men they had carried, one-third of the invading force, were swarming over the shoreline. Muskets were stacked and cartridge boxes and powder horns checked, and men assembled into divisions, waiting for their comrades, waiting to march against Fort Montegu. The American invasion of New Providence was under way.

At the inland edge of the beach a narrow dirt road skirted the shore, leading in one direction southeast to East Point and in the other northwest to Fort Montegu. The fine dust that covered the surface of the road had a light brown color, bordering on white, almost exactly the color of a well-scrubbed deck. Small rocks were scattered about, and a few tenacious plants sprouted in those spots not grooved deep by cart wheels.

On the far side of the road, the inland side, the great green wave of forest crested, threatening to break and spill over the roadway. From that mysterious world came the occasional scream of birds and the constant buzz of insects and Biddlecomb could only imagine what else. Here and there amid the green vegetation, tall, flowering plants burst with color, like shells frozen in midexplosion. It was past noon and already hot, though the heat was tempered by the cool trades that blew over the island.

Biddlecomb looked down the road in one direction, then the other. There was no one to be seen; they might have been invading a desert island, for all he could tell.

He caught a movement in the corner of his eye and looked down. At his feet a patch of rock thrust up from the sand, and on the rock, standing motionless like a delicate china figurine, was a lizard. Then, slowly, aware it was being watched, the creature raised its four-inch body up on spindly legs. It bobbed its head up and down, slowly at first, then faster, and thrust a pink dewlap, like a strawberry, out from under its chin.

Biddlecomb smiled at the sheer audacity of the tiny creature. "I know right well how you feel," he said.

* * *

Fort Montegu was perhaps the most secure place on the island of New Providence. Built of huge blocks of native stone, the fort was nearly one hundred feet square and twenty feet high, with the walls, five feet thick at their narrowest, sloping gently inward from the base to the top of the ramparts. There was only one way in: a heavily secured door opening onto a tunnel with a rounded ceiling running right under the ramparts to the front door of the barracks.

Atop each of the four walls sat a battery of guns, an impressive arsenal of twelve-and eighteen-pounder cannon that commanded a 360-degree field of fire, from the eastern entrance of Nassau harbor to the north, to the single overland approach to the south. The strength of the fort was further augmented by another, smaller battery at the fort's northwest corner. It was little wonder that a former governor of New Providence had declared that, properly defended, Fort Montegu would make the island "the strongest possession on British America."

And to Lt. James Babbidge, standing on the southern wall and waiting for the messenger who a moment before had come charging in from the direction of Nassau, that knowledge did nothing to ease his fear. His short and inglorious career in the army had consisted mainly of parades and garrison duty, along with a brief stint in India. He had never actually been in combat, and he had certainly never been in command of a fortress under attack by an invading army.

Strewn around the upperworks of the fort were the thirty militiamen that had marched with him that morning, along with thirty more who had been sent to augment his force after the enemy's small vessels had been spotted making for East Point. Some were cleaning their weapons, some were sleeping, and others were engaged in card games or arguments. They all appeared relaxed, some even bored, though Babbidge was fairly certain that more than a few were just shamming calm, as he was doing.

He watched the messenger, a sergeant in the militia, come panting up the stairs. He would be carrying instructions, perhaps instructions to abandon Montegu and withdraw to Fort Nassau. That thought gave Babbidge a great sense of relief, followed by a flush of guilt for wishing such a cowardly thing.

"Sergeant," said Babbidge, returning the messenger's salute. As the day had progressed, he noticed, the militia seemed to grow increasingly formal, in the military line. "What brings you?"

"Message from Governor Browne, sir, who's just got back to Fort Nassau. He requests you send a force of men to reconnoiter and, if possible, prevent the rebels' landing, sir."

After a period of silence, Babbidge said, "Is that it?"

"Yes, sir. That's it, sir."

"Oh." Babbidge glanced around. All sixty or so pairs of eyes were on him. The governor, his commanding officer, was ordering him to leave the good stout fort and reconnoiter the enemy, attack if possible. But, no, he had not ordered him, Babbidge, to do it, just to send some of his men.

"Lieutenant Judkin," he began, and even as the words left his mouth, he knew that, terrified as he was, he could not be so craven as to cower in the fort while Judkin marched toward the enemy. He was struck with self-loathing for what he had almost done. "Pick thirty men. You and I will lead them south to see about these rebels."

It took another fifty minutes to pick the men and get them drawn up, with weapons and equipment, into two fairly regular columns on the parade ground outside the fort's gate. "It's like trying to herd cats, like bloody trying to herd cats," Lieutenant Judkin said, several times, as his exasperation got the better of him.

Babbidge was only vaguely aware of the lack of organization or military efficiency that pervaded the militia. He was thinking rather about the upcoming encounter with the large, well-armed, and no doubt cutthroat band of attacking rebels. Should he attack them first? Did he have the men to do that, and if so, did he and his men have the courage for it?

It was useless, he concluded, to speculate until he knew

what he was up against. He might find the Americans were a large and disciplined army, against whom it would be suicidal to move. And again he might find them all dead drunk on the beach. You could never tell with the rebellious type. He would have to wait and see.

"Ready, sir," Judkin reported.

"Right, then." Babbidge turned and looked at the twin lines of men. They did not look any happier than he to be sallying forth to meet the enemy. Some, in fact, looked angry and even frightened, and that gave Babbidge's courage a boost. "All right, you men," he called. "Follow me!" And with that he headed off down the road, and behind him thirty pairs of less than enthusiastic feet followed in ragged order.

Over half of the American invasion force, one hundred and sixty men, were on the beach, with the boats pulling back for the rest, when Biddlecomb saw the militia. He had walked back down the beach, was standing, in fact, with his feet in the surf and looking northwest along the curved shoreline when he saw the marching soldiers over half a mile away. They seemed of no great force, not above fifty men certainly, but they were still enemy troops, marching toward his own.

"Captain Nicholas, Captain Nicholas, sir, a word with you," Biddlecomb called out, splashing toward the marine captain and leading him out of earshot of the others. "I perceive there are enemy troops on the road there, and making for us."

"You're right, Biddlecomb, by damn," Nicholas said, sighting along Biddlecomb's pointed finger. Nicholas was a solid-built man in his midforties. Three months before, prior to beginning his career in the marine corps, he had owned a tavern in Philadelphia, a popular place whose clientele had provided the bulk of his troops come recruiting time. The qualities that made him a good tavern owner—brusque efficiency, frugality, and a willingness to suffer no nonsense—had thus far made him a good captain of marines as well. Of course he had never, until this moment, been faced with an armed enemy.

"Stupid bastards," the marine muttered, loud enough for Biddlecomb to hear. "If they'd attacked half an hour ago, when most of our troops was still on the transports, they might have done for us. Robertson, Faircloth, Michaels," he shouted to three of the lieutenants of marines, "get your companies together and set up some defense there to cover the rest of the landing. Set your companies in a semicircle, First Company there"—he pointed toward the road—"and Fourth there and Sixth over there."

The three lieutenants began shouting orders, though the men in their companies, having heard the captain's instructions as clearly as the officers had, were already snatching up muskets and cartridge boxes and hurrying off to take up their defensive positions.

"There." Nicholas turned to Biddlecomb and smiled, for the first time in Biddlecomb's memory. "That should make them militia bastards think twice about attacking regular troops."

Biddlecomb smiled as well, not so much in delight at the pending action but at Nicholas's reference to his marines as "regular troops," as differentiated from, and superior to civilian militia. "Let us hope, Captain," Biddlecomb said.

While it was unlikely that Lieutenant Babbidge would have considered himself a "militia bastard," he was indeed having second thoughts about attacking regular troops.

They had marched for two miles thus far under a hot sun. He could feel the grit from the road working its way under his clothing—an excessively heavy broadcloth coat, linen waistcoat, and silk shirt and breeches—and sticking fast to the film of sweat that coated his body. The strap of his musket was digging painfully into his shoulder, even after that short time, and every time he looked at the troops behind him, he was convinced that so far at least half a dozen had slipped away, heading back to the comfort and safety of their homes.

The Americans had been in view for the past mile. Indeed, it would have been hard to miss them, so great were their number as they plied between the ships and the shore and swarmed over the beach. This was not some trifling annoyance, it was a full-scale invasion, and Lieutenant Babbidge, vacillating between his fear of combat and his fear of humiliating cowardice, and entirely uncertain of what he should do, just kept marching.

The occasional murmurs from the men still following him grew louder and bolder as they too saw the invulnerability of the attackers. They were just over half a mile from the enemy, and still marching, when a group of rebels broke off from the cluster on the beach and ran up toward the road and, to Babbidge's unhappy surprise, quickly formed into an organized and credible line of defense, aiming at the Bahamians twice the number of muskets that the Bahamians could aim back.

"Halt!" Babbidge shouted, holding up a hand and stopping short.

The murmuring among his troops had turned to loud speculation, and more than a few men offered their opinions of the most prudent course of action. Lieutenant Judkin shouted, "Silence!" and the noise dropped by half.

"What do you think, Lieutenant Judkin?" Babbidge asked.

"There's a bloody lot of them, sir, more than I reckoned on."

"Yes, indeed. Would you agree that an attack is out of the question?"

"Good Lord, yes. We can't attack them, and them already formed up in defense."

"Very well," said Babbidge, greatly relieved that he was not the only officer unwilling to attack. Judkin's reaction was to him a clear affirmation that his decision was based on sound military reasoning and not cowardice at all.

But once again he had to make a decision, and once again he was torn between what he wished to do, which was retreat back to the fort, and what he knew he should do, which was to see what the rebels' intentions were.

Damn it all to hell, he thought. He had never wished to be an army officer in the first place, the whole thing had been his father's idea. And the old man didn't even have enough money to maintain his commission, so here he was on half-pay, neither fish nor fowl. How did it happen that he had to make these decisions?

"Very well," he said, more a sigh than a statement. "We were ordered to reconnoiter. Find me something that will serve as a white flag."

"What do you intend, sir?" Judkin asked.

"I intend to go ask those bloody rebels what they want with us."

CHAPTER 20

Fort Montegu

"YES, YOU ARE RIGHT, CAPTAIN," BIDDLECOMB SAID, STARING AT THE distant militia through his glass. He and Nicholas were standing just behind the line of defense flung across the beach. "The fellow has a white flag."

"Flag of truce! No one fire on it!" Nicholas roared to the men of the three companies, who were all training their muskets with great care on the man with the flag. "And all your damned muskets had best be at the damned half-cock! What do you think he wants, Biddlecomb?"

"I couldn't say. I should think he wants to negotiate, work out some kind of agreement."

"Humph," was all that Nicholas said, then he fell silent as they watched the distant militiaman. They could see, as he drew closer, that his flag of truce was in fact a white shirt tied to a musket. This he was waving wildly, in great sweeping arcs, as he approached, as if he thought the entire American army were half-blind and likely at any moment to shoot him down by mistake.

"We can see your sodding flag, ya stupid bastard," Nicholas muttered to himself, and then in a somewhat embarrassed and confessional tone said to Biddlecomb, "Look here, Captain . . . ah . . . I reckon I'm not much of a talking cove, if you follow me. I mean, this kind of negotiating, this ain't exactly in my line, and you, well, you have something of a reputation as . . . I mean no offense, of course . . ."

"Would you like me to talk to this fellow?"

"If you would be so kind. I'll be right there with you, of course."

"I would be happy to, Captain."

"But don't go promising anything, without we talk to the admiral."

"No, certainly not."

"And don't let on how many men we got. Let 'em think we've got this many again still on the ships."

"Good thought."

"And mind you don't tell him—"

"Captain Nicholas . . ."

"Very well, I was only saying . . ." The marine's words trailed off into a mutter, and he looked with renewed interest at the approaching, flag-waving militiaman.

At last the Nassauvian reached the American lines, and the marines, who were staring at him the way a mean dog will stare at a stranger in its yard, parted and let him through. He had apparently used his own shirt for the truce flag, for he was bare-chested under his broadcloth coat and linen waistcoat.

"I am looking for the officer in charge," he asked of the assembly in general.

"We are the officers in charge," Biddlecomb said, stepping forward. "I am Capt. Isaac Biddlecomb of the United Colonies brig-of-war *Charlemagne*, and this is Captain Nicholas, Captain of Marines of the United Colonies." Even as he said it, he was impressed by the stately, martial sound of those titles.

"Good day, sirs. I am Lt. James Babbidge, assistant to Gov. Montfort Browne, and officer of the New Providence militia."

The lieutenant, seemingly on the verge of panic, had barely enough wind in his lungs to get that statement out.

After an awkward silence, stretching over a quarter of a minute, Biddlecomb asked, "What may we do for you, Lieutenant?"

"I've . . . ah . . . come to see . . . who, in fact, you are and what are your intentions."

Biddlecomb smiled, struck with the directness and naïveté of the question. An enemy force lands on your beach and you march up and ask them who they are and what they want? Well, why not? "We are the naval and marine forces of the United Colonies of America."

"So, you are American rebe—" The lieutenant seemed to suffer a burst of courage, but it quickly dissipated and he fell silent again.

Biddlecomb considered the nervous, shirtless lieutenant, and it dawned on him that, given the right amount of bluster on the Americans' part and backwardness on the part of the Bahamians, this invasion might be carried off without bloodshed after all. "We have been sent by the Congress of the United Colonies in order to possess ourselves of the powder and stores on this island belonging to His Majesty."

"Oh," said Babbidge, and though Biddlecomb waited for him to say more, nothing came.

"Was there anything else, Lieutenant? Would you, for instance, care to negotiate a surrender?"

"I most certainly would not!" This suggestion, apparently, was sufficiently outrageous for Babbidge to forget his discomfort, for the moment at least. "No one short of the governor could do such a thing, and I believe you will find, sir, that he is not disposed to so pacific a course." Then, realizing that he may have gone to far, he added, "You understand, I have no doubt."

"Yes, very well, Lieutenant." Babbidge clearly did not have the authority or the courage to make any sort of decision. "Forgive me, but if you are not here to surrender, then I'm afraid Captain Nicholas and I have a great deal still to do. Not even half of our troops are landed yet, and there's the artillery, which is problem enough, but add to that the cavalry divisions and all their damned horses and . . . well, you can see we are quite occupied."

"Yes, all right," Babbidge said, making no move to leave. The present circumstance was so unlike any social situation that any of the men had encountered before that no one knew just how to proceed.

"Perhaps you had best rejoin your troops?" Biddlecomb prompted.

"Oh. You're not going to take me prisoner?"

"By God, but you're a stupid bastard!" Captain Nicholas spoke for the first time.

"You came under a flag of truce, Lieutenant. You may go."

"Oh. Certainly. Good day, then, gentleman," Babbidge said, a look of profound relief on his face. He turned and hurried back up the beach.

"Well, if that's what we have to contend with," Nicholas said, spitting in the sand, "I reckon we'll be having a rum punch in the governor's house by sundown today."

No more than twenty minutes later, Lieutenants Babbidge and Judkin, at the head of their company of militia, were admitted back through the arched entryway of Fort Montegu. It had taken them considerably less time to return to the fort than it had to sally forth and meet the enemy, this due to a willingness on the part of all the militiamen to move much more swiftly in the retreat than in the advance.

The lieutenant made his way down the long, dark, cool entryway of the fort, then back into the sunshine at the far end. The door to the barracks was in front of him, and on either side stairs led up to the wide landing just below the ramparts and the guns. He chose the stairs to his right, climbing the fifteen feet up to the fort's upperworks.

Governor Browne had arrived during his absence, marching at the head of eighty more militiamen. Browne had pushed his large self into a narrow observation platform cut out of the wall in the fort's southwest corner and was staring intently southward through a telescope. He was in his uniform, his red coat with its epaulets and numerous medals, a wig like a marble sculpture perched on his head.

"Governor, I'll report on the situation, if you wish," Babbidge said, standing on the first step and looking up at the governor's back.

"Just a moment, Lieutenant," Browne said, never taking the glass from his eye.

Two minutes later the governor said, "A lot of those damned rebels, isn't there. Damned good thing I brought more troops, enough to stop those sons of whores in their tracks, push 'em right back into the sea."

"Yes, sir. By my reckoning there were a thousand rebel troops at least, and more to be landed, as well as . . ." Babbidge stopped there. The mention of artillery and cavalry had thoroughly unnerved him on the beach, but now, back in Fort Montegu, he was not entirely certain he believed it.

"Yes, I can see them," Governor Browne continued, "they're on the march already. Damn me, damn me, damn me. They'll cut us off from the town, lay siege to us, and just march right past, sack Nassau, and us cooped up here like a fox in a tree." Along the southern wall of the fort men were standing on the guns and ramparts, peering along the rocky shoreline at the mass of rebel troops that could now be seen marching toward them. The murmuring of the civilian soldiers grew louder with each passing minute.

"Very well," Browne said, squeezing out of the hole in the wall and descending a step.

"Sir, I spoke under flag of truce with their officers, and I was informed that they've come for the King's military stores. Powder and whatnot."

"Military stores, eh? Oh, we'll give them military stores. You there." The governor pointed toward a group of men peering over the south wall. "Clear away three of these guns and load 'em. We'll teach those treasonous bastards a lesson they won't soon forget."

The men began slowly, grudgingly, loading the guns, and

the governor turned to Babbidge. "Lieutenant, get the men assembled. Once those guns are fired, we're going to spike them and abandon the fort. Quickstep it back to Nassau. We must get that gunpowder on Chambers's sloop and off the island, keep it from their hands."

Babbidge wondered about the governor's promise, made just a minute before, to push the rebels into the sea, but he knew better than to ask.

Half the sun was still visible, and the other half was gone, dipped below the western horizon, and Biddlecomb, sitting on the wide stone wall of Fort Montegu, his feet dangling in a section cut out of the southeast corner, felt more genuinely content than he had since leaving Philadelphia.

The taking of the fort had been a bloodless affair, simpler than he had dared dream it would be.

As soon as the marines and sailors had landed, they were formed up in columns, Biddlecomb, Nicholas, and Weatherspoon at the head, and marched off north along the road that skirted the crescent-shaped indent in the shoreline called Sandy Bay.

It seemed impossible to Biddlecomb that the Nassauvians would not try to cut them off on that narrow, exposed, and constricted road, with the jungle on their left hand and the ocean on their right. He knew virtually nothing about land fighting, but that seemed to him a reasonable thing to do.

With that thought on his mind he was not surprised when the first of the fort's great guns went off with that familiar flat boom, followed a second later by the scream of round shot overhead. It was a sound he knew well, but one that he associated with the deck of a ship, not the dusty, hot road of a Caribbean island.

Up and down the column the sergeants called for silence, steadying the men and keeping them marching into the face of it. Another gun fired, and another, and a moment later the enemy's troops came pouring out of the fort, marching double-time, muskets glinting in the sun. Nicholas called for the Americans to prepare to form the column into ranks for firing, and the order was still being passed down the line when it became clear that the enemy was not double-timing it to the attack, but rather making a hasty retreat back toward Nassau. They fired no more guns. They did not even bother closing the gate to the fort.

That evening the victorious invaders had enjoyed an excessive dinner of fresh fruit, vegetables, and sides of beef. That fine repast, most welcome after two months of salted meat and dried peas from a cask, was donated by locals who adamantly proclaimed their sympathy with the American cause, and who went to great lengths to explain to Biddlecomb just which houses were theirs and asked might they be spared when the town was sacked?

Biddlecomb reveled in the splendor of the tropical evening. With the warm trade winds blowing over him, and a belly full of food that had never seen the inside of a barrel, and the rich smells of a tropical island, the *Charlemagne* and Tottenhill and that world of worry seemed far away.

He thought again of the local militia, firing three guns and then marching, practically running, in retreat.

Perhaps, he thought, it is they who are the lizards in this fight, and not us at all.

President of His Majesty's Council Brown could only shake his head, he could not even manage a smile, so much had his former amusement turned to disgust, when the gate of Fort Nassau swung open and Governor Browne marched in like the triumphant Caesar returning to Rome. At his side and two paces back was the parasitic Babbidge, and behind them the militiamen, far fewer militiamen than had sallied forth.

Nothing about them indicated that they had been in a fight, so their much reduced number, Brown supposed, was a result of desertions. That they were here, and not at Fort Montegu where they were supposed to be, suggested that they had abandoned to the invaders the only decent fort in the islands.

"Governor, I'm somewhat surprised to see you," Brown said, walking across the parade ground as Governor Browne halted his troops. "Were you overrun at Montegu?"

"Quite nearly so, to be sure. A thousand of the rascals if there's one. Tried to cut us off from the town—and nearly succeeded, I dare say. But we gave them a good cannonading, almost drove them back into the sea before we was forced to abandon our position and fall back. But I reckon they'll think twice before attacking again."

"I should imagine," said President Brown. The militia, he could see, now consisted of proportionally fewer of the island's gentlemen and prosperous citizens than it had that morning. "Your numbers seem somewhat depleted. Did you have casualties?" he asked, confident that the governor would detect no irony in the question.

"Some light wounds, I think, nothing serious. A few of our number took leave to see to their own affairs."

The few to which the governor referred amounted to at least half of the militia, as far as Brown could see. He could just picture them, slinking away on the dark road between Fort Montegu and Fort Nassau, racing home to collect their valuables and pack them off, along with wives, children, and slaves, to the interior of the island. "And what are your plans, if I may ask?"

"First thing, we have to get some troops up to the Government House. If those rebels take that high ground, they could enfilade this fort. Enfilade it. Then we need every able man or Negro on the island.

"Babbidge." The governor turned to his aide, who looked as if he were about to fall asleep on his feet, in contrast to Browne's overwhelming energy. "I want you to go and issue a proclamation by beat of drum. Offer a reward of a pistol to every free Negro or any others that will enter the fort armed. And those gentlemen that left us back there, send someone to round them up. I want every citizen of note to meet here at . . . what time is it? Half past six? Say eight o'clock, here at the fort. Here we shall make our stand."

The militia, most of whom were now sitting, were something less than stirred by these words. "And what of the military supplies?" President Brown asked.

"The military supplies we hold on to. If we burn every last ounce of powder defending these stores, so be it, but we will not turn them over to rebels."

The governor's voice had a determination that Brown rarely heard, a determination that generally meant that the governor would soon be changing his mind. The one opportunity to stop the Americans, hitting them while they were landing their troops, was gone. Not only were the rebels now ashore, but they already had possession of half of the island's defenses.

"Very good," Brown said, and at the same moment he came to a decision. Conquest by the rebels was inevitable now. If that conquest was to be orchestrated properly, by which he meant orchestrated to his benefit, then he had better start doing it himself.

Biddlecomb came to the far end of the wall, paused, then turned and walked back toward the steps leading down to the ramparts below. It was somewhere around ten o'clock at night. Thirteen hours since they had been driven out of Nassau harbor. Six hours since they had taken Fort Montegu. It had been a hell of a day. It was time to go to bed.

He was halfway there when he heard the sound of oars grinding in tholes and blades dipping in the water. He peered out over the rocky shoreline, and slowly a boat appeared, resolving out of the dark, and in the stern sheets sat Mr. Midshipman Weatherspoon, returning from the flagship, to which he had been dispatched with reports of the day's activities. Biddlecomb sighed. Sleep would now have to wait until he heard what the commodore had to say.

Three minutes later Weatherspoon stood before him, saluting, a sheaf of papers under his arm. "Commodore's compliments to you and Captain Nicholas, sir, and he's more than pleased about taking the fort and without losing a man, sir. He begs you take care to preserve the military supplies. And he sent these along, to be distributed to the natives here."

The midshipman handed the papers to Biddlecomb, who called for a lantern. Each sheet contained the same words, each written in a different hand. Biddlecomb could picture the commodore collecting together every man on the flagship who could write and setting them to it. It must have looked like a seagoing scrivener's shop. He angled the top sheet toward the light and read:

> To the Gentlemen, Freemen and Inhabitants of the Island of New Providence:
>
> The reasons of my landing an armed force on the Island is in Order to take Possession of the Powder and Warlike Stores belonging to the Crown, and if I am not Opposed in putting my design in Execution the persons and Property of the Inhabitants Shall be Safe, neither shall they be Suffered to be hurt in Case they make no Resistance.
>
> Given under my hand on board the Ship Alfred March 3rd. 1776.
>
> E.H. Cr. in Chief.

Biddlecomb nodded his head as he read the manifesto. "Excellent, excellent, I think the people of the island will be most disposed to help us. In any event they don't seem overly disposed to fight.

"Lieutenant Faircloth," he called to the lieutenant of marines, who happened to be in command of the sentries for that watch. "Pray get together a company of your men and distribute these to some of those gentlemen that were here tonight, the ones with homes nearby. Tell them to see these are spread all over the island. Tell them it's their best hope for saving their homes from the torch."

"Aye, sir," said Faircloth, reading the manifesto even as he called for Sergeant Dawes to assemble the men.

Biddlecomb thanked Weatherspoon for his service and dismissed him, then headed for his own bed, suddenly aware of how tired he was. He was halfway along the wall, halfway to the steps, when the sentry on the west wall, facing the town of Nassau, sang out.

"Halt! Who are you, then?" he shouted, his voice loud in the still night. Biddlecomb froze and looked toward the west wall, as did everyone else who was awake. Sleeping men stirred and sat up. A muffled response came from the ground below.

"Sir." The sentry nearly collided with Biddlecomb as Biddlecomb made his way to the west wall and the sentry made his way to the east to find him. "Fellow down there, looks like a gentleman, says he's here to talk to the commanding officer. Do you want to talk to him, sir, or should I get Captain Nicholas?"

"I'm here," Nicholas growled as he stepped up onto the wall, dressed only in breeches and a linen shirt, the long, untucked tails of which hung down in front and behind. As he walked, he buckled his sword belt over the whole thing. "Now who in the hell is this, and what does he want at this hour of the night? If it's some son of a whore pleading with us not to sack his house, I swear I'll burn it down myself just to spite him."

"He won't say what he wants, sir, except to let on he's some important cove."

"Well, if he thinks we're going to just open the gate, he's some stupid cove. You men there, wrestle out that ladder and let it over the side. If they want to storm this fort, they'll have to do it up the ladder one at a time." Then as the men slid the long ladder over the edge to let the nocturnal emissary climb up onto the wall, Nicholas muttered to Biddlecomb in a voice much less gruff and demanding, "Here, you talk to this bastard, like you done the other."

The bastard, if such he was, to whom Nicholas referred made his way to the top of the ladder and stepped awkwardly around and onto the wall. He was dressed in a cotton shirt and breeches. His stockings were silk, not wool, and the buckles on his shoes glinted in the moonlight. The waistcoat that perfectly enveloped his midriff was silk as well, elaborately embroidered. White, ruffled cuffs seemed to explode out of the ends of his coat sleeves.

The man turned to Biddlecomb and Nicholas, seeming to know instinctively who was in command. "Gentlemen, I am President of His Majesty's Council John Brown. I come as an official representative of His Majesty's government."

"Humph," said Nicholas.

"Good evening, sir. I am Capt. Isaac Biddlecomb of the Continental brig-of-war *Charlemagne*. This is Capt. Samuel Nicholas, in command of the Continental Marines. We are here as representatives of the Continental Congress."

"An honor, sir," Brown said, bowing at the waist.

"Now see here," said Nicholas. "If you got me out of bed just to ask we don't burn your house down . . ."

"Oh, never, sir. Never in life. I am as much concerned with the welfare of you and your men as ever I am with my own property. I am . . . a great supporter of your republican ideals."

"Indeed," said Biddlecomb, now fully convinced that this emissary was here primarily on a mission of self-interest. He had seen it before, many times.

"Yes, Captain. I have followed what has been taking place in the American colonies with great interest. In the name of liberty I welcome you to New Providence."

"And in the name of liberty I thank you. Now what can we do for you? Or, more to the point, what can you do for us?"

"Perhaps a great deal. But I must know, sir, what are your intentions here?"

"The entire subjugation of the island. The routing of His Majesty's government, the establishment of an American naval base here, the liberation of all of the island's possessions, and the raising of an army to help in the further subjugation of the Bahamian Islands."

"Oh," was all that Brown was able to say.

"However, we are at liberty to modify those plans to some degree. For example, the extent to which we must rout the present government will depend, of course, on the extent of cooperation that we receive."

"Yes, of course," Brown said, having recovered his wits. "That is precisely my point. The thing of it is, I am much disposed to help you, indeed in the name of liberty I would very much like to assist in the Continental Congress's endeavors. The problem is the governor, Montfort Browne."

"Brown?" Nicholas interjected. "Is everyone here named Brown? Some relation of yours?"

"He is Browne with an *e*, sir, I am Brown without. I think if his removal were to be the goal of the invasion force, I could quite well guarantee the cooperation of the locals. If it is military stores that you need, you shall have them. I have gone to great lengths to see that no damage has come to them, and that none have been removed from the island."

"Is that a fact?" Nicholas interrupted again. "Well, you spiked these damned guns before we got to them. Do you know how much of a problem it's going to be repairing them damned touchholes?"

"That was Governor Browne who did that, not I, which is very much to my point. Sir . . . ," he continued, turning to Biddlecomb, but Biddlecomb's attention was elsewhere. Indeed he had been distracted for the past several minutes by glimpses of something, he could not tell what, bobbing in the surf and nudging against the sandy beach. It looked like wreckage, but not quite, glowing dull in the moonlight fifty yards away on the harbor side of the point. Whatever it was, it was out of place, and he was feeling increasingly uneasy about it.

"I was saying, sir," Brown tried again, but Biddlecomb held up his hand.

"A moment, sir. Weatherspoon"—he turned to the midshipman, who had just appeared on the rampart—"get five of our men together, pistols and cutlasses, and fetch a lantern along. Captain Nicholas, I am going to see what that is out there in the surf. You, sir"—he turned to Brown—"will accompany me."

Four minutes later Isaac stepped from the ladder onto the hard ground surrounding the fort. He led his little troop toward the water, Weatherspoon on his right side, Brown on his left. The hard-packed dirt yielded to soft sand as they made their way toward the edge of the harbor. The water lapped gently at the beach, surging over the sand and retreating again, and into this water he walked, the better part of a lifetime at sea making him quite immune to the discomfort of wet shoes and stockings.

"Bring that lantern up here," he said, never taking his eyes from the flotsam, and a sailor stepped up to his side, holding the lantern over his head.

It was lumber. A great quantity of lumber floating in the harbor and pushing up against the sand of the beach. Long pieces of fresh-cut wood, shining in the lantern light the color of bleached bone.

"Fetch one of those boards out," he ordered. "There, the long one." Two sailors splashed out into the warm Caribbean water, lifted the fresh-cut piece of wood, and brought it ashore.

"Okay, now break it in two. Put it across that rock there." The men placed it like a seesaw over a rock. Three stood on one end and three climbed up on the other, and with a great rending crack—a sound that invariably set Biddlecomb's teeth on edge as it so often signaled disaster on shipboard—it broke.

He stepped up to the jagged, broken edge, motioning for the lantern to be brought closer. The men crowded around, peering over his shoulder, though to the best of his knowledge they had not a clue as to what he was looking for.

"It's dry inside." Biddlecomb turned to President Brown. "It's not been floating long. What do you make of this?"

Brown shrugged and shook his head, clearly hoping to look innocent and failing. "I do not know."

Biddlecomb looked down at the broken plank and then out at the dozens and dozens of others floating in the water. Such perfectly good lumber, drifting away. It put him in mind of those few times he had been forced to jettison valuable stores to lighten his vessel to aid in escape.

He stood up quickly. Jettisoned cargo. It had to be jettisoned cargo, what else could it be? What else would explain so much lumber floating in the harbor? A board or two might be dropped in the water by accident, but not this many, and these were only the ones that he could see.

They were floating down harbor, bound for sea, so they came no doubt from a vessel anchored within. Why would a ship at anchor in a safe harbor jettison a valuable cargo?

"Oh, damn me to hell," Biddlecomb whispered as a possible answer came to him. "Weatherspoon"—he turned to the midshipman—"and you men, take the jolly boat and get out to the flagship. If Hopkins is asleep, wake him, and . . . no, belay that. There's no time." The commodore might well ask for more proof before getting under way, and in the interim lose the stores. But he could order the *Charlemagne* under way with no questions asked.

"Go straight for the *Charlemagne.* Tell Tottenhill I suspect that the island's military stores are being loaded onto a ship with the intention of taking them off the island." The only reason that he could think of for a ship at anchor to jettison a cargo was to quickly make room for another.

He turned and looked at the wood drifting out of the harbor. The tide was ebbing and the breeze was easterly, as usual. "They'll make for the western end of the harbor." He considered going himself, taking command of the *Charlemagne,* but his place was here, where Hopkins had ordered him. As it was, he was taking great liberties sending the *Charlemagne* off without the commodore's permission.

"Tell Tottenhill to just slip the cable and go, try to cut them off. Then tell Hopkins what I suspect. Tell him we must seal off the harbor, stop them from taking the military stores off the island. That is," he added, turning to Brown, "what you are intending to do, is it not?"

"Believe me, sir, I am as betrayed by this as you. I tried to warn you about the governor. He is a treacherous man. Had you arrested him today, you would not have this problem now."

"Well, sir, for your sake, and the sake of this island, let us hope that my men are able to intercept those stores before they leave the harbor." Biddlecomb's hand reached automatically for the hilt of his sword, and he alternately clenched and unclenched the brass-bound handle. He was at once furious and consumed with anxiety. Their entire raison d'être was to fetch military stores, and now those stores were being whisked away.

In the wake of Biddlecomb's genuine anger, President Brown chose to remain silent.

CHAPTER 21

Lieutenants of the Charlemagne

STUPID BASTARD, RUMSTICK THOUGHT. HE LEANED AGAINST THE larboard rail of the quarterdeck and glared at Tottenhill's back as the first officer stared out into the night. It had been like that all day, a sort of informal standoff, since he had first reported back aboard.

He had come on deck just as Biddlecomb's sloop had won its anchor, heading off for the invasion, and he found men sitting, actually sitting, and doing nothing constructive that he could see.

Tottenhill had said merely that there was nothing for them to do, an absurd contention, for there was always something to do. But for every suggestion that Rumstick made, as deferentially as he was able, Tottenhill had some reason that it could not be done. They at last settled on chipping rust from round shot, the least useful thing that Rumstick could think of, and so the men sat and banged away at six-pound cannonballs.

Tottenhill had never been a bad officer, never backward in his duty that Rumstick had seen, merely an intolerable bore. This stubbornness and coddling of the men was something new, inexplicable, and in Rumstick's opinion, dangerous. The first officer seemed to resist any suggestion that Rumstick made, merely because he had made it.

"Hackett," Ezra called down to the waist. On that warm

night nearly all of the hands were topside, but Hackett's watch was officially on deck, and Hackett seemed to be making himself comfortable, too comfortable by half. "Hackett, nip aloft and bust the bunt of that fore t'gan'sl up on the yard and snug up the gasket. It's hanging there like a dead man."

Hackett stood and looked aloft and then looked aft at Rumstick. "That's boy's work. Able bodied seamen don't work above the topsail yard."

Rumstick was silent for a long second, taken utterly aback by this statement. He felt his eyes go wide and his fists clench up. "Able-bodied seamen work wherever in hell I tell them to work, you son of a whore! Get over here, I'm going to rip your fucking lungs out!" he said, his voice starting at a conversational level and building to a roar as he took one step toward Hackett, then another and another.

He was at the quarterdeck ladder, starting to move fast, when Hackett, seeing the probability of serious bodily injury, flung himself into the rig and raced aloft. Rumstick heard snickers from various quarters of the deck, and muttering from others.

"You are a lieutenant, Rumstick, need I remind you?" Tottenhill spoke for the first time in an hour.

"I am aware of my rank, Mr. Tottenhill," Rumstick replied, watching Hackett clamber over the futtock shrouds and on to the foretop.

"Then pray act like it, and not like you were still a bosun or some other rogue. It is not your position to threaten the men with a beating. If you cannot get them to obey your orders through the force of your authority, then you have no business being an officer. The quarterdeck is a place for gentlemen."

"Is that a fact? Well, I don't know much in the gentleman line, so pray, enlighten me. You reckon I should just let Hackett get away with whatever he might please? Or should I have him flogged like you done?"

"Your manner of speaking, sir, is inappropriate, both to your inferiors and your superiors."

"Don't you come it the superior with me. You might have got some patron in the Congress to appoint you first officer on this bucket, but we're in the same gunroom here."

"Why did you pick on Hackett just now?" Tottenhill asked, stepping across the quarterdeck to face Rumstick.

"Because Hackett's a lazy, mouthy son of a bitch of a sea lawyer, and I can see he's poisoning the crew."

"And not because he's from North Carolina?"

"North Carolina? What in hell does that have to do with it?"

"I have observed how you and Biddlecomb give preference to the Yankees in the crew, how you slight those of us from the South. I am perfectly aware of how you undermine my authority, how you pick on the men that I brought with me, and I am quite tired of it. Yes, I am aware of your little Yankee cabal. I have no doubt that this conversation shall be related to Biddlecomb as soon as he is back aboard."

"For one thing," said Rumstick, now equally confused and angry, "it's *Captain* Biddlecomb. For another, what's said in the gunroom stays in the gunroom, I don't tell tales in the great cabin. And if you think any of this has to do with what state you are from . . . good God, you are as dense as the rudderpost! Don't you see what's happening here? God knows we've all tried to work with you, but you are the most intolerable, long-winded . . ."

"Long-winded? Long-winded, is it? You've never tried to work with me, you or Biddlecomb, your Yankee cabal." Tottenhill was building momentum; Rumstick had the impression that he was venting some long-held frustration. "Biddlecomb passes me right by, the first officer. Never has me to the great cabin—"

"He can't endure having you around! Don't you see that? Oh, it might be nice to think that Biddlecomb and me don't like Southerners, isn't that easy," Rumstick said, venting some frustrations of his own. "But it's you we can't stand, can't you see that? You're intolerable. And now you're off on this mad idea about us picking on North Carolina men, and standing up for that son of a whore Hackett, who's playing you like a goddamned flute. My God, sir, but you are a blockhead!"

Tottenhill reared back, a look of horror on his face. "Blockhead? Did you call me a blockhead? A superior officer?"

"Yes, I did, damn your eyes." Rumstick could feel himself going, loosing his grip on whatever it was that kept him from plunging into the abyss of uncontrolled fury. He hated it when this happened—it had nearly gotten him killed on several occasions—but beyond a certain point he could not stop himself.

"You prance around here like some French dancing master," Rumstick continued, louder, his control slipping more and more, "finding plots and undermining the captain's authority. I've had about all I can take, I tell you. I ain't in the habit of taking orders from someone I got no respect for."

"Well, you had best get in the habit!" Tottenhill hissed through clenched teeth. "And as of now you are relieved of your duty, sir. You may go below. In fact, I order you below."

"You order me below, do you?" Rumstick growled, their entire conversation being carried out in low, menacing tones. "Well, listen here, Mr. Gentleman Lieutenant, if you're so worried about me being a gentleman, then why don't you show me how it's done? Why don't you and me go over to that little island yonder and settle this whole thing like gentlemen?"

Tottenhill glanced over at the island, a part of the little archipelago thrown out west of Rose Island, a dark hump on the dark sea, no more than a cable length away. He looked back at Rumstick, his face set in a scowl, and then back at the island.

"Unless you're afraid," Rumstick said, though he knew that Tottenhill was not. His anger and disgust with the man did not so blur his vision that he would unfairly assign cowardice to the lieutenant. He said the words to manipulate Tottenhill into a fight, and as he said them, he thought of himself as an unsubtle version of Isaac Biddlecomb.

"I am not afraid, you bastard, but I have my duty. I am not to leave the ship." Tottenhill was clearly torn between what he wanted to do, which was stick a sword in Rumstick, and what he knew he must do, which was to stay with his command.

Rumstick understood that conflict, for he felt it as well, and even as he pushed Tottenhill into satisfying honor, he wondered if it was such a good idea. But it was too late for such considerations. The blood was up now.

"Come on, you son of a whore," Rumstick said, just above a whisper. "We can't go on like this, we got to settle it sometime. Might as well be now. And it ain't like you're doing anything but sitting on your arse."

"Very well. Mr. Sprout," Tottenhill called forward, "please bring the jolly boat around."

Ten minutes later the small boat ground up on the sandy beach and the two men at the oars—Rumstick on the larboard and Tottenhill on starboard—laid the oars down on the thwarts and jumped into the shallow water. Without a word they pulled the boat up on the sand, then moved twenty feet up the beach, turned, and drew their swords.

The sound of steel grating on steel as the weapons left their scabbards seemed loud to Rumstick on the quiet evening. There was enough of a moon for him to see his adversary quite distinctly. He removed his coat, as had Tottenhill, his white shirt like a ghost against the dark background. The silver blade of his sword stood out against the low, dense foliage of the island.

Rumstick felt a tightening of his muscles, a general tensing. It was not fear, really, not as Rumstick understood fear, but more of a heightened awareness. He had no notion of how good a swordsman Tottenhill was, and it did occur to him that he might be killed in the next few moments, but the thought was more academic, an interesting concept to ponder when he had time.

"To first blood?" Tottenhill said, breaking the silence. "I should not care to hang for killing the likes of you."

"First blood." Rumstick's hot anger had cooled into something more visceral, more permanent. He was not thinking beyond this fight, as Tottenhill apparently was. He intended for first blood to come when he stuck his sword through Tottenhill's heart.

Tottenhill took a sideways step, the tip of his sword making little circles in the air, just visible to Rumstick. Rumstick circled away, moving in the opposite direction. He took an exploratory lunge and Tottenhill deflected the blade easily, lunged himself, and Rumstick, with more difficulty, knocked the sword aside.

This was not at all Rumstick's area of combat, he realized as he circled cautiously. His fighting had been hand-to-hand on crowded decks, riotous and disorganized, or the frenzied mob actions of the Sons of Liberty. It occurred to him as he leapt back from the jabbing point of Tottenhill's sword that for all of the fighting he had done, he could not recall a fight like this, one against one, no one else about. A civilized duel.

Tottenhill lunged again and again, coming on fast, his sword moving with a speed that was hard to follow in the dark, and Rumstick found himself being pushed back, his legs tiring as he tried to move with some agility in the soft sand, his sword just barely able to hold the lieutenant off. This won't do, he thought, this won't do.

Tottenhill lunged, fully extended, and Rumstick managed to deflect the strike, and then with a shout he slashed out at Tottenhill, wild, undisciplined, fighting the way he was used to fighting, as if he were attacking an entire crew of a ship that he had boarded through the smoke.

Now Tottenhill took a step back, and another and another, breathing hard, moving with as much difficulty as Rumstick on the beach. Three steps, four steps, and then he stopped, planting his feet at right angles, holding that spot of ground and making Rumstick stop as well.

He's good, he's damned good, Rumstick thought. There was no sound now, save for heaving breath, his and Tottenhill's, and the clash of steel on steel.

But no, there was something else. Rumstick took a step back, disengaging, and he and Tottenhill stared at one another, hatred flashing like their steel in the moonlight, catching their breath. And over that sound he heard the creak of oars in tholes. A boat pulling toward them.

He had half-turned his head to the sound when Tottenhill moved again, and Rumstick leapt back, clear of the attack. They fought on, but now a part of Rumstick's mind was on the approaching boat, and he could do no more than bat Tottenhill's sword away.

"Sir? Lieutenant Tottenhill?" Midshipman Weatherspoon's voice called out from the water, startling Rumstick. His eyes darted toward the water, a fraction of a second, and he felt the hot, tearing sensation of Tottenhill's blade across his right forearm, felt the warm, wet blood spread across his skin.

"You son of a bitch!" he shouted, drawing back and looking from his cut arm to the lieutenant, who stood back with sword held at his side.

"First blood," Tottenhill said.

"First blood, my fucking arse, I was—"

"Sirs, sirs?" Weatherspoon ran up the sand and stopped a few feet from the combatants. "Sirs . . . sweet Jesus, have you been dueling?"

There was a pause, and then Tottenhill said, "What do you want?"

"I've a message for you, from the captain. Mr. Sprout said you were here, didn't say why. The captain thinks the people in Nassau are trying to send off the island's military stores. He wants you to slip the cable and go after them and . . . what in hell were you two thinking, beg your pardon, dueling like this?"

It seemed oddly appropriate to Rumstick that they should be thus chastised by the midshipman. Now as his anger subsided and the wound in his arm began to throb, Rumstick realized that they had no business leaving the ship to settle their own petty issues.

"Never you mind," he said. "Come along, we best get back to the ship."

"Yes," said Tottenhill. "Now that honor has been satisfied."

"Satisfied?" The words made Rumstick's anger flare again, "Honor has most certainly not been satisfied!"

"Oh, do you say that we have not had a fair fight? What do you say?"

"Sirs, God damn it all to hell!" Weatherspoon shouted and it occurred to Rumstick that the midshipman's voice was getting deeper. "They are getting away with the stores! Now please get in the goddamned boat!"

The two lieutenants stood glaring at one another for a moment more.

"This ain't done, Tottenhill, so don't think you're getting off that easy," Rumstick said, pointing at the first officer with the tip of his sword. Then he slid the weapon back into the scabbard, turned his back on the other two, and clambered into Weatherspoon's boat.

CHAPTER 22

Fort Nassau

PRESIDENT OF HIS MAJESTY'S COUNCIL BROWN STOOD AT THE GATE of Fort Nassau, held open by one of the fort's black volunteer defenders, and waited for a column of militia to pass through on their way out before he could enter. The volunteer, a poor freeman in tattered clothes, stood waiting as well, his new pistol, the bait that had lured him to the fort's defense, thrust in his belt.

The governor's earlier recruiting efforts, his appeal to the islanders' patriotism, and even more so his promise of a free pistol, had yielded good results; when John Brown had left for Fort Montegu, over two hundred men had been mustered to defend their island.

It appeared, however, that their enthusiasm was not long-lived, and now a majority of those who had reported for duty were going home again.

Brown spotted James Gould, Speaker of the Assembly, walking near the end of the line. "Gould, Gould, what the devil is going on?"

"What is going on? We are leaving, sir. We'll not stand by that fool a moment longer. Have you seen this?" Gould held in his clenched fist a copy of the manifesto Hopkins had sent for dissemination.

"If that's the broadside from the rebel commodore, then, yes, we've seen in. Said he'd do no harm if we give him what he wants."

"That's right. And the Lord knows what he'll do now, now that that idiot of a governor sent away the chief of the powder. Loaded it aboard the *Mississippi Packet* and the schooner the *St. John,* and away it went. And then expects us to stand and fight, after the powder's all but gone? I think not." With that, Gould turned and hurried after the last of the retreating column.

At last Brown was able to pass through the gate. He stepped quickly down to the parade ground, to the big fire around which the remaining defenders were clustered. The governor was standing on the far side of the flames, the dancing light flickering off the medals on his uniform coat and the hilt of his sword and the brass-bound butt of the pistol clipped to his belt.

He was listening, close-mouthed and angry, to one of the men, who, judging from his gestures, was in possession of some strong opinions. Gathered in a circle around the fire, the men watched, black faces and white, and nodded or shook their heads in accordance with their own views.

"Ah, here is President Brown," the governor said, as much to distract the man from his point, apparently, as to welcome Brown. "What do you learn from your reconnoiter?"

"What in God's name have you done?" President Brown asked.

"Done? Nothing, beyond the defense of the island . . ."

"Defense? You have just doomed this entire island to the most outrageous depredations. The rebel captain, whom, I might say, is no fool, saw all of the *Packet*'s jettisoned cargo floating in the harbor. It was not hard for him to guess what was acting. He dispatched a man immediately to alert the rebel fleet. So now they not only have the powder but they are enraged that we should try and deprive them of it."

"Well, I am not such a fool," Governor Browne protested. "I did not send all of the powder away. There are still twenty-five or so barrels left. Plenty to defend ourselves and to appease the rebels if we should be taken. What is more, I have sent Babbidge for the troops up at Government House, and they should be arriving directly."

And then the rebels will have Government House, Brown thought, from which they will enfilade the fort. Enfilade it. He looked over the twenty remaining defenders of Fort Nassau, a dejected and nervous lot. "That not withstanding, I think perhaps we should consider capitulation," he suggested.

"What?" said the governor. "Nonsense! Not while we have one man left to fight. We have a sound fort, twenty-five barrels of powder, and men to work the great guns and small arms. Besides, they are only colonial rebels, while we are born Englishmen."

President Brown wondered if the black men there, at least half the men who remained, and freed slaves all, would agree with that assessment.

He could see that he would accomplish nothing by arguing with the governor. If he protested any more, then he himself would be accused of cowardice or compliance with the enemy. Governor Browne was starting to see traitors in every corner. And he was well connected: his wife was a near relation to the Earl of Dartmouth, so it would not do to make him overly suspicious.

What was more, Brown could see that a bloodless capitulation would take place in any event, even with no effort on his part. If the governor was allowed to run amok for another hour or so, then every man in the fort would desert. Then he, President of His Majesty's Council John Brown, could on the one hand claim to have stood by the governor until the end and on the other take credit with the rebels for arranging the island's surrender.

He was distracted from these happy thoughts by the sound of men on the march. He looked toward the main gate of the fort, still open, and saw Babbidge leading forty or so militiamen, the troops from Government House, into Fort Nassau.

Brown watched with a suppressed grin. They came in as an orderly band, stepping together, eyes front. But as they crossed the parade ground to the fire, Brown saw eyes roving around, heads turning, and he knew the thought that was in each head: "Where are the others?" He was eager to see their reactions when they discovered that the sullen band, twenty men strong, huddled around the fire, were all the others there were.

"Gentlemen, welcome," he said magnanimously as Babbidge brought the troops to a halt. "I am pleased to see that there are some on this island willing to fight for their King and their homes. Pray, stack your arms there."

The troops, still furtively searching the dark corners of the fort for the rest of the militia, stacked their muskets where President Brown indicated.

"I think we had best send out a scouting party," the governor said. "Find out what those rascals are up to, so we can be better prepared to meet them. Any volunteers?"

"Beg your pardon, Governor," said Alexander Frazer, lieutenant of militia, one of the men who had just marched from Government House, "but, is this all the men there are? There was better than three hundred men when we left to take our positions on the hill."

"Three hundred damned cowards, you mean. Not one had the backbone to stand and fight, save for the brave souls you see here. But that's no matter. We few are more than enough to fight off any band of rebels."

John Brown turned his head away. Had he not, he would have laughed out loud at the looks of dismay that passed among the men newly joined to the defense of the fort. He did not think that they could look more shocked or unhappy if the governor had informed them that they were to be executed at dawn, which of course was the very thing that they were envisioning. It was once again time for him to be a hero.

"Governor, I would like to volunteer for the scouting party. I'd be honored to ride out and meet these rebels and see what they're about."

"Very bravely said, Mr. President, and I accept your offer. But you can't go alone. Who else will volunteer to go with Mr. Brown?"

Uneasy glances were exchanged among those men who were not staring at the ground in hopes of going unnoticed. "Here," said President Brown, "Lieutenant Frazer, you come with me."

"Well, sir, I . . ." Frazer began.

"Come along, play the man," said Brown. "I'll see no harm comes to you." Brown stepped over to the stack of muskets and took his up, then slung his cartridge box over his shoulder. "Come on then."

Frazer scowled and shot a glance at his comrades in arms, hoping for some help from that quarter, and seeing that none was forthcoming, took up his own musket.

"We shall return as quickly as we can, Governor, and bring you the intelligence you need," Brown said. "But if we are not back by an hour past sunrise, you must assume that we were taken or . . . that we were taken. Come along, Frazer."

With the reluctant lieutenant following behind, Brown marched to the front gate of Fort Nassau. He took up the reins of his horse, handed those of another to Frazer, and the two men sallied forth. The last thing they heard as the gate was closed behind them was Governor Browne's cry of "God speed, John Brown!"

They rode down Bay Street. To their left the rippled water of Nassau harbor glinted in the light of the moon and the tropical winter stars. To their right stood the stout, shuttered coral-brick houses of Nassau. The night was silent save for the birds and frogs and the regular clop clop clop of their horses' hooves on the cobblestones.

Brown pulled his horse to a stop at the head of Charlotte Street and heard Frazer behind him do likewise. He wheeled his horse around until he was facing the lieutenant.

"Your house is just down the street there, is it not?"

"Yes, it is," said Frazer.

"I'll warrant you'd rather be there than riding out to meet the rebel army, am I right?"

Frazer stared at him, searched his face in effort to see what game he was playing. "Sure I would, and my wife and three little ones defenseless in the face of these here enraged rebels. And my aged aunt as well."

Yet another aged aunt, Brown thought. "Well, listen here, Frazer. I'll make a deal with you. I'll let you go home right now and protect your family and your valuables from the enraged rebels in exchange for your word that if anyone ever asks you what happened on this morning, you say that you were captured by the rebels but managed to escape. I'll leave it to you to fill in the details."

"Very well . . ." said Frazer, clearly suspicious of so tempting an offer. "And why are you doing this?"

"Because the governor seems determined to see that the rebels slaughter all the troops in the fort and sack the town, and I am determined to see that they do not. And if you need any further explanation, then I must insist that you accompany me to spy out the rebel forces."

"Oh, no, sir, if you say a thing must be done, Mr. President, then I reckon you know best. You have my word that from this moment forward I was captured by the rebels and somehow escaped. I bid you good day, sir." With that the greatly relieved Lieutenant Frazer wheeled his horse around and charged off down Charlotte Street to the defense of his home and family.

CHAPTER 23

Dead Reckoning

IN THE TEN MINUTES THAT IT TOOK TO ROW BACK TO THE *Charlemagne,* Lieutenant Rumstick put his fight with Tottenhill quite out of his mind. Even as Weatherspoon was binding up his wounded arm, his thoughts were entirely on the job before him.

What he knew of the situation came from the midshipman, who was reporting what Isaac had said. And Isaac had emphasized that he was only guessing, based on scant evidence. His guess was that the Nassauvians had hurriedly emptied some merchantman and loaded it again with the island's precious military stores. Where it was bound or if it had even left at all or if it was escorted, he had no way of knowing.

Well, there is only one course of action, Rumstick thought as the launch pulled up alongside the *Charlemagne*. We slip the cable and go after them and pray to God they are there.

He stood and grabbed on to the boarding steps just as the jolly boat, rowed by two of the launch's crew with Tottenhill in the stern sheets, appeared out of the darkness to lie astern of the bigger boat.

Rumstick glanced at the first officer. He was scowling, angry no doubt that Rumstick was going aboard first, which was not at all proper, but Rumstick could not care less. Indeed, it was not by accident that he had arrived first. He had commandeered the bigger boat for just that reason, so that he could issue orders before Tottenhill was aboard.

He climbed quickly, despite the pain in his arm, and called, "Mr. Sprout!" as he stepped through the gangway.

"Sir?" Sprout approached, a worried look on his face. "Pray, sir, where is Mr. Tot—"

"Buoy the cable, boats, and slip it immediately," Rumstick ordered, and then addressing the brig's company, he bellowed, "Hands aloft to loosen sail, all plain sail and stun's'ls as well! Drummer, beat to quarters, clear for action! Go!"

The ship's company was already keyed up by the day's activities, by the wild rumors floating around and the sound of clashing steel that had come across the water from the small island to which the first and second officers had gone. They paused for no more than half a second, during which they digested Rumstick's orders, before they burst into action.

The topmen flung themselves into the shrouds and disappeared aloft as Sprout ran forward, calling for his mates, and the gun crews began to throw off the tackles and pull the tampions from the muzzles. They worked handsomely and fast, and Rumstick was relieved to see that. He did not know these men well, and he had never gone into a fight with them. They were mostly new hands. All of the older Charlemagnes were ashore with Biddlecomb.

All save for Woodberry, whose one hand was broken, along with a few fingers on the other hand and some nasty bruises on his face. He had obviously been in a fight, and Rumstick could even tell which men he had fought with, for they carried the marks of the punishment that Woodberry had doled out. But despite that evidence Woodberry stuck to the absurd claim that he had fallen down a ladder, and Rumstick knew that no more truthful story would be forthcoming.

He stepped up to the quarterdeck, watching the tremendous activity set in motion by the two dozen or so words he had spoken, as Tottenhill clambered up through the gangway and stamped aft. His eyes were fixed on Rumstick, he seemed oblivious to the activity around him.

"Rumstick," he hissed as he too stepped up to the quarterdeck, "you will not forget who is in command of this vessel, do you understand? I give the orders here!"

"Well, what other orders would you give but to slip the cable and loosen sail? That's what Captain Biddlecomb ordered you to do."

"Biddlecomb is ashore, and when he is ashore, I am the captain here."

"I know that, and I was just trying to anticipate your orders. Captain."

"Don't you play coy with me, Lieutenant, or—" Tottenhill was cut short by Sprout, who hurried aft and said, "Cable's all but out, just the bitter end aboard."

"Very well. Let fall—" Rumstick began, but was brought up short by Tottenhill's black look.

"Mr. Rumstick, go and set the fore topsail and brace it aback, and the fore topmast staysail as well. Mr. Sprout, you may slip the cable when the topsail is set."

Rumstick mumbled something by way of acknowldgment and went forward.

I must keep this battened down, Ezra thought, even as he called for the men aloft to let fall. He was afraid of his own anger, more afraid of it than of anything else he had encountered. He had seen it go before. He had almost beaten the *Icarus*'s boatswain to death when he lost control then. Tottenhill's the captain now, he thought, not Isaac, and sure as hell not me. I have got to remember that. I have got to keep this stowed away.

The *Charlemagne* turned slowly under a backed fore topsail and staysail, swinging away from the anchored fleet, spreading more canvas as she turned. In their wake the jolly boat pulled away, two men at the oars, delivering a hastily written note to Commodore Hopkins, who would no doubt be curious as to why one of his brigs, one-fifth of the fleet, had decided to head off with no word from him.

"That's well, the main topgallant!" Rumstick shouted as the weather sheet came home and the sail stretched tight under the pull of the halyard. He opened his mouth and drew breath, ready to call for weather studdingsails to be set when he thought better of it. He gritted his teeth and stomped aft and looking up at the quarterdeck said, "Permission to set stun's'ls, sir?"

"Yes, very well, and get a man in the chains with the lead, quickly now," Tottenhill said, his eyes fixed on the bow and never meeting Rumstick's. Rumstick heard a triumphant note in Tottenhill's voice, a tone that said that the proper order to the universe had been restored.

Rumstick looked over the bulwark and aft at the fleet, which was all but lost in the dark, save for their anchor lights, which shone like a constellation against the dark water and the islands beyond. The *Charlemagne* had to find a single merchantman somewhere in that darkness and stop it before it sailed away with all of the island's military stores, everything for which the American fleet had come.

To do so they would have to guess where the ship was bound.

Rumstick ran through several possibilities, weighing the likelihood of each. He found himself overwhelmed by the many considerations, the arguments one way and another. He cursed softly. This was Isaac's bailiwick, not his.

"Sir," he said to Tottenhill, as deferentially as he could, stepping up to the quarterdeck. "I was thinking, St. Eustatius might well be their destination."

"St. Eustatius?" Tottenhill glanced at him and then looked away. "I think not."

"And why not?" Rumstick felt the anger mount.

Tottenhill looked back at him and made no attempt to hide his contempt. "Beat to windward and sail right past the American fleet? They are perfectly aware that the fleet is in Hanover

Sound. If they set a course to windward, they should still be in sight when the sun rises. They are heading west, to Florida, most likely."

The first officer said those last words with finality and then looked forward again, into the night, as if it were more desirable to stare into blackness than to look at Rumstick's stupid face.

Rumstick in turn said nothing, just turned his back on Tottenhill and looked outboard. The thing of it was that the son of a bitch was right. Rumstick could see that right off, and it made him more angry than anything yet that night. For all of the thought that he had tried to put into the problem, he had guessed wrong, and Tottenhill, he was certain, had guessed right.

They turned west and ran down the length of Hog Island, which loomed dark against the not quite black sky. The brig was silent, save for the odd cough or murmur fore and aft. There was nothing for the men to do, now that the guns were loaded and all sail set, save sit around and worry.

If Biddlecomb had been there, Rumstick knew, he would have found something for the hands to do, but Tottenhill did not seem interested in doing so. And while he, Rumstick, could think of a number of useful ways to occupy the idle men, he did not speak up. He did not care to offer any more ideas to Tottenhill. He did not trust himself to speak civilly.

For an hour they ran west, plowing through the dark sea, leaving a glowing yellow-green trail of phosphorescence in their long, straight wake. Rumstick began to fidget, began to run his fingers over the hilt of his sword and drum them against his thigh and the caprail. What moon there was gave them some visibility, but not much. Not enough to see another ship at any distance. They would have to be damned lucky to catch this merchantman. It occurred to him that their best chance of seeing the enemy was if there were two ships, rather than one, and—

"On deck!"

All heads turned toward the lookout standing on the slings of the main topgallant yard and hidden by the billowing canvas.

"Deck, aye!" Rumstick called out, regardless of Tottenhill.

"I sees two lights, sir. Look like taffrail lanterns, just a point of the larboard bow!"

Smiles and nodding heads fore and aft. It was what Rumstick had hoped for: two vessels that were burning lights to avoid colliding with one another or becoming separated in the dark. Now the night was their ally, for the two ships would not see the *Charlemagne* coming up in their wake, certainly not if they were looking through the glare of their taffrail lanterns, until it was too late for them.

Rumstick grinned like the rest and thought to tell Tottenhill congratulations. He even turned to do so before he realized that in return he would get something to the effect of I told you so, and that would ruin his grand mood, so he held his tongue. Instead he stepped down into the waist and in a low voice told the men to stand to their guns and to make not one noise.

They plunged on, running downwind with a moderate following sea lifting them stern-first, ever so slightly, and then setting them down again. Their quarry was slow, heavy-laden with military stores, and the nimble *Charlemagne* quickly overhauled them. The taffrail lights grew brighter and more distinct as the Americans came up astern, a mile, and then half a mile, a quarter of a mile, a cable length. Rumstick felt as though he might burst with the anticipation.

He could make out details of the ships now, or more properly the ship, for only one was ship rigged. The other was a schooner, a big schooner, but not as big as the *Charlemagne*. There was no alarm yet on the two vessels that they could see, no attempt to split and run. The enemy just sailed on, unaware of the great predator inching up behind them.

"Mr. Rumstick," Tottenhill said in a low voice, the first

words he had spoken to the second officer in an hour or more. "With what are the guns loaded?"

"Round shot."

"No good. It defeats the purpose to sink these vessels. Draw the shot and load with chain."

"Draw the shot?" Rumstick said, a little too loud. "We're all but on top of them!"

"Then you had better hurry."

"That'll make a power of noise, hauling the guns in! They'll smoke us once they hear that!"

"It's too late for them, we are up with them. They cannot escape now."

"They damn well can! Why, if they—"

"Just do what I tell you, God damn your eyes!" Tottenhill glared at Rumstick with his old fury, and Rumstick felt his own anger stirring.

"You stupid. . . ." Rumstick began, then clamped down hard and through his teeth said, "Aye. Sir," and stomped off forward, giving the orders in a loud whisper, noting the incredulous looks on the men's faces as if he, Rumstick, were insane.

A second later the first of the six-pounders was hauled back from the gunport, the wooden wheels squeaking and the deck rumbling under the weight, and there was no longer any need to speak softly. The two ships that they were pursuing were still a cable length ahead, but even over that distance the Charlemagnes could hear the shouts of surprise, the bellowed orders, the bedlam on their decks as they finally saw the predator, ready to pounce.

The ship swung away south, hauling her wind, heading in a direction that would take her away from the *Charlemagne* as quickly as she could go. "Damn it all to hell, damn it," Rumstick muttered under his breath. He looked back at the quarterdeck to see if Tottenhill had yet realized that he had just made the biggest mistake of his life, a mistake that entirely negated his good work in finding these ships, but from the lack of expression on the first officer's face, he could not tell.

"Hurry it up, you motherless bastards, get them guns loaded!" Rumstick called out for no good reason, save that he had to say something or he thought he might explode.

He stepped up to the bow and onto the heel of the bowsprit and looked across the water to the two British ships beyond. The taffrail lights were extinguished, which was no surprise, and now they would be lucky to take even one of them. Taking both seemed out of the question.

Rumstick could still make out the ship, but just barely, for she was running away to the southward. To his surprise the schooner was not running north but rather east, straight at them, close-hauled, the bone in her teeth reflecting the moonlight as it boiled around her cutwater. He hopped back to the deck and hurried aft.

"Tottenhill, that schooner's making right for us. I think she's a man-of-war, must be an escort to the merchantman."

"Very good. And watch your mouth, I won't tolerate your disrespect any longer."

Disrespect? You ain't seen disrespect, Rumstick thought. He turned toward the waist. "Hurry it up, hurry it up! Load and run out!" Only half of the guns had drawn their shot, and not one of them was yet reloaded with chain.

And then the schooner was on top of them. They could see the big gaff-headed sail looming over the bow as she charged along, close-hauled, flinging herself at a more powerful enemy.

"Hands to braces!" Rumstick shouted.

"Belay that, God damn it!" Tottenhill fairly screamed, "Rumstick, you keep your damned mouth shut!"

"Are you going to let him rake us? Aren't you at least going to show him a broadside, even if we got nothing loaded?"

Whatever Tottenhill had to say to that was lost in the gunfire. Nor would it have mattered, for the schooner had tacked across the *Charlemagne*'s bows and was crossing starboard to larboard, firing as she went, her four-pounder balls tearing the length of the brig's deck.

The captain of number two gun spun around as if he were

dancing and fell, dead before he hit the deck. A ball plowed into the foremast fife rail, smashing it to pieces, tearing up the running rigging made fast there. The jib and the fore staysail collapsed, their halyards parted by the round shot, and fell into the water, dragging under the bow.

"Damn it, damn it, damn it!" Rumstick shouted as he leapt up on the heel of the bowsprit, grabbed on to the headsail sheets, and pulled. "On deck there," he shouted at the nearest gun crew, "give me a hand here, haul these motherless things back aboard!"

The schooner had passed them by, and now it looked as if she was tacking around to deliver another raking broadside. And with the sails dragging in the water and the way nearly off of her, there was nothing that the *Charlemagne* could do about it.

Rumstick let out a bellow, a roar of anger and frustration as he hauled the wet canvas aboard.

CHAPTER 24

Failure and Success

LIEUTENANT RUMSTICK COULD JUST MAKE OUT THE SCHOONER, HALF a cable away, but his vision had been hurt by the flash of her guns at close range. The last of the headsails were pulled aboard and the gun crew returned to their duty. Rumstick dragged the dead gunner clear of the path of his gun's recoil.

The first broadside from the enemy did an extraordinary amount of damage, quite out of proportion to the pathetic weight of iron she threw. That was the price the Charlemagnes had paid for Tottenhill's refusal to fall off, thus allowing the schooner to fire her round shot down the entire length of the brig's deck.

But now the guns were reloaded with chain and running out. "Sail trimmers!" Tottenhill called out. "Larboard tack!" To the helmsmen he called, "Starboard your helm!"

The *Charlemagne* turned to larboard, presenting her starboard broadside to the defiant little enemy. The two vessels were broadside to broadside, sailing parallel to one another, no more than fifty feet apart. This was where the *Charlemagne* could use her superior firepower to good effect.

"Fire when you bear!" Tottenhill shouted, and at that three of the brig's guns went off, blasting their loads of chain shot at the schooner's rig, hoping to render the sails unmanageable while leaving the hull intact.

Rumstick peered through the night, but he could make out only a vague outline of the schooner. Another of the *Charlemagne*'s guns blasted away, then another, lighting the enemy up in the flash. He could see no damage done to the other vessel, and he wondered if any of the shots had told.

Then the schooner's shape seemed to change, seemed to contract, and for a wonderful moment Rumstick thought that they had brought her mast down. And then he realized that they had not. She was just tacking, turning up into the wind, presenting her bow to the *Charlemagne* once the Americans had discharged their broadside.

"She's tacking!" Rumstick shouted aft.

Tottenhill was watching the schooner as well. "Stand by for stays!" he shouted. "Start coming up," he said to the helmsmen. He was going to tack the *Charlemagne,* keep the two ships side by side, but that was the wrong thing to do, and with the headsails gone it was unlikely that they would make it around.

"Tottenhill, listen," Rumstick called, running aft, ready to give advice that he knew was not wanted and would not be well received. "They'll—"

He got no further than that. The schooner was across their stern now and began pouring round shot into the *Charlemagne*'s transom. A ball blasted through the taffrail, spraying the quarterdeck with splinters and felling one of the helmsmen with a chunk of caprail to the head.

"God damn it!" Tottenhill shouted in frustration. The *Charlemagne* was coming up into the wind, ready to tack, while the nimble schooner was already falling off, out of range of their guns. In Rumstick's experience the brig had always been the quick and handy vessel, antagonizing their enemies, sailing rings around them. Now they were the bull, tethered and baited about by a quick and vicious dog.

"Listen, Tottenhill, sod the schooner, never mind them," Rumstick shouted. "It's the ship that has the stores and they're running away from us! Go after the ship!"

"Don't you address me in that fashion, God damn your eyes!" Tottenhill shouted. "Let fly the headsails! Helm's alee!"

The remaining helmsman put the helm over and the *Charlemagne* turned up into the wind.

"Let fly the headsails!" Tottenhill called again, aware, as was Rumstick, of the conspicuous absence of flogging canvas.

"There ain't any headsails, the schooner shot the halyards away," Rumstick said in a caustic tone.

Overhead the leeches of the square sails began to flog. "Mainsail, haul!" Tottenhill shouted, and the mainyard swung around as all of the square sails came aback. The *Charlemagne* turned up into the wind, farther and farther, until the breeze was blowing right down her centerline, and then she stopped.

There was an odd calm, an unnatural sort of quiet, as every man aboard stood waiting for the brig to complete her tack. The schooner was now all but lost from sight, running away to the northwest, and the ship had not been seen for the past ten minutes or more.

"You're in irons," Rumstick said quietly, as if anyone aboard the brig, particularly Tottenhill, did not know that. They had turned straight into the wind and turned no farther, and now the *Charlemagne* sat there, motionless, while all of the military supplies of New Providence disappeared in the night.

"Mr. Sprout," Rumstick shouted, "bend the gantline to the fore topmast staysail and set it that way! On the main braces, brace up sharp starboard tack! Let go and haul!"

"Rumstick, I shall not tell you again, you stupid ox," Tottenhill shouted in a voice that could be heard clear to the jibboom end, "you do not give an order aboard this vessel, damn it!"

"Well, I reckon somebody better start giving orders, giving orders that make some sense! You already lost the ship and the stores, I reckon, the whole goddamned reason we come here, you stupid bastard!"

Tottenhill glared at him. The mainsails remained aback and the headsails remained in a heap on deck, and all of the Charlemagnes stood watching the confrontation. Rumstick was aware of a shuffling, a low murmur from the men like water lapping along a hull.

"That is it, sir, that is it! You shall consider yourself under arrest! You do not speak to me like that!" Tottenhill shouted back, but Rumstick did not hear. The bulkhead had now burst under the great pressure of his anger, anger that had been building since he had lost his position as first officer, and now it flowed in a great violent wave that would not be stopped.

"Under arrest? You're a joke, sir, you little blockhead of a weasel! You calf! Get out of my way, little man!" Rumstick pushed him aside and, shouting forward, yelled, "I said brace them mainsails around, you whore's sons!" but the men in the waist stood sullenly glaring at one another or staring blankly aft.

"Mr. Rumstick is under arrest!" Tottenhill shouted. "No one shall obey his orders. Hackett, Allen, Gray, escort Rumstick below."

In a flash the three men were up on the quarterdeck, led by a grinning Hackett, who had gravitated aft at the first sign of confrontation. Behind them came three more, like jackals to a kill.

"You'll have to come with us, Mr. Rumstick," Hackett said, still grinning. He took a step toward Rumstick, who stood passively watching, his arms hanging loose at his sides. Hackett took another step and paused, sensing the danger. "Here, Allen, Gray, take a hold of the lieutenant."

Allen and Gray, less insightful than their leader, continued to advance on Rumstick. "Come along, sir," said Gray, reaching for Rumstick's left arm.

Like a snake Rumstick's right arm struck out, his heavy fist smashing flat into Gray's face. Blood sprayed from the man's shattered nose as the force of the blow lifted him from the deck and tossed him back against the binnacle box.

Allen was actually backing away when Rumstick's foot caught him in the groin and doubled him over, then the foot came up again directly in his face and he joined Gray on the deck.

"Arrest me, you sons of whores?" Rumstick roared. "Come on then, let's have at it!" He took a step back against the bulwark and his hand fell on the empty belaying pin he knew was there. There was shouting in the waist, the sounds of a tumult, but he could not take his eyes off the men he faced. He jerked the pin from the rail, a foot and a half of solid oak, turned and oiled, just as Hackett and the other three prepared to rush him.

"Stop this! Stop this right now!" Tottenhill screamed. "Rumstick, you will obey my authority!" But Rumstick was not listening anymore. He was well beyond listening.

Nor were his attackers prepared to back off, intent as they were on revenge for some perceived offense—Rumstick could not imagine what, nor, at that moment, did it matter—he had done them.

A sheath knife flashed out, and then another. Rumstick stepped forward, grabbing out with his left hand, diverting attention, and in a great sweeping arc he brought the belaying pin around and dropped one assailant to the deck like a sack of biscuits.

The shouting from the waist grew more frantic, some tumult on the edge of his vision. He had the impression that a great brawl had broken out among the men. But he had no time to look, or even think of what might be happening. Hackett was shouting for more help as the two remaining men came at Rumstick.

Then Weatherspoon was at his side, his dirk, not much longer than the sheath knives he faced, held in his steady hand. "Put those knives away, you stupid bastards," the midshipman commanded with a surprising authority.

"Mr. Rumstick's under arrest! He's to come with us!" Hackett shouted, but he sounded less sure of himself now. He glanced around for Tottenhill, as did Rumstick, but the first officer had abandoned the fight aft and was standing at the break of the quarterdeck, apparently trying, through the force of his authority, to stop the riot that had erupted in the waist.

Rumstick had only a fleeting impression of what was happening, glances stolen while he concentrated on the standoff before him. He saw in the dull moonlight men rushing fore and aft, fists and belaying pins and handspikes rising and falling. Not a thought was left for the enemy ships making their easy escape. The *Charlemagne* was swept up in an internecine battle, a wild brawl in which every man aboard was engaged.

"Put down those knives!" Weatherspoon shouted again, and as if startled from their uncertainty, the two men advanced again, with Hackett standing behind them.

"Son of a bitch!" Rumstick roared, his voice like a cannon blast. The men hesitated, stopped, and then with a sweep of his hand Rumstick brushed aside the knife to his left and swung with the pin. He felt the rip and burn of the other knife plunging into his side. He checked his swing, catching the first assailant on the jaw and spinning him half around.

He turned toward the man who had stabbed him, the knife pulling from his flesh as he did. He was aware of the agony, the burning and the hurt, but he was far to angry to worry about it, or for the wound to slow him down. He wound up with the pin but the man was bent over double, Weatherspoon's dirk thrust deep in his belly, blood running down his slop trousers and onto the deck.

Weatherspoon pulled the dirk from the man's stomach, and with a gasp he collapsed to the deck. Then the midshipman was gone, running and leaping forward, to where, Rumstick could not imagine.

Tottenhill was standing over him now, having abandoned his attempt to stop the riot, shouting, "What in hell have you done?"

"What in hell have *you* done, you idiot!" Rumstick shouted at the first officer. He pointed toward the waist where men struggled as if fighting off a boarding enemy. "Look what your damned coddling has got us!"

"Coddling? Why you arrogant Yankee bastard! I have had no help from you, and no help from Biddlecomb, you have treated me like a leper since first I came aboard! I . . . No!" Tottenhill yelled.

Rumstick frowned, confused by that last shouted word, then felt a great blow to the back of his head, a staggering shock that pitched him forward over the bleeding form of his attacker and down to the deck at Tottenhill's feet. He rolled over, clutching his head, images swimming in his blurred vision. Hackett was there, grinning, a belaying pin in his hand.

And then with the sound of the riot in his pounding head, the sound of the ship's company tearing themselves apart, Rumstick saw Mr. Midshipman Weatherspoon, like some vision, a pistol in each hand and two more thrust in his belt, leap up onto the quarterdeck. He shouted something, fired one of the guns, fired the other, and was reaching for a third when Rumstick finally lost consciousness.

President John Brown pulled his horse to a stop at the White Ground, the sandy point halfway between Fort Montegu and Fort Nassau. He had been riding hard, and for a moment he just sat in his saddle, head thrown back, breathing deep.

The rebels were on the move. It was still dark but they had already assembled and marched out of Fort Montegu and were on the road to Nassau, bent on God knows what kind of mischief. Brown had ridden far enough along the road to see them coming, which was all he needed to see, then turned and rode back to the White Ground. He did not care to talk to the rebels again, not until he had proven himself in their eyes.

They had not been quite as conciliatory as he had hoped; they were apparently quite determined to sack the town if they met with resistance. And what was worse, they would think that he, John Brown, had betrayed them. They were already furious over the loss of the military stores. It would go hard on him if they met with further resistance, the naval captain had promised. Very hard. Brown did not know what that meant, exactly, but he knew that he did not want to find out.

It would take the Americans an hour and a half at least to reach Fort Nassau. He pulled his watch from his waistcoat and squinted at the face. Five o'clock in the morning. By six-thirty the barbarians would be at the gate. He had an hour and a half to convince the governor and the remaining militia to abandon the fort or he himself would be hunted down by the damnable rebels.

He slid down off the horse and looped the animal's reins around a small tree. He took off his coat, then unbuttoned his waistcoat and took that off as well, then pulled his shirt over his head. The morning air was cool on his bare skin, and it felt good after the hard riding he had done. He pushed the arms of the shirt through the arm holes of the waistcoat, then stuffed them back into the arms of his coat. He held the clothes out at arm's length and pulled a pistol from his belt.

He hated this type of histrionics, but it had to be done. The fort had to be emptied before the Americans arrived. He grimaced as he placed the barrel of the gun against the coat at about where his ribs would be, were he wearing it, turned his head, and pulled the trigger. The flash from the pan and the barrel were blinding, and the loud report of the gun made the horse shift nervously, but the animal was trained to gunfire and it did not spook.

Brown examined the hole that he had blasted through three layers of clothing. It was impressive; a gaping wound in the cloth, charred and hanging open. He struggled back into the shirt, waistcoat, and coat.

He pulled a folding knife from his pocket and grit his teeth as he unfolded it, moving quickly before he lost his nerve. He placed the blade against the skin that was exposed by the hole in his clothing and with a jerk of his arm cut his flesh, opening up a wound six inches long.

He gasped, then grit his teeth again and cursed. It was not a deep cut, but still it was painful and, more to the point, bled copiously. He sucked in his breath and held it. He felt the blood running down his side and saw the dark stains it made on the tattered cloth. Satisfied that he had manufactured a quite convincing and, he hoped, frightening wound, he took up the horse's reins, swung himself up into the saddle, and charged off toward Fort Nassau.

Ten minutes later the great front gate of the fort was opened for him, the lookout on the wall having apparently seen him coming. He swung his horse off Bay Street and charged past the surprised sentry and toward the fire in the center of the parade ground, its flames less bright now in the gathering daylight. He pulled the horse to a stop in a great spray of dust and fairly leapt from the saddle to the ground, gasping for breath.

"Brown, Brown, what on earth?" the governor said, lifting his great bulk off the stool on which it was planted and rushing over to him. He put his arm solicitously around Brown's shoulder, saying, "My God, what has happened to you? You're wounded, man! Did the rebels do this?" as Brown, doubled over and gasping for breath thought, "As far as you know."

At last Brown straightened, and his labored breathing, half of it the result of hard riding, the other half playacting, subsided enough for him to speak. "The rebels are a mile or so up the road, Governor, coming on the quick march. I doubt there's above six hundred of them, though in the dark it was hard to see."

"They shot you? Did you try to speak with them? What do they . . . ?" The governor's words trailed off as he stared at the president's bloody wound.

"I tried to speak with them, but they'd have none of it. They called me a bloody rascal and shot me. It's just a scratch, thank God. They're quite enraged, I've never seen the like."

The sixty men who remained to defend the fort were gathered around him now. They listened with eyes wide and growing wider as he gasped out his tale. It needed no art to know what every man was thinking.

"What about Frazer?" one of the citizen soldiers asked. "What happened to Frazer?"

Brown shook his head. "Frazer didn't make it. The rebels captured him. I think they may have . . . I don't know what they did to him."

This last bit of intelligence was enough to send a wave of panicked speculation through the crowd of militia. Brown saw heads shaking and arms waving and fingers pointing at the crumbling walls of Fort Nassau and the heavy gun still lying on its side at the north end of the parade ground.

"Well, damn those rebels to hell, I say," the governor said in a loud and commanding voice. "We'll hold fast here, and when they come, then we'll send them right to hell, help the Lord in his work. We'd best see to manning the great guns."

The militiamen, far from manning the great guns, began to collect their muskets, haversacks, cartridge boxes, and free pistols.

"Beg your pardon, Governor," said the company's sergeant as he slung his cartridge box over his shoulder, "but President Brown said there was six hundred men at least, and they shot him on no provocation. And last night they sent that broadside around, promising no harm if they got what they came for. I don't see the sense in risking the destruction of the town for a few unserviceable cannon and what stores we have left."

That statement was followed with a general murmur of agreement as the militiamen turned and headed for the gate, which, since Brown's return, had remained open. The crowd split up on hitting Bay Street, each man heading off for his own home, and soon they were lost from sight. Brown pulled his watch discreetly out of his pocket and tilted the face toward the fire. Half past five.

"Well, as for me," said Governor Browne, ostentatiously pulling his pistol from his belt and checking the priming, "I shall not leave this fort while any one man will stand by me."

And there was, President Brown noted with some dismay,

even more than one man still standing by him. Besides himself, five members of the council and two lieutenants of militia, as well as Babbidge, still remained. A total of ten men, not one of whom was a professional soldier, to fight off the invading rebels. And it seemed as if the governor still intended to mount some defense. It was absurd. And Brown had less than an hour to get them out of there.

"Governor," said Councilman John Gambier, "I think perhaps we should revisit this defense of the fort," and his words were greeted up by various "Yes's" and "Indeed's" among the councilmen and officers gathered around. "As noble as your effort has been, I think perhaps it is time to abandon the fort to the rebels."

Ah, good old Gambier, ever the voice of reason, Brown thought.

The governor looked at the men around him and was greeted on all quarters by nodding heads. "Babbidge, you're the regular military man here, what say you?"

"I don't think we can hope to defend the fort with ten men," Babbidge said wearily, "and if we try, there's nothing to stop the rebels from just ignoring us and sacking the town."

The governor took one last look around, and Brown could see him, actually see him, come to a decision. "Yes, yes, indeed, we'll let those rebels march right in! And won't they be surprised to find the powder gone and we've outfoxed them again! They won't know if those twenty-five barrels left are all the powder there was, or if we sent it away under their damned noses, and all the time we're in our homes, ready to defend them. Yes, gentlemen, we shall further confound these damned rebels. Let us go now, to the defense of our homes!" At that the governor picked up his musket, handed his stool to Babbidge, and led the last of the defenders out of Fort Nassau.

President Brown, following behind the general exodus, pulled his watch from his pocket one more time. A quarter to six. He had engineered the entire capitulation of the island with forty-five minutes to spare.

CHAPTER 25

The Better Part of Valor

THOUGH THE SUN HAD YET TO APPEAR ABOVE THE EASTERN HORIZON, there was sufficient light for Biddlecomb to see all of Nassau harbor and Hog Island beyond. He looked impatiently at his watch. He had left ordinary seaman Fletcher behind at Fort Montegu to see if the *Charlemagne* was still at anchor. He was to catch up with the invading force and report the moment the sun was high enough for him to see the fleet.

Nicholas had ordered a rest, and now the road was strewn with weary marines and sailors. In ten minutes they would march again, and as yet Biddlecomb had no word from Fletcher.

"Damn that fool's eyes, damn them to hell," he muttered to himself as he walked awkwardly over the sand toward the water's edge. Fletcher was far from the brightest of men, but Biddlecomb had to imagine he could handle so simple a task as the one assigned.

He stopped where the soft, dry sand turned firm and wet and peered off toward the east in hopes of seeing the fleet at anchor. The effort was no more productive than was cursing the unhappy Fletcher, but like cursing Fletcher it eased his discomfort a bit.

The fleet of course was not visible; the eastern end of Hog Island obstructed his view of Hanover Sound, as he knew it would. As he cursed again and began trudging back toward the troops, Fletcher, breathing hard and lathered in sweat like a draft animal, came running up.

"Sir, sir," he called, and Biddlecomb silently retracted all of the curses he had heaped on the man's head.

"Fletcher, good man. Here, catch your breath. Okay, now, tell me what's acting."

"First light, sir, I looked out over the fleet, like you said."

"And . . . ?"

"Fleet's still there, sir, anchored in Hanover Sound."

"And the *Charlemagne*? Is the *Charlemagne* still at anchor?"

"*Charlemagne*, sir?"

"Yes, the *Charlemagne*," Biddlecomb said, mentally adding, you bloody idiot. "You know, the brig I command? That you serve aboard?"

"Oh, bless you, sir, I know what the *Charlemagne* is"—Fletcher grinned—"but I don't know if she's still at anchor or not."

"Well, what in hell were you looking at?"

"I was looking to see if the fleet was still there, sir, which it is."

"You idiot," Biddlecomb said out loud. "I don't give a damn about the fleet, I want to know if the *Charlemagne*'s still there. Now get back to the fort and see if she's there and come back and tell me."

"Aye, sir, tell you if the *Charlemagne*'s there," Fletcher said, saluting and heading back up the beach.

"Oh, and Fletcher?" Biddlecomb called.

"Yes, sir?"

"Run."

With that prompting Fletcher stumbled off over the sand in an awkward gallop. Biddlecomb, watching him retreat, wondered how long it would take him to realize that he could just as easily run on the road rather than the soft sand beach.

Biddlecomb shook his head as he walked back up to the front of the column. Perhaps he should have sent someone a bit brighter this time. No, even Fletcher couldn't twice make a hash of so simple an order.

"Time for us to move, Biddlecomb," Nicholas said. The captain of marines was already standing at the head of the column; indeed, he alone had not sat down for the entire time that the column had halted on the road. "First Sergeant, get the men up. We're marching."

Orders were shouted down the line, and three minutes later the invading army was on the move again, as if it had never stopped. The sun had by then made its appearance, and the island and the harbor were illuminated with the orange light of dawn. Before the marching men, long shadows led the way down the dirt road, and the thick vegetation of the island, wet with dew, was once again alive with twittering and buzzing and shrieking. Lizards still groggy from the morning cool sat on rocks along the road, gathering up the sun on their green and brown backs.

Twenty minutes later the dirt road yielded to cobblestones and the town of Nassau hove into sight. It was as lovely as Biddlecomb remembered: pastel brick houses, battened down with brightly colored shutters, spread over a low hill overlooking the western entrance to the harbor.

They marched on, and the road became Bay Street, lined on the inland side with stores of various descriptions, as well as taverns and less affluent homes. The sergeants no longer called for silence, having themselves joined in the animated discussions among the troops.

"There." Nicholas pointed toward the most imposing and prominent building, perched at the crest of the hill around which the town was built. "That ain't Fort Nassau, is it?"

"No, no," said Biddlecomb. "That's Government House, the governor's residence. Fort Nassau's just up this road a piece, about half a mile."

"Fort's just up this road? So whoever has that house there has the high ground. A couple of guns up there could play well on the fort, it seems. What say you?"

"Well, I suppose you're right. Government House overlooks the whole town, Fort Nassau included."

"Very well, First Sergeant, halt the men," Nicholas instructed his sergeant, who was, at that moment, turned half around and craning his neck to see through the partially open window of a purveyor of wine and spirits.

"Company—halt!" the first sergeant called, to his credit missing not a beat despite yielding to curiosity.

"Flank company!" Nicholas called out. "You'll be taking the big house yonder, on the hill. Drive out any of them rascals that might be there. If the governor is home, then once we have possession of Fort Nassau, I'd be obliged if he would pay me a visit."

"Captain," said Biddlecomb, "it seems we have yet another visitor."

"Oh, son of a bitch, don't these people ever get tired of parlaying?" Nicholas said in undiluted disgust as he watched the figure whom Biddlecomb had indicated approach. He was three blocks away, stepping quickly and waving a white flag. "Hold up a minute, Lieutenant," he said to the officer of the flank company, "we'll see what this whore's son wants."

It was Lieutenant Babbidge. He continued to wave the white flag until he was within a dozen yards of the head of the column, then stopped, came to attention, saluted, and called out, "Lieutenant Babbidge, New Providence Militia, requesting permission to approach. Peaceably."

"What in hell has got into him?" Nicholas asked.

"Yes, Lieutenant, please approach," Biddlecomb called, and Babbidge marched up to the officers and saluted again.

"Captain Nicholas, Captain Biddlecomb, I come from the governor to bring you these." Babbidge held out a big brass ring from which hung three large keys. His face was pale and he seemed even more frightened than he had been before. The keys tinkled like little bells in his trembling hand. "These are the keys to Fort Nassau, sir. You will find it deserted and awaiting your arrival, sir."

"Humph," said Nicholas, snatching the keys from Babbidge's hand.

"Much obliged, Lieutenant," Biddlecomb said.

"And, sir, may I enquire after . . . after . . . Lieutenant Frazer? Sir?"

"Who?" Biddlecomb asked.

"Lieutenant Frazer, sir? The man you captured? The fellow in the scouting party?"

"I don't know what in hell you're talking about," said Nicholas. "Now look here, what about the Government House, eh? You have artillery up there, ready to fire on us once we take the fort?"

"Oh, no, sir, never in life," Babbidge protested.

"Then you won't mind my sending up the flank company to take possession?"

"Oh, no, sir. I'll show them the way, if you like."

"Sweet son of a whore!" Nicholas roared, finally giving full vent to his disappointment. "If we'd have known you were just going to roll over like this, we'd have written ahead to tell you we were coming, save us the trouble of pretending to invade the island. God above, don't you people believe in defending yourselves?"

"Sir," said Babbidge, drawing himself up and mustering his not entirely quashed dignity and courage, "I think you'll find that there are many on this island—and mind you I am not one of them, not at all—who are disloyal to their king and sympathetic with your cause."

"So we've heard," said Biddlecomb. "Now, Captain Nicholas, I think we should go take us a fort."

The keys, as it happened, were superfluous. The front gate of Fort Nassau was not locked, it was not even closed, and the combined forces of the Continental Marines and the navy of the United Colonies marched right through the wooden palisade and on through the tall, castlelike entrance of the fort itself. Over the front entrance a large and tattered Union Jack undulated in the soft breeze.

"Ferguson, you have the flag?" Biddlecomb called out, and the sailor ran up to him, patting the haversack slung over his shoulder. "Good, come with me."

Biddlecomb led the way up a precarious ladder to the base of the flagpole. It was the highest point of the fort's wall and afforded him an unobstructed view of the harbor. "Haul that down and run our flag up," he said, nodding to the Union Jack over their heads. Ferguson cast off the halyard and pulled the British flag down.

Biddlecomb pulled a small glass from his coat pocket and scanned the harbor. Nothing was moving on the water, save for one boat tacking back and forth over the western bar under a single lugsail and jib.

The squealing of the flag halyard's sheave ceased and Ferguson announced, "There she is, sir, and ain't she a fine sight?" At the top of the flagpole the American flag, the Grand Union flag with a union jack in the canton and alternating red, white, and blue stripes, waved gently in the trade winds.

Biddlecomb nodded. It was a fine sight, he had to admit. It marked the successful conclusion of the first American fleet action: the conquest of New Providence Island. And save for the somnambulant marine who had fallen off the wall of Fort Montegu while relieving himself and broken his wrist, it had been done with not one casualty.

Then he recalled the *Charlemagne,* and his warm feeling was gone. He could not enjoy this triumph until he knew that his ship was safe, and that the military stores had not left the island. He scanned the harbor with his telescope once again.

The boat that had been tacking back and forth over the bar had settled on a course making directly for the fort, confirming in Biddlecomb's mind what he had suspected: she was the *Alfred*'s boat, waiting for some sign that the fort had been taken. The change of colors was her cue to approach. No doubt the fleet was under way, probably lying to just the other side of Hog Island.

In the fort below he watched the marines spread out and

search the various storehouses, exploring all the corners of the captured structure. At least they seemed to be enjoying themselves. He looked again at the boat, moving with intolerable slowness. He felt his anxiety and impatience mount with each passing minute.

"That looks like *Alfred*'s longboat, sir," Ferguson offered.

"I believe you're right. You stay here and let me know if the fleet shows up beyond the point, yonder. I'm going down to see what the people in the boat have to say."

The boat would not reach the fort for another fifteen minutes, but he felt that he would explode if he just stood around waiting with his vague and baseless anxiety growing more acute by the minute. He climbed back down the ladder. Ten yards away Captain Nicholas and three of his lieutenants were in animated discussion.

"How goes it, Captain?" Biddlecomb asked, stepping up to the knot of men.

"Not too well, Captain, damn my eyes," Nicholas said, turning and spitting on the hard-packed dirt.

"We've found a prodigious amount of stores," one of the lieutenants said, turning to Biddlecomb. "The great guns you can see, and there's some mortars, as well as round shot and canister and small arms and such. There's a big magazine as well."

"A big magazine? That's a good thing," Biddlecomb said, feeling the first glow of hope that he had been wrong about the lumber.

"There ain't but twenty or so barrels in it, however," Nicholas added. "Twenty barrels of powder for all these guns? You were right, Biddlecomb. I didn't think so last night, thought you were stretching it a bit, but you smoked it. They took our damned powder and made off with it. Son of a bitch!" he added, directed at no one in particular, and stamped his foot on the ground.

There was still hope, of course. The spark in Biddlecomb's breast was dying, but it was not dead. It was still possible that Tottenhill had carried out his orders, had intercepted the escaping ships and recovered the powder.

"I believe a boat from the *Alfred* is approaching," he said. "Shall we go and greet it?"

The front gate, now shut and secured, was opened by the sentries posted there. The two captains stepped out and made their way to the water, walking along the grassy space between the walls of Fort Nassau and the outer wooden palisade. They stepped down onto the beach just as the *Alfred*'s longboat ground ashore, and the midshipman at the tiller scrambled forward and onto the sand.

Biddlecomb felt his hands trembling and clasped them behind his back. This is absurd, he thought, what in hell am I so nervous about? He had no reason to believe that something untoward had happened aboard the *Charlemagne*. It was just the anxiety that every captain feels when away from his command. He vowed that once he learned that all was well, he would worry no more. Neither would he ever leave his ship again for more than a few hours. At least he would not leave it in Tottenhill's command.

"Commodore Hopkins's compliments, sir," the midshipman said, saluting and looking alternately at Biddlecomb and Nicholas, "and please, is it safe to bring the fleet into the harbor?"

"I reckon," said Nicholas. "Biddlecomb?"

"It's safe, at least as far as any threat from the shore goes. But tell me, did the *Charlemagne* get under way last night?"

"Oh, yes, sir. But she's back now, with the fleet."

"And did she take a prize? Did she manage to take the merchantman?"

"No, sir, no merchantman that I know of. She come back alone. But there's no cause to worry. Mr. Sprout sends word that things are fine on board now, and he and Mr. Weatherspoon'll have no difficulty bringing her to an anchor."

"Mr. Sprout? The boatswain? And Mr. Weatherspoon? Where are Mr. Tottenhill and Mr. Rumstick?"

"They're confined aboard the flagship, sir."

"Why . . . ?"

"They were arrested, on account of the riot on board the *Charlemagne* last night. Three men dead, the commodore fit to be tied. Still yelling about it this morning. Did you not know, sir?"

Biddlecomb turned away and stared out over the rippled water of the harbor. He took a deep breath and swallowed hard and twisted his hands together behind his back. He felt his stomach sink away. The nightmare went on and on.

CHAPTER 26

A Court of Inquiry

COMMODORE HOPKINS WAS NOT A HAPPY FLAG OFFICER, AND HE WAS not keeping that fact a secret from Biddlecomb or the dozen or so other men on either side of the table.

The room in which they were meeting, which Hopkins had taken over as the office of the commander in chief, was long and fairly wide with a large table running down the middle. The only natural light came from three narrow windows along the wall facing the parade ground, and Hopkins and the other officers at the inquiry, lining the far side of the table, were forced to hold anything they wished to read at an angle to catch what light they could.

"Well, damn it all to hell," Hopkins growled, not for the first time, "this is one big fucking mess we've got here." He looked up from the reports laid before him, and meeting Biddlecomb's eyes, added, "Again." He leaned back and sighed. "Very well, Captain Biddlecomb, why don't you say what you have to say. And be brief. We've got a prodigious lot to do here, and we can't waste too much time on another one of your foul-ups."

"Very well, sir." Biddlecomb straightened and clasped his hands behind his back. He ran his eyes over the men facing him, the same captains, lieutenants, and marines he had faced at the court-martial. Here he was, as Hopkins said, again.

"Last night around ten P.M., while I was at Fort Montegu, I perceived something floating in the harbor, and on close inspection I found it was fresh lumber. I thought perhaps it might be a jettisoned cargo, and that it might have been jettisoned to make room for military stores that were being spirited away. I sent Mr. Midshipman Weatherspoon to the *Charlemagne* with instructions for Lieutenant Tottenhill to get the ship under way and try and head off any escape. They were to send word to the flagship to inform the commodore of the orders I had given Mr. Tottenhill."

"Why didn't you go aboard the *Charlemagne* yourself?" Captain Whipple asked.

"Well, sir, I did not think it proper for me to leave the landing party without the commodore's permission. I figured I was stretching my authority as it was, sending the *Charlemagne* off, but I thought there was not a moment to lose and it would be faster to just tell Tottenhill what to do than to try and explain my suspicions to the commodore."

"Mr. Tottenhill, what have you to say?"

"Well, sir"—Tottenhill, at Biddlecomb's right-hand side, took a step forward—"last night at just past six bells in the night watch, Mr. Weatherspoon . . . located myself and Mr. Rumstick, purporting to have orders from Captain Biddlecomb. He was not entirely clear as to why the captain wanted us under way, or how he had come to suspect that the military stores or, as we now realize, the majority of the island's gunpowder was being taken away.

"I did not feel certain that Captain Biddlecomb had the authority to order the ship under way, I felt that such an order had to come from the commodore. Lieutenant Rumstick, however, felt strongly that we should get under way without informing the commodore, based on his long familiarity with Captain Biddlecomb. Indeed, I think this committee should be aware of the grievous injuries that my authority has suffered from the onset of this cruise. Captain Biddlecomb and Lieutenant Rumstick have, from the beginning, seen fit to—"

"Thank you, Lieutenant," said Hopkins. "Just tell me, you decided to obey Biddlecomb's orders?"

"Sir, I thought that the most wise course of action should be to—"

"Just a yes or no will suffice."

"Yes, I decided to obey the orders."

"Rumstick?" Hopkins growled, and Rumstick stepped forward.

"Captain Biddlecomb sent the order to get under way. I could see that if the captain was right, which he generally is, we was about to lose the chief thing we came here for."

Rumstick launched into a bare-bones description of the night action: the run west, the taffrail lights, the fight with the sloop. "And then I tried to get the brig under way again and Mr. Tottenhill tried to have me arrested."

"And you resisted?"

"I wasn't in the mood to be arrested, sir."

"You watch that impertinent tongue, mister," Hopkins warned, his anger sparked by Rumstick's insouciance. "And so you set off the brawl among the crew?"

"I don't know what happened, sir, regarding the disturbance forward. I was occupied at the time."

"You were wounded during the fight? Knocked on the head?"

"Aye, sir. Stabbed by some whore's son and knocked over the head."

"You were stabbed?" Hopkins asked, surprised. "You don't seem too damned . . . what? Injured."

"It wasn't too deep, sir. Mr. Weatherspoon cleaned it and bandaged it. I reckon it'll be all right."

"Ah, yes, Mr. Weatherspoon," the commodore said. "As I understand it, you were the one who stopped the riot and restored order. Correct?"

"Well, sir,"—Weatherspoon stepped forward—"respectfully, sir, I think calling it a riot is going it a bit high. It was sort of a scuffle, sir, a bit of pushing and the odd punch, but not a riot. I just fired off a few pistols and that settled the men down again, and we made our way back to Hanover Sound, sir."

Biddlecomb wondered if the officers at the inquiry would realize the extent to which Weatherspoon was lying. Biddlecomb, for one, was not fooled. He had been aboard the *Charlemagne* that morning, had insisted that the *Alfred*'s boat take him out to his ship. The men that he had encountered there—battered, bloody, limping, and bruised—looked as if they had been in a desperate scrape with the enemy. But they had inflicted the hurt on themselves, Charlemagne against Charlemagne, in what had to have been a full-scale internecine battle.

By the time the brig had let its anchor go in Nassau Harbor, the atmosphere on board was no longer explosive. Rather it had settled into something else, a dull and permanent hatred between two factions of the crew.

He was sickened by what he saw. How had it gotten this far out of hand? What had he done differently this time than he had all the other times he had run happy ships with cooperative crews?

It seemed to him that he was no different from that poor stupid bastard Pendexter, captain of the *Icarus,* against whom he had led a mutiny, a mutiny fueled by Pendexter's failure to understand the nature of proper discipline.

As the *Charlemagne* stood into the harbor with the rest of the fleet, he had assembled the men aft. "I am not blind to the problems on board this brig," he had said to the collected crew. "I had hoped that getting out of the ice in Pennsylvania, getting into blue water and getting on with our work, would shake some of that loose, but clearly it has not.

"Whether you like your officers or not makes no difference to me. They were appointed by the Continental Congress and that is the law. But let me assure you that I am back in command here, and I will see this ship is run fairly, and I will see it is run with discipline.

"I reckon we'll be back in the Colonies in not too long a

time, and then we can shake this out. But for now we've got close on a dozen men down with smallpox, we've got work to do, and I expect every man to fall to with a will. You don't have to like your orders, but you have to obey them or you better believe I'll be down on you like the wrath of God. Mr. Sprout, dismiss the men."

"Three cheers for the captain!" Sprout called, much to Biddlecomb's annoyance, and the men in the waist did a tolerable job of belting out their "Huzzahs!'s."

How much had he sounded like Pendexter, just then? Not much, he assured himself. He had not threatened the men to any great degree, had not stopped their tot. No, he assured himself, he was not losing his ability to command men. Nor was he unaware of what was causing this discontent. But they would be home soon, and Tottenhill would be gone, or he, Biddlecomb, would resign his commission. And there was another thing.

"Hackett, lay aft here," he called out, and Hackett shuffled up to the quarterdeck. "Hackett, I know a sea lawyer when I see one, and I know a shifty, lying son of a whore as well. Shut your mouth," he added as Hackett made to protest.

"If I had proof of what I think you're up to, I'd hang you faster than you can spit, do you understand? You just watch yourself, and if I feel generous when we get back to the Colonies, I'll let you walk away from this ship. If you cross me, you'll never walk again. Understood?"

"Whatever it is you think—" Hackett began again.

"Shut your gob, Hackett! I asked you if you understood."

"Aye."

"Good. Get the hell away from me and keep away from me, if you know what's good for you."

Biddlecomb did not think it a great coincidence that Hackett and Tottenhill were both from North Carolina. Tottenhill, it seemed, was seeing Yankee conspiracies around every bulkhead, and Hackett, if he understood the potential power of those differences, which no doubt he did, could be using them to ferment this discontent.

Biddlecomb wanted nothing more than to chain Hackett down in the hold, but such an act, with no proof of what he suspected, would only serve to tear the crew wider apart.

"Well," Commodore Hopkins said after a long silence, "I reckon we've heard enough. Biddlecomb, stay here. The rest of you are dismissed. Oh, one last thing."

The *Charlemagne*'s officers stopped in midturn and turned back.

"There's been some rumors going around about a duel between certain officers on your ship, but since everyone seems to be loyal to one or the other, no one will come forward on that. So let me say this. There will be no dueling between officers. If I find out it has happened, I will drum everyone involved out of the navy. I'll leave 'em on the beach right here, let the citizens of Nassau take care of 'em. If any officer is killed in a duel, I will hang the other for murder. That is all. Now you are dismissed."

Like puppets controlled by the same string, Tottenhill, Rumstick, and Weatherspoon saluted, turned, and left the room. When the door was closed, Hopkins leaned forward and looked down the table to Captain Whipple. "Well, Whipple, what do you think?"

"Damn strange situation," Whipple began. "Biddlecomb was doing what he thought best, and as it happens he was right. Even if he didn't have the authority to order the *Charlemagne* away, I reckon if he had stopped them from taking the powder, we'd be calling him a hero right now.

"Tottenhill made a hash of it, like an idiot, letting them ships get away. Rumstick's a hothead, always has been, but his heart was in the right place. He just wanted to get at the enemy. Hard to see where the blame lies."

"You other gentlemen concur?" Hopkins asked, and he was greeted with various nods and yeses. He leaned back and grunted, staring at Biddlecomb.

"I don't see as there's any action we need to take here. We ain't got time for this goddamned nonsense anyway. But listen here, Biddlecomb. I've known you a long time, always thought of you as a good officer, but you're making a godforsaken mess of this. This is the second time we've had an enquiry into goings-on aboard the *Charlemagne,* and you had to ask me to step in back at Hole-in-the-Rock. I expect more from you."

Biddlecomb gritted his teeth and held Hopkins's gaze. He knew that his face was flushing, and that made him more angry still. He felt like a schoolboy being taken to task by the teacher, or an apprentice catching it from the first mate. It was a sensation he had not had to endure for many years.

He was aware of the weight of his sword on his belt and the clothing—the uniform—he had had made in Philadelphia. The thought of his pompous, self-indulgent love of adulation fanned his present humiliation brighter. If he could just hold it together until their return to the Colonies, he thought again, it would be all right. Until then he would oversee every minute of every man's life aboard the *Charlemagne.*

"In any event," Hopkins continued, "the *Charlemagne,* for whatever reason, missed out taking the merchantman and the powder is gone. Over one hundred goddamned barrels of it is gone to God knows where, and we've lost the chief reason for our coming here. Do you have anything to add, Captain?"

He did. "I am very sorry about this situation, sir, and I will see that the *Charlemagne* is run tighter. As to last night, I was clearly exceeding my authority, ordering the *Charlemagne* away. After all, sealing the harbor and keeping the powder on the island was not my responsibility."

He hoped that Hopkins would catch that subtle dig, and judging from the commodore's frown, he did. But Biddlecomb would not take the blame for the powder. The problems of the *Charlemagne* might be his fault, but failing to blockade the harbor and losing the powder was not.

"Very good, Captain. You are dismissed."

Biddlecomb saluted and stepped from the officers' mess, blinking in the bright sun. He hoped that no one would try to speak with him; he was in no mood for conversation. Looking around, it appeared that there was no danger of that.

Through the open gates of the fort a group of marines led by Lieutenant Trevett of the *Providence* was escorting, indeed practically dragging, a big, heavyset man. The unfortunate prisoner was dressed in some type of uniform coat liberally covered with medals and sashes, his hands bound at the wrists. Some high official of His Majesty's government being brought before the committee, Biddlecomb thought, though watching that man's misery did nothing to ameliorate his own.

Once the ships were loaded with the plunder from the island, they would be heading for America, Biddlecomb reflected. They had to, there was no other logical choice. Too many men were sick and the ships would be too heavy laden for much else. They would head for the Colonies. And then he would clean house.

Hackett sat at a table in the dark tavern surrounded by six others of the *Charlemagne*'s crew. While it could not be said that he sat at the head of the table, the table being round, still it was clear that all attention in the group was focused on him. He would not have allowed it to be otherwise.

The tavern was in fact the gutted front room of a poor private dwelling that opened onto a filthy alleyway. There was room enough to fit three tables comfortably, though seven were crammed in the place. The clientele, save for the American sailors, were largely black freemen and poor whites, and all were drinking great quantities of the island's cheap rum.

The place was far from the waterfront, farther inland even than Government House, in a mean section of town where those marines that the commodore had appointed as provosts were unlikely to venture. It was Hackett's favorite place on the island, a dark hole that he had visited whenever the various ships aboard which he had served called at Nassau.

"Shut up, you stupid bastards," he said to two of his fellow revelers who were engaged in a spirited argument over whether the whores in Bermuda were superior to those in Jamaica. Hackett was fairly certain that neither man had visited either of those places and was sick of listening to them.

The table fell quiet and Hackett knew that they all were watching him, waiting for some word. He, in turn, was staring at the gold watch in his hand, turning it over and enjoying the dull gleam of the metal. It was part of a small but valuable cache that he had stolen from one of the fine homes near Government House, the third he had looted that day.

He smiled a faint smile at the thought of the jewelry and coins he had taken, the small, beautifully inlaid pistol stuck in his belt, and what he had done to the filthy bitch who had tried to fight him off.

Hopkins, that stupid old man, had issued an order that no looting or harm of any sort would befall the people of the island. Hackett snorted and shook his head at the thought of it. Here they were, a conquering army, and they could not loot the island? Not likely.

He looked up at last. "Allen, get us another two bottles," he ordered, throwing two of his recently acquired gold coins on the table. "And tell that black bastard he can keep the change, but we'll be looking for some more from him, and not just his rum that tastes like horse piss."

He was getting drunk and it felt good. He felt the numbness spread through him. It suppressed the anger and it allowed him to think. He understood now why Biddlecomb had given them a run ashore. He never thought that it would happen, but now he understood.

Biddlecomb wanted the men to be happy. He wanted them to work together, and keeping them penned up on the *Charlemagne* while the rest of the fleet took their pleasure on the island would not do much to that end. Instead he kept them aboard for two days, made them think they would not be going ashore, and then on the third day he gave them leave. It made him appear as a benevolent god, rather than the manipulative whoreson that he was. Most captains would have denied leave altogether, and that would just have made the problem worse. But not Biddlecomb.

"Clever bastard," Hackett said out loud as Allen thumped two more bottles down on the table. Played it just right. Just like he did with the deserters, the son of a bitch. But he would not win in the end. That was not tolerable.

"What'd you say, Hackett?" one of his followers asked. The tin cup in front of the man was sitting in a puddle of rum, which grew larger as he poured more liquor.

"I said Biddlecomb's a clever bastard, that's what."

"I always reckoned Biddlecomb for a stupid Yankee whore's son myself," said Allen.

"He's smarter than you are, dumb arse," Hackett growled. "Did you think he was going to give us a run ashore?"

There was a moment of silent reflection. "No."

"And why do you think he did?"

That query was greeted with further silence, which, after half a minute, remained unbroken. "It ain't cause he likes us," Hackett supplied at last. "He wanted us off the ship. It's all part of the plan. You know what the commodore said about looting. Biddlecomb give us a run ashore so Woodberry and Ferguson can put the loot they stole in our dunnage. Then tonight he has an inspection, accompanied by Lieutenant Fuckcloth and his marines, and there you have it. Stolen goods, and we're all in irons and hanging at the yardarm the next morning." Along with holding his rage in check, Hackett found that rum was a great stimulant to his imagination.

The silence that greeted that statement was stunned, rather than confused. Hackett made a great show of reaching for a bottle, filling his tin cup, and draining half of it.

"How do you know that?" Allen asked.

"How do you think I know?"

"Tottenhill?"

"Of course. He don't let that sort of thing happen on board

without I know about it. He knows who's running things on the lower deck."

"Well, what are we going to do?" another asked. Hackett could hear the panic in his voice. After all those long months together he could still be amazed by the sheer stupidity of these bastards.

"I'm having things looked after, don't you worry, my boy," he said, taking another long and histrionic drink. "There won't be one bit of stolen loot in your dunnage, any of you. I seen to that. I reckon Biddlecomb won't even bother with an inspection, once he hears how I fixed things."

Looks of relief flashed among the men at the table.

"But something has to be done. Something permanent, I mean," Allen said. "Biddlecomb'll get us, sooner or later, if we don't stop him."

"Biddlecomb's on his way out," Hackett replied with his usual air of knowing confidence, the attitude that he had long ago realized made men believe anything he had to say. "Commodore chewed his ass for losing the gunpowder. He makes a hash of one more thing or shows he can't hold his ship together, then he's out, and guess who's in."

"Tottenhill?"

"That's right. My friend Tottenhill becomes captain, and won't that be a merry time."

It would be a merry time indeed, Hackett thought, but he was not nearly as confident in its coming to pass as he let on.

Biddlecomb's threats had shaken him. How did that bastard know what was acting? He did not for one moment believe that Biddlecomb would let him walk away from the ship once they were back in the Colonies. No, it would be the chains for him, and the quiet and then the noose.

Killing Biddlecomb might do the trick, but it was unlikely Hackett would get the chance to do it without being caught. And that left just one thing. Biddlecomb had to be made to look a fool, had to be totally discredited, drummed out of the service. And then he, Hackett, would be beyond the bastard's reach.

"So, listen here, gentlemen," Hackett said. "If you don't want that Biddlecomb to do for you, then we better do for him first. You just stick by ol' Amos Hackett, lads, because I have a plan. You had best believe I have a plan."

And looking at their stupid faces, Hackett knew that they did indeed believe it, every word.

CHAPTER 27

The Spoils of War

PRESIDENT JOHN BROWN WAS AWARE, AS HE PEERED THROUGH THE telescope on the veranda of Government House, that he was doing exactly the thing that had so annoyed him when Governor Browne did it. The difference, however, was that he was gathering useful intelligence, whereas Browne had merely been sight-seeing.

"Well, Gambier, I think these damned rebels are soon to leave us," he said.

"What, is there nothing left that they can take? Is there not some trinket that they've overlooked? No, I suspect they'll spend another week at least to make certain they've left nothing behind."

President Brown straightened and turned to John Gambier. The two men were alone on the veranda. "Now, I don't like these bastards any more than you, but you must admit they've kept their looting to a minimum. Really just that incident last week, with that poor woman. Nothing compared to what the Frenchies or the Dons would have done."

"Well, I suppose you have a point. They've behaved themselves for the most part. But you've no doubt heard some of the tales Lieutenant Frazer has been telling, of what they were going to do to him before he escaped. The night they shot you."

"Yes, well, I'm not certain Lieutenant Frazer isn't . . . augmenting his tale a bit. In any event they've picked Montegu and Nassau clean, and it would appear from here that they are sealing up their hatches. From that I deduce that they will soon be sailing for wherever their nefarious plans take them next."

"So it would appear that Governor Browne will be going with them?"

"It would appear so. I have pleaded almost daily for his release, but so far it has done no good. Yesterday they took him from the fort onto the ship that they style the flagship."

"That doesn't bode well."

"No." Brown retrieved his coat from the chair over which it was flung and pulled it on. "I'm off now to meet with that Hopkins, their so-called commodore. Once again. And once again I shall beg for the governor's release."

Since the American rebels had marched into Fort Nassau nearly two weeks before, Brown had been in almost daily contact with Commodore Hopkins, and some of their discussions had in fact involved the governor. Governor Browne had at that time been a prisoner in Fort Nassau, as was Lieutenant Babbidge. With them was a Mr. Thomas Irving, whom President Brown had represented to Hopkins as a powerful and unrepentant Tory and who was, not coincidentally (though Brown did not say as much to Hopkins), one of President Brown's most outspoken critics on the island.

With those administrative nuisances out of the way Brown had been able to accomplish a great deal in the way of American/Nassauvian cooperation. Fresh supplies had been provided to the invaders, and the shops, taverns, and whorehouses had remained open for their convenience and for the not inconsiderable profit to the owners of those establishments.

And more importantly, the looting and pillage of the island had been kept to a bare minimum, and it was widely held that this protection of the inhabitants had been accomplished through the untiring efforts of himself, President John Brown.

In actual fact it was the commodore who, for the most part, held the Americans in check, despite the vocal protests of the sailors, marines, and a surprising number of their officers. This confirmed in Brown's mind what he had long suspected, that being a gentleman was in no way a prerequisite for being an officer in the Continental service. Hopkins, with his crude ways and foul mouth, certainly did not deserve that sobriquet.

Still, the commodore had been cooperative and, whether he meant to be or not, had been very beneficial in advancing President Brown's career.

Brown crossed Bay Street and walked once more through the palisade surrounding Fort Nassau, having left John Gambier at Government House. The fort's big front gate was opened, and no sentries were guarding it. That formality had been abandoned after the first week of the American occupation, after each side had come to realize that the other wished no sort of confrontation.

Brown crossed the parade ground to the officers' mess. Fewer men were in the fort than he had seen since the rebels' arrival, and that further suggested that they were about to up anchor and go. He pushed open the door to the mess. There were no sentries there either, and that was odd. He looked inside.

The room was deserted. All of the papers, the weapons, the cups, bottles, and personal effects that had cluttered the space were gone.

"May I help you, President Brown?" The voice from behind his back startled him and he turned around.

"Ah, Captain Biddlecomb." Brown extended his hand and received a halfhearted handshake in return. "How very good to see you again," he said, though Biddlecomb was in fact the one he least wished to see. Of all the American officers he seemed the least taken by the president's charming ways. He seemed suspicious and not a little hostile. Brown worried about what advice he might be giving to Hopkins. "The commodore is no longer in the fort?"

"No, sir. The commodore has retired to the flagship. We will be getting under way directly. If you have any more military stores on the island, I pray you keep them to yourself as we have no more room for them, even with the merchantman we've contracted. I'm just ashore to round up the last of the marines and see everything secured."

"Well," Brown said. This was excellent news. "I'm sorry to see you go, I was quite enjoying the company. I trust you gentlemen found your stay here agreeable?"

"Very much so, thank you. We were most lavishly entertained by yourself and the other men of note. I speak for all of us when I say that I am grateful for your cooperation, whatever your motives might have been."

"Indeed," said Brown, not certain of how that last should be taken. "Might it be possible for me to speak with the governor once more before you sail?"

"You shall have to ask the commodore that, but I can take you out to the flagship, if that would be convenient."

"That would be most convenient, thank you."

The two men, Brown and Biddlecomb, sat in the stern sheets of the longboat as the boat crew pulled for the flagship, anchored near the western end of Potter's Cay. The boat was silent. It made Brown uncomfortable.

"Captain, that schooner there, the black one that came in the other day. Is she part of your fleet?"

Biddlecomb looked over his shoulder, though Brown had to imagine he knew which schooner they were discussing. "That's the *Fly*. She and a sloop in our fleet, the *Hornet*, collided in a gale on the way down here. We thought she was lost, but she just damaged her rig. Finally caught up with us."

"And the *Hornet?* Was she lost?"

"Apparently not. She seems to have made it back to the Delaware Bay."

"Well, thank the Lord for that." The words did not sound nearly as sincere as Brown had hoped.

Brown was both pleased and relieved to find upon reaching

the flagship that Commodore Hopkins, unlike Captain Biddlecomb, still seemed to regard him as a genuine friend and devotee to the American cause. The president was greeted with military honors as he made his way awkwardly up the *Alfred*'s side, and the commodore shook his hand when the piping was done.

"President Brown, good to see you again, sir. I wish I could ask you to dine, but we're under way on the turn of the tide, which is no more than an hour from now, and we've still a great deal to do."

"I quite understand, sir, thank you. I won't take more of your time. But, if I might be so bold as to enquire, is it your intention to bear Governor Browne and the others off with you?"

"Indeed it is. I reckon you didn't intend to give so much away, but from what you've let slip I've come to realize that the governor is an important cove in the British government, and I imagine he'll make an important prisoner. And like you mentioned, he presumed to fire on my men and to send away most of the island's gunpowder."

"I fear I've been too free with my words in that regard, letting on that the governor is related to the Earl of Dartmouth and such. I suppose I'm enough devoted to the American cause that I have little thought for what bits of intelligence I might accidentally reveal. But pray, might I see the governor one last time before you sail?"

"By all means. Mr. Carey," Hopkins called out to a midshipman standing nearby, "please escort President Brown to the wardroom to see the governor."

The wardroom was two decks below the weather deck with an overhead so low that even Brown, who was of no great height, had to bend at the waist to walk. It was dark as well, being lit by only two lanterns at either end of the room. It smelled like what it was—a tightly packed living space on an old wooden ship.

Gov. Montfort Browne's large bulk was crammed into one

of the small cabins that lined the long room, with two sentries posted outside the door. So miserable did the big man look that President Brown was moved to pity, an emotion that was generally a stranger in his heart.

"Ah, Brown, here you are!" the governor said, standing, bent nearly double, and walking the two steps to the door. The midshipman removed the latch and President Brown stepped into the cabin, shaking the governor's outstretched hand.

"I heard some piping just then, sounded like someone important coming aboard," the governor said with a pathetic note of hope in his voice.

"It was just one of their captains. You know that these rebels treat all of their own as if they were peers of the realm."

"Have you talked to that Hopkins that styles himself admiral?"

"I have."

"And what does he say?"

President Brown shook his head. "All of my pleading and my appeals to his humanity have been for naught. He is determined to bear you away. I even tried to tell him that you were a man of no great consequence, that taking you prisoner would accomplish nothing, but he didn't believe that for a minute. He's well aware of your stature in government and your connections. He won't be disabused of the notion that you would make a valuable prisoner of war."

"Does he know of my relationship to the Earl of Dartmouth?"

"I fear so, and probably did before he sailed from America."

The governor nodded his head slowly. "It is my lot to suffer, then, for my king, and I accept that, sir, I do. But I have been making a list, oh, yes. A list of those that have been too helpful by far with these damned rebels, and, if I ain't mistaken, had a hand in bringing them here."

"Indeed," said President Brown. This was potential trouble. For all of his foolishness, Browne really was well connected. He had the ear of Lord George Germain and the Earl of Sandwich and Gen. William Howe. Not to mention the Earl of Dartmouth, which he did, and often. Any one of those men could make life most uncomfortable for someone accused by the governor of treachery.

"Yes, indeed, a list," Browne continued. "And that damned James Gould is the first on it, and there are others. Here, pray take this." The governor handed Brown a letter. "You are one of the few I can trust, I dare say the only one who has tried to effect my release. This is a letter to Germain with the names of those who are too friendly by half with the King's enemies. They won't give me sealing wax, the creatures, so please seal it with the governor's seal, you know where it is, and post it as soon as ever you can."

"Of course, Your Excellency," said Brown, greatly relieved to find himself in possession of the governor's list. Now he could read the letter without even having to break a seal and would be free to act as the contents dictated.

"And, sir, I have brought some of your papers for you. Your commission appointing you captain general and that constituting you vice admiral of the Bahama Islands. I had thought perhaps they might be of some help to you in negotiating your release."

"Yes, well done, thank you," said the governor, taking the papers from President Brown. From the deck above came a shouted order, too muffled to distinguish the words, and a second later the sound of dozens of men rushing to various quarters of the ship.

"I fear they are getting under way," said President Brown. "I must leave lest we both be carried off."

"Yes, hurry," said the governor. "And please give my regrets to my wife and my aged aunt."

"Yes, Governor, of course."

"And, Brown? Bless you, sir, for all of your faithful service to me."

By the time the *Alfred*'s jolly boat set President Brown ashore on one of the long wharves thrust out from Bay Street, the first of the American fleet had won its anchor and was gathering way for the west end of the harbor. Brown unfolded the governor's letter and read it as he walked up the narrow cobbled street toward Government House. There, as promised, was the name of James Gould, along with Alexander Frazer (a well-known rebel, the governor assured Germain), Thomas Duncoun, Jeremy Newton, John Kemp the Younger, and John Bedon-Adderly. And nowhere in the missive was Brown's name mentioned.

He smiled and folded the letter back up. There might have been some unpleasant repercussions if he had been forced to consign the letter to the fireplace rather than the post, but as it was, he would send it, and gladly. Germain could see those men locked up forever, and with Brown's blessing.

He walked up the familiar wide stairway of Government House and out onto the veranda once more. All of the fleet was under way now, strung out in a long line sailing west with the prevailing wind. The first in line, the *Andrew Doria* if he was not mistaken, had already cleared the far end of Hog Island and had turned away north.

There was a great deal to do. He had first to write to the admiral in Jamaica and see about getting some naval defense for the island, in case those rebellious sons of whores thought fit to return. He had to convene the General Assembly and see about appointing commissioners to undertake repairs to Fort Montegu and Fort Nassau. As long as he was in command, there would be no more invasions of his island.

"Ah, Brown, you're back." John Gambier stepped out on the veranda next to Brown and joined him in watching the American fleet working out of the harbor. "The governor, I assume, is still with them?"

"Hopkins would not yield, plead as I might. But what's done is done, and we've too much work to do to stand around pitying the man. So what say you have the boy fetch us some rum punch and we'll set to it?"

"Very good," said Gambier, heading back across the veranda.

"Oh, Gambier, one other thing. You know, Browne took with him His Majesty's commission appointing him captain general and the one appointing him vice admiral of the Bahama Islands. All he left is His Majesty's instructions to his governor and the great seal. There is no one now on the island with an appointment from His Majesty. In the absence of such, naturally I, as president of His Majesty's Council, assume command of the colony."

"Yes. What is your point?"

"My point is that I think it only proper that from now on I should be addressed as 'Governor Brown.' You understand, protocol and what have you."

CHAPTER 28

False Colors

" 'THEY THAT GO DOWN TO THE SEA IN SHIPS, AND DO THEIR WORK on great waters . . . ,' " Biddlecomb recited. He stared blankly at the Grand Union flag, the very same one that had flown over Fort Nassau, which was now draped over the tightly wrapped body of Jonathan Bailey, foredeckman. Late foredeckman.

"We commend thy body to the deep. May God have mercy on your soul." He nodded to the two men at the inboard end of the plank. They tilted it up and the earthly remains of Jonathan Bailey slid over the side and disappeared into unknown fathoms of water. The third to go that way in as many days.

"Mr. Tottenhill, you may dismiss the men."

"We'll stand down to the watch on deck," Tottenhill shouted. "Dismissed!"

Fore and aft hats were clapped on heads, and the men, melancholy, sullen, and lethargic, marched off to various quarters of the ship. Spirits on board the *Charlemagne* had sunk low, lower even than during the second time they had been trapped in the ice. The men lacked even the spark and energy of their former anger. A morose, shuffling spirit prevailed.

Things had gone well, as well as could have been hoped, during the first week that they had lay on the hook in Nassau harbor, relieving that place of every warlike store that could be found.

The Charlemagnes, for their sins, had expected to be deprived of shore leave, and so Biddlecomb was not surprised to see their attitudes much improved when, after two days confined aboard, he announced that they would get a run ashore after all. It had been a difficult decision, and one with which his wardroom did not agree, but the resulting improvement in humor told Biddlecomb that it had been the right one.

The animosity was not gone by the end of that first week, not even close. But it was ameliorated to some degree through hard work, fine weather, and nights ashore. Tottenhill and Rumstick were less at odds because Biddlecomb was always there, always in command. By appropriating the authority of the officers he helped heal the sectional divide in the crew, and his steadying presence, he knew, had a further good effect on the men. It did little to improve his officers' moods, however, but after the way they had let things run away from them, he did not care.

He had spoken little to either of the lieutenants since the riot, had entertained no one in his cabin for the two weeks since they had left the island.

He stepped up to the quarterdeck, looked at the slate hanging from the binnacle box, then stepped over to the leeward rail. The rest of the fleet was strung out before him, save for the big *Columbus,* a quarter mile away and just a little astern, bringing up the rear.

None of them were sailing fast; the wind was light and dead astern, their bottoms were foul from their time in warm waters, and their holds were heavy laden with cannon, mortars, shot, and all the plunder that New Providence had yielded them. But none of this was slowing them up as much as being shorthanded, and that was due to the yellow jack.

He had seen the first signs during their last few days on the island, and he prayed that it was not so, but when the first man died in a burning delirium, he knew that it was yellow fever. By the time they left New Providence, the fleet had buried ten men, and not one of the ships was free of the disease.

That was almost two weeks before. Since that time the fleet had sailed north, slowly north, bound for whatever destination the commodore had in mind, with the coastline of America a few hundred miles beyond the western horizon. The weather had been calm for the most part and the sea empty, and the men had little to do beyond the routine of shipboard life and watching their mates take sick and die. It was doing nothing to bolster the Charlemagnes' already flagging morale.

"Good morning, Mr. Rumstick," Biddlecomb said. With the voyage near an end he was feeling more charitably disposed toward his officers.

"Morning, sir," Rumstick said. Biddlecomb could see the surprise, and the hint of relief, in his friend's face at the casual and hitherto absent greeting. "This is a hell of a daily ritual we got going here, sir, sending a man over the standing part of the foresheet."

"I can think of better ways to start the day than a funeral."

"So can I, sir, but I don't think we're going to see any soon. Two more from my watch are down, one from Tottenhill's, and three of Faircloth's marines."

Biddlecomb stared out at the fleet, and for a long moment he did not answer. At last he turned and met Rumstick's gaze. They were alone on their little patch of quarterdeck. "We're close to home. By my reckoning we should see Block Island bearing due west by the first dogwatch. I don't know where Hopkins is intending to put in, but damn me if I won't be glad to get there."

"This has not been a real pleasant cruise, starting with being frozen in the damned Delaware River."

"Once our anchor is down I intend to land these sick men and then purge this ship of every son of a whore we took on since Cambridge. I don't give a damn if we spend the next year trying to fill our crew out again, I'll be rid of them or I'll resign my command."

It felt good to talk this way, to confide in Rumstick again the way he had when Rumstick had been first officer. Before he had stopped inviting any of his officers to the great cabin just to avoid having to listen to Tottenhill. It felt good to emerge from his self-imposed exile.

"I don't reckon you'll have trouble filling out a crew, even if you leave every one of these grumbling sons of bitches on the beach," Rumstick said, and with a smile that owed nothing to flattery added, "You're still the famous Captain Biddlecomb."

"God help us all. That's kind of you to say, but I fear the reputation of this ship is sullied now. And my own may be beyond repair."

"Captain, I . . . ," Rumstick began. Clearly he blamed himself in a large way for this blight on Biddlecomb's reputation, and while Biddlecomb did not think Rumstick was entirely undeserving of that blame, he was not in the mood to hear a desperate apology.

"Excuse me, Mr. Rumstick, but I must go below and see to the sick," he said, and with that excuse he made his retreat forward and below.

The sick berth was normally located in the forward end of the tween decks, but normally it never housed more than half a dozen men at any time. That morning a full twenty-five of the *Charlemagne*'s complement were down with yellow jack, two with broken limbs, and seven more with some disease that Biddlecomb did not recognize, and the sick berth stretched from the manger boards forward to well aft of the galley stove.

He made his way forward, stopping at each hammock to inquire of each man how he was doing, in those cases where the sick man was neither unconscious nor delirious.

The smell below was much improved over the last few days since the weather had permitted Biddlecomb to order the tarpaulins peeled back off the hatches and windsails rigged to funnel fresh air below and relieve the fetid atmosphere. Now the dull sunlight came down through the main hatch, a great square block of light moving back and forth with the roll of the ship and divided into many smaller squares by the grating through which it filtered.

Biddlecomb offered what words of encouragement he could, telling the sick men how close they were to their destination and to the further relief that would soon be theirs.

"Georges Bank bears north and east, Wilson," he said to one man, a Gloucester native. "Reckon you'll be hauling cod there again before too long." And: "A day or two, Michaels, and you'll be ashore and we'll see to getting you a doctor who's not so ugly as Thigpen here."

Thigpen was a waister and former apothecary's assistant who had been pressed into service as the *Charlemagne*'s surgeon. He was doing his best, and Biddlecomb was impressed by how good his best was, but an untrained man could only do so much. For that matter, a trained man could only do so much, and Biddlecomb doubted that a board-certified surgeon or even a medical doctor could have effected much more than Thigpen had.

"How are you feeling, Gray?" Gray, it occurred to Biddlecom, was one of Hackett's followers, one of those who had foolishly tried to arrest Ezra and had paid a heavy toll for that ill-considered action. His crooked nose was testament to the inadvisability of coming to grips with Rumstick. Now he lay gripping the edge of his hammock, drenched in sweat despite the cool of the morning.

"Not good, sir," Gray managed to get out. Biddlecomb grabbed his wrist and squeezed it in a reassuring gesture. "We'll be landing you soon, Gray, don't you worry. A nice clean hospital and good food and no bosuns running around shouting."

"Thank you, sir," Gray whispered, genuine gratitude in his eyes and in his voice. Biddlecomb hoped that he was wrong in thinking that Gray would likely be the guest of honor at the next morning's ceremony. Malice was not a part of Biddlecomb's nature.

"Sir, sir," he heard Weatherspoon's voice, low and urgent as the midshipman hurried across the tween deck. "Sir, hail from . . . oh, dear Lord. Gray's done for, ain't he, sir?"

"What is it, Mr. Weatherspoon?" Biddlecomb asked curtly.

"Beg your pardon, sir, but there's a hail from the masthead and they've spotted a strange sail, sir, on the larboard quarter and three miles or so to leeward."

It could be anything, Biddlecomb told himself, and of all possibilities it was most likely an American merchantman bound in or out of one of the many ports along that stretch of seaboard. But all the logic in the world was not able to master the tingling on the soles of his feet, the excitement that he felt at the sound of the words "a strange sail."

"Tell Mr. Rumstick I'll be on deck momentarily." Despite his desire to see what possibilities this sighting offered, he forced himself to continue his rounds, giving each man the attention that he would have received had there been no break in the routine. At last, having finished a whispered and disheartening consultation with Thigpen, he climbed the ladder to the weather deck and stepped aft.

All of the *Charlemagne*'s officers were clustered at the leeward rail, and each was aiming a telescope across the water at the distant sail. Biddlecomb took up his own glass and did likewise. There was little to see, just two topgallant sails and two topsails, gray patches against a lighter grey sky.

"What do you make of her, Mr. Tottenhill?" he asked.

"Brig or a snow, sir, sailing roughly the same course as we are. Can't see any colors."

After ten minutes of observation none of the ship's officers had anything substantial to add to that assessment, nor could the lookout at the masthead give any further intelligence.

"Shall I signal the flag, sir?" Weatherspoon asked. He already had the ensign bent to its halyard, the signal for seeing a strange sail being to hoist and lower the ensign as many times as there were strange vessels to be seen.

"Has *Columbus* already signaled?"

"Well, sir . . . to be sure . . . ," Weatherspoon equivocated. He clearly had not bothered to look.

"*Columbus* has made no signals, sir," Rumstick offered. "I reckon she can't see this fellow, what with the haze."

"Hold a moment on that signal, Mr. Weatherspoon. Helmsman," Biddlecomb said, "make your head north by east, one-half east."

"North by east, one-half east, aye, sir," the helmsman said, pushing the tiller over half a foot and turning the *Charlemagne* slightly, almost imperceptibly, away from the fleet and toward the stranger on the horizon.

"I'm laying aloft," Biddlecomb said at last. His growing sense of anticipation for some pending action was foolish and baseless, he knew, but still it was there, and he could not endure standing around in that uncertain state. "Mr. Rumstick, I'll thank you to get the foresail off her."

"Aye, sir," Rumstick said, doing an admirable job of hiding his curiosity at that strange order and passing the word even as Biddlecomb pulled himself into the main shrouds.

He climbed steadily upward, not so slow as to look bad and not so fast as to be breathing hard when at last he reached the main topmast crosstrees. He was still fifteen feet below the lookout, who was straddling the main topgallant yard as if riding a horse, but he was high enough to get a decent view of the distant vessel.

It was a brig to be sure, they were close enough and he was high enough to see that for certain. She had no colors flying, but a flag was not the only thing that could give a ship's identity away. Biddlecomb rested his telescope on a ratline and peered at her sails, noting every detail; the narrow roach, the cut of the jib, the steeve of the bowsprit. His glass revealed nothing that diminished his feeling of anticipation.

Morale aboard the *Charlemagne* was all but nonexistent, and his own good name, the immediate jewel of the soul, as Shakespeare called it, was much damaged as well. Nothing would go so far to restoring both as capturing a brig-of-war belonging to the Royal Navy.

For the first time in fifteen minutes he turned away from the sail to larboard and looked over the starboard side toward the *Columbus*. With the wind dead astern and the *Columbus* last in line, she would have been the natural choice for Hopkins to order in pursuit of the stranger.

But she was now abeam of the *Charlemagne* and drawing ahead, the *Charlemagne*'s speed having dropped off after Biddlecomb ordered the foresail stowed. And even though she was passing the *Charlemagne,* she was farther away now than she had been half an hour before, a result of Biddlecomb's subtle course change.

If the commodore ever perceived what he had done, holding off signaling the flag until the *Charlemagne* was the closest in the fleet to the enemy, then he would stamp out what little part of Biddlecomb's reputation was still glowing, cussing like a fiend the whole time. And that was only fair; Biddlecomb was aware that his actions were selfish and unprofessional.

And he did not care a whit.

He closed his telescope and stepped down to the topmast shrouds and made his way to deck. "Gentlemen," he addressed the quarterdeck in general, "I believe the sail yonder is a British brig-of-war, about the same size as ourselves. We are going to take it. Please clear for action."

There were smiles all around as this information was digested and the officers envisioned the pending action. Not one among them was unaware of the *Charlemagne*'s tarnished reputation, and though each believed that the others were at fault, all were equally anxious to make improvements in that quarter. With a chorus of "Aye, sir's" and the lieutenants hurried off to their respective stations, shouting orders to the men, who could not possibly move as quickly as the officers would have liked.

"Helmsman, fall off. Hands to the braces, starboard tack!" Biddlecomb shouted, and the *Charlemagne* turned boldly away from the fleet until her jibboom was pointed at the place on the ocean that she and the stranger to leeward would meet if they held their present courses.

"Sir, shall I run up the colors?" Weatherspoon asked.

"No, not quite yet." Biddlecomb thought of the many flags that he had brought aboard, colors of half a dozen countries. There was no reason to reveal themselves this early in the game.

Ten minutes later Weatherspoon reported a signal from the flagship. "White pendant at the mizzen topmast head—that's to speak with us—and a red pendant at the mizzen peak. That's fall into line ahead."

The midshipman's report was followed by silence as Biddlecomb considered the tactical situation. The flagship had finally noticed that something was going on. As well they might; the *Charlemagne* was sailing diagonally away from the fleet, and he was certain now that the fleet could not see the stranger.

The proper thing to do, of course, was to hoist the signal for seeing a strange vessel. But that involved using the ensign, and if this stranger saw the Grand Union flag and recognized it, he might run. Biddlecomb thought it unlikely that the *Charlemagne,* battered about, undermanned, and heavy laden, could catch her.

It had already occurred to him that the captain of the distant brig probably did not know what he was looking at. All of the ships of the fleet, save for the *Charlemagne*, were converted merchantmen, and if he could not see their gunports (which he probably could not over that distance), then he might take the ships for a convoy. That would explain why he was not running away, and Biddlecomb did not wish to disabuse him of that notion.

"The brig is running up colors, sir," Weatherspoon reported. The stranger was less than two miles away now, and even without a glass Biddlecomb could see the patch of color flying from the mainmast head. "Oh." Weatherspoon sounded disappointed. "Oh, sir, he's a Frenchman."

"I have no doubt. And I'm the king of China. Mr. Weatherspoon, let us do this. Signal the flag that there's a strange vessel, but use the British ensign to do it, rather than our flag, then haul the British ensign up and leave it there."

The two vessels, the *Charlemagne* and the strange brig, were converging quickly now with just over a mile of water separating them. The *Charlemagne* was cleared for action; it had taken fifteen minutes with their diminished crew, but now each man stood at his station, guns loaded and ready to run out, match smoldering, as the gun crews fidgeted with rammers, sponges, linstocks, and handspikes.

Faircloth's marines in their green coats, not quite as immaculate as they had been four months before, were poised in the tops and along the quarterdeck. They had an air of great confidence about them, having just conquered an entire British colony with a total of six cannonballs having been fired at them. Biddlecomb wondered if they knew that this little brig was likely to put up a greater fight than had the entire island of New Providence.

And indeed the brig was not shying away from a confrontation. She had turned to larboard and was sailing more directly at them, as if both vessels were sailing down the opposite legs of a great triangle to the apex where they would meet.

"She's hauling down her colors, sir," Weatherspoon reported. No sooner had the French ensign reached the deck than another jerked aloft. Biddlecomb watched the flag through his glass, frowning as he recognized the colors. This was not what he had expected.

"Sir, it's the Pine Tree flag, the Appeal to Heaven, like we used to fly," Weatherspoon observed.

And so it was. Biddlecomb had no reason to think that the Pine Tree flag was any less a subterfuge than was his own

British ensign, but the sight of it made him uneasy and, for the first time, uncertain.

"Very well, Mr. Weatherspoon, please run up the Grand Union flag."

Biddlecomb stepped up to the break of the quarterdeck. "Gunners, listen to me. I want all of the men on the larboard side to help those on the starboard. We'll hold off running out the guns, let these whoresons think they've fooled us. When I give the word, you run out and fire as quick as ever you can. Remember the drills, train your guns before you fire, but if we're as close as I hope, you'll be hard-pressed to miss. Hands to the braces, stand by to heave to."

The *Charlemagne* turned up into the wind. The mainsails came aback and she stopped in her wake with her bowsprit and jibboom now pointing directly at the other brig.

The stranger turned as well, turned toward the *Charlemagne* until she was coming bow-on, charging at the Americans as if determined to crash, bow to bow. Half a mile, a quarter mile, she closed the distance, her yards braced up sharp, the Pine Tree flag rippling from her mainmast head.

Biddlecomb spared a glance at the fleet. They had turned in their course and were heading toward the *Charlemagne*, but it would be some time before they came up to the two combatants. Enough time for the *Charlemagne* to take the other, or for the other to beat the *Charlemagne* to splinters.

Biddlecomb's left hand moved to his side in what was now an unconscious gesture, but nothing was there. He frowned and looked down at his waist.

"Oh," he said, "Mr. Weatherspoon, be so good as to run down to the great cabin and fetch up my sword."

Weatherspoon nodded and disappeared below, and Biddlecomb fidgeted, paced, and wished that the midshipman would hurry. Standing on the quarterdeck, with the enemy bearing down on him, with what was left of his ship and his reputation at stake, his familiar sword absent from his grip, he felt vulnerable, terribly vulnerable. All but naked.

CHAPTER 29

The Bolton, *Armed Brig*

WHAT WOULD HE DO, THE CAPTAIN OF THIS BRITISH BRIG-OF-WAR? Assuming that the vessel with which they were closing was, in fact, a British brig-of-war, what would he do?

Biddlecomb stared at the other vessel churning along through the gray sea. He was oblivious to the tension aboard his own command, oblivious to the nervous yawns and the drumming fingers and the tapping feet.

No British captain would fire until he had hoisted the proper ensign, of that much Isaac was certain. And he was equally certain that this enemy would try to rake the *Charlemagne,* fire on her bow or stern. At least that was what *he* would try to do, were he in command.

"Mr. Rumstick," Biddlecomb shouted. "Please see that the boarders are armed, pistols and cutlasses. If I am not mistaken, we shall be boarding them over the starboard bow. On the foredeck, stand ready on the jib and staysail sheets and halyards. We'll have to swing the bow off the wind quickly. I want them set in a flash on my signal."

"Here, sir." Weatherspoon appeared on deck with Biddlecomb's sword and belt held like some religious artifact in his hands.

"Thank you." Biddlecomb took the belt and wrapped it around his waist and buckled it, adjusting the sword until it hung in just the right spot. His left hand moved back to his side, and this time it found the brass wire-bound hilt that it sought. He felt as if a missing limb had been restored.

The British brig-of-war was one hundred yards off, that distance falling quickly away. And it *was* a British brig-of-war—Biddlecomb had no doubt about that now. The heraldic shield under the bowsprit, the heavy spars, the line of gunports down her black sides, were attributes of a naval tradition hundreds of years old. Nothing about her suggested the upstart rebel Yankee she was pretending to be.

"Foredeck! Set the jib and staysail! On the main braces, let go and haul!" On those orders the men laid into the lines and the *Charlemagne* came to life, swinging away from the wind, presenting her broadside to the bow of the oncoming vessel, a raking broadside that would send round shot hurtling down the length of her deck.

"Starboard battery, run out!"

The enemy was turning as well, turning with the *Charlemagne,* trying to bring her own broadside to bear. Together and fifty yards apart they turned north as if at the start of a race.

The Pine Tree flag disappeared behind the enemy's main topgallant sail as it came shooting down the mast, and on the quarterdeck Biddlecomb could see the yeoman of signals bending the British ensign to the halyard. That was good enough for him. Suddenly his sword was in his right hand, held over his head.

"Fire!" All seven guns in the starboard battery fired within seconds of each other, a great deafening broadside that made the *Charlemagne* shudder and hid the other brig behind a wall of gray and acrid smoke. The last of the *Charlemagne*'s guns had not even come to rest when the Englishman replied, the muzzle flashes of six guns cutting through the smoke, the round shot slamming into the *Charlemagne*'s hull.

Coughing, cursing men moved like machines in the brig's waist, sponging, loading, ramming, running out. The thick cloud of smoke between the ships rolled away downwind, revealing an enemy that, like the *Charlemagne,* was running out its next broadside.

The second broadside, British and American, was fired simultaneously. The *Charlemagne* rolled to larboard under the combined shock of her own guns going off and the impact of the British iron, fired from twenty yards away. Two of Faircloth's marines were dead, and the main spring stay, shot clean through, fell across the wreckage. But it appeared, even through the smoke, that the British had taken it just as hard.

The two vessels were closing fast. In a moment they would hit; the *Charlemagne*'s starboard bow against the British brig's larboard. "Boarders, stand ready! Starboard bow!" Biddlecomb shouted. "Mr. Tottenhill!" he shouted to the first officer in the waist. "Take charge here, I'm going with the boarding party!" and with that he raced off the quarterdeck and forward.

The *Charlemagne* and the British man-of-war slammed together, bow to bow, at the same instant that each fired a broadside. It seemed as if the world were torn apart with noise and shattered wood and shuddering decks underfoot.

"Boarders! Follow me!" Biddlecomb shouted, barely able to hear himself, and waving his sword over his head. He leapt up on the number one gun, ready to leap across to the enemy deck, then saw that he was not the only captain to have thought of this.

The crew of the British brig were gathered in the bow of their own vessel, and even as Biddlecomb prepared to board, so they were readying to leap aboard the *Charlemagne.*

"Son of a bitch," Biddlecomb said to himself, and then the British sailors, ten of them at least, were tossed aside as if the breath of God had blown them away. From the *Charlemagne*'s tops the marines had cut them down with their swivel gun and a withering, accurate musket fire, the result of years of hunting in the Pennsylvania woods.

This was the moment, the second before they regrouped. Biddlecomb turned to his men. "Come on!" he shouted. Faircloth was on the deck below him, literally pushing men out of the way in his desire to be in the forefront of the attack, and behind him were those marines who had been stationed on deck.

Like a cresting wave the Americans poured over the bulwarks and onto the enemy's deck, driving the stunned British before them, sweeping them aft with a momentum that they could not resist. The ferocity in the Yankees surprised even Biddlecomb, a release of months of anger and frustration and humiliation. They screamed like savages, banging out with their pistols and thrusting with their cutlasses at the wide-eyed, terrified British sailors.

A man dropped his sword and threw his hands up, and one of the Charlemagnes hit him square in the face with the hilt of his cutlass. Then another Englishman threw down his cutlass, then another and another, and a moment later only the captain of the brig and three blue-coated officers were still fighting a desperate and futile battle aft.

"Avast! Avast there!" Biddlecomb shouted in that tone that foremast jacks were conditioned to instantly obey. The attackers stopped and stepped back, leaving the officers alone, swords held before them.

"Do you strike, sir?" Biddlecomb asked, pushing through the crowd of men. "I say, sir, do you strike?"

The captain of the brig—he was in fact a lieutenant, Biddlecomb noticed by his uniform—looked desperately around, though what he hoped to see Biddlecomb could not imagine. He was a young man, younger than Isaac, and even his scowl and his fighting countenance could not hide his generally amiable appearance. He flung his sword down on the deck and said, "Yes, God damn it, I strike."

The other officers also dropped their swords to the deck, though with not quite as much violence. Then the captain stooped over and picked up his sword and handed it to Biddlecomb.

"No, thank you, I beg you, keep it," Biddlecomb said, and smiling added, "I have one of my own."

The captain of the brig nodded and looked much relieved, slipping his sword back into its scabbard. His expression suggested that he did not know if Biddlecomb's comment had been a joke. "I am Lt. Edward Sneyd, of His Majesty's armed brig *Bolton*. I congratulate you on your victory."

"I am Capt. Isaac Biddlecomb, of the Continental brig-of-war *Charlemagne,* and I thank you." He turned to issue orders to Faircloth and Rumstick, who now flanked him, and his eye caught a bundle of cloth wedged against the bulwark of the quarterdeck. "Pray, sir, where did you get that flag? The pine tree with the motto An Appeal to Heaven?"

"That's one of your rebel flags, ain't it?"

"It is one of our Continental flags, yes, but I was curious as to where you saw it to get the idea to copy it."

"That was given to me by Capt. Tyringham Howe of the frigate *Glasgow* just before I set out on this cruise. In hopes that it would be of some help in fooling you," he added with a touch of bitterness.

"Howe? I though William Maltby was captain of the *Glasgow.*"

"He was," said Sneyd, "until he had the bad luck to lose a rebel prize as well as a storeship from a convoy he was escorting. Actually, that flag was from the rebel prize. Maltby left it on board the *Glasgow* when he left. I suppose he didn't care to be reminded of the incident."

"Bring that here," Biddlecomb said to a seaman standing beside him.

The man snatched up the flag and handed it to him. He ran the heavy cloth through his fingers. There was that familiar pine tree with the black smudge from the time the flag had got caught up under the topmast backstay, and the small patch the sailmaker had sewn over a tear near the fly. Biddlecomb smiled a broad smile. It was the *Charlemagne*'s flag. They had taken it back.

* * *

The change in the ship's mood was extraordinary. The Charlemagnes could not have been happier if they had been shipwrecked on an island of beautiful women and functional distilleries. Men moved faster, laid aloft faster, chided each other with good-natured banter, and lied outrageously about their exploits while boarding the *Bolton*. To listen to them one might think that no one had remained aboard the *Charlemagne* during the fight, and that all had cowered in fright save for the man who happened to be speaking at the moment.

And nothing put Amos Hackett in a more foul and desperate mood than the jubilation surrounding him. He sat at dinner that afternoon hunched over his food, scowling at the rough mess tabletop, while his five messmates ate in silence, terrified by Hackett's black humor.

"You've got nothing to worry about."

Hackett looked up quickly, startled that someone would dare address him. It was Fletcher, stupid Fletcher, standing there grinning at him. "Ain't no one but me saw you hanging back today, pretending you was hurt, and I won't tell."

Hackett stared at the man until Fletcher began to shift nervously, until he became aware that the crew's general good mood did not necessarily make it safe for him to approach in this manner. "Is that some joke, Fletcher? Are you making a joke?"

"Well, I . . . ," Fletcher stammered, taking a step back. Hackett felt the pressure building inside, the bulkhead about to burst. He stood up and whipped the sheath knife out of his belt. Fletcher stepped back again, dropping the bucket of food he was bringing to his mess table, and pulled his own knife out, holding it before him with trembling hand.

"Is that a joke?" Hackett asked again, advancing. The tween decks was silent now, the buzz of happy conversation gone as the men watched the confrontation.

"I'm sorry, I didn't mean nothing."

"You meant something, you son of a whore." Hackett

stabbed out at Fletcher, and as he did, a big hand clapped on to his wrist and held it fast.

"Leave him be, Hackett," Woodberry said.

Hackett stared at him, jerking his wrist back and forth, but he could not break Woodberry's grip. He could not believe the strength of the hand that had only a month before been broken. He could still see the vestiges of the bruises on Woodberry's face from the time in New Providence that he and Allen and the others had caught him alone in the cable tier and had beaten him half to death. Biddlecomb's little spy on the tween decks.

"Let go of me, you bastard, or I'll get Tottenhill to lock you down again, you sodding bastard."

"You will, hey? Captain's back on board now, and Mr. Rumstick, so you can't go and get your little son of a whore Tottenhill to do your bidding this time. It's only you and me here, Hackett." Woodberry let go of Hackett's wrist, and in the next instant he had his own sheath knife in hand, and unlike Fletcher he held it with a confidence born of long practice, moving it slowly back and forth like a snake ready to strike and beckoning with his other hand.

Hackett was aware of the crowd closing in, the men forming a circle around them, ready for more blood sport, not sated by the morning's fight.

"Of course you're ready to fight, you bastard," Hackett said. "Even if you win, nothing would happen to you. Your little Biddlecomb would protect you, but me, I'd hang for killing you, you Yankee bastard."

"It'd be worth it, wouldn't it, Hackett, just to put your knife in me? Come on, then, give it a try."

"Sod off, you bastard," Hackett said, slipping his knife back into his sheath. "And you, steer clear of me," he added to Fletcher, kicking him hard in the side and then sitting at his mess table again.

"We'll be ashore soon, Hackett," Woodberry said, putting his own knife away, "and then you'll dance to my tune."

"I said sod off," Hackett snarled, and the crowd dissipated as quickly as it had formed.

This was not a good situation. They *would* be ashore soon, Woodberry was right about that, and it would only be a matter of time before Woodberry caught him alone, before he would have to fight the Yankee one-on-one. Woodberry outweighed him by three stone and was strong and quick. In a fair fight Hackett was a dead man, and he knew it.

And even if Woodberry did not get him, Biddlecomb would. Far from being discredited, the captain was some kind of hero again, and the crew's morale was as high as it had ever been. Biddlecomb would be able to do whatever he wished once they made landfall.

"See here, what did I say?" Hackett growled at the other men in his mess. "And doesn't Woodberry look forward to getting ashore? They've got it in for us. Biddlecomb'll leave every one of us poor bastards on the beach, a thousand miles from home and no pay or prize money. That's why he shipped us, so he could leave us off and only him and his Yankee friends to share the prize money, and us doing the worst of the fighting today."

"Tottenhill tell you that?" asked Allen.

"Of course he did. Biddlecomb's got it in for him too, that's why Totty wants us North Carolina men to stick together. And we almost had it set that the commodore was going to drum Biddlecomb out, and now he gets lucky with this rutting brig that practically gives up once it sees us."

That last statement sparked a sufficient amount of muttering among the men that Hackett was able to dig into his dinner and let the talk run high among them.

"So what can we do?" one of the mess asked.

"Nothing," said Hackett. "Not one damned thing. As long as Biddlecomb looks like the admiral of the fucking ocean blue, there's nothing we can do. Except hope that sometime between now and when we anchor he does something stupid again and the commodore wants to get rid of him once and for all. It's him or us, boys."

It seemed a desperate situation indeed, but Hackett, in his own way an eternal optimist, could still see some possibilities.

The prize had demanded a prize crew. He had hoped initially that Rumstick would be sent away in command, but that job had been given instead to Sprout, the bosun. But the rest of the men sent to the *Bolton,* almost without exception, were Yankees. Most of the North Carolina men, and the former prisoners from Philadelphia, most of the men who would do Hackett's bidding with a few chosen words, were still aboard the *Charlemagne*

They were in New England waters. They would be anchored soon. But they were not anchored yet.

Hackett felt a glimmer of hope break through his black mood. As long as they were at sea, there was still an opportunity for mischief. He could still bring Biddlecomb down.

And now with Biddlecomb's threats of discharge or worse hanging over his head, and Woodberry's threats of violence, destroying Biddlecomb was no longer something he might do for amusement. It was something he had to do to survive.

CHAPTER 30

Block Island

THE SUN WAS APPROACHING THE HORIZON, THE EVENING WAS WARM with no more then six knots of breeze, and Block Island, five miles to the west, seemed to glow with the orange light of the sun illuminating it from behind. Isaac Biddlecomb could not recall a time when he had been more content.

On the quarterdeck and down in the waist the ship's company was infused with a similar feeling of goodwill, of accomplishment, of resurrection. He noticed more than one man pause in his work to look over the leeward bulwark and gaze at the *Bolton* two hundred yards away. They were proud of what they had done, as well they should be, he thought. It had been a hard fight, and they had won.

"Tell me, Captain," Tottenhill asked, "would you consider this weather to be unseasonably warm for these waters?" Not even Tottenhill was immune to the mood on board.

"I should say yes, though to qualify that I would add that the weather here at this time of year is the most changeable I've witnessed anywhere."

"I reckon we should carry this weather for the next day or so," Rumstick said, adding his meteorological opinion, "with wind building in the northeast and backing. Course with any luck we'll be swinging at anchor by the time it gets worse."

"Indeed," said Biddlecomb. And so he hoped. But Hopkins,

as seemed to be his way, had not indicated where or when he intended to land, and that did nothing to assuage Biddlecomb's still-gnawing anxiety.

A frightening number of his men were sick, and a good portion of those who were not down were off in the prize. As much as he reveled in the good spirits that once again pervaded his ship, he was quite aware of how fragile they were. It would not take much to make this crowd turn rabid and mutinous again. It was time to head for port.

"Very well, Mr. Tottenhill," Biddlecomb said. "I shall leave you and attend to my reports. And perhaps you and Mr. Rumstick would join me for supper later? I should think Mr. Weatherspoon could take your watch for an hour or so."

Tottenhill's face ran through various shades of expressions before it settled on satisfaction. "Thank you, sir. I should be delighted."

Biddlecomb made his way below, past the marine sentry and into his great cabin. The evening sun washed the white paint and varnished wood in a soft light, making even that battered, spartan space seem inviting, like a library in an ancestral home.

He looked at the white duck curtains (they looked pink in that light), the deep scars in the ceiling from round shot coming through the windows, the solid, rustic furniture made for him by the ship's carpenters. He loved it all, he had to admit, but it was time for a change. Perhaps Virginia would give him some help in decorating the cabin. If ever a place could use a woman's touch, it was here.

And then he remembered. He had promised to marry Virginia. He stopped in midstride. He felt his stomach tighten and the soles of his feet start to tingle, as if he were preparing to board an enemy vessel. What had he said? Had he really committed? Yes, he had. He recalled now. In all of the excitement and anxiety of the past month, he had quite forgotten, but, yes, he had given his word.

He grinned and shook his head. Was this really such a bad

thing, deserving of this much consternation? Had he not been turning the thought of marrying her over in his head for . . . what? Two years? Perhaps after two years it was time for him to make the bold move.

He sat down at his desk, which, in the light breeze, was uncharacteristically level, and positioned in front of him his pen, ink, blotter, and the half-finished report of his action with the *Bolton*. In this brave new world of fleets and commodores and instructions to captains, this was yet another thing to which he was having to adjust: writing descriptions of his actions in words bland enough that they could not be mistaken for hubris.

"About one hour after dawn, sighted strange sail bearing south southeast about three miles distant. Finding myself to be the closest vessel in the fleet . . . " This was not strictly true, of course, and Biddlecomb found himself writing faster, eager to be done with the distasteful writing of words that were something less than the facts.

"The strange sail proceeded to display various false colors, and we did the same. Signaled the flag to the effect of strange sail sighted, and about an hour later came up with vessel, which proved to be the bomb brig *Bolton*, of the British fleet in Newport. Exchanged a brisk fire with them for a quarter of an hour."

How lifeless those words were, how inadequate. Where on that page was the sensation of a broadside roaring out, the shudder and crunch of round shot wounding the ship, the men's fear, their anger and excitement? But those men who had engaged in combat, ship to ship, would read that in those dry words, and those who had not never would, regardless of how flowery his prose.

"After an exchange of several broadsides we ran the *Charlemagne* aboard the brig, by the bow, and boarded her . . . " And so, briefly, the description of their fight on the deck, hand to hand, the horror of wounds made by pistol and cutlass rendered dull in his official style. "Of special note were the actions of Lt. Ezra Rumstick and Elisha Faircloth, Lieutenant of Marines, in leading the boarding party and of Lt. Roger Tottenhill, who acquitted himself most bravely during the entire fight." This was cheap, this willingness to forgive, even to praise Tottenhill now that the crisis was past, but Biddlecomb did not allow himself to dwell on that. He did not mention the flag.

The great cabin door opened and the marine sentry announced, "Lt. Tottenhill, Lt. Faircloth, and Lt. Rumstick, sir."

"Very well. Gentlemen, come in, please. Is it suppertime already?"

The meal passed enjoyably. It was, in fact, the most pleasant meal that Biddlecomb could recall with that group. The sense of redemption, of restoring their otherwise shattered reputation, had infected the officers even more than the men, more concerned as they were with reputation, and having more to suffer by its loss. Faircloth was as loquacious as ever, and he kept the great cabin quite amused with tales of his exploits, romantic and otherwise.

"And this ship you mentioned," Biddlecomb asked Faircloth at the end of one such tale, "she was a naval vessel?"

"No, sir, a privateer. I suspect the goings-on aboard a privateer are infinitely more amusing than aboard a navy vessel."

"Well, Mr. Tottenhill," Biddlecomb said, "you're a former privateersman, what say you?"

"I must concur with Lieutenant Faircloth." Tottenhill smiled, a halfhearted effort. "But I imagine you've heard quite enough of my privateer stories by now," he said, and no more. He seemed content to remain for the most part quiet, not sullenly quiet, but attentively quiet, and Biddlecomb wondered what might have been said, perhaps in those moments before the riot, that had so changed Tottenhill's perception of himself.

From the deck above, the bell rang out eight times, the start of the first dogwatch, and with that cue Tottenhill and Rumstick both stood.

"Change of watch, sir," Rumstick said, "if you'll excuse us."

"Excellent meal, sir, thank you," said Tottenhill.

"Very well, gentlemen, I thank you for your company," said Biddlecomb, and he meant it. A moment later he and Faircloth were alone. "Tell me, Elisha," he said, pouring more Madeira into Faircloth's glass, "what kind of friction has there been in the gunroom? Rumstick and Tottenhill have not been the best of friends, I perceive."

"I shouldn't say that, sir. Like peas in a pod, you know. Which, as it happens, is about the size of the gunroom."

Why did he bother? Biddlecomb felt a twinge of guilt at trying to extract such information from Faircloth; he was putting the marine in an awkward situation and to no end. But Faircloth was a man of the world, with knowledge that Biddlecomb might find most useful.

"Let me ask you this, then," he said as he lit the lantern over the table, the sun having set half an hour before. "I'd like your advice, if I may. There is this woman to whom I am . . . betrothed, I suppose I could say . . ."

An hour later, after a lively and informed discourse on the perils and benefits of marriage, Biddlecomb and Faircloth stepped up to the quarterdeck for a breath of air.

And a breath was all there was to be had. With the passing of the sun, the wind had dropped to less than five knots and the sea was calm. The *Charlemagne* ghosted along near the end of the fleet. Spread out before her were the stern lanterns of the other ships, their sails, all set to topgallants, just visible in the moonlight, deep, deep gray against the sparse stars. A lovely night.

"All's well, Mr. Rumstick?"

"Very well, sir. Nothing to report."

Biddlecomb glanced at the compass. The helmsman was following the flagship, and the flagship was still sailing northeast by north, a quarter north. Rhode Island and Buzzard's Bay both lay more or less under their bows. And that meant they could be on the anchor by afternoon the next day.

The situation, which just the day before had seemed so

bleak, was suddenly so hopeful: a load of military stores, prizes, a successful action against an enemy of equal force, home. Biddlecomb stared out at the fleet, and in his mind he ran over this list of graces he had received.

It filled him with a profound and nameless anxiety.

And so he was not overly surprised when, several hours later, he woke to Mr. Midshipman Weatherspoon shaking him violently and practically shouting, "Sir, sir!" in his ear. It was not the tone he might use to inform the captain of, say, a change in course or something equally mundane.

"What it is?" Biddlecomb was fully awake.

"Signal from *Andrew Doria* to the flag, sir. Two strange sail in sight."

"Very well. I'll be up directly." Biddlecomb tumbled out of his cot and pulled on his breeches and his coat over his bare chest and stumbled up the companionway and onto the deck. It was cooler now, but not uncomfortably so, and the night was as calm as when he had turned in. Tottenhill was standing at the weather side of the quarterdeck and upon seeing Biddlecomb headed to the leeward.

"That's all right, Lieutenant, please stay here. What do you have to report?"

"The *Doria*'s signaling two strange sail. They're out there, sir." Tottenhill pointed forward and to starboard. "See, just beyond the *Doria*."

The American fleet was arranged in two lines, windward and leeward, or nearly so. At the head of the windward line was the brig *Cabot*, and following close behind, no more than one hundred yards, was the flagship *Alfred*. The *Charlemagne* was last in that line.

Downwind of those three, perhaps three hundred yards away, were the *Andrew Doria*, the *Columbus*, and the sloop *Providence*. Trailing astern of the fleet were the prizes and the merchantman chartered in Nassau to carry what booty the others could not.

Biddlecomb followed Tottenhill's finger out into the dark. He could see the great bulk of *Columbus* and the smaller *Doria*. The brig was showing a light from her ensign staff and two false fires: the signal for sighting two strange vessels. The lights did nothing to improve his vision.

He looked past the brig's ghostly headsails, using his hand to shield his eyes from the *Doria*'s lights. The *Charlemagne* was the farthest of the American ships from this strange sail, but he could still make it out. It seemed no more than the suggestion of a ship, out there in the night, perhaps a mile away.

"Yes, I see it . . . " His voice trailed off as he scrutinized the specter. The ship was crossing in front of the fleet, moving left to right. He was looking at a broadside view of her, which made her easier to see.

And then the shape altered, grew more narrow. "She's coming about, she's tacking toward us," Biddlecomb said. This was not a small vessel. What was more, if he, at the far end of the American fleet, could see them, then they in turn could see the entire American fleet. And still they tacked and closed. Whoever they were, they were not afraid. Biddlecomb felt his own excitement mount.

"Mr. Tottenhill," he said, and only through great effort did he make his voice sound noncommittal, almost bored, "please clear for action. But quietly, no shouting. I don't care if it takes a few moments longer."

"Aye, sir," said Tottenhill, smiling as he headed off to deliver his orders in a whisper, rather than the customary shout from on high. Tottenhill, Biddlecomb realized, might be many things, most of them distasteful, but he was no coward.

The *Charlemagne*'s decks came alive with men scurrying up from below and moving quickly through the familiar ritual, but Biddlecomb's eyes never left this strange, distant ship. He watched it as it closed with the fleet, growing larger and more distinct with each cable length gained. It had crossed the *Andrew Doria*'s bow and seemed to be standing toward the *Cabot*.

He could make out the second of the two strange vessels

now. It was much smaller than the first and trailing astern. He felt a growing certainty, and a concomitant excitement and anticipation, a touch of fear and the savory anticipation of revenge, all at once. The soles of his feet and the palms of his hands tingled. He had little doubt that this was a frigate, a British frigate and her tender, standing right into an overwhelming American force.

"Cleared for action, sir." Tottenhill stepped back onto the quarterdeck.

Biddlecomb looked down at the waist. Gun crews were at their guns and sail trimmers at stations, but still the deck seemed like a great open space, thinly populated. When the men were at quarters, it usually seemed as crowded as if a public execution were taking place.

Had Tottenhill not roused the watch below? Had he not tumbled the sleeping men out of their hammocks? Biddlecomb was about to ask the lieutenant if he had done so incomprehensible a thing when he realized that, yes, Tottenhill had turned out all hands. And that was it. With so many down with the yellow jack and so many more off in the prize, those unhappy few were all hands. It did not look like enough men to work the ship in battle, not even close.

"Beg your pardon, sir." Weatherspoon appeared on the quarterdeck. In his arms was a bundle of clothes: shirt, stockings, waistcoat, and hat; under one arm were Biddlecomb's shoes and under the other his sword. "Beg pardon, I took the liberty . . ."

Biddlecomb had all but forgotten he was only partially dressed, which would never do for going into a fight. "Bless you, Mr. Weatherspoon, whatever would I do without you?" he said as he pulled his coat off and pulled his shirt from Weatherspoon's arms, dressing quickly.

Last came the sword. He wrapped the belt around his waist and buckled it and adjusted the weapon with that familiar motion. He still found great pleasure in that act, a sense of strength and legitimacy. He was a naval commander, and all the humiliation he had suffered would not change that, nor would it erase those accomplishments of which he was justly proud.

"What ship is that?" a voice came across the water, faint but clear. Had there been even two more knots of wind, it would not have been audible aboard the *Charlemagne*.

"What ship is that?" the voice asked again. Biddlecomb had thought it was an officer from the *Cabot,* hailing the stranger, but he realized then that it was in fact the stranger, the frigate, hailing the American. And the American was making no reply.

It was quiet again as the big ship and the brig continued to close with each other. John Hopkins, in command of the *Cabot,* must have a good notion of what ship that was, Biddlecomb thought. From three hundred yards away he himself could see it fairly well now: the lofty masts, the steeply steeved bowsprit, the mainsail hauled up. Every bit of her suggested a man-of-war.

The *Cabot* and the unknown vessel were almost on top of each other, with the *Cabot* passing down the other's larboard side. Biddlecomb frowned as he watched the situation develop. *Cabot* was under the man-of-war's broadside now, an uncomfortable place to be.

"What ships are in company with you?" the same voice called, and this time was answered from the *Cabot*.

"The *Columbus* and the *Alfred,* a two-and-twenty-gun frigate!" and from the stranger's waist came a flash and an explosion, loud and brilliant, illuminating like a lightning flash the frigate's barely filled sails, the buff masts, and row of guns.

"Good Lord!" Biddlecomb said out loud, quite taken by surprise. Someone from the *Cabot*'s maintop must have thrown a hand grenadoe onto the frigate's deck.

"Mr. Weatherspoon," he began, never taking his eyes from the combatants, then the frigate fired.

It was not a rippling broadside, not a "fire as you bear," but every gun at once, every gun in the exact same instant. The *Cabot,* thirty yards from the frigate, was nearly blown away. She rolled with the impact, sails and rigging torn up and streaming in the concussion of the great guns, lit from behind by the wall of flames that shot from the frigate's long side and then died away, leaving in their wake darkness and the distant shouting, the screams of the wounded and a ringing in their ears.

The Charlemagnes in the waist were shouting, cursing and swearing at the awesome sight. Few there had seen a frigate fire a full broadside, and none had seen that spectacle at night. Memories of the night that the *Rose* had smashed the *Icarus* to splinters under his feet came rushing back. He pressed his lips together, hard. The darkness that was swept away and then in the next instant engulfed them again made it seem that much more horrible.

The *Cabot* was not dead. She was returning fire, pouring her six-pound shot into the frigate, but to what effect Biddlecomb could not tell. If the fight had been just the *Cabot* against the frigate, then the American would be done for. But it was not. It was the frigate against an American fleet; two ships and three heavy brigs.

"Did you see that, sir?" Rumstick asked. He had just stepped aft from his position in the waist.

"I did."

"You recognize that son of a whore?"

"I did." It had been too much to hope for. Indeed, he did not trust himself to believe it, but here was Rumstick confirming what he, in that brief instant of illumination, had thought he had seen. It was the *Glasgow*.

He smiled and looked at Rumstick, and Rumstick smiled as well.

Biddlecomb felt his hand move to the hilt of his sword. "We're in our own home waters, Ezra, and this time it is they who are outgunned. We're not running any longer."

CHAPTER 31

H.M.S. Glasgow

If there was one thing that Amos Hackett could recognize, with unparalleled insight, it was an opportunity to create havoc. And looking at the wide eyes around him now, the lips muttering shocked curses and the hands clasping and unclasping, he knew he was witnessing just such an opportunity.

"There you go—" he began, then the *Glasgow* fired another broadside, as perfectly timed as the first, a solid wall of sound and flame. The *Cabot* sheered off from the frigate's side, a battered fighter stumbling away from an opponent. Parts of her rig, quite unidentifiable now, hung from her spars, and her own fire, pathetic from the first broadside, grew more sporadic.

"There! That frigate'll do for us like she done for *Cabot!*" Hackett said in a loud whisper, conveying a panic that he did not actually feel.

"Shut your gob, Hackett," someone else whispered. It sounded like Ferguson. "*Alfred*'s coming up, she'll do for them British."

"Oh, *Alfred,* is it? Rotten old merchantman. And anyway, that Biddlecomb'll want to throw us right at them. Ain't he the one craving glory now?"

"I said stow it," the voice came back, a growl like an angry dog's and this time Hackett obeyed. But the words had had an effect, he could see that in the men's faces. They were watching *Cabot* as she tried to get away from the murderous broadsides, but in their limited imaginations they were seeing the *Charlemagne*, a drifting and bloody wreck.

Hackett glanced back at the quarterdeck. There was Biddlecomb, standing there like the admiral of the ocean blue, staring forward at the fight.

He was a clever one, that Biddlecomb. He understood completely what he, Hackett, had done, the part he had played in the riot in New Providence, the general discontent. Once they landed, it would be just like Wilmington: the chains, the dark hold, the jail cell.

But this time there would be no navy to join. And even if Biddlecomb did not arrest him, there was always Woodberry. The son of a whore would stick a knife in him once he got the chance, and Woodberry would make certain that he got the chance.

There was only one way out, and it had to be done now. Biddlecomb had to be disgraced. He had to be cast down to where no accusation from him would ever carry any weight, where Tottenhill would be put in command. And Woodberry had to be killed. But that could be done in the confusion.

"Hey, Allen," Hackett whispered, loud enough for five gun crews to hear. "This is it, mate, we're done for. God speed."

"Shut it, Hackett," someone else whispered. "What are you talking about?"

"We're done for. Look at Biddlecomb there. He's gonna throw us right under the frigate's guns, get us all killed for the greater glory of himself. Well, I hate to die for that, but so be it."

"You shut your gob!" Ferguson hissed back, but it was too late. The murmuring had started, the sweet murmuring, the music of fear and discontent. Hackett heard it fore and aft, saw the men in heated discussion, the seminal act of a riot. He stared out of the gunport at the distant fight. His face was grave, in a deep frown, as he struggled to suppress a smile.

* * *

Biddlecomb was frowning as well, but his frown was entirely genuine. He was hardly aware of the existence of the *Charlemagne*, so focused was he on the fight with the *Glasgow*, which was taking place two hundred yards away. And that fight did not seem to be going well at all, at least not from the American perspective.

Cabot was gravely hurt. She had tacked away, trying to get out from under the pounding of the frigate's broadside. Unfortunately she turned right into the *Andrew Doria*, forcing the other brig to tack to avoid a collision, and now the two of them were downwind and out of any sort of line of battle, all but knocked out of the fight.

The *Alfred* was alongside the *Glasgow*, and the two big ships were pounding away at each other, illuminating the night with their nearly constant gunfire. The great clouds of smoke that hung between them in the light air were shot through with red and orange muzzle flashes. The clouds swirled and danced with the concussion of the guns and grew more dense with each broadside. The pungent and familiar smell rolled down on the *Charlemagne* as she ghosted toward the battle.

The *Columbus*, the second most powerful ship in the fleet, was directly abeam of them and directly downwind. She had turned toward the fight and stopped, wallowing in the gentle rollers. Biddlecomb could see her sails hanging limp, lifeless, not a breath of wind stirring them. The ships and the firefight to windward had robbed her of whatever breeze might have propelled her broad and heavy-laden hull into the melee. He could well imagine Whipple stamping the quarterdeck in all but unbearable frustration.

The *Cabot* was knocked out. The *Andrew Doria* and the *Columbus* were downwind and would have trouble working their way up to the fight. The sloop *Providence* might join in, but she could do little. It was up to them.

Biddlecomb felt a surge of elation, the *berserker* waking from his slumber. They were no more than one hundred yards from the *Alfred*. It was time to fight back. It was time to take on a

British frigate and pound them to splinters, just as he had been dreaming of for a year and more. It was time to join the fight against the *Glasgow*.

"Mr. Rumstick, Mr. Tottenhill, we shall cross the bows of the two ships and engage the frigate on her starboard side," Biddlecomb said. "Helmsman, make your head northeast by north." That would allow the *Charlemagne* to keep clear of the other ships in the American fleet, which seemed to be falling over one another, and get at the enemy's vulnerable bow.

"Listen up, you men!" he shouted down into the waist. "It's our fight now! We'll heave to under their bow where we can blow them to hell! Gunners to the larboard battery!"

"You'll have us under her broadside! She'll kill us all!" a voice shouted back from the dark. There was a rustling, a murmur from the waist.

Biddlecomb's mind had already moved on to the next problem when those words brought him up all standing. Had someone objected to his orders? This was their chance to capture a British frigate, it was right in their hands. He must have heard incorrectly.

"Gunners to the larboard battery! Run out!" he shouted again. Something was thrown to the deck; it sounded like a rammer.

"Look! She's doing for *Alfred!* We haven't got a chance!" another voice, a different voice, shouted out. Biddlecomb spared a glance over the bow. *Alfred* had turned away from the *Glasgow,* and the frigate was pouring shot into her exposed stern, creating God knew what kind of carnage aboard the flagship. The frigate must have shot the flag's helm away; it was the only explanation for her suicidal turn. She was taking a terrible beating and she could not strike back.

"Load and run out! Sail trimmers to stations!" he shouted. It was not possible that his orders could be ignored, yet as far as he could see, with his vision impaired by the flashes of the guns, no one was moving to obey. He could hear voices shouting out protests, and others shouting them down, arguments brewing, and it all mixed with the sound of the cannonade to make a nightmarish cacophony.

"We won't do it!" a voice called out, clear above the others. "We won't die so's you can be a hero!"

Hackett. That was Hackett. Biddlecomb could never mistake that voice, and in that instant he understood exactly what was going on in the waist. Hackett was working the men's fear, undoing all the good that taking the *Bolton* had done. Biddlecomb had been an idiot to think he could wait until landfall to deal with Hackett. Well, he would wait no longer.

"Mr. Faircloth, please place Hackett under arrest. I want him chained up below until this is done."

"You three," Faircloth shouted at his marines, "place Hackett under arrest."

This exchange was met with a howl of protest from half the men on deck, who took a belligerent step aft. All attention was focused on this drama, the *Glasgow* nearly forgotten.

"Hackett, God damn your eyes!" This was Tottenhill now, leaning over the quarterdeck rail and shouting. "Get back to your duty! What are you about? We have a battle to fight! You are a North Carolina man, I will not have you disgrace your home this way!"

"Mr. Tottenhill!" Hackett shouted, his tone a pathetic appeal. "Don't let them Yankees arrest me! You've always been on my side of things, don't let that whore's son do this!"

"What in hell does that mean?" Rumstick asked Tottenhill. There was more accusation than query in his voice, but Tottenhill ignored him.

"Damn you, we are fighting a common enemy here!" Tottenhill shouted back at Hackett. "Get . . . "

Faircloth's marines were down on the waist pushing men aside to get at Hackett and were in turn being shoved back. The shouting was general now, men screaming at each other, faces pressed close. Woodberry took hold of Allen's queue and yanked him aside, kicking him to the deck, then grabbed Hackett around the neck. "Ignore the captain's orders, will you?"

he shouted, and then three of Hackett's men were on him, pulling him off, pounding him with fists and belaying pins.

"Come on then!" Ferguson shouted from across the deck, and he flung himself at the writhing men, half a dozen Yankees at his back.

The riot was fully joined. It swept like a gust of wind along the deck as every man threw himself into the fight, pounding and flailing at his shipmates, American against American.

Biddlecomb was dumbfounded. He stared down at the waist and was, for the first time in his memory, incapable of speech. This can't be happening, this can't be happening, was all the thought that he could muster. They had the *Glasgow* in the palm of their hand, and his men were fighting each other, beating each other senseless.

He turned to his officers, looking for some help, for some salvation from that quarter. Faircloth was screaming orders at his marines, directing them into the fight.

Rumstick threw off the main topsail clewline and pulled the empty belaying pin from the rail. He stepped up to the break of the quarterdeck and grabbed Tottenhill by the arm, twisting him around until they were face-to-face. He held the belaying pin under the lieutenant's chin.

"This here's your fault," Rumstick growled. "Just like before, you done this, because you didn't slap Hackett down when you should have, just let him run on. Too busy telling me to be a gentleman."

And then he was gone, down the quarterdeck ladder and forward, pulling men apart, bellowing, trying to restore order. Sergeant Dawes was there as well, his face smeared with blood, and Weatherspoon, his mouth moving though his voice could not be heard over the din. Only Tottenhill remained, seemingly fixed to the quarterdeck.

Biddlecomb pulled his sword and turned to the first lieutenant. He was going to order Tottenhill to follow as he flung himself into the fight, a last-ditch attempt to restore order, but the sight of Tottenhill brought him up short.

The lieutenant was staring down at the waist, his mouth open in an expression of pure agony. Tears were streaming from his eyes, unchecked, and dripping off his jaw; they seemed to shine in the flashes of light from the *Glasgow*'s guns.

"Rumstick's right, God damn his eyes. This is my fault, God save me, this is my fault!" he shouted, though the words did not seem to be directed to anyone.

"Come, Mr. Tottenhill, pull yourself together," Biddlecomb said, as kindly as the circumstances would allow. "Let's see if we can—"

"No, sir, this is mine to fix," Tottenhill said, looking at Biddlecomb for the first time, the tears still running down his cheeks. "God help me, I never thought it would come to this."

Tottenhill pulled his sword from his scabbard and took a deep breath, his face fixed in a scowl, and then with a shriek—a horrible sound, like that of a soul damned to hell—he flung himself off the quarterdeck and down to the waist below.

"Son of a bitch!" Biddlecomb shouted, racing down the steps after him. The lieutenant was cutting his way toward the place where Hackett, surrounded by a knot of his allies, was holding off Faircloth's marines. There were casualties now, men lying wounded on the deck, and dark patches of blood. Biddlecomb felt his heel go out from under him, slipping in the wetness, and he fell just as a cutlass swiped the air over his head.

Cutlass. Someone had broken open the arms chest, and now the fisticuffs had become something more deadly. He heard a gun go off, a pistol by the sound of it, and then another, but he was concentrating on the crazed man standing over him, cutlass raised like an ax.

Did he understand that it was his captain he was trying to cut down? Biddlecomb recognized the man: Johnson from the larboard watch, waister, North Carolina man. Biddlecomb had given him a new shift of clothing in Philadelphia, had personally set his broken hand after that first storm. Was he so crazed now as to be beyond reason? What did he hope to do here?

"Johnson, you stupid bastard, drop that cutlass!" Biddlecomb shouted as Johnson hacked down at him. He twisted aside, felt the jar of the cutlass striking the deck inches from his head.

This was his man, a member of his own crew, trying to kill him. The thought flashed through Biddlecomb's mind, and with a desperate unhappiness, a sense of total failure, he twisted back and like a machine drove his sword through Johnson's chest. He saw the man's eyes bulge, the blood erupt, as he pulled the blade out, and his only thought was, "Such a waste of time, setting that man's hand," as he pulled himself to his feet and plunged into the fight.

Huddled by the capstan, one of Hackett's messmates was spitting a ball down the barrel of a pistol. Biddlecomb slammed down hard on the man's hands with the flat of his sword. The man dropped the pistol, shouted, looked up, and Biddlecomb smashed the hilt of his sword into the startled face.

He could not shake the unreality of it, the nightmare of what was happening. Here was a desperate struggle, hand-to-hand, as horrible as the half dozen or so he had seen before. But this time it was his own men. It was a riot, a mutiny, and even in his desperation he could not help but see the irony in that, as if the ghosts of those against whom he had led a mutiny were visiting this horror on him. His breath was coming fast and shallow, and it was not from exertion.

The marines were loyal to a man, and with bayonets now fixed they were plunging into the fight. Faircloth, hat gone, hair matted with blood that streamed down the side of his face, was leading them on. The fight surged back and forth, pistols and cutlasses now much in evidence, and beneath the shouting, like a bass line, was the constant rumble of the great guns in the distant fight. The flashes of light in the dark only served to make the scene that much more unreal.

Hackett was standing on top of number five gun, well out of harm's way, urging his men on. Hackett. Now every concern was gone from Biddlecomb's mind, save for his desire to kill

Hackett. But a mass of men stood between himself and that son of a bitch; it would be next to impossible to fight his way through.

He let his sword dangle from its lanyard and stepped up on number eleven gun and then up onto the bulwark, making his way forward, past the fight. He could think of nothing save running his sword through Hackett's chest.

He made his way past the main shrouds and stepped with careful balance, one foot on the bulwark, one on the pinrail, thankful for the calm seas, while beneath him the fight spilled over the deck. Weatherspoon lay in a heap against the main hatch. Biddlecomb paused, horrified, but to his relief the midshipman was still moving.

He looked forward to where Hackett stood on the gun, fifteen feet away, waving a cutlass. The man had not noticed his approach. He took another step along the rail. When he reached Hackett, he would get the bastard's attention and then run him through. He wanted to see the look in Hackett's eyes when he knew death was imminent, he wanted Hackett to know in that final instant who had killed him.

At Hackett's feet was a knot of men engaged in the wildest fighting on deck, a pile of men thrashing, struggling, cursing, and it took Biddlecomb a moment to realize that they were all fighting one man, the whole gang trying to suppress one man, and that man was Tottenhill.

At least Biddlecomb thought that it was Tottenhill. The lieutenant's once fine clothes were in rags, his coat shredded, his breeches torn half off, one shoe gone. But it was his face that was most horrible, most inhuman. His hair was jutting out in all directions, his eyes were battered, his lips swollen and bleeding, and his expression, what expression could be distinguished through the damage, was more animal than man.

"Hold up!" Hackett shouted as the attackers once more fell on Tottenhill. "Hold up! Lieutenant!" The men grabbed Tottenhill and held him as Hackett spoke.

Biddlecomb stood, transfixed, and watched the scene.

"Lieutenant, I thought you was with us, I thought you was a North Carolina man first and always! I just wanted you to be captain here, I just wanted to see an honorable gentleman in command, and not that Yankee bastard. This ain't no mutiny, sir, we're fighting for our rights, and once we gets ashore we can see it all made legal, and you appointed captain, but we have to get that Biddlecomb out of the way."

Tottenhill was silent. He stared up at Hackett, unmoving. And then his entire body seemed to relax and the hatred in his face was gone, as if mind and body together gave in to the man's arguments. Biddlecomb wondered if Tottenhill was about to betray him, the final, complete betrayal. The men holding the lieutenant relaxed their grip as Tottenhill ceased to struggle against them.

And then Tottenhill flung himself at Hackett, launched himself off the deck as if shot from a gun, screaming, "I'll kill you!" louder than one would have thought him able. And Hackett in turn cringed and dropped his cutlass, which fell clanging against the barrel of the gun on which he stood.

He shrieked, a high, piercing scream, like a woman being stabbed to death, cutting through the din of the fight, the sound taking up where Tottenhill's voice left off. All motion on the deck stopped. Men paused in the act of beating one another, and heads jerked toward the horrific sounds of the two men.

Tottenhill snatched up the cutlass and like a flash in a priming pan he was up on the gun, slashing, but he was slashing at air. Hackett, just as fast, had turned and flung himself into the fore shrouds, scrambling aloft, shrieking continuously. Tottenhill flung the cutlass away and clambered after him, right at his heels. Fore and aft men straightened, disengaged from their fight and watched the two North Carolinians race aloft.

Hackett reached the futtock shrouds and scrambled over them, up and out, just as Tottenhill came up below him. The lieutenant grabbed Hackett's foot and pulled, jerking the seaman down as he clung to the futtocks in that awkward position, leaning backward under the foretop.

"No! No!" Hackett shouted, again and again in his high-pitched, hysterical voice as he tried to free his foot from Tottenhill's grasp and Tottenhill, in turn, tried to pull him from the rigging.

Then Hackett pulled his other foot from the shrouds and hanging just from his hands kicked Tottenhill hard in the face, again and again, then jammed the heel of his shoe into the hand that held his other foot. Tottenhill released his grasp and sagged against the shrouds, and only his arm, entangled in the rigging, prevented him from plunging to the deck. Hackett's feet found the ratlines once more, and he scrambled up over the edge of the foretop and into the topmast shrouds as Tottenhill, moving like a drunk, followed slowly behind.

The Charlemagnes were silent, motionless, watching as Tottenhill pursued Hackett through the rig, dark shadows moving against the gray background of the foresails, illuminated in flashes by the distant battle in which no one was taking an interest.

Hackett was halfway up the topmast shrouds when Tottenhill made his way over the edge of the foretop. Hackett's movements were quick, jerky, panicked, in contrast to Tottenhill's slow, deliberate, inexorable pursuit. It must have occurred to Hackett, Biddlecomb mused, that he would soon run out of mast. Soon there would be no place for him to go.

Hackett reached the topmast crosstrees and paused, looking down at Tottenhill. "Get away from me! Get away from me, you son of a bitch, or I'll kill you!" he shrieked, but any threat he hoped to carry was lost in the unadulterated fear in his voice. And Tottenhill did not respond. He just continued to climb.

The sound of Hackett's voice broke the spell, for Biddlecomb at least. "Damn me!" Biddlecomb said out loud. "Mr. Faircloth! I want your marines to shoot that bastard Hackett! Shoot him down!" And then as an afterthought he added, "And shoot any son of a bitch that tries to interfere with you!" But it did not seem as if that would be a problem. No one on deck moved, no one took his eyes from the men aloft, save for the marines who were hastily loading their muskets.

Hackett had stepped from the shrouds onto the fore topsail yard. He was walking along the top of the spar, one hand against the topgallant sail for balance, with the ease of an experienced topman, when the first musket banged out. Biddlecomb could see the hole that the bullet punched in the topgallant sail, ten feet from Hackett's head. Another gun and then another fired, but none of the shots were any closer, and they did no more than hurry Hackett along to yardarm where he stopped and turned inboard. There was no place left to go.

"Give me that, you cockeyed imbecile!" Faircloth jerked a musket from one of the marine's hands and brought the gun to his shoulder, training it aloft.

"Hold your fire, Mr. Faircloth!" Biddlecomb shouted. Tottenhill had reached the yard and was walking out along its length, closing with Hackett. Faircloth was good with a musket, Biddlecomb knew that, but he did not want to take the chance of Tottenhill's being hit or knocked from the yard by the impact of the bullet. Faircloth pointed the gun to the sky and eased the lock to half-cock.

"Get away from me! Get the hell away from me!" Hackett screamed. Tottenhill said something in return, but his words could not be heard from the deck. The lieutenant was advancing on Hackett. He pulled his clasp knife from his coat pocket and held it before him, the blade flashing in the light of the guns.

Hackett had edged out to the end of the topsail yard, seventy feet above the water. His left foot was on the studdingsail boom, even beyond the extreme end of the yard, his right hand holding on to the leech of the topgallant sail for balance.

He plunged his left hand into his shirt and pulled out a small pistol, aiming it with a straight arm at the lieutenant. Even over the distant fire the men on deck could hear the distinctive click of a flintlock pulled back into the firing position.

"Hackett! No! Get back on deck this instant!" Biddlecomb roared. Why had he just stood there, watching this happen? Because, he realized, he had assumed that Tottenhill would kill Hackett. It had not occurred to him that there would be any other outcome.

"Hackett!" he shouted again, and then the whole topgallant sail was illuminated by the flash of Hackett's pistol, priming and powder. The two men seemed frozen like a painting, like an apparition: Hackett with gun held at arm's length, Tottenhill, doubled over, hands on his chest, falling slowly against the sail, mouth open, eyes wide in horror.

In the next instant the vision was gone, and before the report of the pistol had died, Faircloth's musket banged out. Hackett was lifted off the yard like a crumpled paper in the wind. He fell slowly, twisting and shrieking, surrounded by a fine mist of his own blood.

He hit the water flat on his stomach, sending up a great spray; not a neat jet of water like falling round shot, but something bigger and uglier than that. Biddlecomb, still perched on the bulwark, watched the churning, rippling spot on the still ocean to see if Hackett would surface.

And then, ten feet from the spot, there was another splash, another great spray of water as Tottenhill plunged from the high yard. Biddlecomb gasped in surprise, nearly toppling backward to the deck. No one had seen the lieutenant fall.

From behind him Biddlecomb heard Rumstick shout, "Hands to the boat falls! Come on, move it, you lazy bastards!" and then the familiar, comforting sound of bare feet moving quickly to obey. Biddlecomb stared at the twin circles of water spreading out across the glassy surface of the sea, overlapping, pushing each other aside, reflecting the flash of gunfire in broken patterns.

"Mr. Rumstick!" he shouted. "Belay that." There was no

need for a boat. The two men in the water had not yet returned to the surface, and Biddlecomb knew that they never would.

He looked up suddenly, some alarm in his head ringing out a signal of danger.

The circumstances of the battle, still raging half a cable away, were much altered now. The *Alfred* seemed to have regained some control; she was broadside to the *Glasgow,* just beyond the frigate's larboard quarter, and both ships were still blazing away. The *Cabot,* crippled though she was, was off the *Glasgow*'s larboard quarter, giving back as best she could and getting the worst of the exchange. The *Columbus* had managed to find a breath of wind, had drawn up under the *Glasgow*'s stern, and was pouring fire into the frigate's transom.

And this Tyringham Howe, captain of the *Glasgow,* apparently had had enough. The frigate's mainsail tumbled from the yard and was once more set, bellying slightly in the light air. The sheets were hauled aft and the frigate began to pull away from the Americans, all of whom were already astern of her. The *Glasgow* was fast, Biddlecomb well knew that, and the clumsy Americans would never be able to overhaul her.

She was heading north, and that meant Newport and the rest of James Wallace's fleet. And the only thing standing between the great victory of capturing a British frigate and the humiliation of her escape was the *Charlemagne,* and her small, bloodied, and mutinous crew.

CHAPTER 32

The Stern Chase

"LISTEN HERE, YOU SONS OF BITCHES!" BIDDLECOMB ROARED OUT AT the men on the deck below where he stood. Battered and bloody faces turned from staring at that spot on the ocean where Tottenhill and Hackett had disappeared and looked up at him. He could see no anger, no rage, no bitterness, just forlorn resignation. They looked like galley slaves who had long ago stopped caring whether they lived or not.

"The *Glasgow* is making for Newport, and she's leaving the others in her wake. But she's hurt bad, and we have a chance to stop her. If you hope to salvage any dignity for yourselves and this ship, and if you don't want to hang for mutiny, you get to the guns now, man 'em and run 'em out."

He reached over to a marine who had positioned himself between the captain and the rioting men, grabbed the man's musket, and took it from his hands. With great drama he opened the frizzen and checked the priming in the flashpan. There was none—the gun was not loaded—but Biddlecomb did not allow his expression to betray that fact. He clicked the frizzen back in place and cocked the lock. "And I'll shoot the first bastard that even hesitates to obey my orders, is that clear? Now go!"

And they went. And Biddlecomb was not surprised, not entirely. He had reckoned the odds were about even that his orders would be obeyed after the sobering sight of the chief mutineer plummeting, screaming and bleeding, from the topsail yard to be swallowed up by the pitiless ocean.

"Mr. Rumstick, you are first officer once more, I believe," he called out, his voice grim. A week before he would have been happy to see Rumstick back in that office no matter what the price, even one as high as that which had just been paid, but he no longer felt that way.

"Aye, sir," Rumstick replied.

"How's Weatherspoon?"

"He'll live."

"Good. Send him aft." Biddlecomb made his way around the smattering of bloody patches and wounded men back to the quarterdeck. The helmsmen still stood at the tiller where they had remained beyond the fray, unmoving, save for slight adjustments to the helm, exactly as they had been an hour before. They seemed as unreal as all of the other events that had taken place.

He could not think on that now. He turned and looked past the bow. The *Glasgow* had already pulled away from the Americans, and being a fast ship and not loaded to the gunnels with pilfered military stores, she was quickly building her lead.

The *Cabot* had taken an awful beating, and she lay motionless on the sea, her tattered and useless sails hanging from her yards. The *Alfred,* the *Columbus,* and the *Andrew Doria,* badly shot up as well, had fallen into the *Glasgow*'s wake and were doing their best to chase, an unimpressive best in that light air. But the *Charlemagne* was largely intact, save for her battered company, and as the helmsmen had obeyed Biddlecomb's last order and kept her head northeast by north, she was in a good position to intercept the frigate.

The *Charlemagne* could not stop the *Glasgow* by herself, but she could slow the frigate's escape long enough for the big Americans to come up with her again. And if that meant running the brig right into the frigate's bow, then Biddlecomb was determined that that was what he would do.

And as far as he could see, that was what he would have to do.

"Fall off," he said to the men at the tiller. "We'll cross her bow."

The *Glasgow* was one hundred yards away when the *Charlemagne* turned across her path, sailing at a right angle to the oncoming frigate. From that position she could rake the big ship while the *Glasgow* in turn could hit back only with bow chasers, and those only sporadically.

"Starboard battery, fire as you bear!" Biddlecomb shouted. The men did not have to think now, indeed that was the last thing that he wanted. They just had to move like mechanized things, go through the motions that they had been drilled to perform. Rumstick was prowling the waist, walking from gun to gun to make certain they did just that.

Number one gun went off with a brilliant flash, then number three and number five, down the line, blinding, deafening, as the *Charlemagne* sailed past the bow of the *Glasgow*, eighty yards away. The noise hurt Biddlecomb's ears, and the pain felt good, as if his ship were alive again, a single fighting unity.

The men at those guns that had fired were flinging themselves into the reloading. There was nothing sullen in their movements now; their training was taking over and pushing their anger and their despondency aside. He wondered if the gunfire was as cathartic for them as it was for him.

Number seven gun, number nine gun. Biddlecomb could see the shots striking home, tearing sections of the frigate's headrail away, leaving great gaps in her foresail and the fore topsail. He would come up again, close-hauled, and rake them once more, and then if need be, he would crash the *Charlemagne* into the *Glasgow*'s bow and hope he and his men could hold off the boarders until the *Alfred* and *Columbus* came up with them.

Number eleven gun, number thirteen gun, and the starboard battery was finished. The forwardmost guns were already firing their second round, but in a moment they would be past the frigate and out of range. "Sail trimmers to stations, ready to brace for a larboard tack! Gunners to the larboard battery!" Biddlecomb shouted, and the men ran—they ran, they did not shuffle—to obey. "Helmsman, full and bye!"

The *Charlemagne* turned up into the light wind, turning her stern to the oncoming frigate. For a moment the two vessels were on the same course, as if the *Charlemagne* were leading the *Glasgow* north, but the brig continued to turn and slowly the larboard battery came to bear.

Number two gun went off and a part of the *Glasgow*'s headrail plunged into the sea. Number four gun fired. Biddlecomb wondered how long the frigate would take this punishment before she fired back. And just as that thought came to him, the *Glasgow*'s starboard bow chaser went off. He heard the shot whistle overhead, passing through the *Charlemagne*'s rigging and apparently missing it all.

Biddlecomb tore his eyes from the frigate and looked for the American fleet. They were already sagging farther behind, robbed of their air and held back by their own clumsy qualities and the damage the *Glasgow* had inflicted. There was no question about it now; he would have to run the *Charlemagne* into the frigate. There was no other way to stop her.

"Steady up," Biddlecomb barked at the helmsmen, and the brig turned toward the frigate. "Good, steady as she goes." They were on a heading now that would still allow the *Charlemagne*'s guns to bear on the enemy. At the last moment he would put the helm hard over and run them aboard. It was foolhardy, bordering on suicidal, but it had to be done. One British frigate could not be allowed to defeat the entire American navy.

He would not tell the Charlemagnes about this plan.

"Frigate's luffing up, sir," mumbled Weatherspoon, who, a moment before, had limped up to the quarterdeck to take his customary place beside and behind his captain. He made that report at the same instant that Biddlecomb noticed the movement. The *Charlemagne* and the *Glasgow* had been closing on each other at nearly a right angle, but now the *Glasgow* was turning away from the brig, turning up into the wind. There was only one reason for it. She was bringing her broadside to bear.

Biddlecomb turned to the helmsmen. "Luff up!" If he held the course he was on, then the *Charlemagne* would be nearly bow-on to the frigate and the frigate's great guns would sweep down the entire length of her deck. He had seen once before the carnage that that could create, he did not wish to see it again.

The *Charlemagne* turned into the wind, matching the frigate's course, broadside to broadside and fifty yards apart. Overhead the sails slatted and banged as the wind came forward of the beam. The remaining guns on the *Charlemagne*'s larboard side fired at once, four in all, while number two gun was running out again.

"Wait for it—" Biddlecomb muttered, staring at the frigate's side and squeezing the hilt of his sword as he braced for the broadside.

And then it came, twelve big guns at once, the long columns of flame reaching out through the night, the all too familiar sound of iron screaming through the air and the deck jarring underfoot with the impact of round shot.

The *Charlemagne*'s number two gun barked out again, then number four. Biddlecomb stared at the *Glasgow*, trying to see if she was turning, if she was running out her guns or setting more sail, but he could see nothing beyond a vague shape behind the twelve yellow dots that swam in his vision.

He blinked hard and looked down into the waist. As far as he could see, his men were working the guns like things possessed, loading and running out. But those puny six-pounders would not stop the frigate. He had to run the *Charlemagne* aboard her. It was the only way.

"Sail trimmers, stand ready!" he shouted, more to fill the seconds than anything. A minute more and it would be time to turn, to drive his ship into the enemy's.

The *Glasgow* began to fall off onto her old course, her jibs backed and her guns firing, one gun, then another and another, each gun captain apparently taking his time, taking his aim.

"Foredeck, back the jibs there!" Biddlecomb shouted, and then to the helmsmen, "Fall off!"

Shot after shot slammed into the *Charlemagne*'s side, and the sound of iron flying overhead was conspicuously absent. They're shooting low, Biddlecomb thought. He paced back and forth, trying not to look at the frigate, trying to see through the spots in his eyes if any great damage was being inflicted on his command. He could see a section of bulwark gone, and perhaps a wound in the mast, though he was less certain of that.

Ten, eleven, Biddlecomb counted off the frigate's guns. The *Charlemagne* was falling off as well. Twelve. Fifty yards and he could slam into the frigate.

Then the *Charlemagne* turned back, swinging back up into the wind. "Fall off, damn your eyes!" Biddlecomb shouted to the helmsmen, his eyes fixed on the frigate. But the *Charlemagne* was luffing again, as if the helmsmen aft had done the opposite of what he had ordered. "I said fall off, put your helm to larboard, damn you, come right!" He turned to the men behind him, but the stolid helmsmen who had maintained their office during the riot were no more.

One was lying on the deck, thrashing and moaning and clutching at bloody clothes. The other was still on his feet, still holding the tiller, which was no longer attached to anything, and staring at it with eyes wide. The tiller had been shot in two, and the shattered end lay on the deck, having little effect on the *Charlemagne*'s course, despite the efforts of the stunned helmsman, who was thrusting it resolutely to larboard.

"No! Please, God, not the rudderhead!" Biddlecomb fairly screamed as he ran aft, pushing the dazed man out of the way. If just the tiller had been smashed, the disaster was not so great; a spare tiller lay ten feet away, lashed to the rail. It would take less than a minute to put it in place.

He stopped by the rudderhead, that upper part of the rudder that jutted up through the deck to which the tiller was attached. He stared through blinking eyes at what little was left of it. A ball had come straight through the rail and smashed into it, tearing it apart. It looked like the stump of a small tree that had been struck by lightning. The spare tiller would be of no use to them now. Nothing was left to attach it to.

Overhead the sails began to ripple, no more than that in the light air, as the *Charlemagne,* completely out of control, rounded up into the wind. Biddlecomb left off staring at the remains of the rudderhead and raced to the break of the quarterdeck, nearly colliding with Rumstick, who was coming aft.

"Where's the carpenter?" Biddlecomb shouted. "Get the carpenter and his gang aft!"

"Carpenter took a quarter block on the head, he's sleeping like a baby," Rumstick said. "Why—"

"Rudderhead's shot away. We need steering. Damn it, damn it!" Biddlecomb shouted this last as he looked over the larboard bow. The *Glasgow* was all but past them now; in half a minute he would be looking at her transom, and then he too would be part of the useless stern chase, his only real chance to stop her gone. He pushed his frustration aside and forced his mind to work.

"We'll steer with the rudder chains. Run the boat falls from the mainyard aft and we'll hook 'em into the pennants. Mr. Sprout!"

It was a jury-rig, and not a good one. The chains that always remained attached to either side of the rudder were hooked to the lines coming from the ends of the mainyard, those lines normally used to hoist the boat, and by hauling on them they could steer, after a fashion.

But the lack of adequate steering was nothing to Biddlecomb compared with the agonizing six minutes that it took to rig the system up. During those six minutes he paced the quarterdeck, gritting his teeth and forcing himself to resist barking out useless orders, such as telling the men to hurry.

"Foredeck! Back the jibs!" he shouted with great relief as Rumstick cut the bitter end off the last seizing. "Sail trimmers, sharp larboard tack! Let go and haul!" He looked over the odd lash-up controlling the rudder, thought about what had to happen, and said to the men at the boat falls, "Larboard side, ease away, starboard side haul away," and as the *Charlemagne*'s bow turned off the wind and the brig gathered way, he said, "Good, now ease away starboard, haul away larboard . . . that's well . . . steady as she goes . . . ," and the Continental brig-of-war *Charlemagne* resumed the chase.

But it was too late, far and away too late. Biddlecomb knew it. The wounded brig could not catch the frigate now, but he would not admit it, not to himself and certainly not to any of the men on deck, who knew it as well. Rather he sent them aloft to set studdingsails and called for utter perfection in the set of the sails and minor adjustments in the angle of the rudder.

Forty minutes later the *Glasgow*'s transom, which Biddlecomb could dimly make out, was illuminated by the twin flash of two guns going off, the sound coming at the same moment as that of the passing shot. The frigate had rigged stern chasers out of the great cabin to pound away at her pursuers.

"Mr. Rumstick, pray set your best gun crew to the bow chaser and do what damage you can," Biddlecomb called out.

And so on through the night they raced north, exchanging sparse fire, each hitting the other on occasion, but for the most part dropping shot into the sea. And all the while the *Charlemagne* fell farther behind the *Glasgow* and the rest of the American fleet fell farther behind them both.

Biddlecomb clenched his fists and kicked the bulwark on those occasions when his frustration got the better of him. The frigate had sailed straight into the entire American fleet, and they could not stop her! For that brief moment, just before the riot had broken out, he had envisioned the Americans sailing into New London, the *Glasgow* in the center of the fleet, the Grand Union flag flying over the ensign of the Royal Navy, the cheering crowds lining the shore. When, when would he learn to stop letting his imagination run away like that? It seemed that every time, every damn time, it came back to bitterly mock him.

When the sun finally broke the horizon at six o'clock in the morning, four bells in the morning watch, the low shore of Rhode Island was just visible, several miles distant. The *Glasgow* was a mile ahead of the *Charlemagne,* her stern chasers still blazing away, though the threat seemed much less in the gathering daylight. The forwardmost of the American fleet, the big *Columbus,* was three miles astern, and beyond her was *Andrew Doria, Alfred,* and the others, scattered over the sea.

"Signal from the flag, sir," said Weatherspoon. "Disengage and form into a squadron." A minute passed and Weatherspoon added, "Sir?"

"I heard you," Biddlecomb snapped. He remain fixed to the quarterdeck rail, arms folded, staring at the distant frigate, unwilling to break off the chase, to acknowledge the commodore's tacit admission of defeat.

There was no doubt in his mind that the gunfire could be heard in Newport, and that the *Rose,* the *Nautilus,* and whatever other men-of-war were there were at that moment slipping their cables to come in pursuit. It was pointless and dangerous to maintain the chase, but he could not bring himself to break it off.

From somewhere astern a gun banged out. "That's the commodore, sir," said Weatherspoon in a timid voice. "I reckon he wants us to disengage."

"Mr. Rumstick, please step aft," Biddlecomb called, and when the first officer was on the quarterdeck said, "Please take over here. We'll haul our wind and rejoin the squadron. I'm going below to . . . write my report." And with that he stomped off, purposely avoiding every eye on deck.

* * *

First Lieutenant Ezra Rumstick stood in the middle of the quarterdeck and clasped his hands behind his back, running his eyes over the steering lines coming from the mainyard. His mood was an odd mixture of disappointment and anger, relief and exhaustion, pleasure at seeing the familiar headlands of Narragansett Bay and concern at the knowledge that behind them lay James Wallace's squadron. Hackett was dead, and that made him happy. But so was Tottenhill, and that, much to his surprise, did not. He was looking forward to getting the anchor down sometime soon and sorting it all out.

He felt a slight jar beneath his feet as Captain Biddlecomb slammed the door to the great cabin.

"On the braces, get ready to square them up," he called forward, and then to the men on the rudder lines said, "Ease away larboard, haul away starboard. That's well, make off your braces!"

And then from somewhere behind him came the sound of smashing wood and shattering glass, so loud and sudden that he jumped.

"What in the hell . . . !" He ran aft to look over the taffrail.

Floating in the *Charlemagne*'s wake, already fifty feet astern, was a heavy oak chair, which Biddlecomb had apparently hurled, with not inconsiderable force, through the closed aft windows of the great cabin.

CHAPTER 33

New London

THEY SAT IN THE *CHARLEMAGNE'S* GREAT CABIN, THE OFFICERS OF that Continental brig-of-war, huddled over their mugs of coffee and, for the moment, largely silent.

Through the large section of glass and frame missing from the stern window came the smell of damp, warm spring air. Somewhere in the town of New London, a quarter mile away, a blacksmith was pounding away at some work on his anvil. They could not see him; the current and the ebbing tide were holding the anchored brig broadside to the town, but they could hear the sharp, distant ring of his hammer in the quiet of the early morning.

It was Monday morning, the eighth of April, two mornings after the chase of the *Glasgow* had been abandoned, and nothing of any great consequence had been undertaken in that time. Just as Biddlecomb had imagined, the *Rose* and the other men-of-war in Newport had slipped their cables to join the fight, but after poking their noses out of the harbor, they had come to anchor again and not pursued the American fleet.

And that was just as well, for the *Glasgow* and her small tender (the one vessel that the Americans did manage to capture in the melee) had done untoward damage to the Continental ships. The *Alfred* had six men killed and as many wounded, and the *Cabot*, which had borne so much of the *Glasgow*'s fire, had four men killed and seven wounded, few of whom were expected to recover. Among those was Capt. John Hopkins, the son of the commodore.

The *Charlemagne* had six killed and ten wounded, five seriously, and to Biddlecomb's profound shame only two of those casualties had been inflicted by the *Glasgow*. The rest they had inflicted on each other.

He had sat that morning after the fight, hunched over his desk—listening to Rumstick on the deck above leading the men in knotting and slicing the damaged rig, and the carpenter's mate supervising his gang in repairing shot damage—and wrestled with the wording of his report. It would have been the easiest thing in the world to ascribe all of the *Charlemagne*'s hurt to the fight with the frigate, to the greater glory of himself and his ship.

But he could not. He could not compound the shame he felt about the way he and his men had behaved by covering it over with a lie. "Prior to our coming up with the frigate there was another disturbance among the crew such as we suffered in New Providence," he wrote, "and it was in defense of the ship against those cowardly elements that Lieutenant Tottenhill was killed. I regret to say that all but two of our casualties were taken at this time."

There. He had told the truth, and no doubt those same eyes that would see the drama of his fight with the *Bolton* through the dry words of that report would see this shameful mutiny as well. But at least he would not be accused of mendacity. He finished the rest of the report quickly; there was not much to say.

For the remainder of that day and on through the next, the battered fleet had sailed southwest around Block Island, then northwest into Long Island Sound, following the *Alfred*. The winds had been light and variable, and that, combined with the considerable damage done to the vessels' rigging, made for slow progress. They had seen a number of vessels, mostly coasting packets that had spoken to the flagship, but they had been unmolested by the British navy.

They came to anchor three hours before dawn, at slack water, in the wide, straight Thames River beyond the town of New London. Half an hour later they began the long process of sending ashore the dead, the wounded, and the many, many sick men in the fleet. When at last it was done, just as the sun was making an appearance over the low Connecticut hills, a total of two hundred and two men were ashore in the makeshift hospital set up to receive them.

Biddlecomb and Rumstick and Faircloth had stood at the gangway, watching the *Charlemagne*'s boat pulling back to the brig. The vessel had a hollow, empty quality with so many men ashore, and the crew moved quietly and talked in low voices, as if the ship itself were a hospital.

"I'd be honored if you gentlemen would join me for some breakfast, say in half an hour's time? And pray bring Mr. Weatherspoon with you, if he is quite up to it," Biddlecomb said at last.

And so they all sat in the great cabin, as somber aft as were the men forward.

"You say it was a round shot from *Glasgow* that did for your windows here, sir?" Faircloth asked, leaning over and looking closely at the damage.

"Yes," said Biddlecomb.

"Odd, though, it looks for all the world as if the thing that did the damage came from inside the cabin, going out. Here, do you see how the wood projects outward—"

"I was looking over the sick and hurt list, sir," Rumstick interrupted the marine. "Looks like the yellow jack's done the job I was set to do, clearing out them sons of whores forward that we don't care to ship again, including those jailbirds Tottenhill brought with him. A few left, and I'll set them ashore soon enough, but mostly the men we don't want are gone."

"And our company cut to half strength. Less than half

strength. God knows where we're going to get more men, with the privateers taking all the best."

"If I could ask, sir," Rumstick continued, "your report . . . how'd you write up Tottenhill's death?"

"I told the truth. He died defending the ship against a mutinous faction."

"Didn't happen to mention that Tottenhill was the one that coddled them mutineers until they figured they could run things their way?"

"I did not. Nor do I think Tottenhill will bear all the blame. You don't see our own fault in this, Ezra?"

"No."

Biddlecomb took a long pull of his coffee and stared out of the stern window. The gray water below the transom was turning to blue as the daylight gathered strength. He could see beyond the reaches of the river into Long Island Sound.

"Tottenhill was a dead man from the moment he stepped on board," Biddlecomb said at last, turning back to Rumstick. "The poor bastard. He didn't have any idea what was going on around him, who his friends were and who his enemies were, and we didn't do one damn thing to help him."

"Really, though," Faircloth took up the argument, "there was no tolerating the man. Is it our duty to suffer a boor like that?"

"It was our duty to support a fellow officer. Instead, we . . . no, I . . . made him into an outcast, a pariah, just because I didn't care for his company."

"That's no excuse for what he done," said Rumstick, "for undermining the authority of the captain."

"I don't believe he knew what he was doing. It's no wonder he was starting to see Yankee plots everywhere. He was just looking for someone to support him. If I had done so, this all might never have happened."

"He never supported you, or any of us."

"That did not relieve me of my duty to him."

The officers of the *Charlemagne* were silent for a moment.

"Well, he's dead now," said Rumstick at last, "and he'll be remembered as a hero, and I suspect that's the best any of us can hope for."

Breakfast came at last: fresh eggs, fresh bread, fresh beef sliced thin, fresh butter. It was a feast the likes of which they had not seen in some time, and they turned to it with the appetite of sailors, an appetite that even the gravest adversity could not quash.

But satisfied as his stomach was, Biddlecomb's mind could find no peace. Sure, he was more than content at the moment; he loved his tiny great cabin, and he loved the men with whom he shared this meal: Rumstick, his friend from those fine days as a merchant seaman; Weatherspoon, with whom he had shared so much aboard the *Charlemagne;* Faircloth, with his irrepressible humor and unflinching courage and rather skewed vision of the events in which he participated.

But Biddlecomb could not stay in the great cabin forever. There would be a captains' meeting soon, he had no doubt, and he would once again have to stand in front of Commodore Hopkins and explain his failings.

And he would have to go ashore eventually. He would have to walk among the crowds in the streets, crowds that had once hailed him a hero, and explain again and again why the entire American fleet had failed to stop one British frigate, why they had failed to get most of the gunpowder for which they had gone to New Providence, why his crew had twice risen up against him.

By the time he poured his last cup of coffee he was in a thoroughly foul mood, and the others, sensing that, engaged in some inane discussion in which he need not participate. He stared out of the great gap in the stern window at the water swirling away past the *Charlemagne*'s hull.

And suddenly a boat was there, ten yards away, a big boat with six oars per side and crammed with people. Biddlecomb blinked in surprise at the craft's sudden appearance. He thought at first it was the flagship's longboat, but it was gleaming in the morning sun with fresh white paint and was beautifully tricked out with green along the gunwale, far more pristine than any of the much abused boats of the fleet.

"Here, backwater!" shouted the man in the stern sheets, and Biddlecomb realized that the boat was crammed with civilians, men and women, in fine silk coats and dresses. He could see the blink of silver and gold buttons and buckles. He frowned as the boatload of grinning, chatting sightseers came to a stop under his transom.

"Ahoy, there!" the man in the stern sheets shouted with a self-conscious tone, half mocking his own use of the word, the way a landsman will when hailing a vessel, uncertain if that was what sailors really said. "Are you Captain Biddlecomb?"

"Yes. Who in the devil are you?"

But the man did not answer. Rather he turned to the people in the boat and pointing right at Biddlecomb shouted, "There! That's Captain Biddlecomb, the one who chased the *Glasgow* clear into Newport harbor!" The others in the boat, those who were not already doing so, turned and looked up through the windows, waving like idiots and grinning at Biddlecomb as if he were there on display.

"What in all hell . . . ," Biddlecomb said, getting to his feet just as Faircloth, Rumstick, and Weatherspoon crowded around to stare back.

"Huzzah, the Argonauts!" shouted a man in a gold-trimmed cocked hat, and the others in the boat followed his lead with lusty "Huzzah!'s."

"What in the hell!" Biddlecomb said, louder this time.

"Listen, sir," said Faircloth, cocking his head to the open skylight above. "Do you hear it?"

Biddlecomb listened. There was something, a sound like rustling leaves or water moving past the hull. "I hear something. . . . Come, let us go topside," he said, directing one last scowl at the wealthy fools in the boat and pushing past his officers to the door of the great cabin. The last thing he heard before stepping past the marine sentry was a feminine voice from the boat saying, "Look how that horrid frigate has shot out all of the poor captain's windows."

They stepped through the gunroom, through the scuttle, and aft to the quarterdeck. The sun was well up now, revealing a perfect spring morning. The water was a deep blue, far deeper than the robin's-egg sky, and the fields that ran down to the river were a vivid green, broken here and there by tilled patches and stands of trees.

The town of New London was a quarter mile off the larboard side, close enough that the four men on the quarterdeck could make out the finest details of the brick buildings, the storefronts and wharves, the wagons and coaches that filled the streets.

But they were looking at none of that. They were looking, rather, at the crowd.

The waterfront, from the north end of town to the south, was packed with people, and from that mob, which jostled and waved and clambered down into boats along the docks, came an almost continuous cheering. Men were waving their hands, waving flags, and women waved handkerchiefs and children raced around. Boats crammed with people, such as the one under the *Charlemagne*'s transom, swarmed around the anchored fleet like mosquitoes. Biddlecomb had seen nothing like it since the day in Philadelphia when the fleet had gotten under way.

"By God, it would appear that we are heroes, sir!" Faircloth said, grinning from ear to ear. Biddlecomb met Rumstick's eye, and Rumstick grinned, and quite despite himself, Biddlecomb grinned as well.

Faircloth was right. They were heroes, all the brave men of the Continental navy. Word of what they had done, the taking of New Providence, the battering, if not the capture, of the *Glasgow,* must have spread like fire in a bosun's locker, and the town of New London had turned out to hail their conquering countrymen.

"Good Lord in heaven," Biddlecomb said, still grinning and

shaking his head. The yelling from the crowd redoubled, surged and fell like a crashing wave, then surged again.

Whatever did these people think? Biddlecomb wondered. Did they have any idea how little had been accomplished, and at what a price? Did they understand how much more was left to do? How much blood and misery would be involved in winning liberty of these . . . what was it that Adams had insisted on calling them? For these United States?

Historical Note

The men of the first American fleet were indeed hailed as heroes after their return from New Providence. When Hopkins's report of the voyage was read to Congress and published in various papers throughout the Colonies, it generated great excitement and pride at what had been accomplished. President of the Congress John Hancock wrote, "Your Account of the Spirit and Bravery shown by the Men, affords them [the Continental Congressmen] the greatest Satisfaction; and encourages them to expect similar Exertions of Courage on every future Occasion."

Not until a month or more after their return did the bloom come off the rose and Congress begin to question just what it was that Hopkins had done.

Sectional differences, suspicions between the Northern colonies and the Southern, had long been a problem with any organized efforts in America. The Continental Army was constantly plagued by infighting along those lines, though the appointment of a Virginian to the post of commander in chief and a strong Southern military tradition did much to assuage Southern concerns.

The same was not true for the navy. It is hardly surprising, of course, that the majority of captains should come from New England, as that region had the greatest maritime tradition in

Colonial America. Still, the preponderance of Yankee captains made the Southern colonies suspicious of that branch of the armed forces, and most opposition to the creation of a navy came from the South.

Hoping to allay Southern fears, Congress ordered the navy to first relieve the Chesapeake Bay of the despised Lord Dunmore and his small fleet. They were then to make themselves "master of such forces as the enemy might have both in North and South Carolina." It may have been a tall order for that small fleet, but it was a politically astute one.

By ignoring those orders, Commodore Hopkins (about whom Henry Knox said he would have "mistaken him for an angel, only he swore now and then") did nothing to assuage Southern feelings. Why Hopkins chose to ignore the directions of Congress will never be known. In his own defense he said that, after putting to sea, he had "many sick and four of the vessels had a large number on board with the small pox. . . . I did not think we were in a condition to keep on a cold coast."

Having been frozen in the Delaware River for seven weeks had not helped conditions aboard the fleet. And indeed the orders he was given were more than could reasonably have been expected of a small squadron of converted merchantmen. Congress, however, must have considered their orders reasonable, and after sober reflection they were not pleased that those orders had been so thoroughly ignored. Hopkins did not help things as far as the Southern colonies were concerned when, after anchoring in New London, he sent some of the guns taken from New Providence to Connecticut and Rhode Island without even asking permission of Congress to do so.

More questions were raised as to why the *Glasgow* was able to escape from the entire American fleet. The answer, in hindsight, is obvious: the American attack was piecemeal and uncoordinated, and the *Glasgow* was allowed to take on the *Cabot* and the *Alfred* one at a time, while those ships in turn prevented the *Columbus* and the *Andrew Doria* from joining in the fight until it was too late.

Hopkins was blamed by Congress for the debacle and has been blamed by historians for failing to coordinate the attack while it was taking place. But in fact he had provided himself with no means to do so, even if he had so desired. The signals that he devised prior to leaving Philadelphia were crude at best. The only relevant signal he had created for such a situation was for the fleet to attack an enemy, and giving that signal would have been pointless. Beyond that, Hopkins could have done nothing, except hope that his captains would make the best of it.

Nor did the *Glasgow* escape unscathed. Unfortunately, for the sake of morale, the Americans were not aware of how much damage they had inflicted. In a letter to Philip Stevens, secretary of the admiralty, Vice Admiral Shuldham, the commander of British naval forces in North America wrote:

> His majesty's Ship *Glasgow* having on the 6th. Instant off Rhode Island fallen in with and been attack'd by several Armed vessels of the Rebels, in which Action she received so much damage that she was thought unfit to proceed on the execution of the Orders Captain Howe had received for carrying General Howe's and my Dispatches to the Southward, which were unluckily thrown into the sea . . . I find the *Glasgow* is in so shattered a Condition and would require so much time, and more stores than there is in this Yard to put her in proper repair, I intend sending her to Plymouth as soon as she can be got ready.

It is clear that Captain Howe, in command of the *Glasgow*, did not consider his escape to be a foregone conclusion. Only a captain who believes himself to be in imminent danger of capture throws his orders and dispatches over the side.

Though they failed to capture or sink the frigate, the Americans did accomplish the next best thing: they knocked her out of action. It is too bad for Hopkins's career and the reputation of the other captains that the Continental Congress and the nation as a whole did not know that.

Oddly, little seems to have been made of what was arguably Hopkins's biggest blunder: his failure to seal off Nassau harbor and prevent the escape of the *Mississippi Packet*, the *St. John*, and the vast majority of the gunpowder on New Providence. The brief reprieve from criticism that Hopkins enjoyed was largely due to the quantity of military stores he brought to the war effort. Had he also brought New Providence's entire store of one hundred and eighty-five barrels of gunpowder, that lifeblood of all eighteenth-century warfare for which the Americans were always in such desperate need, he might well have escaped further censure. Unfortunately, his numerous mistakes, tactical and political, along with his subsequent inactivity, were enough to put him in disfavor with Congress. On January 2, 1778, Hopkins was dismissed from the service, and for the rest of the war no one was to hold so high a rank in the American Navy.

Just as inexplicable as the behavior of Esek Hopkins was the behavior of Gov. Montfort Browne of New Providence, Bahamas. On February 25, more than a week before the Americans' arrival, Capt. Andrew Law warned Browne that the rebels were coming. How Law knew that is a bit of a mystery, particularly considering that Hopkins seemed to have come up with that destination entirely of his own accord. Perhaps it was a lucky guess on Captain Law's part.

In any event, Browne made no preparations for their arrival and mounted no defense as the American marines splashed ashore near East Point. Not surprisingly, the New Providence militia were not enthusiastic ("rather Backward in their assistance" is how Browne phrased it in a subsequent report) about attacking the Americans once they were landed and formed up. The defense of the island devolved into a series of retreats, with the number of militiamen quickly dwindling. The conquest of New Providence was made without a single casualty.

After being taken prisoner by the Americans, Governor

Browne was quick to see treachery on every hand. He wrote a lengthy report on the taking of New Providence to the American secretary, Lord George Germain, at the end of which he named a handful of men who he believed conspired with the Americans even before their arrival. President of His Majesty's Council John Brown was not mentioned.

Germain agreed with the governor that treachery was involved, and despite the governor's apparently believing John Brown innocent, Germain considered Pres. John Brown to have been an American sympathizer. In a reply to Governor Browne, Germain said, "The refusal of the President and Council to deliver the Ordnance and Stores to Genl. Gage's order, was evidently in consequence of a Plan they had concerted with the Rebels for putting them into their hands."

Germain went on to assure Browne that once the military situation on the American continent was stabilized, a small force would be sent to New Providence for "re-establishing of Legal Authority . . . [and] to discover the principal contrivers and abetters of this traitorous proceeding." Despite Germain's optimism, things on the American continent got worse, not better, for the British army, and no force was ever dispatched to New Providence.

Governor Browne did return to New Providence late in 1778. That none of the Nassauvians seem to have protested his being carried off by Hopkins would suggest that he was not overly popular to begin with. On his subsequent return he did nothing to help that situation by accusing everyone in sight of collusion with the Americans, including, this time, John Gambier and Pres. John Brown. The Nassauvians in turn accused Browne of criminal negligence in surrendering to the Americans. Ultimately, Governor Browne's efforts resulted in his summary recall to London.

Despite the numerous errors made by Commo. Esek Hopkins, as well as the loss of the gunpowder, the raid on New Providence, the first ever by the American Navy and marine corps, was the most successful American fleet action of the

American Revolution. The booty taken from the island was prodigious: 88 cannon from nine to thirty-six pounders, 15 mortars, 5,458 shells, 24 casks of powder, over 2,000 round shot, and much more.

But of greater significance was the threat that the fleet action presented. Suddenly the localized insurrection in the Colonies had become a hemispheric threat, and Hopkins's raid exposed the vulnerability of England's rich Caribbean possessions. Fear of further depredations struck at the heart of London. The Admiralty was forced to pull more of their vessels from home waters and send them to America. This in turn allowed the French fleet, in 1778, to sail unopposed out of the Mediterranean and ultimately to America. This same French fleet would eventually meet the British off the Virginia Capes in 1781 and prevent them from lifting a beleaguered Cornwallis off the beach at Yorktown.

Whether Commodore Hopkins and his captains ever realized it or not, their action at New Providence, with their converted merchant vessels and their sick and ill-trained crews, was one of the vital links in the chain of events that led to the British Colonial Possessions in North America becoming, by 1783, the United States of America.

Glossary

Note: See diagram of brig (page viii) for names and illustrations of all sails and spars.

aback: said of a sail when the wind is striking it on the wrong side and, in the case of a square sail, pressing it back against the mast.

abaft: nearer the back of the ship, farther aft, behind.

abeam: at right angles to the ship's centerline.

aft: toward the stern of the ship, as opposed to fore.

afterguard: men stationed aft to work the aftermost sails.

backstay: long ropes leading from the topmast and topgallant mastheads down to the channels. Backstays work with shrouds to support the masts from behind.

beakhead: a small deck forward of the forecastle that overhangs the bow. The crew's latrine was located there, hence in current usage the term *head* for a marine toilet.

beam reach: sailing with the wind abeam.

belay: to make a rope fast to a belaying pin, cleat, or other such device. Also used as a general command to stop or cancel, e.g., "Belay that last order!"

belaying pin: a wooden pin, later made of metal, generally about twenty inches in length to which lines were made fast, or "belayed." They were arranged in pinrails along the inside of the bulwark and in fife rails around the masts.

bells: method by which time was marked on shipboard. Each day was generally divided into five four-hour "watches" and two two-hour "dog watches." After the first half hour of a watch, one bell was rung, then another for each additional half hour until eight bells and the change of watch, when the process was begun again.
binnacle: A large wooden box, just forward of the helm, housing the compass, half-hour glass for timing the watches, and candles to light the compass at night.
bitts: heavy timber frame near the bow to which the end of the anchor cable is made fast, hence the term *bitter end.*
block: nautical term for a pulley.
boatswain (bosun): warrant officer in charge of boats, sails, and rigging. Also responsible for relaying orders and seeing them carried out, not unlike a sergeant in the military.
boatswain's call: a small, unusually shaped whistle with a high, piercing sound with which the boatswain relayed orders by playing any of a number of recognizable tunes. Also played as a salute.
boatswain's chair: a wooden seat with a rope sling attached. Used for hoisting men aloft or over the side for work.
boom: the spar to which the lower edge of a fore-and-aft sail is attached. Special studdingsail booms are used for those sails.
booms: spare spars, generally stowed amidships on raised gallows upon which the boats were often stored.
bow: the rounded, forwardmost part of a ship or boat.
bow chaser: a cannon situated near the bow to fire as directly forward as possible.
bower: one of two primary anchors stored near the bow, designated best bower and small bower.
bowline: line attached to a bridle that is in turn attached to the perpendicular edge of a square sail. The bowline is hauled taut when sailing close-hauled to keep the edge of the sail tight and prevent shivering. Also, a common knot used to put a loop in the end of a rope.
brace: line attached to the end of the yard, which, when hauled

upon, turns the yards horizontally to present the sail at the most favorable angle to the wind. Also, to perform the action of bracing the yards.

brake: the handle of a ship's pump.

break: the edge of a raised deck closest to the center of the ship.

breast line: a dock line running from the bow or stern to the dock at right angles to the centerline of the vessel.

breeching: rope used to secure a cannon to the side of a ship and prevent it from recoiling too far.

brig: a two-masted vessel, square-rigged on fore and main, with a large fore-and-aft mainsail supported by boom and gaff and made fast to the after side of the mainmast.

brow: a substantial gangway used to board a ship when tied to a dock.

bulwark: wall-like structure, generally of waist height or higher, built around the outer edge of the weather decks.

bumboat: privately owned boat used to carry out to anchored vessels vegetables, liquor, and other items for sale.

buntlines: lines running from the lower edge of a square sail to the yard above and used to haul the bunt, or body of the sail, up to the yard, generally in preparation for furling.

cable: a large, strong rope. As a unit of measure, 120 fathoms or 240 yards, generally the length of a cable.

cable tier: a section of the lowest deck in a ship in which the cables are stored.

cant frame: frames at the bow and stern of a vessel that are not set at right angles to the keel.

cap: a heavy wooden block through which an upper mast passes, designed to hold the upper mast in place against the mast below it. Forms the upper part of the DOUBLING.

caprail: wooden rail that is fastened to the top edge of the bulwark.

capstan: a heavy wooden cylinder, pierced with holes to accept wooden bars. The capstan is turned by means of pushing on the bars and is thus used to raise the anchor or move other heavy objects.

cascabel: the knob at the end of a cannon opposite the muzzle to which the breeching is fastened.

cathead: short, strong wooden beam that projects out over the bow, one on either side of the ship, used to suspend the anchor clear of the ship when hauling it up or letting it go.

cat-o'-nine-tails (cat): a whip with a rope handle around an inch in diameter and two feet in length to which was attached nine tails, also around two feet in length. "Flogging" with the cat was the most common punishment meted out in the navy.

ceiling: the inside planking or "inner wall" of a ship.

chains: strong links or iron plates used to fasten the deadeyes to the hull. The lower parts of the chains are bolted to the hull, the upper ends are fastened to the chainwale, or CHANNEL. They are generally referred to as forechains, mainchains, and mizzenchains for those respective masts.

channel: corruption of *chainwale.* Broad, thick planks extending from both sides of the ship at the base of each mast to which the shrouds are attached.

clear for action: to prepare a ship for an engagement. Also the order that is given to prepare the ship.

clew: either of the two lower corners of a square sail or the lower aft corner of a fore-and-aft sail. To clew up is to haul the corners of the sail up to the yard by means of the clewlines.

clewlines: (pronounced *clew-lin*) lines running from the clews of a square sail to the yard above and used to haul the clews up, generally in preparation for furling. On lower, or course, sails the clewlines are called clew garnets.

close-hauled: said of a vessel that is sailing as nearly into the wind as she is able, her sails hauled as close to her centerline as they can go.

cockbill: said of a yard that is adjusted so as not to be horizontal. Said of an anchor when it is hanging from the cathead by the ringstopper only.

conn: to direct the helmsman in the steering of the ship.

course: the largest sails; in the case of square sails, those hung from the lowest, or course, yards and loose footed. The foresail and mainsail are courses.
crosstrees: horizontal wooden bars, situated at right angles to the ship's centerline and located at the junction of lower and upper masts. Between the lower and the topmasts they support the TOP, between the topmast and the topgallant mast they stand alone to spread the shrouds and provide a perch for the lookout.
deadeye: a round, flattish wooden block pierced with three holes through which a LANYARD is rove. Deadeyes and lanyards are used to secure and adjust standing rigging, most commonly the SHROUDS.
dead reckoning: from *deduced reckoning.* Calculating a vessel's position through an estimate of speed and drift.
dirk: a small sword, more like a large dagger, worn by junior officers.
dogwatch: two-hour watches from 4 to 6 P.M. (first dogwatch) and 6 to 8 P.M. (second dogwatch).
doubling: the section where two masts overlap, such as the lower mast and the topmast just above the top.
driver: a temporary sail, much like a studdingsail, hoisted to the gaff on the aftermost fore-and-aft sail.
elm tree pump: an older-style pump, generally used as a bilge pump, consisting of a piston in a wooden cylinder that reached from the deck to the bilge.
fall: the loose end of a system of blocks and tackle, the part upon which one pulls.
fathom: six feet.
fife rail: wooden rails, found generally at the base of the masts and pierced with holes to accept belaying pins.
first rate: the largest class of naval ship, carrying one hundred or more guns. Ships were rated from first to sixth rates depending on the number of guns. Sloops, brigs, schooners, and other small vessels were not rated.
fish: long sections of wood bound around a weak or broken

SPAR to reinforce it, much like a splint on a broken limb. Also, the process of affixing fishes to the spar.
flemish: to coil a rope neatly down in concentric circles with the end being in the middle of the coil.
fore and aft: parallel to the centerline of the ship. In reference to sails, those that are set parallel to the centerline and are not attached to yards. Also used to mean the entire deck encompassed, e.g., "Silence, fore and aft!"
forecastle: pronounced *fo'c'sle*. The forward part of the upper deck, forward of the foremast, in some vessels raised above the upper deck. Also, the space enclosed by this deck. In the merchant service the forecastle was the living quarters for the seamen.
forestay: standing rigging primarily responsible for preventing the foremast from falling back when the foresails are ABACK. Runs from under the fore top to the bowsprit.
forward: pronounced *for'ed*. Toward the bow, or front of the ship. To send an officer forward implied disrating, sending him from the officers' quarters aft to the sailors' quarters forward.
fother: to attempt to stop a leak in a vessel by means of placing a sail or other material on the outside of the ship over the leaking area. The sail is held in place by the pressure of the incoming water.
frigate: vessel of the fifth or sixth rate, generally fast and well armed for its size, carrying between twenty and thirty-six guns.
furl: to bundle a sail tightly against the YARD, stay, or mast to which it is attached and lash it in place with GASKETS.
futtock shrouds: short, heavy pieces of standing rigging connected on one end to the topmast shrouds at the outer edge of the TOP and on the other to the lower shrouds, designed to bear the pressure on the topmast shrouds. When fitted with RATLINES, they allow men going aloft to climb around the outside of the top, though doing so requires them to hang backward at as much as a forty-five-degree angle.

gammoning: heavy lines used to lash the bowsprit down and counteract the pull of the STAYS.
gangway: the part of the ship's side from which people come aboard or leave, provided with an opening in the bulwark and steps on the vessel's side.
gantline: pronounced *gant-lin.* A line run from the deck to a block aloft and back to the deck, used for hauling articles such as rigging aloft. Thus, when the rig is "sent down to a gantline," it has been entirely disassembled save for the gantline, which will be used to haul it up again.
garboard: the first set of planks, next to the keel, on a ship's or boat's bottom.
gasket: a short, braided piece of rope attached to the yard and used to secure the furled sail.
gig: small boat generally rowed with six or fewer oars.
glim: a small candle.
grapeshot: a cluster of round, iron shot, generally nine in all, wrapped in canvas. Upon firing the grapeshot would spread out for a shotgun effect. Used against men and light hulls.
grating: hatch covers composed of perpendicular interlocking wood pieces, much like a heavy wood screen. They allowed light and air below while still providing cover for the hatch. Gratings were covered with tarpaulins in rough or wet weather.
gudgeon: one-half of the hinge mechanism for a rudder. The gudgeon is fixed to the sternpost and has a rounded opening that accepts the PINTLE on the rudder.
gunwale: pronounced *gun-el.* The upper edge of a ship's side.
halyard: any line used to raise a sail or a yard or gaff to which a sail is attached.
headsails: those sails set forward of the foremast.
heaver: a device like a wooden mallet used as a lever for tightening small lines.
heave to: to adjust the sails in such a way that some are full and some aback so that the vessel is stopped in the water.
hogshead: a large cask, twice the size of a standard barrel.

Capacity varied but was generally around one hundred gallons.

holystone: a flat stone used for cleaning a ship's decks.

hood-end: the ends of the planking on a ship's hull that fit into the rabbet, or notch, in the STEM or sternpost.

hoy: a small vessel, chiefly used near the coast, to transport passengers or supplies to another vessel.

hull down: said of a ship when her hull is still hidden below the horizon and only her masts or superstructure is visible.

jolly boat: a small workboat.

lanyard: line run through the holes in the DEADEYES to secure and adjust the SHROUDS. Also any short line used to secure or adjust an item on shipboard.

larboard: until the nineteenth century the term designating the left side of a vessel when facing forward. The term *port* is now used.

leech: the side edges of a square sail or the after edge of a fore-and-aft sail.

leeward: pronounced *loo-ard.* Downwind.

letters of marque: a commission given to private citizens in times of war to take and make prizes of enemy vessels. Also, any vessel that holds such a commission.

lifts: ropes running from the ends of the yards to the mast, used to support the yard when lowered or when men are employed thereon.

limber holes: holes cut through the lower timbers in a ship's hull allowing otherwise trapped water to run through to the pumps.

line: term used for a rope that has been put to a specific use.

log: device used to measure a vessel's speed.

longboat: the largest boat carried on shipboard.

lug sail: a small square sail used on a boat.

mainstay: standing rigging primarily responsible for preventing the mainmast from falling back when the main sails are aback. Runs from under the maintop to the bow.

make and mend: time allotted to the seamen to make new clothing or mend their existing ones.
marlinespike: an iron spike used in knotting and splicing rope.
mizzen: large fore-and-aft sail, hung from a gaff abaft the mizzenmast.
mizzenmast: the aftermost mast on a three-masted ship.
painter: a rope in the bow of a boat used to tie the boat in place.
parceling: strips of canvas wrapped around standing rigging prior to SERVING.
partners: heavy wooden frames surrounding the holes in the deck through which the masts and CAPSTAN pass.
pawls: wooden or iron bars that prevent a windlass or capstan from rotating backward.
pintles: pins attached to the rudder that fit in the GUDGEON and form the hinge on which the rudder pivots.
plain sail: all regular working sails, excluding upper staysails, studdingsails, ringtails, etc.
port: the left side of the ship when facing forward. In the eighteenth century the word was used in helm directions only until it later supplanted LARBOARD in general use.
post: in the Royal Navy, to be given official rank of captain, often called a post captain, and thereby qualified to command a ship of twenty guns or larger.
privateer: vessel built or fitted out expressly to operate under a LETTERS OF MARQUE.
quadrant: instrument used to take the altitude of the sun or other celestial bodies in order to determine the latitude of a place. Forerunner to the modern sextant.
quarter: the area of the ship, larboard or starboard, that runs from the main shrouds aft.
quarterdeck: a raised deck running from the stern of the vessel as far forward, approximately, as the mainmast. The primary duty station of the ship's officers, comparable to the bridge on a modern ship.
quarter gallery: a small, enclosed balcony with windows lo-

cated on either side of the great cabin aft and projecting out slightly from the side of the ship.

quoin: a wedge under the breech of a cannon used when aiming to elevate or depress the muzzle.

ratline: pronounced *ratlin*. Small lines tied between the shrouds, horizontally forming a sort of rope ladder on which the men can climb aloft.

reef: to reduce the area of sail by pulling a section of the sail up to the yard and tying it in place.

reef point: small lines threaded through eyes in the sail for the purpose of tying the reef in the sail.

rigging: any of the many lines used aboard the ship. *Standing rigging* holds the masts in place and is only occasionally adjusted. *Running rigging* manipulates the sails and is frequently adjusted, as needed.

ringbolt: an iron bolt through which is fitted an iron ring.

ring stopper: short line on the CATHEAD used to hold the anchor prior to letting it go.

ringtail: a type of studdingsail rigged from the mainsail gaff and down along the after edge of the mainsail.

round seizing: a type of lashing used to bind two larger lines together.

run: to sail with the wind coming over the stern, or nearly over the stern, of the vessel.

running rigging: see RIGGING.

sailing master: warrant officer responsible for charts and navigation, among other duties.

scantlings: the dimensions of any piece of timber used in shipbuilding with regard to its breadth and thickness.

schooner: (eighteenth-century usage) a small, two-masted vessel with fore-and-aft sails on foremast and mainmast and occasionally one or more square sails on the foremast.

scuppers: small holes pierced through the bulwark at the level of the deck to allow water to run overboard.

scuttle: Any small, generally covered hatchway through a ship's deck.

service: a tight wrapping of spunyarn put around standing rigging to protect it from the elements.
serving mallet: a tool shaped like a long-handled mallet used to apply SERVICE to rigging.
sheet: lines attached to the CLEWS of a squaresail to pull the sail down and hold it in place when the sail is set. On a fore-and-aft sail the sheet is attached to the BOOM or the sail itself and is used to trim the sail closer or farther away from the ship's centerline to achieve the best angle to the wind.
ship: a vessel of three masts, square-rigged on all masts. *To ship* is to put something in place, thus shipping capstan bars means to put them in their slots in the capstan.
short peak: indicates that the vessel is above the anchor and the anchor is ready to be pulled from the bottom.
shrouds: heavy ropes leading from a masthead aft and down to support the masts when the wind is from abeam or farther aft.
slack water: period at the turn of the tide when there is no tidal current.
slings: the middle section of a yard.
sloop: a small vessel with one mast.
sloop of war: small man-of-war, generally ship rigged and commanded by a lieutenant.
slop chest: purser's stores, containing clothing, tobacco, and other items that the purser sold to the crew and deducted the price from their wages.
snatch block: a block with a hinged side that can be opened to admit a rope.
spar: general term for all masts, yards, booms, gaffs, etc.
spring: a line passed from the stern of a vessel and made fast to the anchor cable. When the spring is hauled upon, the vessel turns.
spring stay: a smaller stay used as a backup to a larger one.
spritsail topsail: a light sail set outboard of the spritsail.
spunyarn: small line used primarily for SERVICE or seizings.
standing rigging: see RIGGING.

starboard: the right side of the vessel when facing forward.
stay: standing rigging used to support the mast on the forward part and prevent it from falling back, especially when the sails are ABACK. Also, to *stay a vessel* means to tack, thus *missing stays* means failing to get the bow through the wind.
stay tackle: system of blocks generally rigged from the MAINSTAY and used for hoisting boats or items stored in the hold.
stem: the heavy timber in the bow of the ship into which the planking at the bow terminates.
step: to put a mast in place. Also, a block of wood fixed to the bottom of a ship to accept the base or heel of the mast.
stern chasers: cannons directed aft to fire on a pursuing vessel.
stern sheets: the area of a boat between the stern and the aftermost of the rowers' seats, generally fitted with benches to accommodate passengers.
sternway: the motion of a ship going backward through the water, the opposite of *headway.*
stow: as relates to sails, the same as FURL.
swifter: a rope tied to the ends of the capstan bars to hold them in place when shipped.
tack: to turn a vessel onto a new course in such a way that her bow passes through the wind. Also used to indicate relation of ship to wind, i.e., a ship on a "starboard tack" has the wind coming over the starboard side.
taffrail: the upper part of a ship's stern.
tarpaulin hat: wide, flat-brimmed canvas hat, coated in tar for waterproofing, favored by sailors.
tender: small vessel that operates in conjunction with a larger man-of-war.
tholes: pins driven into the upper edge of a boat's side to hold the oars in place when rowing.
thwart: seat or bench in a boat on which the rowers sit.
tiller: the bar attached to the rudder and used to turn the rudder in steering.
top: a platform at the junction of the lower mast and the topmast.

tophamper: general term for all of the spars, rigging, and sails; all the equipment above the level of the deck.
train tackle: arrangement of BLOCKS and tackle attached to the back end of a gun carriage and used to haul the gun inboard.
truck: a round button of wood that serves as a cap on the highest point of a mast.
trunnions: short, round arms that project from either side of a cannon and upon which the cannon rests and tilts.
truss: heavy rope used to hold a yard against a mast or bowsprit.
tween decks: corruption of *between decks*. The deck between the uppermost and the lowermost decks.
waist: the area of the ship between the quarterdeck and the forecastle.
waister: men stationed in the waist of the vessel for sail evolutions. Generally inexperienced, old, or just plain dumb seamen were designated waisters.
warp: a small rope used to move a vessel by hauling it through the water. Also, to move a vessel by means of warps.
water sail: a light-air sail set under a boom.
waterways: long pieces of timber running fore and aft along the point where the deck meets the upper edge of the hull. The SCUPPERS are cut through the waterways.
wear: to turn the vessel from one TACK to another by turning the stern through the wind. Slower but safer than tacking.
weather: the same as *windward,* thus "a ship to weather" is the same as "a ship to windward." Also describes the side of the ship over which the wind is blowing.
weather deck: upper deck, one that is exposed to the weather.
weft: used to mean a flag, generally the ensign, tied in a long roll and hoisted for the purpose of signaling.
whip: a tackle formed by a rope run through a single fixed block.
wooding: laying in stores of wood for cooking fuel.
woolding: a tight winding of rope around a mast or yard.

worming: small pieces of rope laid between the strands of a larger rope to strengthen it and allow it to better withstand chaffing. Also, putting worming in place.
yard: long, horizontal spars suspended from the masts and from which the sails are spread.
yardarm: the extreme ends of a yard.